FINDING LYLA

BOOK TEN IN THE BODYGUARDS OF L.A. COUNTY SERIES

CATE BEAUMAN

Finding Lyla
Copyright © January 2016 by Cate Beauman.
All rights reserved.
Visit Cate at www.catebeauman.com
Follow Cate on Twitter: @CateBeauman
Or visit her Facebook page: www.facebook.com/CateBeauman

First Print Edition: January 2016

ISBN-13: 978-1519659996
ISBN-10: 1519659997

Editor: Invisible Ink Editing, Liam Carnahan
Proofreader: Kimberly Dawn
Cover: Demonza

DEDICATION

To Kimberly Dawn, proofreader extraordinaire. Thank you
for all your hard work.

❧ CHAPTER ONE ❧

Moscow, Russia
February 1991

JONATHAN'S HEART RACED AS THE STEADY RHYTHM OF the machines tracking his wife's vitals filled the operating suite.

"Hold me tighter," Mina whispered as she stared up at him and nervously licked her dry lips.

"You're doing great. He or she will be here before we know it," he reassured her, sliding his fingers down Mina's smooth neck and shoulder, one of the few places he could touch on their side of the bluish-green curtain.

"I can't stop shaking."

He glanced at Mina's delicate, trembling arms strapped into place on the table, as if she were affixed to a cross, and he felt his pulse kick up another notch with his sense of helplessness. "It's cold in here." He smiled, kissing Mina's nose and brushing at the silky blond wisps of hair escaping her surgical cap. "Soon this will be over and we'll finally get to meet the little one who's been kicking you for months." He smiled again as Mina did, doing his best to reassure her while his stomach continued its greasy roil.

For hours, they'd waited for their new son or daughter. For hours, Mina had endured the excruciating pain of labor and the frustrations of endlessly attempting to push their child into the world, until the baby's heart rate took a dangerous dip that had yet to recover. Only minutes had passed since the doctors and nurses rushed them down to the operating theater, but it felt like days while they waited for the new life to be born.

"The head's stuck," someone muttered on the other side of the curtain separating them from the gore of Mina's cesarean section.

"Work faster," another demanded quietly as a wet suction sound filled the room. "The outcome will not be good if we don't."

Jonathan sat farther up on the uncomfortable stool as the urgency in the doctors' tones registered. A year ago, he would have struggled to understand the rapid-fire Russian they spoke, but now he understood just fine that even though emergency surgery was taking place, the baby was still in trouble. He swallowed while sweat dribbled down his back and Mina blinked up at him.

"Widen the incision," another doctor said.

"Everything's okay," he mumbled, stroking Mina's forehead, praying his words were true, even though it was clear things weren't going well.

Mina sucked in a breath as her body was roughly jostled. "Why are they pulling so? Even with the drugs, I feel as if I'm being ripped in two."

"It will be over soon—very soon," he promised as the fetal alarms started beeping the way they had when the doctors raced around in the upstairs delivery room.

More tense seconds passed while Jonathan stared into Mina's pretty blue eyes.

"Finally," said the doctor closest to Jonathan's side as he listened to his child's first lusty wails.

The nurse peeked her face over the curtain, holding up a tiny, screaming infant covered in goop and blood. "What do you have, Mina?"

"A girl." Mina grinned as Jonathan laughed his relief.

"We have a daughter." Jonathan followed the nurse's movements with his gaze as she quickly walked his baby over to the warming station. "She's really here." He kissed Mina's forehead and relaxed his tense shoulders for the first time in days. "You did it. You did it, Mina," he whispered next to her ear. "I'm so proud of you."

"I did nothing more than lay here like a log. Kiss me again, my darling, and tell them I need to see her."

He pressed his mouth to Mina's and smiled as he wiped away her tears, surprised that it was possible to love her more than he already did.

"Tell them, Jonathan. Tell them we must see her, or I'll simply die from the anticipation."

Nodding, he chuckled as his daughter's cries echoed, certain he'd never been so overcome with joy. Mina had been waiting for this moment since the doctor confirmed her pregnancy. "Okay." He moved to stand as the nurse walked their way.

"Sit, Papa, and you will hold your daughter."

He settled on the stool again, reaching for the small bundle, careful to support her head. "Hi, beautiful." He brought her close, breathing her in, touching his cheek to her forehead. "You're so warm and soft." He eased her back for another good look, already in love. "I'm your dad."

"Let me see, darling. Let me see."

He angled the baby for Mina's view.

"Oh, she's perfect." She struggled to move her hand secured beneath the restraint. "May I be undone?"

The nurse released her wrist from the tie.

"Thank you. I must touch you. I've longed to touch you, little one." Mina stroked the baby's forehead.

"Lyla, right? We're sure her name is Lyla?"

"Yes." Mina nuzzled the baby's cheek with her own. "Our little Lyla Katarina." Mina awkwardly tugged at the tightly wrapped blanket. "Her feet. I must know her fate, Jonathan. Who will she be?"

He helped Mina unwrap the white cotton, exposing tiny pink legs and feet.

Mina laughed. "She has my arch." Mina kissed miniature soles. "Russia's princess. You, my love, will be Russia's next great prima ballerina."

"Just like your mama." Jonathan caressed his new daughter's knuckles as Lyla's hand wrapped around his finger, unable to get enough of the perfect little girl. "I think she'll have your hair color. She definitely has your nose."

"She has your chin." Mina stroked Lyla's head, stomach, and arms as the baby started to fuss again. "You are dear to my heart already, my girl. So dear." Mina kissed Lyla's palm and dropped her trembling hand back to the table as she rested her head against the small cushion.

"Are you okay?"

"Yes. I'm overwhelmed with happiness." She smiled and closed her eyes. "Wrap our sweet Lyla back up, will you? We don't want her getting cold. We want her healthy and lovely when she makes her debut to the world in the morning."

Newspapers, reporters, and Mina's millions of adoring fans were the last thing on his mind as he struggled to swaddle his daughter while the baby blinked up at him. "I think I've got it." He grinned as he tucked the lip of the blanket in place. "I'll need more practice but—"

"Mina, open your eyes." The nurse gave a rough rub to Mina's pale cheeks as alarms began to beep behind the curtain. "Mina." The nurse gave her another aggressive scrub.

"You must go out now, Diplomat Avery." One of the nurses took Lyla from Jonathan's arms while another helped him from the stool, quickly ushering him toward the doors of the operating suite.

"Stop." He pulled away, fighting to turn around. "Wait."

"Out. Please, Sir." She gave him a small shove.

"What's going on?" he demanded in English and shook his head, remembering that few of the staff members here were fluent in his native tongue. "What's happening?" he tried again in Russian.

"Mina's losing too much blood."

He swallowed a wave of terror. "She's going to be okay? She'll be all right?"

"We will work hard to restore her health." The nurse turned away, and the door to the operating room closed, echoing behind her.

Jonathan glanced around in the silence of the long, dim corridor and sank into one of the plastic chairs in the corner. Clenching his jaw, he bobbed his legs up and down. Mina was so delicate. Her body was strong, but her labor had been so hard. He closed his eyes as he rested his head against the wall, consumed by a sickening dread. They should have gone to The States for the delivery like he'd wanted. The technology was top-notch—some of the best—but Mina had insisted their baby be born here in her country, where the times were still far behind the advances in the West. He should have put his foot down and demanded that they think of both hers and the baby's health and safety, but it was a rare day when he could deny his beloved wife anything she asked.

His eyes flew open and he rushed to his feet when two more doctors ran down the hall and pushed through the doors to the operating room. He blew out a long, shaky breath with a renewed sense of trepidation and paced back and forth while his mind raced. What was taking so long? Why was there no news about Mina? Surely they'd given her blood to counteract the loss and had her ready for the recovery room.

"Diplomat Avery."

He whirled and closed the distance between himself and Doctor Nabatov with several huge steps, as the obstetrician rolled Lyla out in a portable bassinet. "How is she?"

"Your girl is perfectly fine—very healthy."

"How's Mina doing?"

"I'm afraid Mina lost a lot of blood."

"So give her a transfusion."

He took Jonathan by the arm, guiding him over to the row of chairs Jonathan had abandoned. "Sit, please."

The grim apology in the physician's eyes made him hesitate. "I don't want to sit."

"Sit, please."

He did as he was told. "Doctor—"

"Mina has died, Diplomat Avery."

His head went light and he closed his eyes, afraid he might pass out. This couldn't be happening. Only moments ago Mina had been smiling at him and their baby. "How can—Mina *died*?"

"I'm sorry to share this news, Diplomat. This is a huge loss not only for you, but for Russia and me as well. Our—"

"No." He shook his head, ready to stand, but sat where he was, certain his legs wouldn't hold him. "How did this happen? How could this happen to Mina?"

"This birth had many complications."

"Mina is healthy. She's strong. She's so strong." His voice broke as he tried to comprehend that Mina was none of those things any longer.

"Words cannot express my regret." He stood and picked up Lyla, handing her over to Jonathan. "Hold her. Take comfort in your child."

Jonathan settled the baby in the crook of his elbow, cradling her close as tears raced down his cheeks while Doctor Nabatov spoke to him in medical jargon he barely grasped. He struggled to pay attention to the physician's droning words while he stared in shock at his beautiful, motherless daughter.

❧ CHAPTER TWO ❧

New York, New York
January 2016

LYLA PAUSED BY HER DRESSING ROOM DOOR AND SMILED as one of the new interns from the Manhattan School of Ballet passed her in the hallway. "Hi."

"Hello." The pretty teenager waved shyly, smiling back and quickening her pace.

Lyla turned, adjusting her heavy bag on her shoulder, and opened her door, wincing when the troubling ache in her ankle made itself known. "Don't you start," she muttered as she shut herself inside and twisted the lock. "I don't have time for this." Limping slightly, she made her way to the soft, cushy chair in the corner and sat, rolling her stiff joint, attempting to alleviate the issue before it started causing her problems as it had in Boston a few short weeks ago.

Extending her calf and pointing her toes up, she felt the tightening in her tendons and huffed out a frustrated breath. She'd been so *careful* to baby her foot with extra physiotherapy and stretching, but her slight misstep in class today had brought back the familiar discomfort. She pulled her ankle on top of her opposite knee, examining her anklebone for any signs of swelling—a move she never would have attempted in the studio, but no one watched her here. Choreographers and artistic directors weren't there to scrutinize her every move in her dressing room the way they were in the unforgiving lights upstairs.

Narrowing her eyes, she poked at her skin, relieved to see only minor inflammation instead of the major swelling and deep purple bruising that had forced her off her feet and backstage during the last two productions of *Swan Lake* in late December. Luckily there were no telltale signs of her injury. Hopefully she would be able to nurse herself back to health without involving the staff physicians or the private doctor she occasionally consulted with. At this point, no one needed to know that something wasn't quite right. This was ballet after all; the show had to go on.

With a final rub, she stood and caught a glance at herself in the vanity mirror, doing a double take and blowing out a breath as she studied her sweat-soaked hair escaping her messy bun and her rosy cheeks after another grueling set of morning classes. Geoffrey rarely held back on the pace. Today was no exception.

Nibbling her lip, she glanced toward her tiny bathroom and the small shower stall she clearly needed to use, then looked at the clock. Twenty minutes wasn't much time, but she was willing to live on the edge. Showing up to an interview looking like a dirty, drowned rat wasn't exactly professional. She hurried into the bathroom, stripped down, and showered in record time, giving her hair a thorough washing and her body a quick scrub. She wrapped herself in her robe and emerged from the bathroom, grinning as she looked at the clock—six minutes and thirty seconds. "Not half bad."

It was tempting to sit down and prepare for her upcoming question-and-answer session with Roman, but she went to her closet instead, grabbing her bucket, then ice from the miniature fridge/freezer combo, and added several inches of water from the faucet. She plunked down in front of the mirror and sucked in air through her teeth as she submerged her foot in the frigid slush, eager for the glorious numbness to settle into her abused joint.

With her bum ankle seen to for the moment, she got down to business, applying a light coat of powder foundation—her makeup, not the stage gunk she used regularly when performing for the crowds. Today she would be performing again, but this was different. Her yearly interview with Roman Akolov, one of Russia's most well-respected senior journalists, was something she was accustomed to. For the last six years, since her eighteenth birthday, she'd granted him and Russia a glimpse into her private life. Since the day of her birth, her mother's country had been fascinated by her every move. Her father and grandmother had given her the gift of relative normalcy until the day she left for dance school overseas. Agreeing to an occasional interview kept the press at bay and her in control of the media fodder.

She picked up another compact and dashed blush across her high cheekbones, then glided the mascara wand over her long lashes, accentuating her ice-blue eyes before she applied a glossy coat of subtle pink to her full lips. She reached for her hairbrush as her phone alerted to an incoming Skype call, and she smiled, already knowing who waited on the other end. She grinned into the tiny lens as she answered. "Daddy."

His handsome face filled the screen. "Ly-Ly. How's my girl?"

"Good." She angled her phone against the mirror to keep her view of her dad and slide her brush through the yards of her thick blond hair. "Busy."

"How were your classes?"

"A workout."

"Geoffrey's pushing hard?"

She nodded her confirmation as she started the task of twisting her long locks into a French braid. "With the debut show only two months away he doesn't have much choice."

"I guess not." Her father popped something into his mouth and chewed.

"Finishing dinner?"

"I am," he said over his mouthful.

"What did you have?"

"Borscht and a thick slice of homemade bread."

She paused, paying closer attention. "Oksana's homemade rye?"

Her father's grin filled her screen. "You bet."

"She spoils you."

"She does." He wiped his mouth with a napkin. "It's colder than hell. I needed something to warm up these old bones, so Oksana suggested soup."

She scoffed at his comment. He was hardly old—barely fifty-five, and he easily looked a decade younger. "It's thirty here."

"A heat wave by Russian standards."

She chuckled as she secured the tie at the end of her braid. "True. So what's up?"

"Nothing much. I was hoping to catch you before your interview."

She winged up her eyebrows as she met her father's gaze. Thousands of miles separated them, but she knew his intentions weren't quite as casual as his tone. "You were hoping to catch me, huh? Somehow I can imagine you were sitting right there with your meal, counting down the minutes until I would more than likely be back in my dressing room."

He smiled and shrugged. "Maybe."

She laughed. "Definitely."

Some of the humor left his eyes. "This is important, Ly-Ly. I need to make sure we're clear—"

"We're clear, Dad. I'm going to tell Roman I'm postponing my visit for a few weeks until I'm finished with Geoffrey's show, then I'll come over."

"If it's safe."

She fastened simple diamond studs in her ears. "I can't stay away forever."

"There are bomb scares almost daily. One of these times it's going to be real, I'm afraid. I want you staying in New

York."

She sighed as her light mood fell away, thinking of the horrific bombing that killed fifty people in Saint Petersburg on New Year's Eve. The Russian city was several hours away from her father's home in Moscow, but the terrorist group responsible for the attack had struck in the capital before. It was highly likely they would again. "I worry about you."

"I'm fine."

"I worry anyway." She struggled with the clasp on her favorite necklace as she secured it in place.

"Everything's under control."

Yet he wanted her to stay away. "Right." She held back another sigh.

"You're wearing your mother's jewelry."

She pressed her hand to the golden charm settled against her skin. "I am. I just need to change, then I'll be ready. How do I look?" She batted her lashes.

"Beautiful as always."

"Thank you." She rested her chin on her palm. "So, since I'm not coming to Russia, when are you coming home to see me?"

"As soon as I can—when the US position stabilizes. I had a meeting with the President earlier today."

With the tensions between Russia and the US constantly growing worse, she had a feeling she wouldn't be hugging her father for quite some time. "Well, I can't wait to have you here."

"I'm going to miss your birthday."

"That's okay," she reassured with a small smile when she heard the regret in his voice. "You can watch me blow out my candles via Skype."

"Twenty-five's a big deal."

"We'll make it work."

"Have Moses take you out."

"He's busy getting ready for his new production."

He sighed. "Are you helping him?"

"When I can."

"How's your ankle?"

She suppressed a grimace as she attempted to move it in the frigid water. "Much better. No complaints to speak of."

"Not that you would even if there were. You work too much, push yourself too hard."

She grinned. "What's that saying about the pot calling the kettle black, Ambassador Avery?"

He chuckled. "You got me."

She glanced at her watch. "I hate to cut this short, but I need to get dressed."

"Call me when you're finished."

"It'll be late. It's already past eight on your end. You know how Roman loves to talk."

"More like grill you. Don't let Roman bully you."

"I have everything under control."

"Of course you do."

"Trust me." She winked.

"There's no one I trust more. Call me."

"Okay." She kissed her fingers and touched the lens. "Love you."

"I love you too."

She disconnected and pulled her leg from the water, cursing her stiff foot as she hobbled to the closet. She stripped out of her robe and put on underwear, then her creamy tailored slacks and a pale blue sweater. She wearily eyed her two-inch pumps, well aware they would do nothing good for her ankle, and slid her feet into them anyway. Dismissing the nagging discomfort, she grabbed the bottle of ibuprofen on the shelf, swallowed two tablets down with a glass of water, and gave herself a final eagle-eyed appraisal in the mirror—calm, friendly, and completely in control. Perfect.

Lifting her chin, she opened the door, ready to face the press—one of her least favorite things to do. She walked down the hall, smiling when she spotted Roman waiting for her. "Roman," she extended her hands to the tall man with salt-and-pepper hair and a graying mustache and kissed his cheek as he returned her embrace.

"Lyla, how are you?"

"Very well," she answered in fluent Russian.

"Thank you for meeting with me during such a busy time."

"I always have time for friends," she continued in her mother's native tongue.

He smiled.

"Come sit and we'll talk," she invited, gesturing to the chairs closest to the spectacular view of Lincoln Center's grounds.

"Thank you."

She settled in, as Roman did, folding her hands in her lap, ready to begin.

"We should get right down to it, as I know your free moments are rare."

She touched his hand, wanting to soothe the typically intense man. "There's no rush."

"All right." He pressed record on his pocket-sized player and set it on the circular table. "I'd like to document our conversations, if that's okay with you."

"Sure."

He sat back, his eyes sharpening as if they were locking on his prey. "How have you been?"

"Very good. Thank you." She would ask him the same but knew the time for pleasantries had past.

"You spent time in Australia during the fall, dancing *Firebird* and more recently you completed *Swan Lake* in Boston."

"Yes. It's been busy. The troupe and I have been back for about three weeks now."

"You suffered problems with your right ankle that kept you off stage."

"I did, but everything's fine now."

"I'm glad you're well again, especially when it has been suggested that you started back to work before you were given the all-clear by your doctors."

"No. I'm back to full health." She rolled her ankle for his view, clenching her jaw when she felt the sharp ache.

"Congratulations on a full recovery."

"Thank you.

"I know injuries can be quite a scare in your profession."

"If they're serious, yes, but I'm lucky mine wasn't."

"Are you up to traveling again so soon after such demanding performances?"

"Travel is a huge part of my job." An aspect of her career she was growing tired of, but she turned up the wattage on her smile as she dismissed her pessimistic thought. "It's an honor to share the gift of dance around the globe."

Roman nodded. "Your visit this year will be different than most."

"Actually—"

"Tensions continue to grow between Russia and the United States," Roman interrupted. "Where do you stand on the current policies?"

Roman was never one to tiptoe around the big issues. "I love both of my countries."

"One more than the other?"

She shook her head. "Both are my home."

"You live in the United States for all but three weeks. Your father sides with the United States."

She clenched her fingers tighter, unwilling to rise to Roman's bait. "My father is the United States Ambassador to Russia. He sides with the best interests of the two countries he has dedicated most of his life to."

Roman narrowed his eyes, clearly unsatisfied with her answer. "Recently Ambassador Avery was heavily criticized for supporting more US sanctions against The Federation. Are you not bothered by this? Do you feel that your mother would stand by this?"

She couldn't say one way or the other. Her mother was an image she only knew through stories and television footage. "I stick to ballet, to perfecting my techniques and giving the best performances I can."

"Many want to know why it is that you have yet to perform in a country you profess to love? Why is it, Lyla *Markovik*-Avery, that you travel the world sharing your gifts, yet you refuse to share them with Russia?"

Apparently she was going to spend the next several minutes dancing in the fire, but at least the heat was off her father. "I—"

"Perhaps this is your father's influence—the will of the United States?"

Or maybe not. She swallowed, remembering Dad's warnings of the rising tensions. This hostile interview was a clear indication of the strain. "My choice not to dance has nothing to do with my father. It's mine alone."

"So you alone turn your back on Russia?"

She crossed her legs, the picture of calm, even as her temples began to pound with the sudden headache. "I've turned my back on nothing. Dance is personal. My reasons are personal, but I can assure you nothing would make me happier than to see peace restored between the two countries I call home."

"And you will help with this?"

She frowned. "Help restore peace? Roman, you overestimate my influence."

"Perhaps you underestimate your power. Are you not Mina Markovik's daughter? Have you not followed in her footsteps?"

God knows she'd tried. "I will never be my mother."

"But you are 'Russia's Princess.'"

But she wasn't. The weight on her shoulders grew exponentially—as it did every year when the title she'd never asked for was thrown in her face.

"This comes with great responsibility," Roman continued, staring at her, clearly waiting for her response.

She consciously relaxed her hands when she realized her knuckles were white. As their gazes held, she swallowed.

How was she supposed to tell him she had canceled her plans to travel east? By honoring her father's requests to stay in New York, she disgraced the woman who'd died giving her life. With an inner sigh, she sat up straighter, remembering that she owed the beautiful woman who perished nearly twenty-five years ago. "I understand my responsibilities. I accept my duties."

"Russia has heard nothing from you since the tragic bombing in Saint Petersburg almost two weeks ago."

Another request from her father: to distance herself from the politics of extremists and deadly acts against the Russian Federation. "Of course I'm deeply saddened and disturbed by such a horrible tragedy."

"Your father wasn't shy about his condemnation of the attack. He's quoted as calling them guerrilla tactics that cannot be tolerated by the United States any more than they are the Russian Federation."

"Yes. My father is very troubled by the violence."

"Rumor has it your father is discouraging your travels to the Mother Land for fear of your safety."

Her spine snapped straight at such a clear invasion of her privacy. How could anyone know that? She discussed her personal issues with very few people. "The rumors you hear are wrong."

"Ambassador Avery hasn't pressured you into staying home safe and sound in New York?"

"No, he has not."

"So you won't be postponing your trip to Russia?"

"No, I will not. I'll be coming for my three-week holiday as I always do, and I'll be performing *The Markovik Number* at the Bolshoi Theater."

Roman gaped. "You'll dance *The Markovik Number?*"

"Yes."

He edged closer in his seat. "It's never been seen before. The choreography is unknown to all but a few."

"Yes," she repeated.

"This dance is a *pas de deux*?"

She nodded while her mind raced as she dug herself deeper into her current mess. Not only was she now going to Russia, she was also committing herself to imitating the steps of a true legend. Many had compared her to Mina through the years, but that was nostalgia. No one would ever hold a candle to Mina Markovik on stage.

"Who will you partner with?"

"Sergei Ploeski," she decided. As soon as word spread, there was no doubt Russia's best male ballet dancer would be committed to learning the choreography.

Roman's eyes grew wider. "You will dance with Sergei Ploeski?"

"Mmm. A token of goodwill between two beautiful countries."

Roman all but rubbed his hands together. "The headlines will be wild. "Ploeski and Markovik-Avery: History."

"It will be an honor."

"Your father knows of this?"

"He encouraged me to reach out to Sergei, to bring my mother's last dance to life during such uncertain times," she lied without qualm, knowing such a statement would put her father in a positive light.

"This is fantastic, Lyla."

"I'm excited," she fibbed again as she struggled not to fidget.

"And your visit at Orphan House Ten, will you still meet with the children?"

"I plan to carry on with my usual schedule." Which would drive Dad *crazy*.

"With added security and precautions no doubt."

She shook her head. "No. You know I don't use security."

"Surely your father will insist."

"My father and I both believe that we must be cautious with the new threats, but we must also live our lives. I plan to carry on in Russia as I always have—drive my own car, walk the streets without being flanked by any sort of protective personnel, eat out with friends and family."

"You can't exactly call yourself a normal citizen."

"Why not?"

"Normal citizens aren't from the womb of great dancers. Few can call themselves the daughter of an American ambassador."

"I am both of these things, and I've never wanted to be treated any differently than anyone else."

"There is certainly truth in that, Princess." Roman shut off his recorder and stood abruptly. "Thank you for sitting down with me." He bent forward, absently pressing a kiss to Lyla's cheek. "We'll catch up when you land in Russia next week. I want an exclusive."

"Of course," she muttered, waiting for him to disappear around the corner before she let her head settle against the back of the seat. Closing her eyes, she groaned as she rubbed at the throbbing in her temples. What had she done? Dad was going to lose it when she explained what had just happened. She stood and started back toward her dressing room, not looking forward to the call she was about to make. But there was no turning back now. Every word she'd spoken was on Roman's handy little tape recorder.

COLLIN SPOTTED HIS BLACK SUITCASE MAKING ITS WAY down the belt in baggage claim. "Excuse me," he said as he skirted around two women to grab it. He shouldered the thick strap and made his way to his buddy, who was dressed similarly in blue jeans and a white Ethan Cooke Security t-shirt, standing among the chaos of two hundred other passengers waiting for their stuff.

"You ready?" Chase asked him as he shoved his cell phone in his pocket and picked up his luggage sitting at his feet.

"Yeah. Thanks for waiting."

"No problem." They started down the hall toward the parking garage. "I just spoke to Jules. She wants you to come over for dinner."

Cashing in on a hot, home-cooked meal after a long-ass week of travel sounded like an excellent idea, but he shook his head. "Next time, man. We just got home."

"So?"

"So you're supposed to go see your fiancé, have wild 'I haven't seen you for a week' sex, and eat by yourselves—most likely in bed."

Chase grinned. "Jules and I'll get around to having sex—trust me. But I can eat first. I'm flexible like that."

Chuckling, Collin shook his head, glancing toward the winter-darkened skies through the massive panes of glass, dreading the idea of going back to his empty apartment. During the week he and Chase had been on assignment in Iraq, Sydney was supposed to have gotten the rest of her stuff out of his place. "Tell Julie thanks. I'll definitely take you guys up on the offer next time."

"How about a beer first?" Chase slowed his step, gesturing to the tavern as they passed.

He shrugged. "Yeah, sure."

"I'll buy."

He sighed, realizing he'd done a shitty job of keeping his personal life personal over the last few days. He hadn't said anything to Chase about Sydney, but he and his pal knew each other too well not to notice when something was off. Clearly Chase and Julie were on a mission to cheer him up, which he appreciated but didn't need. "I'll get this round."

"If that's what you want."

"It is."

They took their seats at the bar in the simple, dimly lit space.

"What can I get you boys?" the older woman asked from behind the counter.

Collin studied the full sleeve of angels tattooed down her left arm. "I'll take a pale ale."

"Make that two," Chase added.

"Let me see a couple of photo IDs and I'll get them to you."

Collin leaned to the left and grabbed his wallet from his back pocket, showing her his California license as Chase did the same.

"Thanks. Give me just a minute." She turned and poured two perfect draughts, then set them down on napkins and slid the pints in front of them.

"Thanks." Collin took a sip and let loose an appreciative groan as he savored the yeasty flavor. "Beer. *American* beer."

"It's good to be home."

Collin tapped his glass against Chase's and sipped again, grunting his response, not sure that he entirely agreed. It was good to be back from one of the Middle East's most dangerous provinces. He and Chase had completed a successful assignment. Their principals were in one piece and the insurgents had been off wreaking havoc farther north, leaving them alone. They couldn't have asked for a better outcome, but he sure as hell wasn't returning with the same enthusiasm as Chase. No one was eagerly waiting for him to walk through his front door.

Chase set down his glass. "So have you heard from Sydney?"

He shook his head. "I'm sure I won't. We're through."

Chase nodded. "I wish I could say I'm sorry, man."

Collin's gaze whipped to Chase's in surprise. "Thanks." He laughed humorlessly. "Jesus."

"You can do better."

He took another drink, staring out the window and checking the urge to tell one of his best buddies to fuck off. "We don't all get the fairytale," he muttered, trying to ignore the rush of resentment. He was happy for Chase and Julie—and the rest of his friends who were living their happily ever afters, but finding "the one" wasn't in the cards for everyone.

He and Sydney had a good run in the beginning. For the first six months of their relationship, life had been pretty damn close to perfect, but then everything changed—Sydney had changed—and they spent their final seven months together making each other miserable. Eventually they ended it—and tried more than a few times to patch things up, but the on-again/off-again had been too much.

"You deserve better," Chase said again.

"I guess I never realized you didn't like her."

"It wasn't my place to say one way or the other." He drank again. "If you would've started talking wedding rings and long-term commitments, I would've spoken up."

He traced a pattern with his thumb in the condensation on his glass. "Why?"

"Why what?"

"Why didn't you like her?"

"I'm not a big fan of the high-maintenance, bitchy type."

Sydney could certainly be both.

"It was easier to shrug her off when I knew you were happy," Chase continued, "but the day she gave you shit for helping me when Jules disappeared—"

"She'd booked us a long weekend away. I left her hanging."

"Julie's life was in danger." Chase held up his cupped hands as if he were weighing the two options.

"Bros before hoes?"

"Yeah, something like that. But I was thinking more about how you were there for your friend. I can't imagine Jules ever punishing me for doing the right thing. I needed you, and you had my back. You were by my side during one of the worst moments of my life."

Chase was absolutely right. And that's why saying his final goodbye to Sydney after Julie's ordeal had been more of a relief than heartbreaking.

Chase drained the last of his beer. "Are you sure you don't want to come over to the house?"

He shook his head. "I'm good. I'm going to nurse this for a few more minutes." He gestured to his glass.

Chase nodded as he stood. "Invitation's open if you change your mind." Chase extended his hand.

He returned his friend's knuckle bump. "I appreciate it."

"See you around."

"See ya." He picked up his beer, watching the seven-thirty-seven backing away from the Jetway, and pulled bills from his wallet. He set them on the bar by his half-empty glass. "Thanks," he said to the older woman.

"Safe travels, Honey."

He gave her a nod and grabbed his bag, then started down the hall toward his car, hating the idea of heading home.

—◆—

Collin opened his eyes to the bright light pouring in through the window and groaned. He slammed them closed again as he pressed his fingers to his temples, waiting for his head to explode. "Son of a bitch." He rolled to his back and slowly sat up, cautiously opening one eye and glancing down at the blue jeans and white t-shirt he still wore from yesterday.

"Morning, Sunshine."

He turned his head when he heard Chase's voice and immediately regretted the movement. "Damn it."

"I imagine you'll want this." Chase walked to where he sat, wearing a pair of black basketball shorts, and handed over a cup of coffee and a couple of pills.

"Thanks." He slid the Advil past his lips and chased the capsules down with the perfectly prepared brew, caring little that he was scalding his tongue. His mouth felt like he'd chewed on a wad of cotton balls, and the pounding in his head couldn't vanish fast enough. "Thanks," he said again, gesturing to the mug as he studied the framed photographs of Julie and Chase hanging in their cozy living room.

"You're welcome." Chase sat in the plush chair across from him.

"What the hell am I doing here?"

"Smitty called me at two—found my number in your phone. He told me to come get your stupid, drunk ass so he could close up. That's a direct quote, by the way."

He sighed as he rested his head against the cushion.

"Jules and I drove over to the bar. She grabbed your car, and I had the pleasure of bringing you back here to tuck you in."

He set his cup on the coffee table and scrubbed his hands over his face. "Sorry."

"You're up."

He looked up as Julie walked in wearing yoga pants and a snug purple top, her long black hair tied back in a ponytail. She smiled at him, the concern in her big green eyes apparent. "I am."

"How about some breakfast?" She handed him a plate of scrambled eggs and toast.

"You didn't have to make me anything." He moved over a cushion so she could sit down.

She shook her head at his gesture to make room for her. "You need something in your stomach. Chase got you to drink a couple glasses of water before you fell asleep, but breakfast should help too."

"I'm sorry." He looked from her to Chase. "I really am."

She wrapped her arms around him, surrounding him with her pretty scent. "I'm worried about you." She kissed the top of his head.

He returned her embrace, absorbing the comfort his friend offered. "I'm fine—an idiot, but I'm fine."

"Eat up." She gave him another squeeze. "And maybe think about how you're a really great guy." She gave his shoulder a gentle rub. "I'll leave you guys alone."

He took her hand before she could walk off. "Thanks for the couch and for breakfast. Truly."

"You're welcome." She smiled at him, winked at Chase, and disappeared down the hall to the bedroom.

Chase tipped the recliner and crossed his ankles on the footrest as he drank from his own cup. "You should've taken me up on my offer to come over for dinner last night."

He picked up the fork and sampled a small bite of the fluffy, golden eggs, hoping his stomach would behave. "I told you I didn't want to get in your way."

"Jules and I had sex just fine, but we could have fed your dumbass first. I told you I was flexible about that."

He gave a small, brief smile, then stared at the plate in front of him. "What the hell am I doing, man?"

"Is she really worth all this?"

"No." He took a bite of the lightly buttered toast. "No, she's not."

"So what's up?"

He shrugged. "I don't know why the whole empty apartment thing is bothering me so much."

"She came and got her stuff?"

He shrugged again as he met his friend's intense stare. "I couldn't tell you. I got in my car and headed over to Smitty's. I thought a game of pool and another round might help." He ate more of his breakfast, finding the simple food soothing. "Clearly it didn't since I'm waking up here." He sighed and set the remainder of the bread back on his plate. "This is fucking pathetic. *I'm* fucking pathetic. I'm crying in my beer over a relationship that was over months ago. We've been using each other for sex for the last few weeks, hooking up whenever one of us gets itchy—fuck buddies." He laughed humorlessly. "Jesus, that's pitiful."

"You're just down on your luck. You'll bounce back."

He shook his head. "I'm finished with this, with her. I need to get my head on straight."

"It's hard to see things for what they are when your dick's involved."

"She meant more than that—for a long time. I thought we were moving in the right direction."

"Nothing about that woman was right for you, Collin. Just give things some time."

He glanced toward the pictures of the happy, gorgeous couple again and looked away. "I've got plenty of it."

"Maybe that's not such a bad thing."

"Maybe it's not." His cell phone started ringing.

"I'll let you answer that." Chase collapsed the footrest and stood, giving Collin a solid slap on the back on his way by.

As Chase disappeared down the hall toward his soon-to-be wife, Collin glanced at the readout and answered. "Dad."

"You must be back in The States."

"We landed last night."

"Jet lagged?"

He grimaced. "Not quite. I'm sure tomorrow will suck." Although he wasn't exactly enjoying himself right now.

"How's Hawaii?"

"Paradise."

"And Luna?"

"As beautiful as ever. She told me to tell you she's sending positive energy your way."

He grinned, always amused by his stepmother's metaphysical jargon. "Tell her thanks."

"Will do. So how's the empty apartment?"

He sat back against the cushion. "I haven't been home yet. I crashed at Chase and Julie's."

"It's nice to have good friends."

"I have the best." He leaned forward and picked up his coffee, settling again as he drank, realizing he was steadying out.

"Is that girl gone from your life for good this time?"

And Dad cut right to the chase for once. "Looks like it."

"Good."

He winged up his eyebrows. Did no one like Sydney? "I'm glad you think so."

"She has a black aura—muddy with it—or Luna says so, anyway."

"Huh." He smoothed down his hair when he saw that it was sticking up in short, messy spikes as he caught a glimpse of his reflection in the glass across the room. He looked like hell. His brown eyes were bloodshot and his normally clean-shaven jaw was covered with two days' worth of black, scruffy beard. "What's up, Dad?"

"I need a favor."

"Okay."

"It's for a friend, really—Ambassador Jonathan Avery, an old fraternity buddy of mine. I'm sure I've mentioned him before."

Collin shrugged, not recognizing the name. "Maybe."

"Jonathan's in a tough spot."

He took another sip, enjoying the rich flavor of good coffee as his headache began to ease. "How so?"

"His daughter's heading over to Russia for a few weeks, and he would like someone with her—times are rough over there."

"If he's an ambassador, he'll have DSS protection."

"He does, but she doesn't. Initially she canceled her plans to travel, but they appear to be back on for some dance at a fancy theater."

"She's a dancer?"

"Ballerina, I guess—like her mother was."

Collin rubbed at the back of his neck as he tried to piece together the details of their conversation, which were usually all over the place. "So she needs a bodyguard?"

"Jonathan's insisting that she needs you. He and I keep in touch. He knows your background."

"Yeah. Sure. Have him contact Ethan—" His phone beeped with another call. He peeked at the screen. "Ethan's calling me now."

"I imagine he might be. The Averys are good people."

"Let me talk to Ethan, and I'll see what I can do."

"Thank you, son."

"Of course."

"Call soon. Luna wants to speak to you. She says the ballerina has good colors—lots of reds and yellows, but some pastels too."

He rolled his eyes skyward. "What the hell does that mean?"

"Something about needing serenity."

"Dad, I have to go."

"There's more—"

"I'll have Ethan fill me in. Bye, Dad." He and Luna could talk metaphysics later. Disconnecting, he switched over to the other line. "Hey."

"Welcome back."

"Thanks."

"How do you feel about another assignment?"

"Let me guess: Russia and a ballerina."

"You talked to your dad."

"Mostly we talked about auras, but I cut him off before he brought up chakras."

"What?"

He grinned. "You don't want to know. Trust me. So, give me the deets."

"Ambassador Jonathan Avery is formally requesting your presence in Russia for three weeks."

"What about DSS?"

"Lyla's not big on security. She prefers to keep things discreet."

"Okay."

"Her mother was Mina Markovik, so she's a pretty big draw when she's overseas."

He shook his head. "I don't know who that is."

"World-famous prima ballerina—maybe the best ever, according to Jonathan."

"Huh. I'm not really up on my who's who in the ballet world."

"Sounds like you're about to be. Things are hostile over there right now—lots of political tensions and anti-American sentiment, not to mention bomb threats after the detonation in Saint Petersburg a few weeks ago. Avery wants someone on his daughter unofficially."

"Unofficially?"

There was a long pause.

"How am I supposed to run close protection unofficially?"

Ethan cleared his throat. "Jonathan thought it might be best if the public believes you and Lyla are involved."

Collin choked on his coffee. "Excuse me?"

"Of course it's just a front. Who you are and what you do needs to stay under wraps. We would take you off payroll and you would have no ties to Ethan Cooke Security until you get back."

"Are you firing me?"

"Looks like it. Lyla likes to do her own thing. She's never

brought security with her before, and in her interview with Roman Akolov last week, she insisted she would carry on with her life as usual despite the issues in Russia."

"How does she feel about me tagging along?"

"Jonathan says she's agreeable."

"So you're setting me up with a ballerina and paying me too. Is this legal?"

"I'm sure somewhere it's not."

He smiled. "When do I leave?"

"You and Lyla will head over to Russia Wednesday evening, but she's in Manhattan now. It wouldn't hurt if you spent a couple of days getting to know each other."

"I'm ready to go whenever."

"I'll book you another flight. For this afternoon?"

"Yeah. Sure. Text me the information and I'll head out."

"*Do svidaniya.*"

"Huh?"

"It means 'goodbye' in Russian."

"Right. Back at ya." He hung up, slightly relieved that he'd already been reassigned. He needed to get out of here for a while and start over. He'd never been to Russia before— it would be a good way to shake things up. The whole fake relationship was a new twist. He'd seen a lot in this business, done a lot, but he'd never pretended to date a client. He shrugged. At least it would keep things interesting while he got his life back on track.

ᴄ₰ Chapter Four ᴂᴖ

LYLA LEAPED HIGH, SCISSORING HER LEGS AND ARCHING her back with the punch of dramatic flair the dance demanded of her. She soared through the air, making certain her fingers were posed perfectly, and clenched her jaw, bracing for the pain that would surely accompany her landing. Her foot made contact with the floor, and she grit her teeth, ignoring the discomfort radiating through her lower right leg as she kept moving in a series of pirouettes across the dimly lit space. She followed her sequence of energetic twirls with a smooth *arabesque penchee*, then raised herself up on pointe in a basic *sous-sus* before executing the final *grand jete* of the intricately choreographed piece she was determined to get right. She kicked out her legs, flying high once again, and readied herself for the agony of impact. Her toes hit the sprung floor panel and she gasped, losing control of her movement and rolling her ankle. Her momentum took her down hard, and she caught herself on her hands and knees, gasping again when small chunks of rosin cut into her palms.

"Ow. Ow," she panted out as she plunked herself down on her butt and closed her eyes, gripping her foot. Her chest heaved as each unsteady breath echoed in the room while the music she'd listened to a dozen times played through the speakers. Sweat trailed down her face and neck, dripping into the front of her snug, black unitard. For the last three hours she'd rehearsed, taking advantage of the mostly empty building. Her technique was still flawed, her movements too jerky, but her battered body couldn't take anymore.

She swiped at the drops of perspiration tickling her skin and stared at herself in the mirror, tracking her gaze down her long, muscled frame and locking on her right ankle, which was throbbing in time with the rapid beat of her heart. Her Achilles tendonitis was definitely rearing its ugly head again, and today Doctor Chu diagnosed her with a minor ankle sprain, adding yet another injury to her growing list of body woes. Doctor Chu was strongly recommending a six- to eight-week hiatus from dance to allow her leg the opportunity to heal, which was absurd and precisely why she'd sought out a diagnosis from her personal physician instead of seeing someone here on staff at the theater. Legally and ethically Doctor Chu couldn't say anything about her current conditions—and that was exactly the way she wanted it.

She couldn't afford to lie around on her couch. There were no breaks in this business. It was rare if she took one day off, let alone a week. Two months was like suggesting a year. Geoffrey was constantly on her, demanding perfection for his new show. Now she had *The Markovik Number* to think about as well. According to Dad, Russia was abuzz with the idea of their beloved princess bringing Mina's last dance to life. The Bolshoi Theater was already sold out for the "historic event." The pressure to perform was always there—had been since she was ten, but lately the challenges seemed daunting.

She moved to stand and winced when her ankle protested. Swallowing, she rested her forehead on her knee as her eyes welled—part pain, part...defeat? She shook her head, knowing that such weaknesses were intolerable. This wouldn't be the first time she'd suffered for her art nor would it be the last. In the end, she always came out stronger, no matter the obstacle. Her current situation would be no different.

She met her gaze in the mirror for the second time, noting the misery in her eyes, and snapped her shoulders straight as she raised her chin. What was she doing? She didn't have time for this. Sick of her own mood, she gained her feet and hobbled over to her MP3 player, shutting it off. For tonight, she would relent and let herself rest. Tomorrow was another full day—company class, physiotherapy, and an afternoon rehearsal with Moses.

"Ly-Ly?"

She whirled, smiling when she spotted the pretty redhead standing in the doorway. "Hey there."

Jennifer walked to where she stood, dressed in a black wool pencil skirt and white top, her high heels echoing with every step. "What are you still doing here?" she asked as she wrapped her arms around Lyla.

Determined to shake off the remains of her pity party, she returned her friend's embrace. "You might not want to be hugging me. I'm really sweaty."

"Aren't we always?"

Chuckling, Lyla eased back. "Pretty much."

Jennifer settled her hand on her hip. "I thought I saw you leave hours ago."

She shook her head and drank deep from the water bottle she always kept handy. "I needed to practice."

Jennifer rolled her eyes. "From what I saw today, you looked pretty darn perfect."

She smiled at her fellow dancer. "I feel like I can't get the last sequence right."

"Geoffrey wasn't bitching when he left, so I think you nailed it."

There was always room to improve, always something to prove, even if it was just to herself. "Thanks." She picked up her towel and blotted her face and neck. "So what are *you* still doing here?" She poked Jennifer's shoulder playfully. "You and Tony were magic this afternoon. You really brought that scene to life."

"Damn straight."

Lyla laughed, enjoying Jennifer's energy.

"I'm here with the sole purpose of flirting with Matty, which has absolutely nothing to do with work." She hoisted herself up on the window ledge. "So how's it going with *The Markovik Number?*"

"Good." She turned up the wattage on her grin, trying to convince Jennifer as much as herself that what she said was true. "Great."

"Are you finally going to give it a rest for tonight?"

She took another sip of her water as she nodded. "I am."

"A bunch of us are going out for a late dinner—Matty, Deb, Tony, Gail, and me. Do you wanna come? We're all dying to hear more about Russia."

There was nothing she wanted less. She craved the quiet of her cozy apartment, a couple of ibuprofen, and a decent meal. "Mmm, can I take a rain check?"

Jennifer tsked as she shook her head. "One of these times, Lyla, we're actually going to get you to come out."

She wrinkled her nose. "I haven't been very social lately, huh?"

"The word hermit comes to mind. Or granny. Or—"

"Okay," she said with a laugh. "I get your point. Next time I'll come, I promise." She tossed her dirty towel in her bag. "When I get back from Russia, I'll have everyone over for dinner as penance for my hermit-like ways."

Jennifer's eyes widened in what could only be delight as she hopped down from her spot. "You've got a deal. I'm requesting those sinful brownies you make, the ones with the beans or whatever it is you put in them that makes them taste so *good.*"

"Done," she said with a decisive nod.

"I should go." Jennifer pulled her into another hug. "If I don't see you before you head overseas, I'm telling you to break a leg now."

Her ankle felt like it was already halfway there. She kissed her friend's cheek. "Thanks."

"See ya." Jennifer tossed her a wave and started toward the door.

"Hey, Jennifer?"

Her friend turned.

"You look amazing. Matty doesn't have a chance." She winked.

"That's what I'm counting on." She wiggled her eyebrows and walked out.

Chuckling, she waited for Jennifer's footsteps to fade down the hall before she took off her pointe shoes and dug into her bag for the ankle stabilizer Doctor Chu had given her. She slid the compression-type sock in place and rotated her foot, finding a bit of relief. Standing on her tiptoes, she found her movements weren't completely excruciating. See? Everything was going to be fine. She would dance in Russia and for Geoffrey, then move on to her next big role.

Relieved and mostly cheered up after her chat with Jennifer, she slipped on her sneakers and debated whether or not she wanted to walk all the way down to her dressing room for today's change of clothes. Quickly dismissing the idea, she pulled on her jacket, plunked her pale blue beanie-style hat on her head, and started down the hall, eager to be home. Lately, that was the place she craved to be. For months she'd been "on," having little time to herself. When the day was over, she wanted out of the spotlight. In her apartment she was just Lyla, not the daughter of a legend, not Manhattan Ballet's famous Principal Dancer.

She pushed open the door and stepped out into the shocking cold, adjusting her winter gear as a nasty gust of wind blew down the street. Moving toward her building, she stared up at the hundreds of lights ablaze in the huge skyscraper a half-block away. She was almost there—only moments away from locking herself in for the night. Her gaze wandered to the heavens above, and she shook her head, smiling as she wondered why she was always surprised by the lack of stars. They were up there somewhere, but the hazy city glow made them impossible to—

She slammed into someone and gasped as the impact knocked her back a step. "Oh my gosh."

The man turned, grabbing her arm before she could fall off the sidewalk.

She blinked her surprise when he flashed her a smile instead of swearing at her or flipping her off. "I'm so sorry."

"That's okay."

She shook her head as she freed herself from his grip. "I need to pay more attention."

"You're good. There's a lot to take in around here." He gestured to their busy surroundings.

She smiled, studying his strong jaw and the planes and angles of his handsome face in the dim light. "There is."

He narrowed his eyes, the color impossible to see in the play of shadows. "Are you—are you Lyla Markovik-Avery?"

She debated whether or not to deny who she was. He was a big guy, a good seven or eight inches taller than her, and his bulky winter jacket did little to disguise his broad shoulders and solid build. He seemed nice enough, but that didn't mean he was.

"The dancer?" He pointed to Manhattan Ballet at her back.

With an inner sigh, she nodded. People usually didn't recognize her here, which she loved, but she'd bumped into him after all. If he tried anything funny, she would scream bloody murder. He probably wanted an autograph, maybe a picture, then he would be on his way. "Yes, I'm Lyla."

He flashed her another one of his devastating smiles. "How about that? I'm Collin Michaels."

She narrowed her eyes this time, trying to place the name. "From Ethan Cooke Security."

It wasn't often someone could surprise her twice. She grinned. "My new boyfriend."

He let loose a quick laugh and extended his gloved hand.

"That's what I've heard."

She accepted his greeting. "Welcome to Manhattan."

"Thanks." He let her go and adjusted the huge bag on his shoulder. "I landed about an hour ago—thought I would come scope things out."

"I was just on my way home." She gestured with her chin to her building as the wind kicked up again.

"I'll let you go then. It's pretty damn cold—"

"Would you—would you like to come up?" she interrupted, not quite sure what she should do in this situation. This was her guest—kind of—and the man who would be spending the next three weeks with her in Russia.

He frowned. "You're inviting me up?"

Swallowing, she shrugged. "Sure. I mean—"

"But you don't even know me. From a close protection standpoint, that kinda makes me cringe."

She laughed, liking him already. "You *are* Collin Michaels, right?"

"That's me."

She stepped closer and lowered her voice. "My dad said you would be landing sometime today, and since he and I are the only ones who know you're coming, I feel pretty safe that you're you."

He swung his bag onto his other arm. "You should at least ask to see some ID or something."

"Okay. Can I see your ID?"

He grinned as he pulled his wallet from his front pocket.

She leaned in, reading his credentials on the Ethan Cooke Security badge that reminded her of a driver's license. *Collin Michaels. Close Protection Agent.* His picture was slightly grainy in the poor lighting, but what she could see of it was definitely the man standing in front of her. "It looks like you're really you."

His smile reappeared as he shoved his wallet back in his pocket. "Better safe than sorry."

"I couldn't agree more. How about some dinner?"

"Are you sure? It's pretty late."

"I'm sure that I'm starving, and there's plenty of food."

"All right then."

"Come on. Let's get out of here."

"Thanks."

They started walking, and she caught a better glimpse of his face in the row of bright streetlights: firm lips; straight, longish nose; even longer eyelashes that clashed with the rugged, edginess she sensed—gorgeous. But the color of his eyes was still a mystery. They crossed at the crosswalk and quickened their pace as the wind gusted mercilessly the closer they moved to her building.

—◆—

Collin stood by Lyla's side as the doors slid shut, closing them in the blissful warmth of the elevator. He glanced her way as she pressed the button for the twentieth floor, studying her wool hat resting low on her head, making it hard to get a good look at her face, but what he could see was nothing short of spectacular. He'd had an idea of what to expect. While he waited to board his plane, he'd searched for her picture online. Her status as Mina Markovik's daughter and one of Manhattan Ballet's most revered principal dancers made her image easy to find, but he'd been to more than one photo shoot in his day, watching makeup artists and cameramen toy with a person's looks until their subjects resembled someone else entirely. So far, Lyla Markovik-Avery was the real deal—a genuine blond goddess.

The elevator car gave a hard lurch as it started its way up, and he automatically pressed his hand to the wall. "Whoa."

"I should have warned you about that," she said as she turned her head, aiming a friendly smile his way. "This thing can be pretty slow."

He stared, taking in her straight white teeth; creamy, smooth skin; and shocking blue eyes that reminded him of the calm waters of a tropical beach. Definitely a stunner. "I guess we'll get there when we get there."

"Hopefully. Last week some people got stuck on the thirty-sixth floor for a couple of hours."

"That must've sucked."

"I guess some lady was screaming hysterically. The man trapped in here with her threatened to knock her out." She chuckled as she shook her head. "The police and fire department came. Apparently it was quite a show."

"Gotta love city life."

"Mmm." She held his gaze. "They're brown."

"Huh?"

"Your eyes. I couldn't tell outside."

"Oh. Yeah. Brown."

She leaned against the wall and smiled again, then looked down.

He wanted to say something in the slightly awkward silence, but his mind went blank, a phenomenon he rarely experienced. Luckily the door dinged and opened. "Looks like we won't be camping out in the elevator tonight."

"Phew." She wiped her hand across her brow, feigning her relief. "I'm down to the right."

"Great." He shouldered his bag and followed her.

"So, um, thanks for coming all the way out here." She stopped in front of 2007 and unlocked the door.

"No problem."

"Come on in," she invited, flipping on the light in her kitchen as she walked in.

He took a small step, hesitating. "Are you—are you sure this is okay? I definitely didn't plan on crashing your evening."

She shook her head. "You're not."

"If you have other stuff to do..." Someone who looked like Lyla more than likely had other stuff to do.

She put her keys down on the counter and opened the door wider. "I'm home for the night, so this is actually great."

"Okay." He stepped farther inside, breathing in the same flowery scent he caught when she slammed into him on the sidewalk.

She tugged off her hat, revealing a head full of shiny blond hair pulled back in a messy bun. "My dad said you just got back from being overseas."

"Yeah, Iraq."

"Wow, that's a long flight. And then to come here." She took off her jacket next, giving him a good look at her excellent body in the snug black one-piece spaghetti-strap outfit she wore. He'd been expecting skin and bones, but her arms were long and well-muscled, her breasts were surprisingly full, and her legs went on for miles on her slim five-five frame. "I was in rehearsals." She gestured to her clothes.

"I thought maybe you were just getting back from the grocery store." He set down his bag and unzipped his jacket. "I usually wear something like that when I go."

She grinned. "I would never consider this an option without properly accessorizing with leg warmers—preferably pink."

He returned her grin—gorgeous and a great sense of humor. He was going to have to remember to thank Ethan. "Purple or red could work too—really any color."

"Black is versatile." She hung her coat in the small closet. "I can take your jacket if you want to stay awhile."

"Only if you're sure I'm not in the way."

"Of course not. I'm about to help myself to a bowl of chili if you want some."

"Sounds great." He handed her his coat, the warmest one he had in preparations for the brutal Russian temperatures they would face.

"I'm going to catch a quick shower and change. Go ahead and make yourself at home. There're drinks in the fridge."

"Thanks. Don't rush on my account."

Nodding, she disappeared into a darkened room off the living room and closed the door.

He stepped farther into the kitchen, sniffing the glorious scent of what had to be their dinner in the Crock-Pot. The place was small—cozy, nothing over the top, but her view was spectacular. He moved to the wall of windows in the section of living room she'd transformed into an eating nook with a tiny table and two chairs. It was getting late, past nine, but cars and people bustled about twenty stories below as if it were noon. He tore his gaze from the hustle on the streets and stared farther into the distance at the expanse of black emptiness that had to be the Hudson River before the city lights continued on as far as the eye could see.

Turning, he gave his attention back to Lyla's home. Hardwood floors decorated with pretty floral rugs, plush beige furnishings, and black and white photos of famous Russian architecture hung framed on the wall. He wandered to the bookshelf crammed with several cookbooks, studying pictures of her smiling with the ambassador or an older woman with gray hair. His eyes stopped on another photo of Lyla grinning, snuggled up next to a handsome black man. Her boyfriend maybe?

"I'm back." She stepped out of her bedroom dressed in jeans and a pink sweater. She'd twisted her wet hair into a long French braid, leaving her face unframed. Somehow the blue of her eyes seemed more vivid, and her eyelashes impossibly longer. Lyla was a true beauty. "You didn't help yourself to a drink."

"No, I was checking out your view. It's amazing."

"I can stare out there for hours. I think that's why I love the city. It's always alive." She smiled. "How about some chili?"

"Yeah. Definitely." The in-flight peanuts he ate over three hours ago weren't doing much to satisfy his hunger.

"If you wouldn't mind grabbing us something to drink from the fridge, I'll scoop us a couple of bowls."

"Sure."

"How hungry are you?"

"I'm never afraid to eat." He opened the refrigerator door

and gaped at the stockpile of fruits, vegetables, and bottled green and purplish juices. "Are we due for a storm?"

"Huh?" She glanced over her shoulder and laughed. "No. I forgot to cancel my grocery order last Friday."

He snuck another peek at her small build. "You eat all of this in a week?"

"Mmm."

"By *yourself*?"

"For the most part." She scooped food into bowls. "Sometimes I have to grab more fruit. The power greens are really good—the green juice there."

His gaze wandered to the dark green concoction in the plastic bottle, and he barely suppressed a grimace.

"If you wouldn't mind grabbing me one of those and the salad too?"

"Sure." He snagged the nasty-looking green stuff, a bottle of water for himself, and the colorful salad.

"Oh and the—" She turned as he did, and they almost collided in the galley-type kitchen.

"Whoa." He breathed her in while they stood inches apart.

"Sorry. Small space. I forgot to mention the dressing." She eased the salad out of his arms, then took the drinks and set them on the counter. "Do you like balsamic?"

"Uh, I'm not sure. I usually go for ranch."

"It's homemade."

"I'll give it a try."

"Great." She leaned in front of him, her shoulder brushing his chest, as she grabbed the dressing and set it on the tray with the rest of the meal. "I think we're ready."

"I'll take this." He headed over to the table, staring at the tomatoes, beans, and some other stuff he couldn't identify, noting the lack of beef in the bowls. If this was supposed to be chili, he didn't recognize Lyla's version of one of his favorite dishes. He glanced from the salad to the bottle of power greens and swallowed, wondering what in the hell he'd just gotten himself into. "Here we go."

"Thank you." She pulled out her chair and sat down. "Please help yourself to as much as you like."

"Thanks." Taking his seat as well, he reluctantly grabbed his dish and silverware, scooping up a healthy spoonful of whatever this was. Trapped by manners, he slid the stuff past his lips and nodded as spices melded nicely on his tongue. He chewed his mouthful of beans and tiny pieces of something that reminded him of...he didn't know what. "This is really good."

She smiled. "You sound surprised."

"I've never seen chili like this before."

"It's vegetarian."

"Huh. What's this stuff?" He pointed to the small yellowish pieces.

"Quinoa."

"Never heard of it."

"It's a grain. It's loaded with protein and fiber."

"A health nut?"

She shrugged. "I try to be healthy."

"So you're not a carnivore?"

"I like fish."

"But you don't eat beef or chicken?"

She wrinkled her nose as she chewed her meal.

He couldn't imagine giving up burgers or anything slathered in barbequed sauce. "Different strokes for different folks. I guess it's not so bad though if stuff tastes like this." He wagged his spoon at his bowl.

"I make all kinds of delicious food."

"I take it you enjoy cooking."

"When I have time. Even when I don't," she amended. "What about you?"

He shook his head. "I'm more of a sandwich maker."

She smiled. "We'll try to do better than that over the next few weeks."

"We'll have to talk about that at some point: logistics and whatnot—the whole relationship thing. Probably not tonight, but maybe tomorrow we could go out for dinner and figure out how we're going to play this."

"How about I cook for you instead?"

"I don't mind home-cooked food." He helped himself to more of his chili.

"Is this going to be too weird for you, the relationship aspect?"

"Nah. You're okay with it?"

"I kind of made this mess so the least I can do is play along." She twisted open her bottle of green sludge and drank.

"You're not a big fan of security?"

She shrugged again. "It makes me different, inaccessible. I just want to be like everyone else."

Interesting answer. He stared into her eyes as he pondered her statement.

She looked down as she forked up lettuce leaves and tomato. "So do you do this often—have pretend girlfriends?"

He grinned. "I can definitely say you're the first."

Smiling, she swallowed her bite. "How long have you been a bodyguard?"

"For a few years."

"How does one become a bodyguard? Is there a bodyguard college or something?"

His smile returned, enjoying Lyla's questions. "Most of us come in with a military or law enforcement background. After Ethan hired me, he sent me over to Europe for a couple of months to get the extra training I needed."

"Which one were you: military or law enforcement?"

"Military."

She nodded. "A former military man turned bodyguard. I'm sure you have lots of stories."

He shrugged. "Maybe a novel or two."

She smiled. "We have a long flight Wednesday. Perhaps you can tell me a few."

"Sure." He scooped up the last bite of vegetarian chili.

"This was really good. Thanks for the meal."

"I'm glad you liked it." She stacked her bowl on her empty salad plate.

He pushed back from the table, seeing that as his cue to be on his way. "I hate to eat and run, but I should probably head out."

She stood and piled the dishes back on the tray. "Where are you staying?"

"Some place a couple blocks east of here. I haven't checked in yet."

"You could—you're welcome to the couch if you want. It's a pullout."

He felt himself frown.

"You certainly don't have to. If the invitation makes you uncomfortable—"

"No. No." He rubbed his jaw.

"I've never been in this situation before, so I don't really know how it works—what I'm supposed to do."

This was a unique situation for him as well. He looked to the window and the frigid skies beyond the glass, then at the love-seat-sized couch tucked in the corner of the small living room. "I just don't want to put you out."

"You wouldn't be. I won't be here much tomorrow anyway. I have classes and rehearsal."

"I thought you were on vacation."

She chuckled as she brought the tray to the counter. "In my career, there's no such thing as a vacation."

"You've got three weeks on the books, right?" He helped her put the plates and bowls in the dishwasher.

"Yeah. Three weeks."

He looked at her back as she grabbed the dirty silverware and put it in the basket on the door, not missing the weariness in her voice as she answered.

She washed her hands and wiped them on a cloth, smiling as their eyes met.

He studied her closely, holding her gaze. Something

about Lyla wasn't quite adding up for him, but he made his lips curve anyway. "I guess I'll take the couch." It would probably be better this way. If anyone from the press was keeping an eye on her, this would look more authentic: significant other's in town; significant other stays the night.

"I'll warn you, I'm usually up pretty early."

"So am I."

"Okay then." She walked to the tiny closet that held a stackable washer and dryer and pulled extra blankets and a pillow from the top shelf. "Here you go."

"Thanks."

"If you get cold, there's another afghan on the couch."

"I'm sure I'll be fine."

"The bathroom's right through there." She gestured to the closed door by the laundry area.

"I appreciate it."

She pressed her hand to her mouth, suppressing a yawn. "Well, I think I'm going to head to bed. Help yourself to the TV and whatever you want in the fridge."

"Thanks."

"Goodnight."

"Goodnight." He watched her walk away, frowning when he realized she was limping a little.

CHAPTER FIVE

THE OBNOXIOUS BEEP STARTED BLARING ON LYLA'S phone, startling her out of a deep sleep. Groaning, she blindly slapped at the screen until the alarm went silent, then rolled to her side, tucking her arm under her head as she stared out at the dark sky through her window. Five a.m. always came too soon, but today seemed worse than usual—probably because she hadn't been able to shut off her mind until the wee hours of the morning.

When she was lucky enough to be home in New York, she always followed the same after-work routine: shower, dinner, and a little TV while she stretched her body one final time before she crawled under her covers. Bedtime was sacred—by nine or sooner whenever it was humanly possible. Sleep was a luxury she often did without. Her life was typically crazy with photo shoots and flights to some around-the-world destination. If she wasn't on stage performing in packed theaters, she was in a studio enduring endless classes or rehearsals. When she had the chance to catch some decent shuteye, she took advantage. But her plans for a quiet evening vanished the moment she bumped into her guest. Collin had occupied her thoughts since he'd smiled at her on the sidewalk. They'd barely spoken, not much more than small talk over a simple meal, but already she could tell he was unlike anyone she had met before.

He seemed nice—funny—and he was definitely a good sport. It wasn't every day a complete stranger was willing to play along with a fake relationship to help out their father's old friend. And he was polite. She smiled, remembering the way he'd eyed the chili in his bowl while he sat across from her at the dining room table. He'd been wary, yet he ate every bite. Her smile faded as she thought of the hints of intensity she had seen in his eyes. There was something about him that made her think he wasn't always as easygoing as he appeared to be. The next few weeks were bound to be interesting as they got to know each other better. Luckily she and her bodyguard seemed to be off to a good start. Her bodyguard...

Frowning, she shook her head at the idea of having her very own security agent for the first time in her life. She'd never needed one before and probably didn't now, but Dad had asked her to make a concession just this once. If having Collin tag along eased Dad's mind, it was fine. Perhaps she might actually have a good time on this visit.

She sat up and yawned, fighting the urge to lie back down. Technically she had the day off, but with Geoffery's show right around the corner and *The Markovik Number* just a couple of weeks away, she didn't dare sleep in. Another busy day lay in wait. It was time to get moving.

She tossed her covers back and got to her feet, instantly regretting her urge to rush when pain radiated through her ankle. "Damn. Damn," she whispered as she fell back to the mattress and reached for the brace on her side table. She pulled the snug compression sock in place and cautiously flexed her tender joint, glancing at the time on her phone as she realized she was going to need plenty of time to warm up her muscles before class. It wasn't uncommon to experience aches and pains in the morning—they came along with the territory—but this was different, far more serious, and something she was going to have to work through.

She stood again, finding the same bit of relief she'd treasured last night, and grabbed yoga pants and one of her comfy Manhattan Ballet sweatshirts from her drawer. She put on her clothes and opened her door, wincing when the doorknob squeaked. She stepped out into the living room, pausing mid-step and doing a double take as she looked over at Collin, boxer clad and sprawled out on the full-size mattress. Her eyebrow shot up as she trailed her gaze over his body. She was around muscled men every day, but they didn't look like this—broad and bulky and...billboard perfect. The dancers she worked with were strong but more leanly built. Collin clearly lifted weights regularly.

He rolled to his side and she jumped, pressing a hand to her chest. The last thing she wanted was for him to open his eyes and see her staring down at him like some weirdo. She moved to the kitchen with breakfast on her mind—something warm and energizing on this chilly morning. And maybe something that would prove to Collin once again that healthful meals were not only the way to go, but could be really darn delicious. He'd mentioned that he was a sandwich guy. Who knew what else he ate on a regular basis, but for the next three weeks, she would be adding a little variety to his diet. Quietly, she turned the dial to preheat the oven and gathered the items she needed from the cupboards and fridge to begin creating one of her most favorite wintertime treats.

Half an hour later, the scent of cinnamon and apples filled the room while Lyla started her morning stretches. She glanced at the kitchen clock, making certain the minutes didn't get away from her. She still had fifteen before she would have to scramble up and shut off the timer. Sitting in a split on the tiled floor, she flipped through a magazine in the dim light shining through the oven window and gasped in surprise when her phone started ringing. "Shoot," she whispered, reaching up and grabbing it off the counter. She frowned when she realized that Jennifer was calling. "Hello?" she said quietly.

"Ly-Ly, it's Jennifer."

She closed her magazine when she picked up on the tension in her friend's voice. "Is everything okay?"

"No. I mean yeah. Nothing major's wrong. I'm going to be late for class."

Her shoulders relaxed. "You scared me there for a second."

"I'm sorry."

She moved to lie on her back, pulling her leg up until it touched her forehead. Closing her eyes, she welcomed the wonderful sensation of her muscles going loose. "No, it's okay."

"I just woke up like five minutes ago and I'm all the way over in Tudor City."

Her frown reappeared. "What are you doing in Tudor City?" Then she smiled. "Doesn't *Matty* live over that way?"

"Yes. Apparently he liked the pencil skirt. It's a nice change from a leotard, you know?"

Her smile turned into a grin. "Of course."

"We never got around to setting an alarm—"

"Sounds exciting."

"I'm not complaining, except for now I'm late. Will you cover for me? Tell Geoffrey I was abducted by aliens or something."

She chuckled as she switched legs, once again touching her forehead. "Yeah, I'll come up with something, but I'll make it a little more believable."

"Thanks."

"You're welcome." Jennifer liked to have fun on her free time, but this was the first time Lyla could ever remember her friend being tardy for class. "I'll bring you a bowl of oatmeal. It'll be in your dressing room waiting for you."

"And that, Lyla Markovik-Avery, is why I love you to pieces."

"That's what friends are for. I'll see you soon."

"'Kay."

Pressing "end," she set the phone next to her on the floor

and closed her eyes, focusing her attention back on her routine.

"Morning."

She opened her eyes, staring up at Collin dressed in a pair of black athletic shorts. A night's worth of scruff shadowed his jaw, and his hair stood up in messy spikes. "Good morning."

"I didn't realize you were a contortionist."

She grinned. "I'm stretching before my class."

"I don't think I could *ever* get my leg to do that. Maybe if you ripped it off first..."

She laughed. "If you did this every day for the better part of twenty years, you wouldn't have any problems." She let go of her leg and sat up.

"Are you standing?" He held out his hand.

"Sure." She took it and gained her feet. "Thanks."

"It smells great in here." He sniffed. "Like apple pie."

"It's apple cinnamon oatmeal."

"*Homemade?*"

"Of course."

"How do you feel about ditching ballet and moving to LA with me?"

She narrowed her eyes as if considering the idea. "Mmm. That's tempting, but we should probably make sure you like it first."

"If that tastes even half as good as it smells, I might ditch close protection and move in with *you*. The couch is comfy, and my boss would understand."

She laughed again, enjoying him. "I was going to make a smoothie too and maybe scramble some eggs."

"I thought ballet dancers munched on carrots and celery all day."

She scoffed out another laugh as she pulled the dish from the oven and scooped Jennifer's serving into a Tupperware bowl, then dished out a second for her friend Charlie. "If they plan on falling on their faces before class is halfway over, maybe."

"So it's a myth then."

Years ago, she'd restricted her calories dangerously when Alina convinced her that her body would never be right for ballet, but then her grandmother and father stepped in. "Unfortunately some people in my profession undereat, but I've found that nourishing your body is the better way to go."

"What were you thinking about putting in that smoothie you mentioned?"

"Spinach, banana, strawberries, and a little protein powder."

"I'm game."

"Perfect. I'll have everything ready in about fifteen minutes."

"I can help."

She wasn't used to having handsome, shirtless men in her kitchen. "Yeah, sure. Um, if you want to grab the fruit and spinach from the fridge, that would be great."

Within minutes, eggs were scrambled and protein drinks ready. She glanced at the clock and winced. Class started in less than thirty minutes. "I'm going to have to take my smoothie and run."

"You don't want any of the eggs?"

She pulled off the Velcro icepack she'd secured around her ankle and tossed it back in the freezer. "I'll probably swing by later and grab a snack."

"You're off to class?"

"Yes."

"If you're a professional, why do you go to class every day?"

"Because there's always something new to learn or improve on."

He nodded as he scooped up a huge bite of eggs. "I can see that."

"I'm sorry. I don't mean to be rude, but I really need to go."

"Yeah, go ahead."

She hurried to her room, grabbing her bag, and came

back, pulling off the ankle support and shoving it to the bottom.

"You dance when you're hurt?"

She paused as she slipped on her shoes. "We're always hurt to some degree—usually minor aches and pains."

"Hmm," he said as he swallowed some of his smoothie.

She secured her hair in a quick bun and put on her jacket and hat. "What?"

"I thought I saw you limping last night, and the brace thing you've got there." He pointed to her bag.

"It's just a support." She had to be more careful. If a complete stranger was picking up on her injury, Geoffrey was bound to catch on. "I'll, um, I'll see you later. Probably for dinner."

"Great." He spooned up more of his meal. "Man, this oatmeal's *insane*," he said over his mouthful.

She grabbed her friends' breakfast and her smoothie. "I'm glad you're enjoying it. Bye."

"Bye."

Collin flipped to one of the many tabs he had open on his computer screen when his e-mail alerted him to another incoming message. "Here we go," he muttered as he clicked open the copy of Lyla's finalized schedule for the next three weeks. He'd been waiting for most of the day for the ambassador's team to confirm Lyla's appearances and for Ethan to send the information along. "Jesus," he said, frowning as he scanned the long list, wondering when in the hell Lyla was supposed to sleep: dance rehearsals from five a.m. till noon, quick lunches at home, then she was off to visit schools, hospitals, and orphanages among other places. There was even a televised cooking lesson with the Russian President's personal chef on the agenda, along with countless interviews, and a parade planned for the day after her dance at the Bolshoi Theater. So much for Lyla's vacation. Her weary response to his question last night now made perfect sense. Her visit overseas had nothing to do with R&R and everything to do with moving from one event to another. It looked like he was going to have plenty of time to sit or stand around and watch Lyla work herself to exhaustion.

Shaking his head, he made notes on a pad of paper, reminding himself of a couple of things he needed to look into, then glanced at the time, surprised to see that it was already after three. The day had gotten away from him while he worked at the little table by the window. Why was he just now realizing that Lyla never made it home for a snack or even lunch?

He stretched his arms over his head and looked outside through the huge panes of glass. It was snowing—not hard enough to call in the plows, but the fat white flakes were bound to make the sidewalks sloppy. He continued his study of the spectacular view, noting that Lyla's apartment faced the opposite direction of the Manhattan Theater, so it was impossible to see what was going on half a block away.

On impulse, he shut his laptop and walked to the closet for his jacket. Maybe he could track her down and see if she had any idea of what she wanted for dinner. He could run to the store for whatever she might need, which was the only real help he could offer. His skills in the kitchen were pathetic at best, so having something hot and ready for her to eat when she walked through the door wasn't an option.

He moved his wallet from his back pocket to his front and zipped his coat, ready to take on the grocery store...and maybe catch a glimpse of Lyla in action. She was supposed to be spectacular on the dance floor. According to the articles he'd perused on the flight east, she was one of the best dancers ballet had seen in a long time. He was eager to get a look for himself.

Locking up, he walked to the elevator and waited through the slow descent to the bottom floor. Moments later, he was pushing open the glass door and stepping out into the cold. "Dammit." The winds blew the snowflakes about, and he took his wool hat out of his pocket and settled it on his head, not quite used to the frigid temperatures of the Northeast. He and Chase had caught a lucky streak in Iraq. The days had been relatively warm—mid-fifties to sixties—and LA was usually mild by most winter standards.

Another gust of wind carried through the rows of buildings, and he pulled his gloves out next, fighting with the index finger of the stiff leather as he jammed his hand in. He skirted around a woman and her dog misbehaving on his leash and knocked into a man smoking a cigarette feet from the crosswalk. "Sorry about that."

"No problem."

He crossed with the flow of pedestrians and hustled to the back entrance of Manhattan Ballet, following two women dressed in sweats and heavy jackets. They carried bulging bags on their shoulders similar to the one Lyla had walked out with earlier this morning. "Thanks. Go ahead," he said, taking the door they held open for him and stepping inside after them, welcoming the warmth. He tugged off his gloves and started down the hall, having no idea where he was going. Piano music played in one of the rooms he peeked in. A man and woman danced, but the woman wasn't Lyla. He moved along, glancing in two more rooms, but she wasn't there either. "Excuse me." He stopped a pretty redhead as she passed by.

"Yeah."

"I'm looking for Lyla."

She raised her eyebrow as she studied him.

"Lyla Markovik-Avery," he clarified, just in case there was more than one Lyla in the building.

"Who are you?" the redhead asked.

"I'm, uh, I'm her boyfriend," he coughed as he said it, still trying to get used to his new role for the next few weeks.

The woman scoffed. "Ly-Ly doesn't date, but nice try,

buddy." She scoffed again and walked off.

He rubbed at the back of his neck. That didn't go the way he'd planned. He spotted a younger man, a kid easily in his teens, and hurried ahead. "Hey. Excuse me."

The kid turned.

"I'm looking for Ly-Ly," he tried using her nickname, hoping that might get him further than he just got.

"She's not here."

"Oh."

"I think she went over to The Y on Sixty-Third Street. I heard her saying something about *The Markovik Number* in class this morning. I know she's been rehearsing with Moses."

"Sixty-Third Street?"

"A couple blocks east of here. Over by Central Park West."

"Thanks." He moved back down the hall and pulled out his phone, typing *YMCA Sixty-Third Street* into Google Maps. Within seconds, he found the location and put on his gloves as he stepped back into the cold. A nasty gust of wind made itself known before the door closed behind him, and he debated whether to hail a cab or walk the four or five blocks to The Y. He stopped in his tracks, blinking and staring up at the huge billboard hanging on the side of the building with Lyla's image in its center. She wore pointe shoes and some sparkly, fitted mid-thigh-length dress that exposed her midriff. Her long hair was curled and spilling around her as she lay down. Lyla's name and the dates for some new ballet were written in fancy bold letters, but he couldn't take his eyes off of the beauty advertising the upcoming performance.

There was another picture of Lyla in a smaller poster-like advertisement in front of the theater for the same show. She wore a light blue tutu covered in sparkling sequins, but her hair was in a bun this time and she stood on pointe with her right leg lifted well behind her as she smiled. "Damn," he muttered, shocked by the power of his attraction to a picture. Lyla made what she did appear effortless. He definitely wanted to get a look at what she could do for himself.

Turning away, he started down the block, growing increasingly more curious about his new principal—a beautiful ballerina who could cook like a dream, offered her couch to men she barely knew, and apparently didn't date. He narrowed his eyes. Why didn't she date? She was gorgeous and friendly—clearly very successful. Lyla seemed to have the whole package, yet she was content to keep to herself.

He crossed at the corner and glanced into the windows of the natural foods market as he past, kept going, and turned around. He walked in and grabbed a basket as he stepped farther into the store. The place was busy and full of every fruit and vegetable known to man. He hadn't been able to touch base with Lyla, so he would have to come up with a plan for dinner on his own.

Rubbing at his jaw, he perused the produce and stopped when he spotted the large selection of kale—a superfood, according to the sign. He grabbed a huge bunch of the dark, leafy greens and put them in his basket, then moved through the store, worrying some when he passed the organic juice bar and the selections of chia seeds and maca powder, waiting for something to inspire him—or for something to at least look familiar. He turned another corner and smiled when he came upon the seafood counter. There were numerous options of fish, shrimp, and other goods from the ocean. This was something he recognized.

"You got a number?" the man asked from behind the glass.

He shook his head, not exactly sure what to choose. He was an expert in cold cuts—ham, turkey, a good rare roast beef—but fish was way over his head. "No."

"What do you want today?"

"Uh." He scanned the selections again and picked at random. "Cod. Two pounds. No, three. Three pounds," he decided, afraid two pounds wouldn't be enough.

Within minutes he was shoving his wallet back in his front pocket and walking back out into the cold with the makings for a decent meal in hand...he hoped. Before long, he was pulling open the door to the YMCA, hoping he hadn't missed Lyla while he was shopping. He moved to the information booth and smiled. "Hi."

The woman seated behind the desk dog-eared the page in her book and set it down. "Hi."

"I'm looking for Moses. The dancer," he assumed out loud.

"He's upstairs—third floor."

"Great. Thanks."

He hustled up the two flights of stairs and moved down the hall. Much like he had at the Manhattan Ballet, he peeked in several empty rooms, following the heavy bass of hip-hop music on the other end of the building. Frowning, he shrugged and kept going as a deep voice counted off steps in a series of eight over the loud beat. He looked in the room and spotted Lyla sitting in a chair by a long wall of mirrors as the man from the picture on her bookshelf—Moses, he assumed—moved to the music then stopped.

"So what do you think?"

"It's good—really great, but what about a fast side-step at the end before coming together?"

"Show me."

She stood, wearing a white leotard, loose gray crop pants, and shoes instead of ballet slippers. When she left this morning, her hair had been piled on top of her head in a tight bun. Now it ran free—yards of shiny golden locks stopping just past her butt. Bopping her head, she snapped in time with the music. "Pick it up with me."

"You know I will."

She nodded. "Five, six, seven, eight." Lyla kicked her leg out to the right and rolled her hips in several fast, sinuous jerks while her arms moved above her head in an impressive combination that matched her partner only a few steps away. The two continued on, and Lyla laughed when the choreography brought her and the man face to face. "More like that," she said.

"Perfect."

Collin's frown deepened. This wasn't at all what he'd been expecting. There was no way in hell this was *The Markovik Number*.

Lyla laughed again as the music faded and Moses clapped. "Hell yeah. The kids are going to eat this one *up*. Does it get the official Ly-Ly seal of approval?"

"It's a good one," Lyla confirmed with a huge smile. I just hate that I won't be here to see the final production."

"It's just a few weeks—" Moses stopped when his eyes met Collin's. "Can I help you?"

Lyla looked over her shoulder and smiled again. "Collin." She walked his way, her cheeks rosy, her skin dewy. "What are you doing here?"

He adjusted the bag in his hand, suddenly feeling slightly stalkerish. "I was out and about and heard through the grapevine that you were over here."

"Come on in and meet my friend Moses." She guided him farther into the room. "Moses, this is Collin Michaels. Collin, Moses Hagerty."

"Nice to meet you." Moses held out his hand.

Collin returned his shake. "You too. Those were some impressive moves there."

"Thanks." Moses dabbed at his sweaty forehead with a towel he grabbed off the floor. "So you're the Collin Michaels taking Ly-Ly across the pond?"

"Tomorrow," he confirmed.

"Good for you. Looks like you're up for the job." Moses looked Collin up and down, clearly sizing him up.

He glanced toward the wedding band on Moses' finger, trying to get a read on what role this man played in Lyla's life. "Always am."

"Good."

Collin returned his attention to Lyla. "I picked up some

stuff for dinner."

"Oh." She walked closer and peeked in the bag, smelling as good today as she did last night.

"Kale. It's supposed to be pretty good for you."

She grinned. "It is."

"I grabbed some fish too—cod. Three pounds."

Her eyes widened.

"If that's not enough—"

She chuckled. "No. That's more than plenty and very sweet of you. Thanks."

"You're welcome."

Her cell phone rang across the room. "Hold on just a second. Let me get that." She hurried off, leaving Collin with Moses.

"I didn't realize Lyla danced hip-hop."

"Only unofficially." Moses draped the towel over his shoulders. "She likes to come over here to the Y and help me out with my classes—likes to get in on the preschool ballet whenever she can."

"Do you work with her at Manhattan Ballet?"

"No. This is my gig. I used to dance at Julliard. That's how Ly-Ly and I met. Manhattan School of Dance and Julliard share dorms."

He nodded. "So college then?"

"Sort of—for me. Ly-Ly was already dancing with the company even though she was pretty young—sixteen or seventeen, I think. She was still living at Residence Hall when I was a freshman at Julliard. I messed up my knee a couple years ago, so the professional stage went out the window." He snapped his fingers, demonstrating how quickly his career ended.

"That's tough."

He shrugged. "It happens."

"You definitely didn't seem injured to me."

"Surgery fixed me up pretty good, but I wouldn't be able to keep up night after night like Ly-Ly does."

Lyla laughed as she continued her conversation on the phone.

Moses and Collin looked her way.

"It sounds like this should be an interesting trip. Ly-Ly usually travels overseas alone."

He didn't have any trouble reading between the lines, noting the protective edge in Moses' voice. Clearly Lyla told her buddy that they would be posing as a couple. "The ambassador thinks this is the best way to handle things for the time being."

Moses nodded. "Things seem like they're pretty intense over there."

"Her schedule's packed. We should be able to keep her out of the worst of it."

"I'd appreciate you getting her back to us in one piece."

"That's always the plan." Collin glanced toward Moses' wedding ring again, wondering if this was the reason why Lyla didn't date.

She looked their way and smiled as she held up her finger for one more minute.

Collin smiled back.

"That's a good woman right there," Moses continued, "the best I know besides my wife, of course."

Perhaps he was reading the situation wrong but he couldn't be sure just yet. "She seems great—has a great sense of humor."

Moses nodded. "Ly-Ly definitely knows how to laugh, but sometimes you have to look beyond her smiles. She lets people see what she wants them to see."

Collin opened his mouth to ask Moses what he meant, but Lyla hung up and grabbed her coat and bag.

"Okay. I'm ready to go. Should we blow this pop stand?"

"Sure."

She hugged Moses. "I'll see you in a few weeks. Tell Charlotte we'll get together when I get back—my place this time."

Moses kept his arms hooked around her waist. "I'll let her

know."

"I'm going to have to work hard to impress her after the shrimp she made last weekend."

Moses laughed. "You know she'll be pleased to hear that."

Collin studied Lyla and Moses closely, mostly convinced that he was seeing nothing more than a warm friendship.

"You listen to Collin and don't forget to break a leg."

"Okay." She kissed his cheek and said something quiet to him in Russian as she smiled.

He nodded as he let her go and held out his hand to Collin once again. "It was nice to meet you."

"You too."

Lyla put on her jacket and hat. "Let's go." She hooked her arm through Collin's, and they walked downstairs.

"I didn't realize you did hip-hop or whatever that was."

"Just for fun."

"It looks like you have a backup career if the whole ballet thing doesn't work out."

She laughed as they stepped outside. "Thanks. Cab or should we walk?"

He glanced down at her wrapped ankle. She said the brace was for support, but he wondered about that too. "Cab." He raised his hand, hailing a taxi, and did a double take when he noticed the man he'd bumped into by Lyla's building standing on the corner across the street. He opened the back door for Lyla and got in next to her as Lyla told the cabbie her address.

He looked out the rear window, thinking back to the moment he smacked into the man's shoulder and apologized. The guy had an accent—perhaps Russian, but maybe not. It was interesting how most people were in a hurry to get out of the miserable weather while the man they left behind enjoyed a cigarette in the cold. He turned around, keeping his eye on the side view mirror, watching for a tail. "I saw your billboard by the theater."

She smiled. "It went up today for Geoffrey's new show."

"You must get hassled by the press some—and fans."

"Not as much here as in Russia. Sometimes before performances, but that's about it. In a city this big, it's pretty easy to get lost in the crowd."

He nodded, looking toward the mirror again. It was easy to get lost in the city, so how was it that the man knew how to find her? Collin didn't know who he was, but he would certainly be paying attention from now on.

❧ Chapter Six ❧

LYLA FORKED UP ANOTHER BITE OF THE SAUTÉED KALE Collin had prepared under her direction. The touch of kosher salt and minced garlic added to the amazing flavor, complementing the mashed sweet potatoes on her plate. "This is *so* good. You did a great job."

"Only because of you." He sampled more of the baked cod she'd drizzled with fresh lemon butter. "This right here," he gestured to the fish with his fork, "this is out of this world. I haven't eaten this well in months—since Hawaii."

She smiled brightly. Her friends always appreciated the treats she often shared, but Collin's adoration for her cooking was a solid stroke to her culinary ego. "There's plenty more."

He looked over his shoulder toward the full platter of fish on the counter. "I definitely got a little carried away. Three pounds of cod goes a long way. It's a shame we'll have to toss that out."

She shook her head. "We won't. I'll pack up everything and send it over to my neighbor." She picked up her white wine, an indulgence she rarely allowed herself, and sipped, enjoying the subtle hints of buttery vanilla and peaches— almost as much as she was enjoying her quiet evening with Collin. Blue jeans and sweatshirts were tonight's dress code, but even better was the laughter and easy conversation they'd shared while working together in the kitchen. Sitting across from him, completely relaxed, was pure bliss. "So, did you vacation in Hawaii?"

He shook his head as he swallowed the last of his fish and set down his fork. "No. My parents live there."

Her eyes widened. "You're from Hawaii?"

"I was born and raised there. Both of my parents are mainlanders. They moved to the island a few months before I made my debut. They divorced when I was eleven. My mother took me to Chicago with her, which pretty much sucked."

She raised her brow. "That's quite a change."

"I hated every second of it. When you surf and fly planes almost every day of your life, then move somewhere where you can't do either, it makes for a rough existence."

Lyla frowned. "I thought you said you moved when you were a little boy."

He nodded as he wiped his mouth. "I did."

"You flew planes when you were eleven?"

"Nah." He snagged his glass of wine and sat back. "My dad let me at the yolk when I was six."

She gaped. "You flew planes when you were *six*?"

He grinned. "Sure. Dad owns a small charter service that flies tourists between the islands. I used to go with him any chance I could get. If he didn't have passengers on return flights, he would let me go at it."

She pressed her hand to her heart, trying to grasp the idea of a child flying an airplane. "Is that *legal*?"

"Yup. I'm licensed now."

"There better not be a six-year-old flying our plane tomorrow."

He laughed. "A CPL's a whole different ballgame. I think it's pretty safe to say we won't see any grade-schoolers in the pilot's seat."

She traveled constantly and had yet to warm up to air travel. "I appreciate the reassurance. What's a CPL?"

"Oh, a commercial pilot license." He sipped from his glass. "So, I imagine we should talk about Russia—how we're going to make all of this work."

She pushed her plate away and settled against the back of her chair, crossing her ankles beneath the table. "Since we *are* dating, we should probably know how we met."

He grinned. "Probably." He took another sip of his wine. "How about we go with something simple, like we bumped into each other on the sidewalk."

She smiled. "We *did* bump into each other on the sidewalk."

"Exactly. Sticking as close to the truth as possible is always a good policy. Why fabricate if we can be honest?"

She nodded, appreciating his logic. "So we'll leave our dads setting this whole thing up out of it?"

"I think we should. It seems kind of arranged marriage-ish." He sent her a friendly wink.

She paused with her glass halfway to her mouth and laughed, realizing the whole situation absolutely did. "I never thought about it that way, but you're right." She laughed again. "We'll keep marriage out of this."

"It's a little sudden."

She smiled, staring at the gorgeous man looking at her, completely relieved that if she had to be a part of a farce for the next few weeks, she had Collin as her partner. "So, how long have we been dating?"

He pursed his lips and narrowed his eyes. "A month?"

"Do you think that's long enough? Bringing my significant other overseas really says commitment, especially when I always travel alone."

He shrugged. "So we're hot and heavy."

"The media's pretty sly. They'll pick up on whether or not we're hot and heavy." She swallowed, thinking of the press's scrutiny, never giving her a moment to breathe.

"We'll be convincing. I should probably call you Ly-Ly, since that's what all of your friends say."

"Good thinking." She sat up, resting her elbows on the table as a new thought occurred to her. "Are you—this isn't going to be a problem for your personal life?"

"No." He sat up as well, mirroring her gesture as he set his elbows on the small table. "Sydney and I broke up about six months ago."

"I'm sorry."

He shrugged again. "We tried to make things work, but sometimes they don't, especially with a job like mine."

She frowned. "A job like yours?"

"The traveling, being gone for long stretches of time. It's hard on the other person."

She nodded, well aware of what he was talking about. "That's why I don't date. But you know what I never understand?"

"What's that?"

"I've always been told by my exes that I give my career too much, that I travel too much, but when we first met, my job was exactly the same."

His brow furrowed as he made a sound in his throat.

She stared at the golden wine left in her glass and traced the stem with her finger as she sensed the sudden tension in the room. Clearing her throat, she looked at him. "I hope I didn't say something to make you uncomfortable."

"No. You gave me something to think about."

"Oh." She licked her lips, still not quite sure that she hadn't somehow offended him. "Something good or bad?"

"A new perspective. Those are always good."

She nodded, certain she and Collin were going to walk away from the next three weeks as great friends. "I think I'm going to like this—our pretend relationship."

"Oh, yeah?"

"Yeah." She smiled as he did. "No complications. I'm not big on drama, or maybe I'm just too selfish to make time for someone else, but either way, this is going to be good."

"You've been single for a while?"

"Four years."

He widened his eyes. "You haven't gone out on a date in *four* years?"

She shook her head. "In the last two days, I've been on two dates with the love of my life who I'm extremely hot for."

He looked over his shoulders playfully, giving her a confused expression.

She laughed. "I like you. I like that you make me laugh."

He chuckled. "It's a good sound—easy on the ears."

Polite, funny, intense, *and* charming—Collin Michaels was a dangerous combination. She stood, wanting to end their evening right here. "I'm going to pack this up." She gestured to their leftovers.

He got to his feet and started stacking dirty dishes. "I'll give you a hand."

"Thanks. If we can put some of the fish and vegetables into tinfoil that would be great. The rest can go in Tupperware."

"Yeah. Sure."

Systematically they wrapped everything up and put the items from her fridge in cloth grocery sacks. "I think this is it. If you wouldn't mind helping me bring this next door."

"Your neighbors hit the jackpot."

"Mrs. Franelli lives on social security for the most part. Her son does what he can to help, but her medications are really expensive." She'd picked up the tab Medicare didn't cover more than a few times—and the cost was staggering.

Collin grabbed four of the bags, leaving the lightest for her. "Let's go hook her up."

Lyla led the way, knocking on the door across the hall.

Minutes later, the door opened and her elderly neighbor smiled. "Ly-Ly."

"Mrs. Franelli, you didn't ask who I was," she scolded gently.

"It's always you, dear."

"One of these times it might not be though."

Mrs. Franelli opened the door wider, dressed in her typical royal blue robe and matching slippers that Lyla had given her for Christmas. Her thinning white hair needed a wash and cut. "What have you got here?" Her eyes brightened considerably when she spotted Collin. "And who's this young man?"

"This is Collin."

"Oh." She clasped her arthritic hands together, then reached for Collin's arm, guiding him inside. "This is wonderful, just wonderful. Ly-Ly doesn't have many people over, certainly not men—and none as handsome as you."

Collin smiled. "Thank you."

Lyla shut the door, making sure Mrs. Franelli's half-dozen cats stayed in the apartment. "I want to put this stuff in your fridge. I have some of the power greens you like—enough for you to have one a day until Frank can bring you more."

"She's a good girl. Likes to fill me full of fruits and vegetables," Mrs. Franelli said to Collin. "Says it keeps me young and healthy."

"She's a good cook."

"A ballerina and a chef. You should hold on to this one. You will if you're smart." She gave a gentle tap to his shoulder.

Lyla smiled apologetically at Collin. "Mrs. Franelli, would you like some cod? It's still nice and warm."

She nodded. "That would be lovely, dear."

"We made some mashed sweet potatoes and kale."

"A feast. The kitties want some too."

Lyla reached into the cupboard for a plate. "I'll get you taken care of first. How are the litter boxes?" she asked, even as she smelled their odor.

"They might need a change."

"I can handle that," Collin offered as he set down the bags.

Lyla stared at him as he took the hand Mrs. Franelli offered him and walked with the hunchbacked octogenarian to the odorous boxes lined up by the window. He crouched down to take care of the problem while cats slithered around his legs and sweet Mrs. Franelli talked his ear off. Big, tough Collin Michaels was a sweetheart. She was going to have to be careful around him. He had the potential to be trouble.

Shaking her head, she gave her attention back to the Tupperware, portioning out Mrs. Franelli's meal and putting pieces of fish into six small bowls. "Come on kitties." She set the bowls down, and the cats immediately abandoned their new friend for their dinner.

Mrs. Franelli smiled as she watched her cats eat. "They sure love a nice meal, don't you boys and girls?"

Collin glanced over his shoulder. "They certainly look like they're happy."

"They are. They are, dear."

Taking a paper towel from the roll in lieu of a napkin, Lyla brought Mrs. Franelli's plate to the table. She went to the fridge next and poured a glass of filtered water from the pitcher she'd bought a couple months ago, then grabbed the small handful of prescription pills dosed out in the reminder box and set them on the placemat. "Here you go, Mrs. Franelli. I think that's everything."

"You're a dear," Mrs. Franelli said as she made her way to her seat.

Lyla crouched down next to her. "I'm going to be gone for three weeks. I leave tomorrow afternoon. Frank's going to bring by your groceries on Thursday, and Lisa will be here to clean next Wednesday."

"I remember."

"If you run out of anything, you call Frank and have him put it on my account."

"And I'll pay you back."

"You can pay me back with a game of cards when I get home."

"I have the set right here." She pointed to the deck of cards by the salt and pepper shakers.

"I'll see you soon." She stood and hugged the frail old woman in her chair.

Mrs. Franelli returned her embrace, gently patting her back. "You take care of your ankle. Remember the Epsom salt."

She kissed Mrs. Franelli on the cheek and eased back. "I will."

Collin dried his hands at the sink. "It was nice to meet you, Mrs. Franelli."

"I'll see you in three weeks too, dear."

Lyla and Collin exchanged a look, then Lyla smiled at her neighbor. "Take care of yourself."

"Of course, dear."

"Bye." She opened the door, waited for Collin to step out, and locked up. Sighing, she met Collin's stare. "Thanks for helping."

"Is she okay to be living on her own?"

That was a question she'd asked herself every day. "She really needs part-time care. Her son's trying to get things figured out."

"Where's he at?"

"In New Jersey."

"Huh."

They went back into her apartment, and she filled a mug with water, putting it in the microwave as she looked toward the windows, staring out at the city lights. It was cold tonight, brutally so.

"How about I get started on the dishes?"

She shook her head as she met Collin's gaze. "You don't have to."

"They aren't going to do themselves."

"You're my guest. I can take care of it."

He looked toward the mess. "I'm pretty sure we both had a hand in making that." He slid up his sleeves as he moved to the sink and started filling it with water.

"You really don't have to."

He squirted in a glob of dish soap. "It's fine."

"Thanks." She glanced toward the windows again, thinking of Charlie, and snagged the navy blue wool cap she'd made off the entryway table, along with the other stuff she would need for her friend. She put it in one of the cloth shopping bags they'd brought back from Mrs. Franelli's as the microwave beeped.

Collin glanced over his shoulder and frowned. "What are you doing?"

"I need to run downstairs real quick." She grabbed her coat from the closet.

"You're going *outside*?"

She put the hot water and a teabag into a Styrofoam cup, secured a lid in place, and headed for the door. "For a second."

Collin abandoned the sink and pulled his own jacket from the closet. "Why don't I come with you?"

She shook her head. "You don't have to."

"It'll be good to get some air."

She opened her mouth to argue and closed it when she saw in his eyes that he wasn't going to take no for an answer. "Okay." She twisted the doorknob instead.

They took the elevator to the ground floor and pushed through the glass door, stepping out into the wretched cold. She quickened her pace, wanting to avoid questions as she turned the corner and headed down the darkened alley behind her building.

Collin grabbed her arm. "Lyla—"

"This will only take a minute. You can go back inside and wait."

"I'm not leaving you in an alley by yourself."

But she wasn't by herself. She pulled away and walked farther into the dark. "Charlie?"

The homeless man popped his head out of the thermal sleeping bag she'd bought for him. "That you, Ly-Ly?"

"It is." She crouched down in front of him in the dim light shining from the hundreds of windows, knowing his sight was getting worse. "I brought you some dinner—some hot tea and some fish and vegetables."

He sat farther up, bundled in his coat and hat. "That's nice of you. Soup kitchen served up stew tonight, but nothing as good as your food."

She smiled. "I made you another hat. I know you said your friend liked the one you have." She handed it over. "It's navy blue."

Charlie squinted, bringing the knitted piece closer to his face. "Gus'll be real grateful. Who's he?" Charlie gestured to Collin.

She didn't bother to glance behind her. "My friend Collin."

"He's not gonna try and make me leave—"

"He's not going to try and make you leave." She pulled the large serving of healthy food from the bag, along with plastic utensils, hoping to soothe his ruffled feathers.

Charlie took the bulky aluminum foil and cupped it in his hands. "Nice and warm."

"It should be." She cleared her throat. "I made a couple of calls today after my class. There are a few doctors downtown who might be able to help you with your eyes."

"My eyes are just fine."

"We could probably get you a pair of glasses."

He tore open his second dinner and settled it on his lap. "I found myself some in the bin over at the shelter."

"We can get a prescription that's just for you."

"The one's I found are working just fine."

She nodded, knowing that arguing wouldn't help. "You'll have to let me know if you change your mind. We can take a cab down and get you fixed up."

"Can't leave my stuff." He gestured to his cart.

"We could put it in my apartment. No one would touch it there."

"My glasses are fine," he said again.

Burying her frustration, she smiled. "Okay. I'm going to be gone for a few weeks."

He dug into the meal. "Off to do your dancing?"

"Yes."

"Where this time?"

"In Russia. If it gets much colder, you should sleep at the shelter. I don't want to come home and find out they found a popsicle in the alley."

Charlie laughed. "My new bag keeps me toasty. And the winds not too bad back here."

"I'm glad, but that sleeping bag is only good to twenty below."

"It works fine."

"I'll make you some custard when I get back."

He smiled his mostly toothless smile. "A real treat."

She took his filthy hand. "You be careful out here, Charlie."

He gave her a gentle squeeze. "You be careful too."

"I will." She stood and reluctantly left him where he wanted to be, hurrying back down the alley into the warmth inside as Collin followed. She avoided meeting his gaze as she pressed the button for the elevator, sensing his disapproval.

They stepped into the car for the slow journey to the twentieth floor. Silent seconds ticked by as they ascended.

"That's pretty dangerous."

She looked at him. "Charlie's harmless."

"It's pretty dangerous," he repeated as he stuffed his hands in his pockets and leaned against the wall.

"He helped me this summer when he startled off a couple of jerks who were going to mug me. Bringing him food and tea on a cold night is the least I can do." The door dinged and slid open.

"Why doesn't he stay at the shelter?"

She started down the hall. "People take his stuff. I tried to find him a job and a small place, but he doesn't want the help. His wife died a few years ago. He started drinking and lost everything."

"There are people at the shelters who can help him."

She slid her key in the lock and met his eyes again, absorbing the quick stab of disappointment. "I'm not turning my back on Charlie. Too many people see a homeless person and have no problem looking the other way. I'm not one of them." She opened her door and stepped in. "I'm going to take a shower and get packed for tomorrow."

"I guess I'll see you in the morning."

"Yeah." She did her best to ignore her irritation with the situation in general. "I'll see you in the morning." She sent him a small smile and closed herself in the bathroom, aware that her explanations had done little to convince Collin that feeding homeless men in the dark was the right thing to do. But she didn't care. No one could convince her she was wrong. She would continue to provide Charlie dinner until he told her he wanted her to stop.

—◊—

Collin settled beneath the covers on his temporary bed as the dim glow of city lights radiated through the windows. He reached out, grabbing the remote off the coffee table he'd pushed off to the side, and flipped through several channels, stopping on SportsCenter. Scores and updates ticked by on the bottom of the screen, and he moved on, not all that interested in hockey stats.

He stopped again when the live footage from Saint Petersburg, Russia caught his attention. With the volume on mute, he searched for the closed caption button and sat up, reading the news report while the station switched back and forth between the newscaster and images of the police surrounding a trolleybus in the middle of a downtown street. The reporter spoke of a bomb discovered during the busy morning rush hour, mere miles from the plaza where dozens had been killed on New Year's Eve. Luckily a citizen had been paying attention, and the explosive device had been deactivated, stopping another disaster.

Early reports were suggesting that the same rebel group

responsible for the December thirty-first bombing, Chechen Freedom, had attempted to strike again. The news segment switched to snippets of the video released weeks ago, shortly after the slaughter of innocent civilians, where the masked men promised more violence in retaliation for The Federation killing one of their leaders. The man pointed at the camera, vowing to continue with his plans to destroy Russia until the regime relented and gave the Chechens back their country.

Sighing, Collin rubbed at his jaw. Why did he feel like he was walking into a losing situation? Everyday there was something new going on over there. If it wasn't bomb threats and anti-American rallies, it was anti-Putin demonstrations outside the Kremlin walls, which often ended with tear gas and riot gear. And he and Lyla were only hours away from their late-afternoon flight.

The issues in Saint Petersburg weren't necessarily one of his concerns. The city was a good nine hours away from their destination. It was the possibility of terrorist attacks in Moscow and Russia's discord with the United States in general that had him on edge. The fact that Lyla was a dual citizen of two countries at odds had the potential to work for her... or very much against her. Only time would tell which way things were going to go, and they would be along for the ride while they waited to figure it out.

The news coverage moved on to the local forecast. He hit the power button, looking toward the locks on the front door he'd made certain were secure before calling it a night. His thoughts turned again to the mystery man he'd bumped into on the corner. When he and Lyla went outside several hours ago to deliver Charlie his dinner, he hadn't seen anyone lurking around, but there were numerous vehicles parked close to the building. Anybody could have been sitting in one of the cars or SUVs using the darkness to their advantage. His gut told him that spotting Cigarette Man twice in one afternoon hadn't been some strange and random coincidence. Lyla was being watched. He was willing to bet someone waited twenty floors below even now.

Clenching his jaw, he laid back and tucked his arms behind his head. He needed to talk to Jonathan and get the ambassador's take on who might be following his daughter, but that was going to have to wait until they could speak face-to-face. From this point forward, Collin was on his own. All ties to Ethan Cooke Security had officially been severed. If anyone did any digging into who he was, they would be led to believe he'd walked away from the company the day he got back from Iraq to follow his girlfriend on her journey around the world.

Restless, he turned on his side, studying the pictures of the Russian architecture hanging on the wall, trying to settle. It was well past three, and the jetlag of returning from Iraq then hustling off to New York less than eighteen hours later was setting in, but even as his body yearned for sleep, his mind wouldn't rest. Already this assignment had him on high alert, yet there was nothing he could or needed to do for Lyla at this point.

He yawned as he thought of the woman sleeping in the next room. What was it about her that constantly kept her in his thoughts? Her beauty was distracting, but that wasn't it. There was so much more to Lyla than her looks—dancer, chef, caretaker to elderly neighbors, and a private soup kitchen to the homeless who lived in cold, dark alleys.

He'd spotted her note and generous tip for Frank stuck to Mrs. Franelli's fridge, reminding the deliveryman to charge the sweet old woman's bill to Lyla's account for the remainder of the month. Then there had been the longer letter Lyla had composed to Lisa, the housekeeper, asking that Lisa help Mrs. Franelli with her laundry. Lisa was supposed to call Lyla to settle up for the extra cleaning duties, which was complete bullshit. Supposedly Mrs. Franelli's son did what he could for his mother, but from what Collin could see, it looked like Lyla was the only one stepping in.

And then there was Charlie. Collin hadn't missed the high-end sleeping bag the homeless man had been laying in when Lyla dropped off the warm meal. There was no way in hell Charlie had picked that up in the bin at the shelter. If Charlie would have been willing to take Lyla up on her offer to visit the optometrist, Lyla would have been responsible for that bill too.

He steamed out a breath, shaking his head at the entire situation. Lyla certainly had her hands full. She danced full-time, and in her spare moments, took care of everyone else. Her career was lucrative and her mother had amassed her own fortune, undoubtedly leaving Lyla without financial worries. Clearly she could afford to help others, but it was a rare person who chose to take on the problems of the world. Her selflessness appeared to be genuine and was undeniably attractive. He wanted to know more about the woman who couldn't seem to turn a blind eye to others' needs.

He glanced toward the pictures on her bookshelf and frowned, realizing for the first time that he had yet to see anything in Lyla's home that gave anyone a clue as to who she was when she walked out her apartment door. Down the street, her image covered a huge billboard. Her employer was one of the world's most prestigious dance companies—and she was their star, yet there were only photographs of family and friends among the stacks of cookbooks filling her shelves.

Perhaps it was the aura of mystery surrounding Lyla Markovik-Avery that kept him intrigued. More than once he'd replayed his conversation with Moses.

She lets people see what she wants them to see.

What was Lyla trying to hide? Why did he care? Lyla was certainly nice. Working with her for the next three weeks was going to be a refreshing change of pace. The two of them were bound to have a good time—they already did, but it was clear he and his principal would part ways as nothing more than friends.

Who knew? Maybe Lyla's company would help him return to Los Angeles with that new perspective he was searching for. She'd already brought up a good point about his breakup with Sydney. His ex had dropped more than one ultimatum toward the end: her or his career, and he'd always felt like a dick because he hadn't been willing to choose the woman he was supposed to love more than his job. Hopefully Lyla had a few more pearls of wisdom up her sleeve. Perhaps when he went home this time, entering his mostly empty apartment wouldn't sting so much.

CHAPTER SEVEN

LYLA RESTED HER HEAD AGAINST THE EDGE OF THE plane's window, watching their descent toward the runway. She swallowed, pressing her lips together as the jumbo jet tilted left then right in the gusty winds, but it wasn't the dips and sways that made her hands sweat. She'd flown too many times to worry about crashing, but the airport coming in and out of view through the clouds, that definitely made her heart pound.

During the overnight ten-hour flight east, she'd slept little, anticipating and dreading this very moment. Soon they would coast to the ground, and the game would begin. In fifteen minutes or less, her life would cease to be her own. The anonymity she treasured in Manhattan would vanish, and for the next three weeks, she would be speculated over and spied on. Every corner she turned would be a photo opportunity for the press, and the comparisons to Mina would start immediately—her looks, how she walked, talked, danced, smiled. Every minute was like being on a stage where the curtains never closed, but the euphoria of the dance wouldn't be there to take her into another world where music and movement were all that mattered.

The sudden urge to yank free of her seatbelt and flee overwhelmed her, so she clasped her fingers in her lap and shut her eyes. Fourteen days. In fourteen days she would dance at the Bolshoi. For years, she'd dodged the pressure to strap on her pointe shoes, choosing instead to use her trips to Russia as an opportunity to spend time with her father and support the causes most important to her. Her mother was a legend, an icon she could never live up to—and didn't want to. Now she would have no choice but to try.

She clenched her jaw as her chest constricted, and she exhaled a quiet, shaky breath. Every year she hoped things would be different—that she might feel differently, but being under a nation's microscope had always been tough to bear.

"Looks like we're here." The weight of Collin's shoulder rested against hers as he leaned closer to stare out the window.

She forced herself to open her eyes as she inhaled the woodsy, musky hints of his aftershave, finding comfort in the newly familiar scent. "Just about. Another minute or two."

He frowned. "Are you okay?"

She nodded. "The landings are always a little rough," she fibbed, wishing the plane would gain altitude and turn around.

"You're kind of pale."

"I'm just tired." She was exhausted and raw—a familiar sensation she knew would vanish the moment the plane took off for home twenty-one days from now.

"Maybe you should think about a nap after we get settled."

She sighed longingly at the idea. "That sounds perfect. You look pretty tired yourself."

He stretched as much as the small space would allow. "This isn't exactly your comfy pull out." He gestured to the coach-class seating.

"No, it's not."

"Something tells me your pal Charlie might've been more comfortable in his swank sleeping bag than we are right now." He gave her arm a teasing jab with his elbow.

She smiled, finding the pressure in her chest easing. Bringing Collin along for security purposes was probably overkill, but as she stared into his steady brown eyes, she couldn't be sorry he was here.

"Excuse me," the flight attendant said as she stopped and beamed at Lyla and Collin in their seats. "Ms. Markovik-Avery, I would like to let you know that arrangements have been made for your luggage. You and your companion won't need to bother with baggage claim."

She wanted to tell the woman not to worry about it, that she was perfectly capable of gathering her own things just like everyone else, but then she glanced around at the other passengers sitting close by and realized that she was already drawing people's attention. "Thank you."

"Enjoy your stay in Russia. We always love to have our princess back."

Lyla barely suppressed a groan when the woman curtsied—as if she were truly royalty. She smiled politely instead. "I always do. Thank you."

Collin raised his brow as the flight attendant walked off down the aisle. "Did she just *curtsy*?"

Lyla winced. "I'm afraid so."

His eyebrows drew together. "Huh."

"My mother was known as 'The Queen of Dance.' Everyone loved her. When I was born, the media nicknamed me 'Russia's Princess.'" She cleared her throat, always slightly humiliated when she was forced to offer up an explanation. "Unfortunately it stuck."

He hummed in his throat as he nodded. "So since we're dating, does that mean I get to be your prince?"

She grinned. "If you want to be."

He shrugged. "I've never had the option before, so it could be fun."

She rolled her eyes. "Being dubbed royalty isn't all it's cracked up to be. I promise."

"I guess we'll see." He wiggled his eyebrows.

She laughed. "You'll have to let me know what you think on the way home."

"Deal." He sent her a friendly wink.

She smiled again, deeply appreciating that none of this seemed to matter to him. Collin saw her as Lyla—just Lyla. He couldn't possibly understand how much that meant. She blinked as the wheels made contact with the tarmac, realizing that she was joking around while they made their final descent, instead of struggling not to be ill—a first in all the years she'd traveled to Russia.

"Overall that was a pretty smooth landing considering the wind," he said as he glanced out the window again.

"How would you rate it, Pilot Michaels? A solid ten?"

He grinned. "Let's go with an eight-and-a-half. There's always room for improvement."

The flight attendant moved their way again, using the seats to steady herself as the plane pulled up to the Jetway. "Ms. Markovik-Avery, Sir, if you two could please come with me."

"Oh, that's okay," she said as she slapped her hand over Collin's, halting him from unbuckling his seatbelt. It was one thing to accept the baggage claim favor, but this was too much. "We can—we can wait our turn."

The woman shook her head. "Letting you deplane first is best. Please follow me."

And so it began. With little choice, she did as she was told, grabbing her carry-on and moving toward the door with Collin behind her, listening to the murmurs of the other passengers.

"Yup, I could definitely get used to this," he said close to her ear as they stood side by side, waiting to be let out while everyone else remained seated.

She glanced at him, trying to smile, knowing that he was attempting to keep the mood light. Undoubtedly he was used to special privileges due to the line of work he was in. The rich and famous were treated differently no matter where they went.

"Thank you for flying with us. It has been our pleasure to serve you." The stewardess opened the door. "Welcome to Moscow."

"Thank you."

"Follow this man please and he will take you where you need to go."

She and Collin started down the Jetway, following behind the guest services employee who led them down a private hall, bypassing the typical walk she took through the airport.

"Nervous?" Collin asked.

"No," she said too quickly. "No, I'm fine."

"You look good—a hell of a lot better than anyone has a right to after ten hours on a plane."

She'd spent at least twenty minutes in the tiny bathroom applying makeup and doing her best to unwrinkle the long navy blue sweater she'd paired with black leggings and her favorite Uggs. "Thank you."

"I was kinda hoping you were going to say something similar to me: 'The color of your shirt brings out the gorgeous brown in your eyes,' or, 'Does it ever get old being so damn handsome, Collin?'"

She faltered mid-step, looking at him as he stared at her with humor dancing in those gorgeous brown eyes of his. He was certainly a head-turner, dressed just as casually as she was in his dark-wash jeans and a snug gray v-neck top that emphasized his tough build, but she wasn't about to tell him he was worth a second glance. Her incredulous scoff turned into a laugh. "You really are something else."

He shrugged. "That's what I've heard." He took her hand as they approached the main entrance of Sheremetyevo International. "It's show time."

They turned the corner, and a loud cheer rose up from the huge crowd of waiting fans. She blinked in defense against the blinding flashbulbs, allowing Collin to guide them as they walked parallel to the barriers separating them from the waving people calling out to her.

"Take my flowers, Lyla," a small child with red hair pleaded in Russian.

She stopped, letting go of Collin, and smiled, crouching next to the little girl. "Are these for me?"

"Yes, but they're not as lovely."

Her smile turned into a grin as she hugged the child who reminded her so much of Jennifer. She pulled one of the sunny daisies from the bouquet and slid the flower into the redhead's hair. "Thank you for such a wonderful gift."

"You're welcome."

She moved along, taking the time to shake hands and pose for photos as she and Collin approached the press waiting at the end.

"Who is your companion, Lyla?" several of the reporters shouted.

She looked at Collin.

"What?" He stepped closer to her side, tickling her ear with his breath as he asked, "What's wrong?"

"They—they want to know who you are."

"So tell them."

She swallowed. "I don't think I can lie."

He held her gaze and took her hand, lacing their fingers and bringing her knuckles to his lips for a kiss.

"Uh," she shuddered out as the warmth of his mouth against her skin made her pulse pound.

He pulled her along down the hall, away from the crowds. "I think that gave them a pretty good idea."

She nodded, looking down at their fingers still intertwined.

"There's my little girl."

Her gaze flew to the sound of the familiar voice, and she smiled. "Daddy." She broke her connection with Collin and hurried forward, skirting around the DSS agents surrounding her father.

"Ly-Ly." He wrapped her up in a tight hug. "It's always good to have you home."

She returned his embrace, ignoring the lightning-like flashes of more camera bulbs as the press followed them. If her privacy had to be invaded, at least she hoped people would see that supporting her father wasn't an awful thing. She eased back, smiling. "Daddy."

He kissed her cheek. "You're as stunning as always."

His hair was more gray than black, and the fine lines around his blue eyes were more pronounced, yet he still looked fit and handsome. "You're looking good yourself."

"This must be Collin."

"Um, yes." She tucked long strands of her hair behind her ear, remembering she had a part to play. "Dad, this is Collin Michaels."

Dad shook Collin's hand. "It's nice to meet you."

She cleared her throat as more cameras flashed for the momentous occasion of boyfriend meeting father for the first time.

"You too, sir."

Dad smiled, looking from Collin to Lyla. "What do you say we get out of here?"

She nodded. "Sure."

Collin took her hand, and they started toward the private exit. She waved and smiled as people stopped to stare at her, knowing her duty, pretending she didn't hear any more of the questions the press hollered about the man at her side or *The Markovik Number*. Tomorrow she would be forced to answer, but she didn't have to right now. Today she and Collin would have a chance to settle in and hopefully catch up on a little rest.

———◆———

Collin sat by Lyla's side as the ambassador's security team drove them back to Spaso House, the long-time residence of the United States Ambassador to Russia. He stared out the window, taking in the snow-covered sights of Moscow as father and daughter chatted it up in the back seat. He half-listened to Lyla answer Jonathan's questions: Yes, her ankle was fine, and of course she was thrilled to be home for a few weeks.

The conversation died down, and Lyla stared straight ahead as the small caravan of cars attempted to make their way through the congested traffic. Despite her happy responses for her father, her stiff posture and the way she gripped her hands together in her lap told Collin a different story. He studied her closely behind the cover of his dark sunglasses, trying to equate Manhattan Ballet's Prima Ballerina with Russia's reluctant princess.

He was only just beginning to figure Lyla out, but one thing he knew for certain was she didn't like all of the attention she received. She'd tried to hide her discomfort with smiles, but he'd taken Moses' suggestion and looked beyond her pretty grins. Lyla Markovik-Avery made her living on the stage. She danced before thousands of people on a regular basis, but she appeared to hate the spotlight and went out of her way to try to blend in.

Jonathan made mention of her popularity overseas, and Lyla had eluded to the fact herself, yet the huge crowds waiting to welcome her back to her birth country had taken him by surprise. Hundreds of people had shouted at her, eager for pictures or to hand her flowers or balloons. Princess Lyla was a high-caliber star, on par with some of Hollywood's biggest names, but as he looked at the beautiful blonde, he saw the sweet neighborly caretaker who secretly danced hip-hop with her friend at The Y.

I just want to be like everyone else—her words echoed through his head as he remembered one of their conversations over dinner. Unfortunately for Lyla, being ordinary wasn't in the cards.

Her gaze met his and her lips curved. "When we get to the

house, I'll show you your room."

"Oksana's eager to feed you lunch," Jonathan said to Lyla. "She was rushing around the kitchen when I left."

She grinned. "I can't *wait* to see her. Collin, you're in for a treat. Oksana's been taking care of Dad for the last fourteen years."

"Since I became ambassador," Jonathan confirmed.

"Everything she makes is amazing." Lyla smiled again, this time for real.

"You know I'll never turn down food."

The car turned off the main road, down a quieter street, and slowed, stopping at the wrought-iron gates in front of the huge yellow-and-white-pillared house. Lyla waved at the women and children bundled up in their winter gear. They held up signs Collin could only assume welcomed Lyla home.

"They've been waiting for you for about an hour."

The car pulled through the side entrance.

"That's very sweet. I'll come out and say hello after I give Oksana a hug. Maybe we can bring them some hot chocolate."

"I'm sure they would appreciate it."

The vehicle came to a stop, and one of the DSS agents opened Collin's door.

"Thanks." He stepped out and clenched his jaw in the shocking chill. The sun shined bright in the pretty blue sky, but the temperatures were brutal nevertheless.

Lyla got out and crossed her arms against the cold. "Yikes, it's freezing out here."

Collin bobbed his head from side to side. "It's a little cool—slightly arctic, but who needs the tropics when you've got this?"

Her breath puffed out in a white cloud as she chuckled. "Should we go in?"

He was ready for a decent meal and a long shower. "Definitely."

"Welcome to Russia by the way."

"Thanks."

They walked up the stairs and stepped through the front door into a grand entryway, with Jonathan following behind.

"Ly-Ly." A thin, black-haired woman of about fifty yanked Lyla against her, showering her cheeks with kisses as she spoke to her in Russian.

Lyla grinned. "Oksana." She kissed her cheek in return and gave her a big hug. "It's so great to see you."

"You are well?" Oksana asked, this time in English. "You are well, my girl?"

She nodded. "I'm very well."

Oksana stepped back, looking at Collin. "I see you've brought someone with you this time. Someone special?"

She nodded again. "Oksana, this is Collin Michaels."

Oksana held out her hand. "It's nice to meet you, Mr. Michaels."

He returned her greeting. "Collin. It's nice to meet you as well."

"You make my little girl happy?"

"I hope so." He looked at Lyla as he spoke, genuinely hoping he did.

"He makes me very happy. We laugh a lot."

Oksana made a sound in her throat as she grinned and clasped her hands together. "This is what I've been hoping for."

A tall man with clean-cut mahogany hair and a decent build stepped from one of the rooms down the hall, followed by a short, older, bald man with a manicured, pewter-colored beard.

"Sergei," Lyla said with a hint of confusion. "Fedor."

"You have guests," Oksana said, not bothering to mask her annoyance.

The tall one, Sergei, Collin assumed, said something in Russian, his nasty tone unmistakable despite the foreign language.

Lyla nodded and glanced from her father to Collin. "Collin, this is Sergei Ploeski, my dance partner, and Fedor Yeltsov, the choreographer for *The Markovik Number*. Sergei and Fedor want to hold rehearsals."

Collin frowned. "Right now?"

"Yes."

"Excuse us," he said, pulling Lyla into one of the small sitting rooms. "Lyla, we just got here. Don't you want lunch? And you said you were tired." Despite the time she'd spent on her makeup, she *looked* tired.

"I'm fine. I can eat and rest later."

"They can come back later."

She shook her head. "No. We'll run through the dance a couple of times and get to know each other as partners. We don't have a lot of time to get this right."

He narrowed his eyes. "This is what you want?"

"They have the ballroom set up for us, and I pushed this on Sergei without even asking him first. We have to get started at some point. It might as well be now. Are you going to be okay on your own for a while?"

"I'm here to work around *you*. Go ahead and do what you have to."

She nodded again and stepped back into the entryway, curving her lips in a polite smile, speaking to the men in Russian. She said something to Oksana next and went upstairs.

Oksana led Lyla's dance group in the opposite direction, and Jonathan gave Collin a firm nod.

"Welcome to Spaso House. I hope you'll be comfortable here."

"I already am."

"Oksana will bring by tea and some lunch shortly if you would like to join me in my office."

He nodded. "Sure."

They walked down a long hall, and Jonathan shut the door behind them, immediately moving over to the radio across the room and turning it on fairly loudly. He took his seat behind his desk, and Collin sat in the chair in front of him.

Some of the lightness left Jonathan's eyes. "I take it your flight was uneventful."

"Yeah, pretty standard," he said quietly, well aware Jonathan was concerned that the room was bugged.

"Good. I'm sorry you're here. I'm always happy to visit with my daughter, but under the circumstances all I want is for her to be safely back home—civil unrest, anti-American sentiment, the constant threat of the next bombing..." He used a remote to turn the music up louder and leaned in closer. "They're watching my every move, now yours as well."

"Who exactly?"

"FSB."

"Lyla had a tail in New York. As far as I know, they didn't follow us here."

Jonathan's cheeks pinked up as he clenched his jaw. "This is bullshit. She has nothing to do with any of this."

"We'll keep her out of it."

"That might not be possible. Although we're standing strong with The Federation on the recent terrorist attack and continued threats, our stance on Ukraine damn well makes me close to an enemy of the State." He rubbed at the back of his neck. "I want you two to play up the relationship—keep it in the media. I want everyone distracted with her love life. She needs to stay busy—dancing, touring the city, keeping up appearances with her humanitarian causes. I want anyone that matters to see that their problems are with me and our government, not my daughter."

Collin nodded.

"We're cutting her trip short. She's leaving after she dances."

"Does she know that?"

"No one will until after the parade. She's going to fall ill and need to get home to The States."

"There's gonna be backlash."

"And she'll be thousands of miles away. I'll make arrangements with your boss to keep you on in New York until we know she's safe—until you can confirm that the bastards have stopped following her."

He nodded.

Jonathan turned down the music and sat back in his chair. "I know Lyla's looking forward to showing you around the city."

"She's mentioned a few restaurants and some of the museums," he improvised.

There was a knock at the door, and Oksana entered with tea. "Ambassador. Collin. I hope you'll enjoy a cup of tea."

He preferred coffee, but he sat farther up, nodding. "I will. Thank you."

Oksana set up tea service for two. "I'll be back with lunch shortly. Lyla asked me to bring the women and children by the gates drinks and cookies first. Such a good girl she is."

Lyla was exhausted, and if he was gauging her right, maybe even a little bit miserable, but she hadn't forgotten about the kids standing outside holding up their signs. "She's the best," he said.

Oksana beamed at him as she closed the door behind her.

Collin's friendly smile faded as he looked at the ambassador again.

"Trust no one," Jonathan said as he helped himself to the teacup sitting in front of him.

ෆ CHAPTER EIGHT ෨

LYLA APPLIED A SWEEP OF BLUSH ALONG HER CHEEK-
bones and a light coat of mascara to her lashes as she
sat in front of the mirror in her temporary bedroom.
She glanced at the clock on the vanity and sighed as she
pushed the wand back into the tube of black liquid, realizing that the last thirty minutes had gotten away from her. If
she didn't get herself in gear, she was going to be late.

She picked up her brush, running the bristles through
her damp hair, then twisted her golden locks into a French
braid. The first official duty of her visit to Russia required
she keep her hair pulled back—and if she could muster up
a little energy... She exhaled another long breath and shook
her head, trying to force herself out of her funk.

Typically she looked forward to her afternoon at Orphan
House Ten, one of Moscow's smaller orphanages. The kids
were sweet and welcoming, and they always enjoyed the extra attention she tried to pay each of them. But today she
couldn't find her usual enthusiasm. Perhaps it was because
the skies were a gloomy gray, or maybe she was simply exhausted from the three days of dancing from dawn to dusk.
For some foolish reason, she'd been hoping for a morning
to sleep in and recover from the jetlag and long flight after
her journey east, but catching up on her rest wasn't in the
schedule.

She secured her braid with a hair tie and stood, sucking in a sharp breath when her ankle reminded her that her mind wasn't the only part of her body that was tired. Nibbling her lip, she moved her joint in cautious circles—left to right, then right to left—gauging her discomfort and knowing that she was overdoing it in rehearsals. Babying her foot for any decent length of time hadn't been an option. Fedor was relentless and Sergei rude and unforgiving. She was used to working with demanding partners—she could be one herself—but this was a different category of intense, something she was going to have to endure for the time being.

More than once she'd been tempted to tell them both to take a hike, but they were under the same amount of pressure she was, probably more. Although she'd never actually danced the steps of *The Markovik number* before her announcement to the papers nearly two weeks ago, she'd seen her mother's rehearsal tapes several times, which gave her an advantage her partner didn't have.

"Come on, Ly-Ly," she muttered as she hobbled to her bureau, dressed casually in jeans and a bold red sweater. She dug through her drawer for the compression brace she was coming to rely on more and more and pulled the snug sock in place, giving her ankle a wiggle, finding little relief even with the extra support.

Swallowing, she stepped closer to the window, staring out at the grounds of Spaso House, the only home she'd known in Russia, except for her three years at the boarding school in Saint Petersburg. As she glanced around at the familiar landmarks in the distance, she didn't feel the peace that met her when she studied her view from her apartment.

She shook her head with the rush of regret. Why did it have to be this way? She'd been *born* in Moscow. Her mother had been *revered* here. She'd visited for three weeks in late-January for the last ten years, trying her best to embrace the people who adored her and proudly claimed her as their own, yet she felt no connection, nothing familiar except for the waves of guilt that always consumed her.

She pressed her fingers to her temple as the dull ache started in her head, and she turned away from the window, sitting on her bed and staring at her tender toes exposed in her brace. Blisters. She was going to have to take better care of her feet if she planned to get through the next week and a half without adding bloody stumps to her problems—an affliction she'd suffered a time or two and did her best to avoid. She pulled Band-Aids from her bag, protecting the sores, then slid on socks and tied her Adidas sneakers as someone knocked on her door. "Come in."

Collin stepped inside, dressed in jeans and another long-sleeved t-shirt that accentuated his broad shoulders and muscular arms. "Hey, stranger."

She smiled. "Hi."

"How's it going? I haven't seen you much."

He wasn't kidding. They ate dinner together every night and that was about it. "Not half bad." She stood, cautious of her sore ankle.

"Rehearsal went well today?"

She nodded as she secured simple silver earrings in her ears instead of vocalizing her lie.

"Oksana said you were in the ballroom at four thirty this morning."

Sergei's call to her cell phone at four demanding they get an early start had been an unpleasant surprise. "We don't have a lot of time to get this right."

He closed the distance between them and took her chin between his fingers as he narrowed his eyes.

She blinked, surprised by his forwardness, fighting the urge to step back. They were supposed to be playing a couple deeply in love; she needed to get used to his touch.

"You need more sleep—at least a solid twelve hours."

She frowned, pulling away and studying herself in the mirror. The purple bags beneath her eyes had been covered with concealer. The blue of her eyes was bright and her cheeks a healthy, subtle pink, thanks to her expert hand with a makeup brush. "I look fine."

"I couldn't agree more, but that doesn't mean you're not tired."

Her brow furrowed again, reflecting back at her in the glass. She wasn't so sure she liked that Collin seemed to see what she tried so hard to hide. "I'll go to bed earlier tonight." She faced him and realized he was still staring at her. "What?"

He shook his head. "Nothing. How about some lunch?"

She nodded. "I'm hungry."

"Then let's eat."

"We'll have something quick and get to the orphanage. The children are expecting us."

"I'm game for whatever." He held out his hand.

For the briefest of seconds, she hesitated. They weren't on display here at the house, but she settled her palm against his and left her room, walking side by side with the pretend boyfriend she'd spent a total of two hours with over the last three days.

—◆—

"You make lovely flowers," Lyla spoke in Russian to the blond sitting by her side in the small arts and crafts room.

"Your snail is friendly," the girl replied, gesturing to Lyla's paper. "He smiles at us."

"Yes, he does. He's very happy." And so was she. For the first time since they'd arrived in Moscow, she felt a sense of peace—and the energy she couldn't muster up at Spaso House had thankfully returned. On the twenty-minute drive to Orphan House Ten, Collin had joked her out of her melancholy mood. By the time he'd parked the car at the curb, her usual enthusiasm for one of her favorite visits was back.

She dabbed her brush in the cup of cloudy water as she studied all of the pictures the four youngsters seated around her were painting. "Look at all of this beautiful artwork."

A few of the children peeked up from under their lashes and smiled, their shyness vanishing as the afternoon went on.

For over an hour she and Collin had sat front and center in the tiny music room where the nine residents of the orphanage, ages six to nine, took turns playing songs on the ancient piano or singing something special for their guests. Now she did crafts with the girls while Collin played games with the boys across the hall.

She glanced toward the window when a movement outside caught her attention, and she immediately looked away when she spotted the growing crowd of reporters gathering on the sidewalk, waiting to pounce. For days she'd been locked behind the gates of Spaso House. The media had camped out for the first forty-eight hours, eager for a princess sighting, but Sergei and Fedor had been the only ones to leave the grounds during that time. By some miracle, she and Collin had managed to escape the camera's probing eye earlier this afternoon when they left through Spaso House's back entrance and her father sent a decoy vehicle out the front, but the press was here now. "I, um, I hope you'll let me take some of these pictures with me," she said, trying to focus only on the children and what they needed from her today.

All four of the girls grinned, and her heart melted. She wished she could take them home. "Perhaps we can—" She paused when she heard the commotion in the next room: a loud bang quickly followed by roars of laughter.

Dasha, the caretaker supervising Lyla's visit, muttered something as she hurried to the closed door across the hall.

Something knocked against the wall again, making one of the children flinch, and Lyla frowned, gaining her feet and following the only woman in the house who spoke a few words of English. "Dasha, is everything okay?"

"Your partner makes a commotion," she said in a scolding

tone.

Lyla looked through the rectangular panel of glass, and her eyebrows winged up in surprise as little boys crawled over Collin. Growling, he rushed up, hefting two of the youngest kids on his back. The remaining three children giggled and quickly took chase around the train table as the boys clinging to him laughed hysterically, clearly having the time of their lives. Grinning, she barely suppressed a chuckle. Apparently Collin was excellent with kids.

He stopped abruptly, and the three kiddos running after him slammed into his backside. His gaze met hers through the window, and he grinned, winking at her as he set the two youngest down.

Without warning, one of the boys grabbed a pool noodle toy and smacked Collin on the temple.

Lyla winced, then laughed as his eyes rolled back in his head and he fell to the floor in an excellent imitation of a faint.

There was another uproar when the boys dove on top of him in a pig pile, and soon Collin had his work cut out for him, fending off the attention-hungry children.

"He makes them *crazy*." Dasha frowned.

"But they'll sleep well tonight," Lyla tried to soothe, reverting back to Russian so the woman at her side would have a full understanding of what she said.

The woman cast her a disapproving glance. It was clear they were wearing out their welcome.

"I'll take him home and send him to bed. You see for yourself that he's a big child. I'm not sure who's having more fun."

Dasha sent her a reluctant smile.

Lyla glanced at her watch, knowing her time at Orphan House Ten was coming to an end. Typically she stayed for two or three hours, and they were inching closer to the latter. "We should be leaving soon."

"Princess." Katria, the girl who'd sat by her side at the table, tugged on her sweater.

Smiling, she crouched down. "Did you finish your picture?"

"Yes." She handed over the brightly painted paper filled with flowers and butterflies. "It's for you to take home. So you won't forget me."

Her heart broke as she stared at the little girl with pigtails and blue eyes. How could no one want this beautiful child? "I could never forget you." She pulled Katria close. "I'll hang up your picture so I can see it every day."

Katria smiled. "At Spaso House?"

She nodded. "For now. When I go to the United States, I'll take it with me."

"Okay."

Moments later, Collin opened the door, stepping out of the playroom. His shirt was wrinkled and his hair a mess. "That's an intense crowd."

Lyla gave Katria a final hug and stood. "You got everyone riled up."

He shrugged as he pushed up his sleeves. "They had fun."

"Yes, they did."

"I had no idea what they were saying and vice versa, but who needs words when you're rough housing?"

She smiled as she reached up, smoothing his hair back into place.

"Thanks."

"You're welcome."

"Children, Princess Lyla and Mr. Michaels will leave us now," Dasha called to the kids.

Several groans filled the room.

"What's going on?" Collin asked.

"She told them we have to go."

"Sounds like they're going to miss you."

"I think they're going to miss *you*." She gave him a poke in the stomach. "You were a human jungle gym. I simply painted."

"Everyone likes a jungle gym."

She grinned as he did and returned her attention to the children as the boys were ushered into the room with their cheeks rosy and eyes full of delight. "I hope all of you will come give me a hug," she said in her mother's language.

Several teary girls took their turns hugging her.

She loathed this part, saying goodbye to children who didn't belong here, who would more than likely still be stuck in Orphan House Ten when she came back next year. "I'll visit next January and you'll all have wonderful new stories to tell me. But for now, I hope you'll enjoy a few gifts."

On cue, Dasha rolled out a cart with bulging party bags in the center, each containing a few favorite sweet treats and several age-appropriate books, along with hair ribbons for the girls and matchbox cars and trains for the boys.

The children swarmed Dasha, eager for their new items.

"Goodbye," Lyla called as she put on her jacket and hurried outside, wanting to go while the kids were occupied, a trick she'd come up with a couple of years ago when leaving had almost been impossible. Now when she closed the door behind her, she knew the children were smiling instead of crying. It was better for everyone.

"Princess, did you enjoy your visit?" someone shouted at her as the media immediately surrounded her and Collin.

"I always do," she answered as Collin took her hand and they walked toward their car. "There are so many children in need of good homes."

"How do you feel about Russia's ban on American adoptions?"

"Children need love no matter where it comes from."

"Will you and Collin start a family?"

She moved faster to the vehicle, gripping Collin's hand tighter, not interested in speaking about her personal life—even if it was pretend.

Collin opened her door for her.

"How does it feel to date the princess of Russia?" she heard someone ask him in broken English as she settled in the passenger's seat.

"Ly-Ly and I are very happy. Excuse me. We need to get home." He started around to his side, far more at ease with the press than she was.

"Do you consider Russia your home?"

"Russia is one of Ly-Ly's homes. I feel very welcome here. We'll see you later." He opened his door and got in.

"I'm sorry," she said as he buckled his seatbelt.

"Don't worry about it." Turning over the engine, he gave several toots of the horn, moved slowly through the crowd, and took off with a quick acceleration the moment the wheels were clear.

❦ CHAPTER NINE ❧

COLLIN DROVE THROUGH THE BUSY DOWNTOWN streets with a brigade of reporters following behind. He gave the gas pedal an extra punch when one of the vehicles tailing them moved to the right, getting too close on Lyla's side as a photographer in the backseat tried to get a shot of the princess finally out and about. Collin maneuvered to the left, sandwiching their car between two SUVs he was certain had nothing to do with the press. Keeping his pace steady with the surrounding traffic, he glanced Lyla's way as she stared at her lap, tracing the edges of the paintings she'd brought with her from the orphanage. "I see the media's as crazy here as they are in The States."

"Mmm. They'll do whatever it takes to get their story."

Silence filled the car again as she continued following the outline of the page with her finger. She'd been quiet at lunch and on the drive over to the orphanage—pretty much since they landed in Moscow three days ago. They didn't see each other much, but the Lyla sitting next to him wasn't the Lyla he'd met in New York. Luckily that changed when they stepped inside Orphan House Ten. It was then that he saw the bright, cheery woman he remembered from Manhattan. She'd been great with the kids—kind, warm, attentive, and more than willing to accept the dozens of hugs the children were eager to give her throughout the afternoon. She'd enjoyed her time with the kids as much as the children had themselves—and she hated leaving.

"So that was a nice visit," he said, hoping to start a conversation.

"It was. Spending time with the kids is my favorite part of coming overseas."

Horns blared behind them when the eager driver of the silver vehicle trying to get pictures of Lyla moments ago cut someone off.

She scoffed, shaking her head as she looked in the rearview mirror. "They're truly awful."

"It's pretty pathetic," he agreed.

"You must deal with this all the time—the constant chase in your line of work."

He spent his days helping his clients avoid overly eager fans and the press—an entirely different experience than being sought by them the way Lyla was now. "Sort of."

She nodded and started tracing the paper again.

"You know not speaking Russian has me at a disadvantage. I can't help you much with their questions when I don't understand what they're asking you."

"They want to know if we're planning to have children." Her finger stropped abruptly against the page as her gaze flew to his.

He smiled. "Your father forgot to tell me that was part of the deal."

She smiled back, but her eyes were sad. "It's not."

"So you said you visit the kids every year?" he asked, changing subjects. Lyla didn't seem to be in the mood to laugh.

She nodded. "My mom did a lot with that specific orphanage. It was pretty close to the house where she and my dad lived before she died."

"I thought I heard that Russian orphanages were in rough shape. That one seemed okay."

"That one is okay. I've never been allowed in any of the

others."

Interesting. "It's nice that you were able to pick up where your mother left off."

"Yes."

The quiet stretched out again as he waited for her to say something more, but she didn't. "Are you all right?"

"Of course." She sat up straight in her seat, pasting on a sunny smile. "I'm fine."

Why did that annoy him? "You don't have to do that."

"What?"

"Pretend."

She frowned. "I'm not."

"Those kids don't have homes, and they should. That sucks any way you look at it. It's okay to be a little down in the dumps."

She snapped her shoulders straight as her frown deepened. "I don't typically dissect my emotions. I wasn't planning on starting now."

Ouch. Sore spot. Apparently Lyla had a little bite when she felt backed into a corner. "I didn't say I want to be your shrink. I'm just saying it doesn't always have to be okay."

She looked out her window but said nothing.

He turned off the main road onto the quieter street close to Spaso House and stopped in front of the security gates with the damn silver car following behind.

The guard stepped from a small house outside of the property, looking at him, then at Lyla, and let them through. Collin pulled into the parking space where the DSS agent had told him to leave the Ambassador's private vehicle and shut off the engine.

"I think Roman's here," she said as she opened her door.

"Your interview."

She nodded.

He met her at the hood of the car, bundling his coat tighter around himself in the hellish cold.

"This shouldn't take too long. He usually gets right to the

point."

"We'll go in and let you get to it."

She took a step toward the house and stopped. "Thank you for coming with me today, for being so wonderful with the children."

He assumed that was her attempt at smoothing things out between them. "You're welcome." He took her hand as they started toward the steps, not because they were putting on an act for the journalist who was waiting, but because she was upset and didn't think she could show it.

⸺◆⸺

Lyla and Collin walked into the house and were immediately greeted by Oksana.

"Roman's here," she said, kissing Lyla's cheek. "Go ahead and give me your coats. I'll take care of them for you."

"Thank you." Lyla took hers off, handing it over as Collin did the same. "When did he arrive?"

"About thirty minutes ago. He's having tea with the ambassador in his office."

Lyla barely suppressed a wince as she imagined the hellish half-hour poor Dad must have endured with one of The Federation's staunchest supporters. "Will you let them know we're home?"

"Right away. I'm sure your father could use a break." Oksana hurried off down the hall.

She sighed a weary breath as she walked over to the entryway mirror and slid the loose wisps of hair escaping her braid back in place. Very soon it would be her turn to contend with Roman, which was only fair. He was here to see her after all. It was unfortunate Dad had gotten caught up in the bad timing.

Collin stepped up behind her, his gaze meeting hers in the glass. "You look great."

She opened her mouth to offer an apology for her behavior in the car, and closed it as Roman walked into the large space with her father following closely behind.

Lyla turned from the mirror, smiling even as she noted Dad's clenched jaw and the battle light in Roman's eyes. She stepped forward, taking Roman's hands. "Roman, it's so nice to see you here at Spaso House," she said in Russian.

He kissed both of her cheeks. "I'm always happy to pay our very own princess a visit."

She smiled again. "I hope you feel welcome."

"I do." He gave her fingers a squeeze. "Since we are among so many who speak English," he gestured to Collin, "we can happily continue in your first language."

She nodded. "Roman, let me introduce you to Collin Michaels."

Roman shook Collin's hand. "Welcome to Russia, Mr. Michaels."

"Thank you. Go ahead and call me Collin."

"We hope you find Moscow to be friendly."

"So far, so good."

"Good." Roman gave him a decisive nod. "Should we get started?" he asked, returning his attention to Lyla.

"Whenever you're ready," she agreed. The sooner they began, the sooner they would be finished. She faced Collin, not quite sure of what to do or say after their awkward last few minutes in the car. She wasn't used to snapping at people any more than she was used to others' reading her thoughts and emotions so well. "Um, make yourself comfortable." Swallowing, knowing all eyes were on her and Collin, she took his hand, hoping the gesture didn't appear stiff. PDA and relationships in general weren't her thing.

"I'll be upstairs." Collin slid his thumb over her knuckles and closed the distance between them, kissing her cheek with far more affection than Roman's quick brush of lips.

She fought the urge to retreat as her heart beat faster. He always smelled good. "I, um, yes." She cleared her throat and turned, hoping her cheeks weren't as hot as they felt. "Okay.

Let's go. I'm ready."

Roman studied her with his eagle eyes. "I would love to have Collin join us if he will."

She blinked her surprise. "Oh." Roman typically preferred to grill her without the company of others. "Uh—"

"Sure." Collin stepped closer and ran his palms down her arms. "I'd be happy to sit in."

"I'm going to take my leave," Dad said. "It was nice to see you again, Roman."

"And you, Ambassador."

Dad smiled at Lyla and walked back toward his office, leaving the three of them alone in the entryway.

"After you," Collin gestured to Roman and hooked his arm around Lyla's waist. They started toward the less formal living area. "Relax," he whispered next to her ear.

How was she supposed to do that when his lips and hands were all over her? "He's very sharp," she muttered. "He doesn't miss much."

"I guess we should give him something to talk about then."

She swallowed, ignoring the goose bumps puckering her skin as his breath tickled her neck with every word he spoke. Nodding, she took the cushion next to Collin on the loveseat as Roman settled across from them in a chair in one of the private rooms meant more for family and close friends than the press.

Roman pressed "record" on the tape recorder already set up on the coffee table and folded his hands in his lap. "Lyla, how is *The Markovik Number* coming along?"

Apparently they were going to begin. She struggled to relax as she leaned back against the couch cushion. "Very well. Sergei, Fedor, and I have gotten together several times since Collin and I arrived on Wednesday."

Roman's lips curved humorlessly. "I spoke with Sergei earlier. He says you're a sloppy couple. Fedor mentioned there's much progress to be made."

She laced her fingers, silently cursing her new team. "I think anytime you work with someone new, there's a learning curve. We're compensating for each other's styles as we perfect the choreography."

"Fedor also stated that *The Markovik Number* was to be Mina's most demanding dance. You're well-respected—considered one of the best, but do you feel that you can take this on?"

And here came the comparisons she loathed so much. "I can only hope my mother would be happy. I certainly plan to give this all of my effort."

"The Bolshoi Theater will be filled to capacity. All tickets have been sold at a steep price for a twenty-minute dance."

But no pressure. "Sergei and I will have to make sure our performance is worth everyone's time."

"Yes." Roman rested his ankle on his knee as he made himself more at home. "You went to Orphan House Ten this afternoon."

She nodded. "We did."

"On the way out, you said you believe Russia's ban on Americans adopting is wrong."

She frowned, hating that he was trying to twist her words. "No, I said anyone who can offer children a good home should be allowed to do so, no matter where they live."

"One would imply this means Americans as well."

"Yes, it does," she answered smoothly, well used to Roman's games. "All children have a right to be loved, to be offered the best that a family can provide. If a little boy or girl can find that here in Russia, that's wonderful. If they can find that in China or England or the United States, that too is a wonderful thing."

"Would you consider adopting?"

"Perhaps someday, but my career doesn't offer me much time to devote to children right now."

"But you have time for a relationship?" He raised his eyebrow in Collin's direction.

She looked at Collin. "It isn't always easy, but we're making it work."

"You made no mention of your relationship when we spoke in New York."

"Ly-Ly's entitled to a private life, don't you think?" Collin interjected.

Roman's eyes sharpened on Collin. "Mr. Michaels, you live in New York City?"

If Collin realized he was about to be interrogated, he didn't show it as he sat back with his arm slung over the cushion, as comfortable as Roman seemed to be. "No, I'm from Los Angeles."

Roman's brow furrowed. "How did you and Lyla meet if you live across the continent?"

"I was in Manhattan on business. We bumped into each other on the sidewalk," he said without batting an eye. "Ly-Ly took my breath away."

She swallowed, holding his gaze. Collin was certainly convincing.

"What do you do for work, Mr. Michaels?"

"I'm in between jobs at the moment, which actually works out well." He slid his hand down her braid, never taking his eyes off her. "When Ly-Ly invited me to join her on her trip east, I jumped at the chance."

"How long have you been together?"

"A month," they said at the same time.

She grinned at Collin, remembering their conversation over cod and sautéed kale.

"Lyla, you typically travel alone. One would assume this is serious. Will you marry?"

She sat up straighter as she looked from Collin to Roman and back. "Uh—"

"We're taking things a day at a time—enjoying each other as it comes," Collin cut in.

"We'll see where our relationship takes us," Lyla added.

"You'll watch her dance, I assume?"

"I wouldn't be anywhere else." He winked at her.

"I think that's enough for now." Roman stood, ending the interview as abruptly as he'd started it. "I'd like to get a picture of you both."

She apologized with her eyes as she looked at Collin again.

"Shoot away," he offered.

"I usually bring a photographer, but today I'm on my own."

"That's okay," Lyla assured.

"Stand for me and smile."

Lyla moved over by the fireplace, and Collin came up behind her, wrapping his arms around her shoulders and resting his chin on the top of her head.

She hesitated, noted that Roman was watching closely, and settled her hands on Collin's arm. This was nothing more than a dance. Her partners embraced her all the time. This was no different. Relaxing with the idea, she rested against him, realizing that her father and politics had barely come up at all. She smiled as Roman pointed the camera their way. Tomorrow the paper would be full of her and Collin, the perfect distraction to take some of the negative attention off of Dad.

"How about one more? Perhaps sit on the loveseat again."

"Okay," she said as Collin took his original spot on the small couch. She sat down, leaning her back against his side as she crossed her ankles and let them rest on the opposite end—like a cozy couple enjoying a night in front of the TV. Collin settled his arm around her waist, and she laced their fingers, resting her opposite arm on his thigh.

"Smile."

She did, struggling not to blink as the flash blinded her again.

"Thank you for your time." Roman shook Collin's hand then kissed Lyla's cheeks. "We'll talk before the dance."

She nodded. "Yes. I'll see you out."

"That would be appreciated."

They walked Roman to the entryway and waved, waiting

for him to make it to the car. She closed the door and sighed, leaning against the wood. "I'm so sorry, Collin."

He frowned. "For what?"

"For all of this." She glanced over at one of her father's security agents loitering in the hall and stood straight, lowering her voice as she leaned closer. "For lying. For dragging you into this entire situation and for me being okay with it if it means we're taking the heat off of my dad for a while."

He stuffed his hands in his pockets. "I've already told you I'm fine with this. I don't have a problem with it. I wouldn't have taken the assignment if I did."

She nodded. "I'm sorry for my behavior in the car too. I shouldn't have snapped at you—"

"Relax, Lyla. Go up and catch a nap before Oksana calls us for dinner."

She stared into his eyes, confused by the intensity she saw there, and suddenly she was as tired now as she had been when he knocked on her bedroom door several hours ago. "I think that might be a good idea."

"I know it is." He gave her shoulder a friendly pat. "I'll wake you up when it's time to eat."

"Thanks."

CHAPTER TEN

COLLIN YAWNED AS HE PULLED A MUG FROM THE CUP-
board and poured himself a cup of coffee. He followed
up his first yawn with a second and swore, finding it
impossible to shake his grogginess after another shitty night
of sleep. He'd tried a workout and a shower before he headed
downstairs, but neither option had helped him much.

The time difference between Iraq, then the US, and now
western Russia was definitely screwing with him. He and
Lyla were heading into their fourth full day in Moscow, and
he still couldn't acclimate to the time changes the way he typically did. His initial conversation with Jonathan upon their
arrival had kept him on edge, making a good night's rest impossible. He found himself studying everyone he met, trying to figure out who was on Jonathan's side and who might
hurt the ambassador and his daughter just to prove a point.

Sighing, he slid his hand through his damp hair as he
walked to the kitchen table wearing a pair of blue jeans and
a plain black t-shirt. He glanced at his watch, noting that it
was just barely seven. The house was still quiet except for the
murmurs of music and voices occasionally escaping from
the closed ballroom doors down the hall.

He sat down, spotting the small stack of newspapers by
one of the placemats, and took his first sip of morning java,
his eyes going wide as he choked on the *strong* black coffee.

"Son of a bitch," he said as he coughed and set the mug down with a clatter. "Son of a *bitch*," he repeated as he pushed the cup away, certain the damn thing would get up and walk off on its own. If Oksana was trying to kill him, it was possible she might succeed. Another sample of that thick sludge and he was bound to go into cardiac arrest. "Jesus." He shuddered as the bitter taste remained stubbornly on his tongue.

He stood, intending to take the disastrous brew to the sink and pour himself a glass of water, but he sat again when the picture on the front page caught his eye. He pulled the newspapers closer, examining himself and Russia's Princess sitting cozy on Ambassador Avery's couch. They looked good together—like any typical couple, but as he scanned line after line of the Cyrillic script, he found he couldn't read what Roman Akolov had to say.

He was fluent in Arabic and Farsi. He could read both languages; their alphabets were similar, but the letters scrolled across the current page looked like artistic symbols.

Picking up the next paper, he studied the picture of him and Lyla walking hand in hand away from Orphan House Ten. Lyla certainly made headlines here.

"Good." Jonathan walked into the room dressed for the day in khaki slacks, a crisp white shirt, and olive green tie, his blue eyes hard and his jaw set. "You're up."

"I have been for a while."

"You saw the paper?"

"I see the pictures."

"Why don't you bring your coffee down to my office."

Collin glanced at his cup, barely suppressing another shudder, and stood, bringing the newspapers with him instead.

Jonathan closed the door behind them, and as he had four days ago, turned on the radio.

Collin studied the papers once again and could only assume that Jonathan wasn't happy with the headlines. "What's going on?"

"Take a seat." Jonathan sat down as he invited Collin to do the same in the chair across from him. "Roman did his homework," he said as he slapped his hand on Roman's article. "He's questioning the authenticity of your romantic relationship with Lyla."

Collin looked at the couple smiling on the couch. "Be more specific, because we're pretty cozy here."

"He knows you were a Ranger. He knows you've been working private security for several years."

His eyes met Jonathan's. "Was. On paper I've left my job."

"You're a decorated soldier with one of the United States' most elite military teams."

"I'm not anymore—haven't been for a while."

"They're suspicious." Jonathan stood again and started pacing. "There are rumors you and Lyla aren't together, that you're here for other reasons."

He leaned back in his seat, crossing his ankle on his knee. "Like what?"

He shook his head. "I can't be sure."

"Am I supposed to be a spy?"

Jonathan whirled back to face him. "Perhaps."

"So because I'm former military and a bodyguard, I'm a spy?"

"Anything's possible."

"Lyla too?" He sat up farther in his chair. "Come on, Jonathan. They can't be that delusional."

"I don't know." He shook his head again as he rubbed at the back of his neck. "The Kremlin is very paranoid right now, especially where I'm concerned. Perhaps I'm paranoid myself."

"We just need more time. Lyla and I need to be seen together and give the people of Moscow more opportunities to see that we're legit. God knows she can't breathe without being photographed."

"I don't like this whole thing."

"With all due respect, this was your idea."

"Not the *relationship*," Jonathan said impatiently. "The rest. They're watching us all, scrutinizing. I don't like it," he muttered more to himself than Collin.

Yet this was the situation they were in, and they needed to deal with it. "Today she's cooking with the chef over at the Kremlin. She and I can go for a stroll afterwards or head over to the ice festival tonight."

Jonathan shook his head. "I don't like her out after dark. I don't want her anywhere near the crowds. The terrorists are constantly looking for their next opportunity to make a statement. I don't want Lyla getting caught up in that."

"That's why I'm here—to keep her safe."

"I wish you weren't. I sure as hell wish my little girl was back in New York."

He opened his mouth to remind Jonathan Lyla had been followed in Manhattan as well, but there was no point. "We'll be out of here before you know it. We just have to make it through next week."

Jonathan clenched his jaw. "That's a long damn time."

He shook his head. "A week and a half is nothing. I know you're concerned, but I can guarantee you I've been in far worse situations than this."

Jonathan nodded as he picked up his tea then frowned. "You forgot your coffee."

"I'm trying to lay off the caffeine."

Jonathan laughed. "Oksana makes far better tea." He gestured to his cup.

Collin grinned. "That's some pretty powerful stuff she left for me in the kitchen."

Jonathan chuckled. "You're all right, son."

"Thanks."

———◆———

Lyla piped sinful chocolate mousse into quarter-sized, paper-like cookies as cameras rolled in the Kremlin's famous kitchen. The scent of delicious treats filled the huge room while Russia's most well-known chef stood by her side, giving her occasional pointers. "These look *amazing*," she said in Russian, grinning at the handsome man.

He smiled back. "You have a knack in the kitchen—a gift like your dancing."

"Thank you." She glanced over her shoulder as Chef Orlov's assistant attempted to tutor Collin in the fine art of preparing decadent whipped cream. She bit her cheek, fighting back another grin as her poor bodyguard and the cook struggled with their language barrier. Both men were trying their best, and Collin's willingness to yet again be a good sport made him all the more adorable.

When they arrived a couple of hours ago, Collin had been happy to sit back behind the scenes and let her have the spotlight, but the producer of Moscow Cooks had insisted Collin put on a chef's coat and join in on the fun.

And this was fun. Although she was on television and a few of Moscow's more popular reporters were hovering in the background, their environment was relatively chaos-free—and she was doing one of the things she liked best: creating in the kitchen. There were no questions here. No one wanted to know about her personal life or whether she was more pro-Russia or backed the United States. Chef Orlov simply wanted her to finish with the huge tray of confections so he could get back to his preparations for tonight's State Dinner, which her father would be attending.

The cameraman moved from Collin's table back to Lyla's when Chef Orlov started speaking to her again.

"For time's sake, we will have you finish the row." He skirted to Lyla's right and tapped Collin's shoulder. "Please prepare a bag of whipped cream for the final touches," he said in very good English, then shared his request with his assistant in their native tongue.

"Coming right up. Ly-Ly, I have—"

She turned as Collin said her name and gasped as they

slammed into each other.

"Whoa." He hooked his arm around her waist, preventing her from stumbling back into the prep table.

"Oops." She winced as she dropped the half-empty piping bag to her side and studied the glob of mousse Collin now wore on the chest of his bright white chef's jacket.

He looked from the blob of chocolate into her eyes. "I thought we were going to save that for the cookies."

She grinned as he did. "That was the original plan."

"Here." He set the piping bag on the table and lifted his hand, sliding his fingers along her cheek, tucking loose strands of her hair that had fallen free from her French twist behind her ear. "We'll get those out of your lip gloss."

"Thanks."

The camera crew kept rolling, and a few camera bulbs flashed while he continued holding her close.

"How about we ask for a cookie?" he suggested.

"I'll never turn down a cookie."

His brow winged up in what could only be surprise. "I didn't realize you ate cookies. I'll have to keep that in mind."

"Sweet treats make life worth living."

"They certainly do." Collin broke their connection, and they both turned as Chef Orlov's assistant slid a plate of roasted eggplant and tomato topped with a garlic aioli in front of them. Two mousse cookies piped with a small dollop of whipped cream came next.

"Please enjoy the creations you made with me today," the chef invited, stepping back.

She cut into the vegetables and garlicky parmesan-mayo they helped prepare during the first segment of the show and sampled a bite of pure heaven. Rolling her eyes, she moaned quietly. "Oh my *goodness*."

Collin groaned his opinion and cut into the tomato and eggplant again. "We're going to make this at home, right?" he asked with his mouth full.

She laughed. "Absolutely."

"Will you try the cookies?" Chef asked.

Collin lifted the delicate treat and surprised her when he held it to her lips.

Enjoying the fun in his eyes, she picked up the other treat and held it to his.

"Go for it, Ly-Ly," he encouraged.

She opened her mouth as he did the same.

"Oh my God," they said in unison and chuckled.

"That's it. I'm moving in," Collin said.

She laughed again and reached up, wiping a smear of mousse off the side of his mouth. "You have—"

He grabbed her wrist and guided her finger into his mouth, his slippery tongue teasing her skin as he made the last of their treat disappear.

She swallowed, snagging her lip between her teeth as her stomach fluttered with dozens of butterflies.

He wiggled his eyebrows as he let her arm go. "We need to make these too."

"Mmhm," was the best she could do as she turned away, looking around, realizing the entire room had stopped and was watching them. She glanced to her side, peeking at one of the cameras, remembering she and Collin were going to be on television.

"We've got what we need," one of the men said to her, speaking in Russian.

She nodded and gave her attention to Chef Orlov. "Thank you so much for having us today. Everything is absolutely delicious. I know my father will enjoy his meal tonight."

Chef Orlov took her hand. "You are truly lovely. Please come back anytime."

"How about next year?"

He chuckled. "I'll see you again next January." He looked at Collin. "You're a fine cook, Collin. Take care of our princess."

He nodded and held out his hand for a friendly shake. "Thank you. I definitely will."

CHAPTER ELEVEN

LYLA HELD COLLIN'S GLOVED HAND AS THEY WALKED among the crowds in the cold. Everywhere she looked, Moscow's citizens were enjoying the final days of the city's famous Winter Festival. She smiled, caught up in the energy and noise, bright lights and music, and the delicious scents of amazing food no matter where she turned.

"This is quite a party," Collin said as he glanced around, bundled up in his winter gear.

"It's a pretty big deal. Wait till you see the ice sculptures. They're always spectacular." She spotted a sign for home-made bagels and jam. "We have to go *there* right this second."

"Where?"

"To the bagel stand." She pulled him toward the concession booth. "You're in for a treat."

"You know how I feel about food."

She grinned, relaxed as they strolled around in the dark. No one recognized her with her hat tucked low and her scarf wrapped snuggly around her neck. She stopped at the counter, curving her lips in a friendly smile. "Can we get a bagel with raspberry jam, please," she asked in Russian. "And a hot tea as well."

"Please wait," the woman said, turning away, then gasped, whirling back. "Lyla." She shook her head. "Princess Lyla."

"Shoot," she muttered, glancing at Collin and stepping

closer to his side.

His brow furrowed slightly. "What?"

"She knows who I am."

He draped a protective arm around her waist as his gaze darted around their surroundings. "Play it cool and we'll get out of here."

She nodded.

"The princess is here!"

Lyla winced, glancing over her shoulder as people stopped and started taking notice.

"Collin. Lyla's love," the woman continued in Russian as she grabbed Collin's hand then shoved the evening edition at them through the concession window.

She studied the close up of herself and Collin staring into each other's eyes as he held her in his arms in the Kremlin kitchen. By all accounts, she and Collin had managed to erase any speculation that their relationship wasn't the real deal during their two hours in front of the television cameras. "Let me sign this for you," Lyla offered, hoping they could finish this and be on their way.

The woman gave her a pen.

To the lovely lady who makes heavenly bagels and delicious tea.

—Lyla Markovik-Avery.

The woman pulled the newspaper back inside the booth, read what Lyla wrote, and burst into delighted tears. "Our princess." She touched Lyla's hand. "How we love you so. How we loved your mother."

"Thank you."

Collin grabbed a wad of rubles from his wallet as another woman brought the bagel slathered in jam, along with the tea, to the window.

"*Nyet.*" She shook her head, pushing Collin's money back

at him.

"Please let us pay," Lyla insisted.

"*Nyet.*" The woman shook her head again. "*Nyet.*"

Collin tucked the bills in the tip jar by the window. "*Spasibo*," he said, thanking her in Russian.

The woman grinned, nodding, clearly delighted that he was making an effort to speak the language.

"Let's get out of here." Collin picked up their snack and they turned, blinking against the blinding flashes as several people took their picture.

Her heart sank as the crowds continued to gather and she realized her evening was going to turn into a mob scene and autograph session. "Hello," she said to everyone, always wanting to be kind, even if she yearned for escape.

"Please sign. Sign this please," a teenager shoved a piece of paper at her.

She looked at Collin and took the small scrap from the young woman, writing her name. "Here you go," she said as she handed it back.

"For me too, please," a little girl said.

She crouched down. "What's your name, sweetie?"

"Nikita."

She included Nikita's name as she signed the paper bag that had contained a treat not too long ago. "Have fun tonight." She hugged the little one and stood.

Collin put the tea and bagel in one hand and linked his arm through hers. "Start walking or we're going to get stuck."

They moved through the crowds as fast as the groups of people would allow. She stopped periodically to sign a napkin or shake a hand and snap a quick picture.

"Over here, Ly-Ly." Collin gestured to the empty troika, gently pulling her toward the horses and sleigh as a good seventy-five to one hundred people started closing in around them, making it hard to move. "We need to get out of here before I lose control of the situation."

She signed one more paper, knowing it wasn't possible to

sign the rest, and got in the back of her improvised getaway vehicle. "I'm going to go now," she called to the small mob. "It was nice to see everyone."

Collin took his place at her side. "Let's go."

"We're all set," Lyla said to the driver as people continued to call to her, begging for one last snapshot or autograph.

The horses took off, and a few of the children ran alongside the carriage. She waved as her eager fans lost pace with the powerful animals pulling her and Collin down the snowy path. Sighing, she turned, settling back in the seat. "Sorry about that."

"No problem. Unexpected surprises come with the territory."

"I guess they do." But she wished desperately that they didn't.

Minutes passed as they moved through the park, taking in the ice sculptures lit up in the night while tinny music blared through speakers along the trail.

"Bagel?" Collin pulled off his gloves and handed her half on a napkin.

She almost refused, thinking of the calories in the doughy bread and jam. She'd already indulged with cookies and aioli. A bagel was too much. Her show was days away and her costume unforgiving. "I'll have a little nibble. I ordered it for you."

"You didn't eat much at dinner."

A salad topped with poached shrimp had satisfied her. "I ate plenty."

He held the bread to her lips.

She bit in, savoring the melding of yeasty perfection and sweet fruit, staring at him as he devoured a decent portion of his snack in one bite.

He chewed and swallowed. "This is insane."

"The jam is homemade."

"I can tell." He ate more. "Tea?"

"Yes. Thank you." She took the paper cup from him and

sipped. "Mmm. The tea is always delicious."

"Last bite?" he asked.

She shook her head and drank again as he polished off the rest. She paused with the cup at her lips for a third sample when they passed a huge icy replica of St. Basil's Cathedral. "Wow."

"Spectacular. Here, let's do this," he said as he covered them with the blanket and settled his arm around her shoulders.

She glanced around. What was he doing? No one was watching them here.

"This is pretty great."

"It is," she agreed, studying him more than the sculptures. She understood the game they were playing and appreciated that he was willing to give up his privacy to help her and her dad, but he didn't have to keep up the charade when they were mostly alone in the dark. He was doing a very convincing job in his role as her boyfriend. The people of Russia were falling in love with "Lyla's Prince Charming." And she was finding herself confused. Occasionally she forgot that they were acting, that she wasn't supposed to be attracted to the gorgeous man snuggled next to her on the peaceful carriage ride.

He pulled her closer, tucking her against his side. "They should do something like this in The States."

She fought to keep her shoulders relaxed as her temple brushed his jaw and she breathed in his aftershave. "I'm sure they do...somewhere."

"I'll have to look it up." He glanced her way, doing a double take. "What?"

"What?"

"You're frowning."

She shook her head. "No. I'm just—I think I'm ready for bed."

"Really?" He eased away some, his own frown growing more intense as he studied her in the multi-colored lights.

"Are you feeling okay?"

Their faces were inches apart, their breath mingling as her pulse pounded rapidly in her throat. "Yes," she answered quickly.

The troika slowed, then stopped as the ride came to an end on the opposite side of the park. Cameras flashed while a new group of people loitered around the exit.

Collin pulled back the blanket and got out first, tipping their driver. "Word must have spread that you grabbed a carriage."

She let loose a quiet sigh as she studied the people waiting for a glimpse of her. Enough was enough—of this day, of her spending too much time in such close proximities to her bodyguard.

"Let's get you back to Spaso House."

Nodding, she took the hand he offered her, and they hurried through the new crowd, stopping only once to sign autographs for a set of adorable triplets.

Collin pulled her against him, signaling to the crowd that they were finished.

"Goodnight," she called.

They walked quickly to the curb and hailed a cab in the busy traffic. Within seconds, they were settling into the warm backseat. Lyla told the man their address, making certain that as she sat back against the cushion, she and Collin didn't touch. She needed some space.

Finally they were out of the spotlight. Finally she could *think*. Wiggling her ankle, she tested her level of discomfort and found the pain bearable. She yearned to dance—to get lost in the music until she remembered that what she and Collin shared was nothing more than a product of her father's wishes.

Eventually the cab stopped in front of the gates and was quickly let through when the guard confirmed who was in the car. She and Collin paid the cabbie, got out, and went inside.

"Thanks for showing me around the Festival," Collin said as he pulled off his hat and took off his jacket. "The bagel with jam was truly killer."

"You're welcome." She smiled, just wanting to be alone. "I'm going to go up."

"Yeah. Goodnight."

"Goodnight." She turned, craving a change of clothes and her pointe shoes. Tonight she would dance until her mind was blessedly clear.

Collin walked downstairs in the dark, on the hunt for an after-midnight snack. He wasn't wearing much, just his favorite pair of black athletic shorts, but it was nearly one, and his stomach wouldn't stop growling. Lyla may have found the shrimp tossed salad they ate hours ago to be filling, but he needed *food*. The bagel and jam at the festival hit the spot for a little while, but he wanted something more. Hopefully there was some of that teacake left Oksana had offered them after dinner. Jonathan's cook and housekeeper couldn't make a cup of coffee worth a damn, but she could definitely bake.

His foot hit the bottom step in the quiet house, and he made his way toward the kitchen, stopping when he heard music floating down the hall. "What the hell?" Turning, he walked in the opposite direction, recognizing the classical number Lyla and her partner practiced to every day. There was no way Sergei was here at this hour, so what was Lyla doing?

He stopped in the shadows, peeking in the massive ballroom, expecting to see Lyla twirling across the floor, but her back was to him as she leaned her arms on one of the ballet bars and breathed as if she'd just run a race. She didn't look like the ballet goddess he remembered from the billboard in Manhattan. Instead of sparkling sequins and a stunning tutu, she wore a pink leotard soaked with sweat, a tiny skirt that barely covered anything at all, and white legwarmers on her long, muscular legs.

He stepped closer, on the verge of walking in to make sure she was all right, but paused when she turned, facing the long wall of mirrors. Her golden hair was wrapped in a tight bun and damp around her temples; her face was dewy and flushed. She was stunning, her physical features could be called nothing less, but her eyes were hauntingly sad. He frowned as he watched her unforgiving gaze trail up her body, clearly seeing something wrong that he didn't. And he realized that he was catching a glimpse of Lyla Markovik-Avery unmasked for the first time.

Who was she? Who was this woman—not the one who offered up smiles and hugged orphaned children, but this one here who broke his heart just from staring at her? Lost. Lonely. But Lyla was happy...or so he'd thought. He couldn't deny that she seemed a little rundown and wary of her celebrity status. She liked her privacy, but who didn't? Yet the misery in her icy blue eyes hinted at something more.

She raised her arms above her head as she stood on pointe, her graceful movements appearing effortless, but the illusion was shattered when she winced and whimpered, her small cry of pain echoing over the music. She snapped her head straight, and the expression of agony left her face as she held her position despite the trembling in her right foot. She dropped down to her soles and limped to her MP3 player, switching it off.

Lyla was injured, far worse than she'd been letting on. For days now, she'd told everyone her ankle was fine, but clearly that was bullshit.

What the hell was going on? He wanted to go to her and demand that she tell him—as much as he wanted to pull her into a hug—but he stepped back into the dark instead, knowing she wouldn't want his help, that she dealt with her pain alone.

He glanced toward the ceiling, to where Lyla's father

slept in the room above. Did Jonathan know this side of his daughter? Collin didn't, but he planned to before their trip was over.

Turning away, he walked upstairs, completely forgetting about Oksana's teacake as he thought of the miserable ballerina he'd left downstairs.

Collin leaned against his doorframe, staring at Lyla's closed door. For several minutes, he'd been listening to the murmurs coming from her television, debating whether or not he should let the whole thing with her go for now or just walk right into her room. He'd assured himself tomorrow would be soon enough to see what was what where Lyla was concerned. He'd even tucked himself back into bed, but then he heard her walking down the hall, her hobbled gait unmistakable.

He thought of her sad eyes and took a step across the hall, stopped, then turned back to his own room before swearing and whirling around again. "Screw this." He gave a quick knock on her door. "Lyla."

"Come in."

He stepped inside, blinking in the dim light, and watched Mina Markovik dance across some stage. Moments ticked by while Lyla sat on her bed, freshly showered and dressed in her simple shorts and tank top, saying nothing as she stared at the TV.

"They always play her productions when I come—hours worth of footage."

He stepped farther in and closed the door behind him. "You look a lot like her."

She smiled sadly. "Yes."

"She's an amazing dancer," he tried, not quite sure what to say to her right now.

"She's classic, effortless, a legend—impossible to live up

to." She shook her head as if she was coming out of a trance and turned her head, smiling at him. "It's really late. Is everything okay?"

He crossed his arms, wishing he'd thought to put on a shirt. "You tell me."

She frowned. "What do you mean?"

He shook his head. "Nothing."

She pulled her feet from a large bucket of ice water and set them on a towel.

Squinting in the poor lighting, he crouched down in front of her as he caught a glimpse of at least a dozen nasty sores. "Jesus, look at your feet."

She drew her legs up, turning away as much as she could in a self-conscious gesture. "I have ugly feet. Ballerina's typically do."

"You're covered in blisters." He spotted her pointe shoes in the corner by the bed, noting the blood staining the bottom edges of the satiny fabric. Horrified, he yanked on her calf muscle, pulling her foot up for a closer inspection. "What the... Lyla—"

"I'm all right."

He'd never seen anything like this. Her nail was bruised, her calluses cracked, and her toes inflamed at the joints and missing several layers of skin. She had to be in horrible pain. "You aren't going to be able to walk tomorrow."

"I did just fine today." She pulled out of his grip and stood, catching her weight on the side of the bed.

Christ, she could hardly stand. "What are you doing?"

"Getting my cream from the dresser." She pointed to the tubes and bottles across the room.

"Sit. I'll get it for you."

"I can—"

"Take a seat," he said with less patience, trying to figure out why she was doing this to herself. No job could be worth all this on a regular basis.

She sunk to the bed as he grabbed the medicated aloe

vera and Icy Hot for her ankle.

"Go ahead and sit back."

She stood again instead, holding out her hand. "Thanks but I've got it."

He deflected her, holding the stuff out of her reach. "I'm going to help you out."

"I'm perfectly capable of tending to my own injuries." She lunged toward his hand and sucked in a breath as she jostled her right ankle. Seconds ticked by as she clenched her jaw with her eyes closed.

"Just sit down and humor me," he said with less heat. "Over the last few days, I haven't been able to help but notice that you take care of everyone else. Who takes care of you?"

"Me."

He shook his head. "Not tonight."

She hesitated, then sighed as she sat again.

He made himself comfortable on the opposite side of her bed, capturing her legs between the V of his thighs. Wincing, he scrutinized her injuries again. "These look raw."

"They *feel* pretty raw."

He stretched forward, grabbing the package of Q-tips from the side table, and applied small globs of the medicated cream to her blisters. "Are you a masochist or something?"

"I think all dancers are to a point."

He glanced up, and she smiled at him. The composed Lyla was back. Her hair was wet from her shower, leaving damp trails down her thin white spaghetti-strap top and little to the imagination. Her breasts were beautiful—perky, fuller without a bra. They would easily fit in the palms of his hands... Swallowing, he looked down and focused on his work. Touching Lyla was the last thing he needed to be thinking about. "You need to let these wounds air out and heal."

She let out a small laugh. "They'll have a week after Sergei and I finish *The Markovik Number*."

"You're pushing yourself too hard. The hours you're working are—"

"This is my job."

It was more than that. What exactly was she trying to prove? "You're not eating enough."

Her eyes sparked as she yanked her foot away. "I have a father down the hall."

"I don't have any interest in being your father, Lyla." He took her leg back, doctored up her right foot and put cream in his hands, rubbing her ankle.

She frowned, biting her lip. "That hurts."

"I can imagine." He moved his fingers in slow strokes along her tendons. "You're swollen."

"It's a little aggravated," she shuddered out, bunching her fists, clearly in a world of hurt.

"It's *sprained*."

"Are you a bodyguard by day and masseuse by night? You seem to know what you're doing."

"I broke my ankle on my final mission overseas. I had my fair share of physiotherapy, physical therapy, doctor appointments..."

"I didn't realize you were a Ranger until I read it in the paper."

He shrugged. "I haven't been for a while."

"Did you like it?"

"I served my country for six years and pissed off my mother at the same time, which was a pretty great bonus."

"She didn't want you to serve in the military?"

"I was supposed to go to college."

"You two don't get along?"

He traced her ankle in firm circles. "We don't speak—haven't for ten years."

"I Skype with my dad almost every day. I can't imagine not talking to him for a decade."

"I'm not broken up about it."

"Clearly. You're close to your dad, though? My dad speaks

very highly of him."

"My father and I have always understood each other. We're into the same things. And Luna, my step-mom, has been pretty awesome since day one."

"That's nice that you have them."

"I can't imagine not talking to *them* for a decade."

She nodded.

He rested her foot against his stomach, working the tendons by her heel. "It must be tough not having your mother."

She shrugged. "I never had her, so I can't really say." She huffed out a quiet breath. "That sounds cold."

"It sounds truthful."

"I had my grammy and my dad."

"What about your mother's family?"

"She didn't have any. Her parents died long before I was born, and she was an only child."

"Huh. Your dad's been over in Russia for a few years?"

"Since I was ten. After I was born, my dad brought me back to New York. We lived with my grammy in a little town a few miles outside of Albany."

"When did you start dancing?"

"When I was three—it's all I wanted to do. My dad started going overseas a lot when I was six, but it never bothered me much. I had my own things to do, my own dreams to chase. When I was ten, he was offered the ambassador position here in Moscow. I went to a dance school in St. Petersburg for a couple years, but it didn't work out, so I went home and stayed with Grammy until my teachers told her there was nothing more they could do for me. I needed better instructors who could keep up with my abilities, so I moved to Manhattan right after my fourteenth birthday and started my career."

She'd been taking care of herself for years. "That's a lot for a kid."

She shrugged. "I've never been a normal kid."

But she was an extraordinary woman. "I guess we all make

the best of what we've got."

"Pretty much."

"You're good though, huh? One of the best?"

She jerked her shoulders. "That's what they say."

"What do you say?"

"That there's always room to do better, to improve." She nestled deeper into her pillows as he sensed her relaxing. "So what about you? You told me you flew planes at six and moved to Chicago at eleven."

He smiled. "And got myself into a lot of trouble."

"Oh, yeah?"

He nodded. "I went to school enough to pass—a private, snooty place, but I'm not a private, snooty person."

"Was it co-ed?"

He grinned. "Hell yeah."

She rolled her eyes. "I'm sure the girls loved you."

"And I loved them right back." He winked, earning one of her genuine smiles.

She looked at her foot, watching his fingers work, and tried to pull away as he slid his hands farther up her leg. "That's probably good."

He held her still, waiting for her eyes to meet his. "Does this make you uncomfortable?"

"No. But we're alone."

He glanced around the quiet room, trying to figure her point. "We have been."

"You don't have to...pretend." She sat up again.

"I'm not big on pretenses. I rarely pretend anything."

"I'm talking about us—the hand holding and cookie sharing." She swallowed. "The whole finger in the mouth thing at the Kremlin kitchen."

"I would've done that whether there were cameras there or not." He struggled not to smile when her eyebrows winged up.

"Oh."

He gave her ankle a final rub and stood. Lyla was vulnerable and incredibly sexy. It was time for him to go before he started thinking about things that were bound to get him in trouble. "You should get some sleep."

"I will."

"I'll see you sometime tomorrow." He stopped by the long black garment bag hanging on the closet door. "Costume for the theater or dress for tomorrow night?"

"For tomorrow night."

He looked forward to seeing what she was going to wear to the benefit. It was bound to be spectacular. "Good night."

"Good night. Thanks," she said before he stepped out. "My ankle feels a little better."

"Good." He tossed her a wave and closed the door behind him, realizing that their little encounter hadn't left him unscathed. Lyla seemed to be in decent spirits, but being in the same room with her, touching her and smelling her shampoo, made him want things that weren't good for either one of them right now.

☙ CHAPTER TWELVE ❧

LYLA SECURED HER NECKLACE IN PLACE AS SHE STOOD from her chair in front of the vanity, then slipped her battered, Band-Aid-clad feet into her two-inch heels. Her ankle made its objection known with a sharp stabbing ache, and she longingly stared at her fuzzy slippers, wishing she were wearing those instead of her tortuous stilettos. Sighing, she dismissed her indulgent ideas, well used to her duties as Ambassador Avery's daughter. Tonight she would stand by her father's side again.

This evening's gala was bound to draw a huge crowd, with the proceeds from the star-studded event going to different charitable organizations helping the victims affected by the New Year's Eve bombing. Sergei would be there, along with several other popular Russian celebrities and many foreign dignitaries eager to show their willingness to support The Federation in their fight against terrorism.

She stepped closer to her mirror, studying her dramatic evening makeup. She'd worked her magic, playing up her eyes with clever slides of eyeliner and several sweeps of mascara. Instead of her typical pink-hued lipstick, she'd chosen shimmery clear gloss. Satisfied with the effects, she made certain her French twist was secured and gave the loose tendrils framing her face a quick fix. With an approving nod, she slid her hands down her simple yet snug long-sleeve black dress that stopped a good six inches above her knees. Her look was a little more daring than usual, but still classy. Her goal for the next several hours was to raise big money for those in need and keep the attention on her and Collin. Her father was finally getting a chance to breathe with her love life filling the newspaper columns; she had every intention of making sure it stayed that way.

She exhaled a long breath, thinking of the gorgeous man in his bedroom across the hall. Somehow she'd managed to keep her distance from Collin throughout the day. Sergei and Fedor had tied her up in rehearsals until almost three. After they left, she devoured a late lunch Oksana had happily made, then showered, but her two-hour nap hadn't been planned. She'd laid down only for a second, letting her eyes droop, and woke up in time to see that she needed to expedite her gala preparations or she would make everyone late.

Someone knocked on her door, and her shoulders automatically tensed. It was bound to be her delicious date. If their afternoon in the Kremlin kitchen and slightly romantic troika ride hadn't confused her enough yesterday, their conversation and the way he touched her late last night had only added to her uncertainties. She frowned, remembering his proclamations about not being much of a pretender. What did that mean exactly? How could he hold her hand and look at her the way he did and not be faking? Wasn't that their objective: act like they felt things for each other that they didn't? The knock came again, and she shook her head, already flustered. "Yes. Come in."

Collin walked in, pursing his lips and nodding as his gaze trailed down her body. "Damn, Lyla. You look amazing."

She was still trying to get used to his forward compliments. "Uh, thank you." He looked amazing himself in his tux—not elegant the way her father always did. The black suit and bowtie somehow accentuated his tough, sexy edginess. "You're very handsome."

"Let me fix this." He stepped closer, his fingers brushing

her skin as he centered the silver and diamond pendant on her necklace. "That's an eye catcher."

She touched the quarter-sized circle. "My mother gave this to me." She shook her head. "It was my mother's, at least."

He leaned in, touching her jewelry again. "What does it say?"

"'Love' in Russian. Dad had it made for her when they found out she was pregnant."

"It's nice. You smell good."

"Yes, well. Um, you too." She glanced up, meeting his eyes. Even in her heels, he had her by a good seven inches.

"I missed you today."

She darted her tongue across her lips. Why did she always feel slightly off kilter when she stood in the presence of Collin Michaels? "You did?"

He nodded. "Lunch wasn't the same, and I like heading out on the town with you."

"Oh." She swallowed under his penetrating stare. "You were bored."

"No." He slid his finger down one of the curls in her hair.

She struggled not to fidget, waiting for him to explain.

He smiled. "Should we go?"

Her heart was beating faster than it should be, and her stomach muscles were clenched painfully tight. They definitely needed to go. She nodded. "I imagine my father's waiting for us."

"He's downstairs." He extended his arm to her.

She linked hers with his, and they started down the hall. She smiled when she spotted her father speaking to his security as they descended the long staircase.

Dad stopped talking and turned, grinning as their eyes met. "Ly-Ly, look at you, honey. You're a vision."

She smiled again as she reached the bottom step and freed herself from Collin's grip, kissing Dad's cheek, eaten up with love for the man she didn't get to hug enough. "You're very dashing." She fixed his tie. "Are you ready for some gala fun, Ambassador Avery?"

"Of course. There's been a small change in plans, though." He gave her hand a gentle pat.

"Oh?"

"I'm going to meet you and Collin at the event." He exchanged a quick glance with Collin.

She frowned as she shook her head, looking from her father to her bodyguard. "No. We can go together."

"We'll meet there." He patted her shoulder this time. "I've arranged for you to have your own car and driver."

She wanted the three of them to walk in together—to remind everyone that the man the media was chewing up was her dad and Mina's devoted widow. "But—"

"I won't stay long tonight. I have an early morning."

She nodded when she wanted to argue, but the finality in his tone demanded that she drop the subject. "We'll see you there."

"I'll see you both soon." Dad turned and left with two more agents following him than usual.

She studied the group of men who hung back with her and Collin, new security agents she'd never seen before, then looked at her date again, taking his hand and pulling him with her into the corner. Something was wrong. "What's going on?"

"We're going to a party."

She narrowed her eyes. Apparently Collin practiced in pretenses when they suited him. "Why are we going in separate cars? Why do we have our own team of DSS agents? I get roped into at *least* one formal event every time I'm here, and my father and I always travel together with far fewer men than this."

"Times are different now."

"Yes, but I've never seen my dad surrounded by a small army before." And it terrified her.

"Tonight's a big draw—lots of important people all in one

place giving a group of terrorists the finger. Everyone's going to be surrounded, Ly-Ly. Even us."

Her bodyguard needed a bodyguard. Why had she agreed to this? Why was Dad putting himself in this situation? She and Collin easily could have gone alone to represent the US and Ambassador Avery.

"Keeping everyone separated is just precautionary," Collin continued. "Other foreign consulates are taking the same precautions—husbands and wives traveling separately."

She nodded even though she didn't like any of this.

"Let's get out of here. We'll go have some fun and meet your dad there."

She wanted to get there and make sure Dad was safe. It was hard to pretend that he wasn't the ideal target for the guerilla group constantly trying to gain the upper hand on the Russian government. Killing a US Diplomat to Russia would only heighten tensions between two countries and create more unrest right here in The Federation, which would strengthen their desire for destabilization. Taking out Mina Markovik's husband would be quite a statement. "Okay."

Collin helped her into her cashmere coat, and they walked out to one of her father's cars, settling in the back seat. It wasn't long before they were on their way.

Lyla stared out the window at the busy traffic as her stomach churned with nerves. During the ten years her father had lived overseas, this was the first time she'd truly feared for his life. The possibility was always there with the type of high-profile job he did, but tonight somehow emphasized how vulnerable Jonathan Avery's situation was becoming. It was time to start talking him into coming home to The States.

"So how did today go?"

She focused on Collin. "Fine."

"Your feet were okay?"

"Yes. They're good."

"One more week."

She nodded, trying her best not to think about it. She and Sergei were running out of time, and they still had a long way to go. The man's ego was huge and continued to get in their way. "I'm looking forward to it," she lied.

"I'm looking forward to seeing you dance—other than hip-hop that is."

She grinned, her shoulders relaxing slightly. "Hip-hop's for fun."

"Ballet isn't fun?"

Ballet hadn't been fun for years. "It's different." How could she properly explain her pleasure and loathing for her career?

"It's a love/hate thing, huh?"

She studied his eyes in the light of the passing cars, continually surprised that he seemed to be able to read her mind. "Yes, I guess so."

The car slowed as they approached beams of searchlights swaying in the night sky, immense crowds, and a traffic jam of limos.

"Wow." Collin whistled quietly through his teeth. "Reminds me of the Academy Awards."

"You've worked the Academy Awards?"

"Every year if I'm not overseas—an all hands on deck kind of night. It's a fucking zoo."

"I bet." She smiled, imagining Collin standing next to one of Hollywood's most popular stars, offering them protection. "Hopefully tonight won't be too boring if you're used to a zoo."

He grinned, holding her gaze. "I don't know how it could be. My date's a hottie."

Her pulse accelerated. Why did he have to *look* at her like that?

The car stopped and Collin's door opened.

He stepped to the curb and got out, extending his hand to her.

She got out to the screams of hundreds of adoring fans. Her fingers automatically laced with Collin's as she waved with her free hand while security walked close to her and her date—something she wasn't used to. Typically Dad's team kept their distance, but tonight they were no farther than a shoulder's length away.

"Collin!" several of the teenage girls yelled.

She smiled. "I think the ladies have a crush on you."

He lifted his hand and waved, and they screamed again. "Huh. Usually I just stand in the background and keep my eyes open for threats." He raised his hand for the second time, inciting more screams. "How about that?"

She laughed as she met his amused gaze.

"Collin, Princess Lyla, stand over here," several photographers demanded.

"They want our picture."

"So let's give it to them."

They took their place by the huge board advertising tonight's sponsors, and Collin wrapped his arm around her waist. Flashbulbs went off in a frenzy.

"Lyla, over here. Lyla," one of Russia's morning show hostesses hollered among the chaos.

Lyla smiled at Dobra Petroff. She'd always liked Dobra. More than once she'd helped Dobra greet Moscow on a weekday morning with tea and conversation, enjoying herself every time.

"You look lovely tonight, Princess," Dobra said into her microphone as a television camera rolled by her side.

"Thank you. So do you."

"It's nice that you were able to come out this evening."

"I'm happy I can be here to support such a worthy cause."

"I see you've brought your Prince Charming."

She laughed uncomfortably as she glanced at Collin while he looked at her, glad he had no idea what Dobra was saying. "Yes."

"As an American citizen, how does Mr. Michaels feel

about such a special event for The Federation?"

She met his gaze again. "Dobra wants to know how you feel about the gala."

"I'm glad I can be here for you, and to support the victims of the Saint Petersburg attack."

Lyla translated back what Collin said.

Dobra nodded and smiled. "Thank you, Princess."

"Thank you." She stepped back as another celebrity made his way toward the door and more cameras flashed.

"Enough of this." Collin took her hand, guiding her inside. "Hopefully we'll be able to see again before your performance."

She chuckled, taking off her jacket and draping it on her arm. "Should we find my dad?"

"Definitely." He led her through the crowds with his hand on the small of her back. "It's time to get this party started."

"Mmm," she agreed as she looked around at the dozens of security agents mingling among the guests. Hopefully Dad would keep his word and head home early.

———◆———

Collin wiped his mouth with a cloth napkin as he finished the last of his crazy delicious dessert and glanced at Lyla, who was toying with her fruit tart. She'd eaten every bite of her salad and half her cup of soup, but she'd barely touched her entrée and now the final course of their spectacular dinner. She danced for hours each day and ate like a rabbit—or she did now that they were in Russia. Her appetite had been just fine when they sat at her dining room table in New York.

Sergei muttered to her, something Collin couldn't understand, and Lyla's shoulders snapped straight as her hot eyes met her dance partner's.

Damn, it was frustrating not understanding the language, but he didn't need words to comprehend that there was major tension brewing between Lyla and Sergei. Collin hooked his arm around her shoulders in a gesture of support as he made eye contact with Sergei. "It looks like tonight's a success." He offered a friendly smile, hoping to diffuse some of the hostility here at table twenty-nine. For two hours, Sergei had tossed remarks at Lyla in Russian, even though his English was just fine.

"Yes," Sergei said, sitting back in his chair. "Although I find it dangerous. We've all written checks for the cause, haven't we? Why do they insist on gathering Russia's most important people in one room to taunt a group of madmen?"

"But the food's delicious." Collin gestured to his empty plate, ignoring Lyla's quiet scoff in response to Sergei's pompous remarks.

"You liked your meal?" Sergei asked as he peeked at his watch, clearly bored with the evening.

Collin nodded. "Very much."

"I was just telling your girlfriend she needs to eat. Her costume will look poor if a skeleton wears it."

He glanced from Sergei to Lyla, noting the battle light in her blue eyes.

"I had no idea you studied nutrition as well as ballet," she responded coolly.

"Ly-Ly looks great. We ate before we came," Collin lied as he brushed his hand down her arm. He couldn't be certain she'd had much of anything all day, but she would certainly be eating something when they got home. He wouldn't be giving her an option. "So, what do you have lined up after *The Markovik Number*? I know Ly-Ly's doing the new Geoffrey production in Manhattan."

"Skiing. A week away with Ava." Sergei touched the black-haired, olive-complexioned beauty at his side. Sergei's girlfriend was a class act. Unfortunately Collin couldn't say the same for her date.

"That sounds great. What slopes do you plan to hit?"

"Asha Resort in central Russia for sure, then maybe something else farther east or perhaps somewhere entirely different."

"Sounds pretty adventurous."

"I fly myself, so we come and go as we please."

Collin perked up. "You're a pilot?"

"*Da*. I learned about two years ago. Ava's papa is a pilot as well. He allows me to use his planes on occasion when Ava and I are ready for a vacation."

"No kidding. I fly as well."

"Perhaps a few days at Asha Resort would be good for you. The skiing is acceptable, but it is the privacy that I love. Ava and I will leave immediately after the parade."

"Sounds good." He looked at Lyla as she played with the crumbs on her plate. "If you'll excuse us, I'm going to take this lovely lady for a spin on the dance floor." He extended his hand to her.

She took it, and they stood.

Sergei muttered something else in Russian as they walked away.

He pulled Lyla close as they stepped in the center of the room among the other dancers. "So, I had no idea you and Sergei hated each other's guts."

She laced her fingers behind his neck. "Hate's a strong word."

"I thought I was going to have to keep you from crawling over the table and clawing his eyes out."

She grinned. "I was trying to be subtle."

"I know you better than most." Or he was starting to. "I *am* your Prince Charming."

She laughed. "Ava's wonderful, but he can be a bit much."

Sergei had insulted her time and again—or so he assumed—and she still had nothing particularly unkind to say. "Arrogant?"

She rolled her eyes. "Yes."

"Rude?"

She chuckled. "*Incredibly*."

"I could hold your coat if you want to pop him one."

She grinned. "Don't tempt me."

"How about we stay over here and keep dancing for a while?"

"Maybe you could punch him for me."

He shook his head. "I'd knock him out, but it wouldn't be as satisfying as if you did it yourself."

"True. But I would treasure the silence however I had to get it."

He grinned, locking his wrist with his opposite hand at the back of her waist as he sensed her relaxing. "You really do look amazing tonight—by far the most beautiful woman in the room."

"Thank you. I—" She trailed off as she looked over his shoulder, and the bright light he'd brought back to her eyes disappeared again.

"What?" He glanced behind him, trying to figure out what was bothering her.

"My dad. He's unhappy."

He spotted Jonathan speaking to a couple of men. "He looks okay to me."

She shook her head. "No. He's not. I can tell."

"He'll be okay."

She shook her head again. "I'm afraid things are getting worse for him here. I never realized..." She swallowed. "I want people to focus on me—on us."

"You hate the spotlight."

She tore her gaze from Jonathan, focusing on him. "I love my father."

He stroked her cheek. "He's all right, Ly-Ly."

Her brow stayed furrowed as they held each other's stare.

"He's all right," he repeated.

She nodded.

"Dance with me, make fun of Sergei a little, and try not to worry." He pulled her closer and gently turned her away so that her view would change. He studied Jonathan, seeing the strain on the Ambassador's face himself and the body language that said the conversation going on across the room was not a friendly one. He looked around, his eyes landing on Roman Akolov as the reporter spoke to a man Collin was certain he'd seen on TV before—a higher up in the Russian government.

The official said something to Roman, and they both glanced at Jonathan then toward him and Lyla. He clenched his jaw, not liking whatever the hell was going on. People laughed and enjoyed wine and good food, but the air was unmistakably hostile at an event that was supposed to be bringing groups together in the face of adversity.

Roman looked back towards him and Lyla.

Collin eased back, smiling at Lyla, focusing on his principal and the role he was playing. "How's the ankle?"

"Okay," she said, almost hiding her grimace.

"Has anyone ever told you you're a *horrible* liar?"

She smiled. "All right. I'm looking forward to a bucket of ice water. How's that for the truth?"

"Better." He felt eyes on them again and slid his thumb along her jaw.

She blinked as she jerked. "Collin—"

Doing what he thought was best, he pressed his lips to hers.

She tensed, her fingers curling into the collar of his jacket. "Collin—"

He held her confused gaze as he captured her chin with his fingers and kissed her again, tasting the slightest hint of Lyla's sweet flavor as he drew out the moment longer than the first.

She shuddered out a breath. "What are you—what are you doing?"

He rested his forehead against hers. "Roman's watching us. I don't like him or the way he looks at us—like we're full of shit."

"We are."

He chuckled despite the intensity snapping between

them. "No one needs to know that except for us."

She settled her hands against his biceps and closed her eyes. "Don't kiss me again, okay? Hold my hand, but don't kiss me."

He swallowed as he slid his palms up and down her waist. "Why?"

She let loose another unsteady breath. "Just because."

"I didn't—"

"It's time for us to go," Jonathan said as he walked over to stand next to them, his irritated tone unmistakable.

Lyla broke their embrace, taking a step closer to her father. "Why? What's wrong?"

"We've been here long enough."

"Daddy—"

"One of the police dogs picked up a scent in the basement. They've declared it a false alarm, but I want you home anyway. You and Collin leave first. I'll follow."

"No, I want us to go together—"

"That's not possible. Do as I ask, Lyla. Please," Jonathan added, gentling his voice.

She opened her mouth, closed it, then said, "Okay."

"I'll be right behind you, Ly-Ly." Jonathan kissed her cheek.

"Come on." Collin slid his arm around her waist as they walked to the table to grab their coats. He watched more than one security agent speaking into their communication pieces. There wasn't a bomb this time, but that didn't mean there wouldn't be the next. He glanced around at eyes on them and pulled her closer. There was nothing romantic in his gesture or desire to further cement their façade. His only goal was to get her out of there and keep her safe.

⊰ Chapter Thirteen ⊱

Lyla hobbled from the bathroom with her wet hair dripping drops down her shoulders and her body wrapped in a towel. Goose bumps puckered her skin in the slightly chilly air as she fought off a wave of wracking shivers. It had been tempting to stand in the shower and let the stream of warm water baby her fatigued muscles, but heat wasn't her friend right now. Her ankle was swollen after another grueling practice. She needed a bucket of ice, a late lunch served up with a bottle of ibuprofen, and oblivion. Fedor was growing more relentless as the week carried on. In the three days since the gala, she'd rehearsed endlessly, often for ten to twelve hours, until she and Sergei could barely stand. She reached for her ice bucket, craving the blessed numbness the icy water would bring, and paused when someone knocked on her door. "Just—"

"Hey," Collin said, poking his head inside.

She stood upright, clutching the towel tighter around her. "I just need a minute."

He walked in, wearing blue jeans and a navy blue long-sleeve tee, holding up a bulging plastic bag as he shut the door behind him. "I brought you ice."

Did he not see that she was practically *naked*? "Thanks."

He dumped the ice in the bucket and moved to her windows, closing her curtains. "You've got some hopeful stragglers out there this afternoon."

"Yeah." She cleared her throat. "Uh—"

"Damn, Lyla, look at your ankle." He cut across the room in three quick strides, snagging her by the arm. "Let's get you off your feet."

"Collin." She pulled away. "I just got out of the shower."

"I see that."

"I'm wearing a towel." She tugged on the hem, emphasizing her point.

"I've heard that's what those are called."

She scoffed. "You need to leave so I can get dressed."

He grinned. "How about I fill up your bucket while you put on some clothes?"

"Fine." She limped over to her drawers, pulling out panties and a bra, and glanced over her shoulder, realizing Collin was already off and at work on her bucket. She hurriedly grabbed dark gray sweat shorts and a soft white cotton sweatshirt and put everything on before Collin came back in.

"All set?" he asked from the bathroom.

"Yeah."

"Here you go." He put the bucket down in front of her bed where she typically parked herself to soak.

"Thank you." She hobbled back to the mattress and sat, submerging her foot and sucking in a breath from the shock of icy cold.

"Hurts so good."

She laughed. "Yes, it does."

There was another knock on her door. "Lyla, I have some lunch for you," Oksana called.

She frowned. "Why does Oksana have my lunch?"

"I asked her to bring you something."

"She's not my servant."

"No, but she knows you've been working hard." He opened the door. "Hey." He smiled, taking the full tray. "This looks amazing."

Lyla studied the large salad topped with grilled salmon

and the bowl of lentil soup, then smiled at Oksana. "Thank you so much, Oksana."

"Fedor pushes hard. You'll need this good food to regain your energy."

"I already know it's going to be delicious. I appreciate it."

"Eat every bite."

"I will."

Oksana gave her a firm nod and stepped out as Collin brought her the tray, setting it next to her on the bed.

"Thanks."

"No problem." He sat down on the opposite side of the mattress, making himself at home where he had the other night. "Sounds like today was rough. I heard the hollering through the ballroom doors."

She rolled her eyes, remembering the ridiculousness of her rehearsals. "Sergei enjoys his tantrums."

"What's his problem?"

"He's an amazing dancer, but his ego gets in the way. I thought he and Fedor were going to come to blows." And it was nice to not be the center of ridicule for once.

"I had no idea there was so much drama in the dance world."

"It's a pretty intense art." She took a huge bite of perfectly prepared fish and leafy romaine. "Mmm. This is *great*."

"Looks like it."

She extended the plate to him. "Do you want some?"

He shook his head. "I ate a couple hours ago."

With her ankle comfortably numb, she pulled her foot from the water and settled in the center of her bed, leaning back on her pillows as she dug into her lunch.

Collin grabbed the bottle of lotion on her side table and tugged on her leg, bringing her swollen foot closer. "Looks like hell."

She paused, then kept chewing, growing more accustomed to Collin's constant need to touch.

He squirted a glob of lavender-scented moisturizer in his

hand and rubbed her ankle, starting with long, slow sweeps with his warm fingers.

She closed her eyes, trying not to purr.

"Too much pressure?"

She shook her head as she opened her eyes, and their gazes met. "No. It's perfect—amazing."

"Good." He circled his thumbs around the bone. "I've gotta tell you, I don't think I've ever seen uglier feet."

"Gee, thanks," she said over her mouthful.

He grinned. "You look like magic on that billboard in Manhattan. You make standing on the tips of your toes appear effortless. I guess there's a price to pay for that type of beauty."

She swallowed, staring at him. Big, bad Collin Michaels was a poet. "You have a way with words."

He applied more lotion to her foot. "I don't know about that."

"You're rough and edgy, but you're also sweet."

He winced. "Sweet?"

She laughed.

"I don't think I want to be known as sweet."

She set down the half-empty plate and went after the soup next. "It's an excellent quality."

"I prefer 'Collin Michaels: badass.'" He puffed up his well-built chest.

She laughed again as he chuckled. "Stick with sweet. Trust me."

"Is that what you want, Ly-Ly?" He gentled his fingers, the kneading more a tender caress. "Sweet?"

She licked her lips as the fun light in his eyes changed into something she didn't quite recognize but knew was dangerous all at the same time. "I don't—I don't—" Her phone jingled with an incoming text, and she set down her bowl, relieved to have a distraction as the intensity that had swirled around them on the gala dance floor came back.

Are you free for dinner tonight? she read, smiling at Pasha's message.

I'm not sure. Let me talk to Collin.

"Good news?"

She nodded and sat up farther, breaking their connection. "My friend Pasha wants to get together for dinner."

"Pasha?"

She smiled again, loving the idea of seeing her old friend. "Yes. He's a journalist here in Moscow. We met in Manhattan when he was interning with the *Times*."

"We can do that if you want." He stood and walked to the windows, opening the curtains. "Is he going to come here?"

She shook her head and let loose a small laugh. "No, that wouldn't be a good idea. Pasha works for one of the smaller, more liberal newspapers here in the city. He's not particularly popular with the regime or Moscow's more conservative audience."

"Do you think this is something you want to be doing right now?"

She finished rubbing in the moisturizer he'd missed. "He just wants to get together for some conversation and a meal."

He rubbed at his jaw. "I don't like the press."

"Pasha's not looking for a story, Collin. He's my friend."

"This is entirely up to you. I'm here to tag along. If you want to have dinner with your pal, we will."

She gained her feet, testing her ankle, and walked to where he stood, staring out at the people lingering around the gates with their posters, even in the twenty-degree weather. "I would love to see him. It's been so long. We met up for coffee last year when I was here."

"So we'll go."

"What about that?" She pointed to her eager fans. "Last year I snuck out the back gate after it got dark, and he picked me up a couple blocks away. I wore my hair in a bun and a hat, and no one noticed us..."

"It's my job to deal with the logistics. We'll do our best to avoid another night like we had at the Winter Festival. Have Pasha set something up and make sure he requests private seating—something away from windows and doors but close to the kitchen so I can get you out the back entrance if I have to. Then give me the details."

She smiled. "That shouldn't be a problem. No one really knows who Pasha is. His paper has a very small following, so I don't think we'll have to worry about our plans getting leaked to the media if he uses his name and keeps mine out of it."

"He *is* the media, Lyla."

She shook her head. "Not the way you think. Trust me. This is going to be fun. You'll like Pasha. He's a great man."

He let loose a long breath. "I can't wait to meet him."

———◆———

Collin stared at Lyla as she laughed. The candlelight accentuated her flawless complexion and stunning face as they sat at their quiet table tucked toward the back of *Kafé Pushkin*. Pasha had asked for privacy, and the staff at the high-end restaurant honored his request. He took another bite of his extraordinary beef stroganoff, unable to take his eyes off of Lyla.

Her shoulders were bare in the charcoal gray top she'd paired with snug, stylish jeans, and her blond hair cascaded down her back. She'd added loose curls to several glossy locks and had done something different with her makeup. He wasn't exactly sure how she'd managed to make her eyes appear larger or her lips more shimmery and kissable, but she'd pulled it off nonetheless.

She forked up the last of her grilled sea bass as she and Pasha laughed. This right here was what she'd needed. Here was the woman he hadn't seen since Manhattan. Lyla's smiles were big and genuine, and her shoulders relaxed. Somehow he'd been able to pull off getting them out of Spaso House's back entrance without being noticed. For the last hour and a half, Lyla had been enjoying a normal evening—for the most part. A few patrons recognized her as they walked through the restaurant, but they'd given her space.

"You'll have to come see the show," she said to the clean-cut blond at her side as she blotted her lips and set her napkin back in her lap. "You know my couch is always available."

"I'll be in New York later next month. I'll be sure to stop in." Pasha focused on Collin. "I hope I'll see you as well, Collin."

Lyla opened her mouth and closed it when her eyes met Collin's. She smiled guiltily at her friend and picked up her water glass.

Collin took Lyla's hand across the small table, giving her fingers a not-so-gentle squeeze, well aware that she was about to spill the beans to her buddy about their not-so-genuine relationship status. Lyla trusted Pasha, but he didn't. He was a reporter, and Lyla a hot story. "We look forward to it. I should be moved in with Ly-Ly by then."

Lyla choked on her drink.

"Are you okay?" Pasha asked, patting her on the back.

She nodded as she cleared her throat. "Yes. Yes, I'm fine."

"You're moving in?" Pasha asked, his hazel eyes full of surprise.

"We figure why not, you know?" Collin sat back in his chair, certain he'd made his silent reminder for Lyla to keep her mouth shut clear. "Ly-Ly wants me to find a job in Manhattan, so it makes sense."

Pasha looked from Collin to Lyla.

She nodded again. "It'll be great having him close. Long-distance relationships are tough."

"You're not going to give up dancing?"

"No. Never."

"Collin, will you still do security?"

He shrugged. "Most likely." And that's all he planned to say.

"I will certainly look forward to seeing you both—" His phone vibrated with a text. "Excuse me." Pasha looked toward the table, tipping his phone and reading his screen. "I'm afraid I'm going to have to cut this short." Pasha signaled for the check.

"Oh, so soon?" Lyla asked, her disappointment unmistakable.

"Yes, they need me back at the office." Pasha gestured to his phone.

The waiter brought over the bill.

"We'll have to treat you in New York," Collin said as Pasha reached for his wallet. "I've been wanting to take Ly-Ly to Tavern on the Green. It's not far from her apartment."

"That sounds wonderful." Pasha laid down several bills. "I hope you and Lyla will stay and enjoy dessert."

"We'll walk you out," Lyla offered. She stood and pulled on her long coat. "I hate to say goodbye already. Luckily we'll see you very soon."

"Yes," Pasha answered distractedly as he glanced at his phone again before shoving it in his pocket.

They walked through the restaurant and out the door into the horrid cold. "Pasha, thank you so much." Lyla hugged her friend, who wasn't much taller than she was, and kissed his cheek. "I'm so happy we could do this. It's always so fun."

He kissed both of her cheeks. "I'll see you after your performance if I'm able to get backstage." He took her hands and said something to her in Russian.

Lyla smiled and responded in the language Collin didn't understand.

"Collin, thank you for letting me steal some of your and Lyla's precious free time."

Collin shook his hand, noting that Pasha's friendly tone had gone serious. "It's always nice to meet Ly-Ly's friends."

"Yes, well, I should be on my way."

"Thanks for dinner."

"I'm always happy to treat special people."

Lyla hugged him again. "You be careful. Those articles you write are bound to get you in trouble."

"The truth is often dangerous." Pasha hailed a cab. "Goodbye." He got in, waved, and the car drove off.

She sighed, her breath pluming out in a puff of white. "It was nice to see him again. I hate that we can't get together very often."

"He seems nice."

She narrowed her eyes. "You don't like Pasha."

"No. He's fine. But he's still a reporter."

She shook her head. "He's my friend first. He wasn't here for the scoop on the princess and her new boyfriend."

He would believe that when he didn't see their conversation in the paper tomorrow. "Should we get a cab?"

She nibbled her lip and shook her head. "No." She took his hand and started walking. "I want to show you some of my favorite places in Russia."

"Lyla, it's freezing."

"We'll buy you a hat."

He pulled on her hand, stopping her. "I'm not worried about me. You have to dance tomorrow. The last thing you need is to be sick."

"I don't want to think about dancing. I just want to be. For an hour I just want to be, Collin. Play tourist with me."

There was something desperate in her voice. "Okay. Show me Moscow."

She grinned and pulled him ahead.

He wrapped his arm around her waist, and they walked down the busy sidewalk in the raw temperatures. "What's our first stop?"

"I'm not sure, but I'll know it when I see it." Within moments she was leading him to a gift shop. "We have to get something to remember our trip."

The woman behind the counter perked up as they stepped

inside.

Lyla smiled and continued down the rows of gift options. "So what do you think?"

He stared at dozens of items and blew out a noisy breath, shaking his head. "I don't even know where to begin."

She laughed. "How about one of these *ushankas*?"

"What's that?" He frowned, moving closer to where she stood with her back to him.

She held up a big furry hat. "It's pretty iconic." She gained her tiptoes, plunking the bulky black hat on his head and laughed again.

"I look that good, huh?"

She took a step back and put her hands on her hips, clearly considering. "It's actually not too bad. You're pretty handsome so you can pull off just about anything."

"Thanks." He grabbed a lady-sized hat in white and plunked it on her head.

She smiled. "Well?"

"It's perfect." He pulled out his phone and stood next to her. "Sometimes you have to take a selfie."

"Definitely." She grinned with her thumbs up.

He took the picture and they both studied the results. Damn, she was spectacular, especially when she was at ease. "I think we have to buy these."

Her eyes went huge. "Really?"

He nodded. "Definitely. I need to get something for Luna. She would never forgive me if I didn't bring her something home."

"Let's take a look." She took his hand, lacing their fingers.

He walked just behind her in the close quarters, wondering if she realized she'd reached out to him. Typically he was the one to take the lead in their "relationship," but not right now.

"How about this?"

"What?"

She picked up an intricately painted, roundish wooden

doll-type thing. "It's a *matryoshka* doll."

"A what?"

"A *matryoshka* doll."

"And what's the hat called?" He gestured to his head.

"An *ushanka*. Because the earflaps cover your ears. *Uk-hos*." Smiling at him, she touched his ears.

He leaned against the shelf and slid his thumb along her jaw. "It's sexy as hell when you speak Russian."

She grabbed his wrist and licked her lips. "Do you—do you like the doll?"

What he liked was her. What he wanted was her, whether it was stupid or not. "It's nice."

"It, uh, it has more dolls inside." She pulled the doll open, setting the next out and the next until there were five progressively smaller figurines standing side by side. "They're a symbol of mother or matriarch—fertility."

He sucked in a breath through his teeth. "Luna's younger than my dad, mid-forties, but I don't think she's looking for any help in the fertility department."

She laughed.

"I was kind of a handful."

She grinned, shaking her head. "I bet you were." She put the doll back together. "This is a pretty popular Russian-inspired gift."

"So we'll take it."

"Okay. Anything else?"

He shook his head. "We're off to a good start. What's next?"

"We'll pay, then I'll take you underground."

"Underground? Sounds pretty wild." He wiggled his eyebrows.

She rolled her eyes. "What am I going to do with you?"

"I'm not sure."

"Come on. Let's pay."

The woman took the tags from their hats and bagged up the doll.

"*Spasibo*," Lyla said, and they left.

He extended his arm to her. "Should we go underground?"

"Yes." They walked a quarter-mile in silence, and she sighed.

"What?"

"I love this."

"The city?"

"Yes. When I get to walk around freely and be a part of it like any other person."

"Do you ever think about giving it up?"

"All the time." Her eyes widened, and she stopped as if she'd surprised herself by her own answer. "I don't know why I just said that."

"Maybe you mean it."

She shook her head. "I was born to be a dancer. That's what I'm meant to be."

"You can be anything you want to be."

"Sometimes you can't."

The unhappiness was back in her eyes. He wanted to see it gone. He gave her arm a gentle bump. "So where's this mysterious underground you're taking me to?"

"We're getting closer." They crossed the busy street with several pedestrians, and she stopped by a set of stairs. "Right here."

He frowned. "The Metro?"

"Just wait and see."

"I've been on a subway before."

"Not like this." She walked backwards, pulling on his hands. "Come on." She gestured with her head to the stairs. "I promise you've never seen anything like this."

The fun was back in her eyes. He would do just about anything to keep it there. "Hold on." He eased her to the side, handed her the white hat she wore, and gathered her yards of soft, cold hair, twisting it and piling it on top of her head. "Put on your hat."

She did, managing to catch most of her hair in her *ushan-*

ka before it fell. "What's this for?"

"To give you some privacy."

"Good thinking."

He stared at her, not sure the attempt at a disguise would help. She was striking, eye-catching whether she wore her hair up or down. People were bound to take notice of her, not for any reason other than she was beautiful. It wouldn't take them long to realize she was Lyla Markovik-Avery if they were paying attention. "Ready?"

"That's what I should be asking you."

"Okay. Ask me."

She smiled. "Are you ready, Collin?"

"I'm ready to be amazed."

They walked down the steps, stopped quickly to buy two tickets, and pushed through the turnstiles. He stopped again and stared, taking in the ornate, museum-like quality of the Metro stop—marble sculptures, golden gilding along the archways. "Holy shit."

"I told you."

"This is a *subway* stop?"

"Mmhm."

"Wow. I'm officially blown away."

She pulled out her phone. "Selfie in the coolest stop you've ever seen?"

"Hell yeah." He stood next to her, and they captured their smiling faces in front of one of the intricate paintings. "Good stuff. Where to now?"

"Spaso House."

"Are you sure?"

"Yeah. Sergei and Fedor will be by early tomorrow."

"Take a day off."

"I can't."

"Even if it's just like this?"

She shook her head. "I can't."

"Okay." He glanced around, noting that they were starting to attract attention in the bright light of the huge space.

A train pulled up, stopping to let people off.

They stepped on, and he tugged her closer as the car started filling up. "Turn around," he said next to her ear.

She did, and he wrapped his arms around her, hiding her face from the public. He stared at their reflection in the glass. They looked like any other couple embracing, out enjoying the city's energy.

He leaned against the pole as the car started moving.

Lyla wrapped her arms around him, keeping her balance.

He studied the man and woman in the glass again as he rubbed his hands up and down her back, finding himself wanting something just like this—a warm, sweet woman who was strong yet vulnerable because she thought she had to take on the world by herself. Minutes later the train pulled up at their stop. "Ready?"

She barely met his gaze as they exited the car, hand-in-hand, and started up the stairs.

"I know it's just a couple blocks home, but we should probably hail a cab from here."

"Sure."

They pushed through the door and stepped out into the cold. Collin lifted his hand, and a car eased up to the curb. Like hell he was getting into just any vehicle. It was common practice for cars to stop and play taxi, but not tonight. He waved it on. A marked cab stopped when he put up his hand again. "Spaso House, *spasibo*."

The cabbie nodded, and they were off.

Lyla stared out her window as he played with her fingers. Something was different—had changed while they were on the Metro.

"Is everything okay?" he asked quietly.

"Yes. Of course." She sent him a small smile.

It wasn't. He knew her well enough to recognize her false reassurances and the placating curve of her lips. "Good."

Before long, they were let through the gates, the crowds finally gone as the late-night temperatures grew brutal. Collin paid the man off and they got out, moving quickly up the front steps as the wind slapped at them.

Lyla let them in the house. "Thanks," she said as she walked farther into the entryway. "I'm going to go up. I'll see you tomorrow." She hurried away up the steps, her slight limp slowing her down.

He stared after her as he took off his jacket. Something was definitely not okay.

She disappeared down the dim hall.

He could let her go, which was probably the smart choice, or he could catch up and figure out what was going on. "Hey, Lyla." He took the stairs in twos, pulling off his new hat as he went. "Lyla," he called again, watching her hesitate and keep going. "Hey." He jogged after her. "Hey." He grabbed her by the arm.

She turned. "What?"

"What's up?"

"Nothing. I just need to ice my ankle and get to bed."

It wasn't lost on him that she looked over his shoulder as she spoke, avoiding eye contact.

He leaned to the right, hanging his coat on his doorknob. "I thought we had fun tonight."

Her gaze snapped to his. "We did."

"What happened between the Metro and home?"

"Nothing." She unbuttoned her coat and took it off.

He pulled off her hat, watching her hair cascade past her naked shoulders as he let her hat fall to the floor. "Nothing," he repeated as he tucked a curling tendril behind her ear, wondering what in the hell it was that he was doing.

She stepped away.

Now he was supposed to let her walk into her room and shut the door, because he was the bodyguard and she his principal. Instead, he closed the distance between them as he held her gaze. "Why don't I believe you?"

"I'm not sure." She cleared her throat.

This wasn't getting him anywhere. Clearly she had no intentions of telling him what was bothering her. "So thanks for helping me pick out Luna's gift."

"You're welcome."

"You laughed a lot tonight. I like watching you smile—really smile." He watched his own fingers reach out and stroke her soft cheek. This right here was a fatal mistake. This right here wasn't going to help him get his head on straight... So why didn't he care?

Her coat fell to the floor as she placed a halting hand on his chest.

He touched her wrist, feeling the rapid beat of her pulse. "I like being with you—just you and me."

Her breath shuddered out.

"When no one else is watching." He eased forward as she gripped his shirt. "I want to kiss you, Lyla. Not for an audience—just for us." He rubbed his lips against hers, testing, teasing as he had at the gala, but now they were alone. "The other night I barely got a taste..."

Her eyes fluttered closed as her hands moved to clutch his elbows.

"No one's here but you and me," he whispered against her mouth.

She lifted her chin, deepening the kiss, surprising him when she rose on her tiptoes and wrapped her arms around him.

He groaned, pushing her back against the wall, and plundered, sliding his tongue against hers as her hands wandered into his hair. This Lyla was all heat. She was fire, and he wanted to be part of the inferno. He pulled her closer, feeling her breasts firm against his chest.

She whimpered, holding herself against him.

He combed his fingers through her hair, tugging gently and easing her head farther back, hungry for her, diving.

Her hands were everywhere, running up and down his back, along his sides, his stomach.

He grabbed her by the wrists, lifting her arms and pinning them against the wall, lacing his fingers with hers. Heat snapped. Electricity sparked as she gained her tiptoes again and snagged his bottom lip.

Something creaked down the long hall, and a door closed, startling them both.

He dropped her hands and stepped away, his chest heaving as hers did.

She licked her swollen lips. "I, um—I don't know why... I guess we shouldn't have done that."

"Probably not." He rubbed at the back of his tense neck, still tasting her on his tongue.

She groped for the doorknob behind her. "I should go."

"Lyla... We can't do that again." But he wanted to.

Swallowing, she nodded. "We'll just hold hands," she said, stumbling into her room and closing her door.

He clenched his jaw, staring at her coat and hat she'd forgotten. He balled his hands into fists, aching to finish what they'd started. He could walk in. He could make Lyla his lover right now. But it wouldn't be right for either of them. Steaming out a long breath, he turned away and went to his own room, ready for an ice-cold shower.

CHAPTER FOURTEEN

L YLA STUMBLED THROUGH THE LAST STEPS OF *The Markovik Number*, and Fedor swore.

"Three days, you blockhead! This must be perfect in three days!"

She stood with her hands on her hips, struggling to catch her breath as she cautiously rotated her screaming ankle, well used to Fedor's insults. "If you'll let me rest—"

"There's no time for rest," he shouted over the music, moving his arms about wildly.

"I need water and food. I haven't sat down in almost eight hours," she snapped. "You won't get perfection like this."

Fedor dismissed her complaints with a wave of his hand and a string of curses. "Lazy! You're a shame to your mother's *name.*" He emphasized with a stomp of his foot. "Where is your ethic? Mina could dance circles around you, little fool. You will *work*! You will earn your birthright!"

She'd had enough—more than enough. "Tomorrow." She grabbed her empty water bottle and opened the door, leaving whether Fedor was ready for her to go or not.

"Ly-Ly." Her father rushed over to greet her as she hobbled up the first step on her way to her room. "You look like you've bathed in sweat."

"I'm fine," she said as she adjusted his collar and tie. Or she would be after a shower and a meal.

"Ly-Ly." Dad took her hand.

She frowned, realizing he wasn't worried about her physically. "What's wrong?"

"Pasha's in the hospital."

She gripped his fingers. "Pasha?"

"Yes. They found him outside his office. Beaten."

"*Beaten?*" She rubbed at her temple, trying to comprehend. "*What?*"

"He's in intensive care. His jaw is broken, and there was some internal bleeding. His spleen and kidneys are in rough shape."

She shook her head, not wanting to believe it. "No. Why?"

"I'm—I'm not sure."

She narrowed her eyes. Dad never faltered. "You have an idea."

"There's footage on the news of you and Pasha having dinner last night."

"With Collin."

"Yes."

She shrugged, not following. "We had dinner at *Kafe Pushkin.*"

"Can you walk?"

"Yes. Of course."

She followed him to his office, watching as he closed the door and turned on the radio. "What are you doing?"

"Taking precautions. Come sit."

Her father was suddenly The Riddler. "Precautions?"

"Sit, Lyla."

She did as she was asked, taking the seat across from him at his desk. "What is going *on* around here?"

"We're under scrutiny. Our every move is being watched and speculated over. You and Collin are making a big splash. The citizens are taking note—they're fascinated. You have influence here."

"I realize that. I'm doing what I've always done—what my mother had always done."

"And she would be so proud of you, honey. Times are different now—much like they were when you were born."

"Tell me what happened to Pasha."

"You know Pasha is unpopular with the Regime. He bashes the President almost daily. His last statements went too far. The article he published yesterday morning accusing the government of not doing all that they can to catch the terrorists was dangerous." He steamed out a puff of air. "Now you're associated with that."

She gaped, trying to see the ludicrous connection. "We only had dinner. Work never came up."

"It was enough just to be *seen* together. It looks as if you sympathize with his ideas. Your popularity might make others start to question—"

She rushed up as his implications finally rang clear. "This is my fault?"

"No." He leaned across his workspace, taking both of her hands. "These are the times we live in. This isn't the Russia you've enjoyed over the last few years."

"When will it stop?" She yanked away from his gentle hold. "When will you come home and give this up?"

"I can't."

"Yes. At any time you can tender your resignation—make a call to Washington and tell them you've had enough."

"Your mother dreamed of a democracy for the people—for peace and stability here and between our two countries. I can't turn my back because times are tough."

How could she argue with that? He'd loved her mother deeply, had lost his wife to gain a daughter. But it didn't make this any less hard. It didn't banish the wave of resentment she felt for the woman she never knew or the guilt that quickly followed. "You could help from the US."

"You know I have to stay here."

He wanted to stay here, and she wanted him safe. "What happens when they get to you, when I get a phone call that you've been left beaten in the cold or worse?"

He stood, walked around the desk, and settled his hands on her shoulders. "I'm well protected."

"They can get to you—to any of us." She hugged him despite her sweaty clothes and his dapper suit, clutching him tight. "Your agents are an illusion of safety." She sighed with the weight of worry as heavy on her shoulders as it had ever been.

"Ly-Ly, this is what I have to do."

She eased back, staring into his determined eyes, and kissed his cheek, well aware arguing was fruitless. "I know." She moved to the door. "I have to get ready for my afternoon."

"You can cancel."

She paused with her hand on the doorknob. "No."

"It's not safe."

"So you can be in the crosshairs, but I should sit back safely?"

"Lyla—"

She shook her head. "I have Collin. We'll go to the Maternity House and then to visit Pasha."

"That's not a good idea. You need to keep your distance."

"I'm going to see my friend. I'll do just about anything for you, Daddy, but not that. I've done nothing wrong. Pasha has done nothing wrong except speak the truth as he sees it." She turned and opened the door, slamming into Collin on her way out.

"Whoa." He caught her around the waist.

"Sorry. Excuse me." She broke free of his hold and moved toward the stairs as quickly as her ankle would allow. If she didn't get away, she might explode.

Collin fell into step next to her as she started up the steps. "I take it you heard about Pasha."

"Yes."

"We should probably think about wrapping things up around here after your dance."

She stopped dead. "I should run away?"

"No, you should heed a warning."

She scoffed and kept walking down the hall. "I have to get ready to go."

"I think we should cancel today."

"I won't."

They stopped outside her room, much like they had last night, but hot kisses in the dimly lit hallway were the last thing on her mind at this point.

"It's not really up for discussion."

Who did Collin think he was? Why did everyone suddenly believe they could tell her what to do? "Fine. You stay at Spaso House and I'll go." She opened her door.

He grabbed her arm. "We go to your stuff together or we don't go at all."

"I've always come and gone as I please. You being here isn't about to alter that." She closed the door in his face, locking it, and sat down on her bed, covering her face with her hands and rocking gently as she fought to steady her breathing. Poor Pasha. And her father. *They're always watching.*

She glanced toward her windows, stood, and stared out the panes of glass at the fans waiting beyond the gates with signs for her and Collin. "Damn it." She snapped her drapes closed and flipped on the television, eager to find an update on Pasha. Her eyes grew wide as she watched herself and Collin in the surveillance videos at the gift shop they'd visited last night. They'd tried on hats and took a selfie. Collin stroked his fingers along her face and watched her as she displayed the *matryoshka* dolls on a shelf. The surveillance continued as they walked down the streets on their way to the Metro and their long embrace when Collin slid his hands up and down her back as the train brought them closer to home. She powered off the TV and threw the remote on the bed. There was no privacy here. Not a single moment was hers alone.

Her breathing came fast again as the walls closed in around her. There was nowhere to go. There was no place she could get away. She was thousands of miles from her apartment—the only place that felt like home. She shut herself in her bathroom, stripped off her clothes, and stepped into the shower, hoping to gather a few moments of peace.

———◦———

Collin sat next to Lyla in the backseat of the cab as they made their way to one of Moscow's state-run maternity hospitals. So far, the ride through the city's busy streets had been quiet. He and Lyla hadn't spoken much since she met him downstairs, dressed for the afternoon in jeans and a pretty pink sweater instead of the sweaty dance clothes she'd been wearing when she slammed her door in his face an hour ago. He'd expected Lyla to take the news about Pasha hard, but giving Jonathan the business, then more or less telling him to go to hell had taken him by surprise. Clearly Lyla was feeling backed into a corner—the only time in his experience that she didn't smile and pretend everything was fine.

He studied her profile as she leaned against the door and stared out the window, gripping her hands together in her lap. He wanted to hug her against him and reassure her that her father was okay and that Pasha was going to make a full recovery, but he glanced at the cab driver instead, uncertain whether the man was just any other cabbie or a spy being paid by The Regime to keep tabs on the Avery clan. At this point, nothing was off the table. They were in a foreign land with a different set of rules, and he was on guard.

He looked at Lyla again, sorry that the fun they'd had only hours ago was now overshadowed by a series of troubling events. He'd slept little, replaying their kiss several times throughout the night, but their hot little lip lock in the hall at Spaso House didn't seem to mean much now. They both agreed the whole thing had been a mistake, so why in the hell was he eager to make another one?

The cab pulled up to the maternity hospital outfitted with a brand new NICU—the purpose of Lyla's visit. The city was proud of its advances in a healthcare system that was years behind their Western counterparts.

He studied the crowd of reporters waiting for Lyla by the entrance. "You don't have to say anything today. We can go straight inside."

She nodded.

"Ready?"

Finally, she looked at him. "Yes."

"Are we holding hands or giving it a rest?" He wanted the contact—needed it, he realized, to provide comfort and because it just felt right to touch her. He opened the door and waited for Lyla to slide his way.

She got out and took his hand.

He intertwined their fingers, relieved that last night's little slip-up and their small hiccup today didn't appear to have ruined anything between them. "Let's go."

They walked a quick pace past the cameras and microphones shoved their way. On occasion, he was able to identify Pasha's name being hollered at Lyla among the barrage of questions. They weren't just interested in Lyla and her new love anymore. They wanted dirt on her friend—and he'd be damned if they were going to get it. "Come on." He wrapped his arm around her shoulders, quickening his step until they made it through the building's sliding doors.

"Lyla," a black-haired, middle-aged woman wearing a white physician's coat smiled, greeting them as they stepped farther inside. "I'm doctor Dernov, Head of Neonatology."

Lyla smiled, accepting her hand as camera bulbs flashed outside the barriers of glass, invading Lyla's privacy even still. "It's nice to meet you. Doctor Dernov, this is Collin."

"Thank you both for joining us today." She shook Collin's hand.

He was just happy she spoke English. "I know Ly-Ly's been looking forward to this."

Lyla smiled at him.

He could barely see the strain on her pretty face as he

held her gaze, but it was there. Princess Lyla was a good actress, but she had a long way to go before she fooled him.

"Can I take you for a tour?" Doctor Dernov gestured to the pale-beige hallway beyond a wooden door.

"Yes, please." Lyla smiled again. "We would love it."

He reached out to her this time, sliding his arm around her waist.

"We'll start in our maternity ward. We've made many improvements, which are creating better outcomes for our mothers and new babies."

"That's wonderful."

"I know this is a cause close to you, especially as your birthday nears."

Lyla nodded.

Collin glanced at her, foolishly realizing for the first time that Lyla's birthday was also the anniversary of her mother's death. How the hell did she celebrate a day like that? His heart went out to the woman at his side. Lyla had certainly dealt with her fair share of hard knocks. He lifted her hand, giving her knuckles a quick kiss as they started down another maze of hallways that appeared new but still looked nothing like the accommodations his friends were accustomed to back in The States. Over the last couple of years, he'd made more than one trip to the maternity ward to drop off flowers and hold a newborn as the Ethan Cooke Security family grew.

A woman moaned in a room as they passed just as someone farther down the hall screamed. Grimacing, he paused, struggling not to turn around and walk back out.

"Today is busy with new life," the doctor said.

As if Lyla knew what he was thinking, she hooked her arm around his waist, ushering him along until they stepped into a pretty kitchenette filled with tables and chairs, several potted plants drinking in the sunshine by the big windows, and a counter space stocked with cups, saucers, and numerous tea options.

"This is for our mothers waiting for birth or those who have recently delivered. They often enjoy the view with their cup of tea."

"Lovely," Lyla replied. "Very warm and comforting."

They walked out a door on the opposite side of the room, into a hallway where several mothers-to-be waddled about in their hospital gowns. Collin glanced behind him, noticing the lack of men. "Where are their husbands?" he whispered to Lyla.

"Most women birth alone," she answered quietly.

He frowned. "The father doesn't come and help?"

"Some men do. Many don't."

He would. He would be there for his partner—to do what he could to comfort her and welcome his baby into the world. "They should come."

"There are different customs here."

"I would be here," he said, even as a mother-to-be cried out in agony in a curtained-off section of a not-so-private room.

She smiled at him. "See? Sweet."

"It has nothing to do with being sweet. That would be my wife—my baby."

Her eyes softened, and she rested her head against his shoulder. "Sweet."

"We will go to our NICU." The doctor pressed the button for the elevator.

The three of them stepped into the elevator car and rode up two floors. The doors slid open, and they walked into a brand new wing decorated with a classy, European flair.

Several of the nurses at the nurses' station stood from their chairs, smiling at him and Lyla.

"Hey," he said, nodding as Lyla stopped to speak to the women in Russian.

The women talked back in excited bursts.

Suddenly Lyla laughed and looked at Collin. "Rozalina wants a picture with you."

He grinned at the strawberry blond blushing behind the counter. "Huh. Looks like you've got some competition, Markovik-Avery."

Lyla chuckled.

"Come on." He gestured with his head to the woman.

Rozalina's cheeks burned brighter.

"Come on," he encouraged again when she did little more than stare and bite her nail.

She walked over and stood next to him as several cameras came out.

He slid his arm around Rozalina's shoulder and smiled as flashes went off.

Rozalina said something to him in rapid-fire Russian.

He looked at Lyla for help.

"She's hoping they can get one of the two of us."

"Sure." He took Lyla's hand and pulled her against him, wrapping his arms around her waist.

Lyla returned his embrace. "They think you're very attractive—like an American movie star," she whispered with mischief in her eyes.

His fingers found their way into her hair, playing with the soft tips as he smiled at her and another round of flashes went off. "I am Prince Charming."

She rolled her eyes as she laughed. "Yikes. We're not going to be able to get you on the plane when it's time to go home. Your head's too big."

He secured his arms tighter around her, winking as they grinned at each other. Their playful banter was so much better than this afternoon's arguing.

"Over here," one of the nurses said in broken English.

They looked at the group, waiting for the ladies to ready their cameras, and smiled.

"You will make beautiful babies," another said.

"Interesting." He wiggled his eyebrows. "They think we should make beautiful babies."

"I think we should stick with a tour of the NICU," she

muttered as she eased away from him and took his hand.

"You're probably right." Although he'd certainly had more than a few vivid dreams about taking Lyla to bed after he finally fell asleep last night.

"Are we ready to continue?" the doctor asked.

"Yes."

They moved through the heavy wooden doors into the space much more subdued than the nurses' station.

"We will ask you to put on gowns, masks, and gloves before we go in these rooms."

He and Lyla put on the appropriate gear and stepped into a dimly lit room.

"This is where our most critical patients will live for the next several months," the doctor said quietly. "The lights are kept low and stimulation to the babies is limited to mimic the womb as most of these infants are preemies."

They stepped closer to the incubator, staring in at a tiny preemie covered with numerous tubes.

"Oh, you poor, sweet baby," Lyla whispered. "He's so little."

"Yes. He weighs less than a kilo."

"Oh." Lyla shook her head, glancing in at the baby again, her concern for the new life unmistakable. "Will he be okay?"

"With the new advances available to us, we can hope for a favorable outcome, but it's never guaranteed I'm afraid. Let's move on."

The doctor removed her protective gear. "We'll change again at the next location."

Lyla nodded as she pulled off her gloves and mask then sought Collin's hand.

"They have a shot here," he reassured, noting the worry still clouding her eyes.

She nodded again.

They moved on to another room, peeking in at a new mother holding her tiny child against her chest. Lyla waved to the woman.

The woman smiled back.

"This is kangaroo care," Doctor Dernov explained. "Babies and mothers both relax when they can spend time together."

"That's wonderful." Lyla smiled at the mother again.

They walked down the hall, listening to the doctor's spiel about the equipment and new hope for Moscow's tiniest population. "And this is what we work so hard for," she said. "If you'll please put on gloves."

They did what the doctor asked and were brought into another room where five much bigger babies slept in their cribs. A few had tubes in their noses but they appeared to be in much better shape.

"Many of these infants are days away from going home."

Lyla grinned as she moved closer to one of the cribs. "Twins."

"*Da*. They came a few weeks early. We like to keep them together as they would be in the womb."

"They're so beautiful." Lyla beamed. "And healthy looking."

"If all stays well, they will go home next week."

"How precious."

A woman walked in, dressed in a yellow gown much like they wore. She said something to Lyla in Russian.

Lyla's eyes widened. "Oh."

"What?"

"This is the twins' mother. She says we can hold her babies."

The mother spoke again as she gestured to the crib, and Lyla nodded.

"She would *really* like for us to hold her daughters," Lyla said to Collin.

"Uh, I don't know." He backed up a step, hating the idea. "They're bigger than the kiddo down the hall, but I don't think I should." It was one thing to hold a full-term munchkin, but these little girls were still pretty delicate looking.

"Right over here." The doctor ignored his hesitations and

guided them over to the side-by-side rocking chairs.

With little choice, he took his seat next to Lyla. "How about you hold them and I watch?"

"It's okay," Lyla reassured, clearly delighted by the idea of snuggling a little one.

"You may take off your gloves if you sanitize." The doctor squirted a cold glob of alcohol into their hands. "Rub well and please keep your fingers away from their noses, mouths, and eyes."

"Yes. Of course." Lyla settled herself more comfortably in her seat as the babies were brought over and placed in their arms. "Hello, beautiful." Lyla touched the baby's fingers and stroked her forehead.

The twins' mother spoke again.

"How sweet." Lyla grinned. "The girls' names are Mina and Lyla."

Collin glanced from the baby he held to Lyla. "A namesake. Who do I have?"

Lyla asked their mother. "You're holding Mina," she said to him.

Baby Lyla began fussing, and Lyla cooed something to the infant in Russian.

He stared at her as she smiled at the little girl. He wanted children—had for a while now. When Ethan and Sarah started growing their family, he'd gotten itchy for one of his own.

Mina joined her sister and began to cry.

"You're okay." He rocked a little faster and wiggled his arm, settling the baby down.

"A natural." Lyla smiled at him.

"That's what they say. When my friend Ethan has parties, they always hand me the fussy kids. They usually zonk right out."

She smiled again. "You just might be irresistible."

He held her stare. "I was thinking the same thing."

She swallowed and looked down, giving her attention back to the baby.

"Picture," Mina and Lyla's mother said, holding up a camera.

"Sure," they said at the same time.

Lyla and Collin smiled and the flash went off as an alarm started going off in one of the rooms down the hall.

"I'm afraid I must go." Doctor Dernov hurried out.

One of the nurses from the nurses' station, far more serious now that she had a job to do, came over and took the first baby from Collin, then she came back for Mina's sister. "We will move on," she said in broken English. "A new baby is in need of Doctor Dernov."

"Yes. Of course."

The nurse took them to the last room—a small area for tired parents to rest.

"This was lovely. Thank you for sharing your facility with us. I hope you'll thank Doctor Dernov for us."

She nodded. "I will."

Another alarm sounded farther down the hall. "Excuse me, please. I must go help."

"Yes."

They walked to the elevators and stepped in as the floor started getting busy with parents visiting their little ones and new admittances. "That was pretty amazing—a cool experience."

"It was." She hesitated as the doors slid open in the main lobby to reveal the pack of reporters hovering outside, waiting for her.

"You don't have to talk to them."

"Yes, I do. Part of my purpose here is to let Moscow know how pleased I am with the new facility."

"There's nothing wrong with keeping it quick."

She nodded, and they stepped out into the firestorm.

Questions were asked and Lyla answered. He had no idea what anyone said, but she kept it short. The cab that had dropped them off waited in a parking space. They got in, and Lyla told the man new directions.

Collin hesitated then wrapped his arm around her shoulders, holding her against him as he sensed her tension coming back. "Home?"

She shook her head. "I need to see Pasha."

He wanted to remind her that it wasn't a good idea, but how could he discourage her from seeing her friend? "Let's go see Pasha."

———◆———

Lyla stepped into Pasha's hospital room and froze, staring in horror at her good friend she barely recognized. Slowly, she walked to his bedside, swallowing as she studied his swollen jaw, puffy black eyes, the bandages wrapped around the top half of his head, and the thick tubes protruding from his mouth, breathing for him. "Oh, Pasha," she shuddered out, touching his fingers peaking from the cast on his hand. "Look what they've done to you. Look what they've done."

Pasha wasn't the first to be harmed by The Regime. Several journalists had been hurt or worse over the years for criticizing and questioning. Pasha's cell phone had been confiscated and any footage from the surveillance cameras by his office building had mysteriously disappeared. The news stations spoke of thugs or other muggers, but she knew better, as did her father and Collin and so many others. Pasha's attackers would go unpunished because someone had been contracted to shut him up. "You were supposed to be careful," she whispered as her lips trembled.

He didn't respond. He couldn't. The doctors had put him into a medically induced coma.

"You were supposed to be careful," she repeated, clearing the choking emotion from her throat and speaking louder, hoping that he might be able to hear her. "If I would have known meeting you for dinner was going to lead to this, I would have stayed away." She blinked back tears. "I'm so sorry, Pasha. I'm so sorry."

The nurse she'd been nasty to several minutes ago opened the door, her posture stiff and her eyes full of disapproval. "You'll have to leave now. The patient must have quiet to heal."

When Lyla arrived at the hospital, they'd been ready to turn her away, but she'd demanded to see Pasha. Never had she used such bully tactics. Never had she acted like some spoiled star, but she'd needed to see for herself that Pasha was being treated well and was going to be okay. She nodded and kissed his bandaged forehead, giving his fingers a gentle squeeze. "Rest well, my friend. I'll come back and visit again before I go home. Hopefully your eyes will be open by then." She walked to the door and glanced over her shoulder once more before walking out to the hall where Collin stood, waiting.

"How's he doing?"

"I wouldn't have known who he was if they hadn't told me that was his room." She swallowed as her throat grew tight again.

He stroked her cheek. "I'm sorry, Ly-Ly."

She let her head rest against his chest for mere moments, taking the comfort he offered, and pulled back, trying hard to bury her fear and outrage of such a horrendous attack.

"Let's go home."

She nodded and started down the hallway, careful to avoid Collin's touch. She'd allowed herself a minute to grieve, now it was time to put the pieces back together...on her own. They turned the corner and walked down a flight of stairs before she stopped short and closed her eyes, sighing at the group of reporters hovering around the exit. Was there no peace? Could she not even visit a friend without being stalked?

"The cab's still waiting. We can have him meet us around back?"

"Does it really matter?" They were always waiting, suffocating her until she was certain she might go crazy. "Let's just go." She pushed through the doors into the madness.

"How is Pasha? Did he say who harmed him? How do you feel about Pasha's situation?"

She stopped dead. How did she *feel* about Pasha's situation? "I feel saddened to say the very least."

"Ly-Ly," Collin said next to her ear, his warning tone unmistakable.

She took a step away from him.

"What did you talk about last night? Before he was hurt?" another reporter demanded.

They meant punished, for certainly Pasha was being taught how to behave. Someone had beaten him within an inch of his life. "Pasha is my good friend. I wanted him to meet the special man in my life."

"Your friend criticizes," Roman Akolov said, shoving his damn recorder closer to her face.

She stared right at him. "Isn't that the beauty of democracy—to be able to speak freely and ask questions without fear of retribution?"

"So you agree with Pasha's statements?" Roman challenged.

"My feelings are my own, and they will stay that way, but clearly Pasha believes more can be done to find the terrorists responsible for the slaughter of so many innocent people."

More questions were fired her way, but she'd had enough—said enough. "Let's go." She walked off with Collin following.

"What the hell just happened there?" He hurried to catch up, falling into step beside her. "It really sucks that you guys don't speak English or Farsi or Arabic—the three languages I actually know."

They got in the cab, and she said nothing else, closing her eyes and resting her head on the back of the seat. She needed music and her pointe shoes despite the pain in her ankle. She craved to dance. Luckily, they were only two miles away from Spaso House.

Vehicles honked behind them, as cars were cut off—the

chase was on, and it was all she could do not to cover her ears and scream. The taxi pulled up to the gates and was quickly let through, leaving the mess behind for now.

Collin paid and she got out, hurrying up the steps and inside.

"Ly-Ly." Collin tugged on her arm.

"Not now." She stopped, aware she was being rude. "Later." She kissed his cheek and pressed her palms to his face as she rested her forehead against his chin in a moment of weakness. "We'll talk in a little bit."

"Okay."

She ran upstairs, ignoring her protesting foot, needing to be alone.

✄ Chapter Fifteen ✄

LYLA MOVED TO THE MUSIC, NOT THE SONG SHE DANCED to when she rehearsed for *The Markovik Number* but to one of her favorites she'd danced to as a child. She lifted her arms above her head and closed her eyes, trying to focus on the melding of piano and weeping violins, but the gruesome images of Pasha lying bruised and battered in his hospital bed came back to haunt her again.

Clenching her jaw, she snapped her backbone straight and raised her chin, annoyed by another intrusion. Thoughts of her father and Pasha, worrying for both of them, was eating her alive and making it all but impossible to concentrate. She arched her arms for the second time and did her best to think of the choreography for Geoffrey's upcoming show—and *only* Geoffrey's show.

"One and two and three," she counted off, moving from a *croise* to a *glissade*, followed smoothly by a *sous-sus* on pointe. She winced as the familiar stabbing pains seized her ankle from holding fifth position, and her foot began to tremble as she refused to cave to the agony and drop back down onto her soles. Her joint buckled, and she stumbled slightly, missing her timing and ruining a basic step she'd learned as a young girl. "Come *on*, Lyla." She stood with her hands on her hips, huffing out a breath and staring at her own look of disapproval reflecting back at her in the mirror. Tonight dancing brought her no comfort. For over three hours now, she'd been locked away in the ballroom, yet she'd accomplished nothing.

With a frustrated sigh, she walked over to her MP3 player, pulled the converter from the wall, and stepped into the hall, shutting the door behind her. "Dad," she called, moving down the hallway toward her father's private quarters. "Dad," she said again, frowning when he didn't answer. She stopped in the doorway to his study, staring at herself on the large TV screen. The volume was barely above a whisper as she spoke to the media outside of the hospital, answering Roman Akolov's questions and causing a firestorm with her remarks on her friend and her interpretations of the meaning of democracy. The news station cut to the demonstrators currently occupying Red Square, shouting their outrage about the violence against Pasha, censorship, and numerous other anti-regime sentiments.

She glanced at her father's reflection in the windows to his left as he sat with his back to her in his chair, rubbing his hands over his face then knocking back two-fingers of vodka. Today she'd made everything worse. Her plan to come to Russia and soothe tensions had backfired in the most horrendous of ways. Dad's situation had quickly become dangerous, Pasha was in the hospital, citizens were rioting, and it was all her fault.

Pictures of her and Collin in the NICU flashed on screen: Collin smiling with the shy nurse, Collin holding her close as they grinned at each other in the nurses' station, and the two of them cuddling twin girls almost ready to come home. The coverage cut to the surveillance footage from last night as she and Collin walked through the city then back to the disorder at Red Square.

She shook her head and turned away, rubbing at the drumbeat in the base of her skull as she started back down the hallway toward the stairs. There was nothing she wanted more than to walk into her room, pack her suitcases, and get the hell out of here, but she couldn't. She wasn't about to leave her father alone in Russia to deal with this. This was her mess—her problem.

As she climbed the steps, she found herself craving Collin. Maybe he would watch a movie with her and make her laugh. That's what she needed right now—the man hunkered down in the room next door to hers. She hurried into her bathroom, pulled off her clothes, and hopped in the shower. She wanted his company tonight. Maybe he would rub her ankle and stare at her in that way that always made her heart pound. Maybe he would kiss her again...

She scoffed and rolled her eyes, chastising herself as she soaped her body and shampooed her hair. They both agreed that holding hands was best, to play up their "romance" for the cameras, but she snagged her lip between her teeth, remembering the way it felt to be pinned up against the wall by his hard, tough body. She'd been stupid and reckless, yet she wanted to be again...and more.

Butterflies filled her stomach as she rinsed away the conditioner, replaying the strokes of his finger against her jaw, his mouth capturing hers, and his skillful tongue teasing hers. Last night she and Collin easily could have been lovers. If she'd invited him into her bed instead of closed her door, he would have been hers. Tonight he could be... "Oh, God," she shuddered out on a rush of nerves as she shut off the water and wrapped her hair in a towel then dried off. "Foolish," she muttered, but she grabbed the cream Collin seemed to like so much and slathered herself in it, wondering what it might feel like to have him kiss her belly, her breasts, to feel him inside of her. She steamed out another trembling breath. If all went well, she would soon find out.

Hurrying into her room before she lost her nerve, she slid on her favorite black camisole she never wore for anyone but herself. She didn't take lovers. Intimacy was a complication she avoided at all costs. But Collin was different. She pulled the towel from her hair, combed her fingers through the tangles, and gripped the doorknob. "What are you doing? What are you doing?" she chanted as her heart pounded in her chest and echoed in her ears. She wasn't exactly a seductress, but her mind was made up.

She opened her door and started across the hall. It was now or never—before she had time to think. For the next little while she just wanted to feel—something she rarely allowed. She stopped in front of Collin's half-open door, staring at him, bare chested and dressed in his typical black athletic shorts, lying on his bed in the dark with his phone at his ear.

"No, Sydney. It's not like that."

She raised her hand to knock and paused when she heard him say his ex's name.

"It's for show—an act. She's just... I'm just trying to do my job."

Lyla let her hand fall to her side, flinching from his verbal blow.

"Sydney—" Collin turned his head, meeting her gaze.

She turned toward her room, hearing Collin say he had to go as he rushed up off his bed.

"Lyla."

She shook her head.

"Lyla." He grabbed her arm and yanked her around.

"Don't." She pulled away, crossing her arms.

"That wasn't what it sounded like."

It sounded like he'd just told his ex-girlfriend that she was nothing more than his job. "I overheard a private conversation."

"I don't know why I said that." He shoved his fingers through his hair as he steamed out a long breath. "She started crying, and I—"

She held up a hand, not interested in his explanations. "It's none of my business."

"Lyla, I—don't look at me like that."

She clutched her arms around herself again and glanced

at the floor, knowing Collin always saw too much. "I don't know how I'm looking at you."

"Like you're trying to hide the fact that I just hurt you."

She shook her head, denying the truth to herself as much as him. "You're entitled to your private life."

"I haven't even thought of her since I left LA." He reached out, trying to touch her shoulder, but she evaded him. "You're the only one I've been thinking about, Lyla."

She scoffed her disbelief. And she'd thought he was different. Collin Michaels was just like any other guy. "It's really no big deal. We barely know each other."

"Bullshit," he punctuated, taking a step closer to her.

"We're playing a game." She walked into her room. "Good night." She closed the door and sagged back against the wood, pressing a hand to her sick heart.

"Lyla," he called through the door.

She shut her eyes and pressed her lips firm as they tried to tremble. Twisting the lock in place, she exhaled a long, steadying breath, burying any sort of regret as she stared into her devastated eyes reflecting back at her in the mirror across the room. This was why she stayed away from relationships—from disappointment. Luckily Collin helped her realize her mistake before she made any more. They'd spent a little time together, had some fun, but nothing had changed. She wasn't part of some happy couple. She was a dancer—only a dancer: her mother's wish for her. And her life was falling apart.

She limped to her bed, not bothering with her ritual of ice and ibuprofen. Instead, she got under the covers, elevated her foot on a pillow, and blinked in the dark until exhaustion finally allowed her to sleep.

⎯⎯◆⎯⎯

Collin stood outside Lyla's room, clenching his jaw and staring at her door as he fisted his hands at his sides. He reached for the knob, hesitated, and took a step in retreat. "Son of a *bitch*." What the hell was his problem? Why did he even bother answering his phone when Sydney's name popped up on his screen? He and his ex were nothing but destructive forces in each other's lives: case and point.

He scrubbed his hands over his face, fighting the urge to give the wall a solid punch. He should have hung up when she started crying, but he'd fallen back into old patterns, trying to explain to her the pictures she'd seen of Lyla and him in some of the papers back home in LA. He and Lyla were making a splash all over the world, especially now that Moscow was in an uproar after her comments outside of the hospital earlier today.

For some stupid-ass reason, he'd started justifying his "thing" with Lyla, finding excuses as if he was some sort of guilty party. He and Sydney were finished. He didn't even *want* her. Now that he'd had time away—a real opportunity to clear his head, he could see that he'd been willing to put up with her insecurities and frequent demands, to fool himself into pretending he was happy because he was ready to settle down.

He wanted what his friends had: a wife to come home to, kids running around at family parties, and a home he could be proud of. He wanted that with someone he could laugh with, someone he enjoyed spending time with. He needed someone special who saw beneath his rough exterior to the man he really was—someone who made him a better person. He craved a woman who spoke sexy languages and found simple things like Metro stops fascinating.

He stared at Lyla's door again and sighed. He wanted a gorgeous blond with pretty blue eyes—eyes he'd made sad because he was a complete dumbass. He rested his forehead against her doorframe then turned away. Lyla had locked her door, making her feelings perfectly clear. Tomorrow they would talk and he would explain.

COLLIN WALKED DOWN THE STAIRS AND GLANCED TO-
ward the closed ballroom doors—again. He steamed
out a frustrated breath and took a step closer to the
space off limits to anyone except Lyla, Sergei, and Fedor
during working hours, tempted to just walk in. Instead, he
sat in one of the chairs in the huge entryway, hoping Lyla
wouldn't be too much longer. He peeked at his watch, noting
the time, and muttered a swear. For *hours,* he'd been waiting
for Fedor to release Lyla from practice. Sergei left at eleven
thirty, but Lyla had yet to appear.

Resting his head against the wall, he rubbed his tired
eyes, fighting the fatigue of a mostly sleepless night. At some
point during the wee hours of the morning, he'd dozed off
and sprung out of bed at a little after four, intending to catch
Lyla before she started her work for the day, but when he
knocked on her door at five, her room had been empty and
the music already playing in the ballroom. There was no telling how long she'd been at it, but she had to be exhausted.
His ass was dragging and he didn't dance for hours on end.
Lyla couldn't have gotten much rest, and in less than two
days, she danced for a packed theater.

Luckily the riots at Red Square had settled down to a dull
roar. The police had the situation under control, but Lyla's
sound bites about Pasha and democracy continued to fill

the airwaves. There was talk of the Bolshoi Theater and Mina's daughter's dance. There were even articles about himself and Lyla in the papers, but the news was also back to focusing on Jonathan Avery and the US's destructive agenda against Russia.

"Collin."

He whipped his head around when Jonathan called his name. "Yeah?"

"Come on down to my office."

"Sure." He stood, glancing at the ballroom doors again, and headed toward Jonathan's office when he would've preferred to wait for Lyla. If he could just explain...

"Come on in."

Collin closed the door and sat across from Jonathan at his desk, studying him dressed in his usual suit and tie, trying to gauge his mood, especially when Jonathan didn't bother to turn on the music for privacy.

Jonathan folded his hands on the blotter. "How are you today?"

"Fine, thanks."

"Good. Good." He shifted in his seat. "How's Lyla?"

He shook his head. "I couldn't tell you. I haven't seen her since last night."

Jonathan grabbed one of the newspapers sitting among the stacks on his workspace and slid it toward Collin. "There's a lot going on."

He looked at the photos of the police dragging protesters off the street. "There is."

Jonathan turned to the next page and pointed at another picture—of him and Lyla grinning at each other as they wrapped their arms around one another in the NICU's nurses' station. "Things seem to be going well between you and Ly-Ly."

Mmm, not so much. He hooked his leg up, settling his ankle on the opposite knee. "They appear to be."

The light in Jonathan's eyes changed as he looked at Collin again. "Be careful with my little girl."

He frowned and dropped his foot back to the floor as he sat farther up, taken completely by surprise. "I thought you said this was what you wanted." He pointed to the picture this time.

"I want the act, but I don't want her heart broken. She's been through a lot—too much."

He shook his head. "I'm confused—"

Oksana knocked on the door and brought in tea. "Here you are."

"Thank you, Oksana." Jonathan's smile was friendly for his housekeeper. "I'll serve us today."

"Very well." Oksana closed the door behind her.

Jonathan poured himself a cup. "Do you want some?"

He shook his head. "No. Thank you." What he wanted was for Jonathan to explain what in the hell was going on. "I thought you wanted Lyla in a relationship."

"I did—do. But I don't want her hurt."

Jonathan wouldn't be pleased to know he'd already fucked up that part of the assignment. Lyla was safe, but he'd definitely hurt her.

Jonathan left his cup to steam and walked to the fireplace, picking up a picture of a young Lyla grinning in a photograph. "She's always been beautiful—so much like her mother." He sighed, putting the frame back. "I've been careless with her—selfish."

Collin leaned back in his chair again. Jonathan was all over the place, so he would take their meeting as it came. "You two seem to get along fine."

"My daughter's too good to me. I've spent my life honoring my wife's memory—her hopes for Russia—and neglected Lyla in the process. I imagine Mina would kick my ass for that."

He scratched at his jaw, not sure how to respond.

Jonathan moved to the window, staring out. "Has Lyla told you about Saint Petersburg?"

"Just that she went to school there."

Jonathan shook his head, looking at Collin. "Lyla doesn't tell anyone much of anything."

He'd noticed.

"After Mina died, I took Ly-Ly home to New York. My mother helped me raise her. I was gone a lot—politics keeps a man busy." He sat in his seat at the desk again. "Lyla never seemed to mind. She had her friends, but mostly she had ballet. From the time she was three, she enjoyed her classes. By the time she was five, she was obsessed and talented well beyond her years. It was all she talked about—all she wanted." Jonathan let loose a humorless laugh. "Maybe it's all she thought she could want. I talked about her mother so often, filled her head full of stories—the way Mina captured an audience."

I was born to be a dancer. That's what I'm meant to be.

You can be anything you want to be.

Sometimes you can't.

Collin swallowed, remembering his conversation with Lyla just days ago. Was that what she'd meant by her response?

"When Lyla was ten, I was offered the Ambassadorship here in Moscow. Saint Petersburg Dance Academy also extended Lyla an invitation to attend after she took first place for her age group at the Youth America Grand Prix."

"Pretty big stuff?"

Jonathan chuckled. "Doesn't get much bigger. It's the world's largest ballet competition. She blew the judges away. Lyla was better than most of the seventeen- and eighteen-year-olds. They were already comparing her to her mother."

"So she decided to go to Saint Petersburg?"

Jonathan nodded. "Mina studied there—was the teachers' pride and joy. Lyla was over the moon and wanted to go. She spoke fluent Russian and was plenty skilled enough to keep up with the demands, so I let her. She spent three years there, learning and perfecting her gift, visiting with me during holidays and going home to my mother for a week or two in the summers."

"Sounds like a good deal."

"I thought so—until my mother called, insisting I go up and check on Lyla one afternoon after the two of them had gotten off the phone. Mom was certain something was wrong. I took a flight up and walked in to hear Mina's long-time instructor screaming at my child—horrible, horrible ridicule: downright verbal abuse. I took Lyla back to The States the next day and realized she'd developed an eating disorder and spent the majority of her three years in Saint Petersburg in utter hell."

Clenching his jaw, Collin rubbed at the back of his neck as Lyla's less-than-happy life story started to unfold. "That sucks."

Jonathan stood again, walking back to the fireplace, clearly restless. "She was a tough cookie—always has been. Or it was easier to believe that. She worked with a therapist for a while. She started eating again, and enjoyed the cooking classes my mother suggested. Soon she was dancing and smiling. The psychologist assured me Lyla was doing well, but she warned me about her tendency to repress her emotions—a coping method she developed that might cause her problems with close relationships or some psychobabble like that." Jonathan waved his hand in a dismissive motion. "Ly-Ly's never had a shortage of friends, so I shrugged away the doctor's concerns."

Collin bobbed his leg up and down. Lyla's knee-jerk reaction to shut down now made perfect sense.

"Luckily, life got back to normal. Lyla excelled, and I came back to Moscow. She moved to Manhattan a few months later when her local instructors assured me she was ready. She was taking her classes by storm and dancing some pretty big parts for the company. My mother became ill and died about a year later. Basically, my daughter's been on her own for a long time. She's done a damn fine job with herself."

"She's a beautiful woman."

Jonathan studied him from across the room with hard, measuring eyes.

He held the Ambassador's stare, refusing to be intimidated, if that was Jonathan's intention. "Why are you telling me all of this?"

"Because of that." He gestured to the picture of him and Lyla. "Lyla doesn't let people get close. She doesn't date or share her worries. I can't remember the last time I saw her cry."

The jokes he and Lyla made about arranged marriages over their dinner in her apartment came back to haunt him. "Jonathan—"

"I saw you two in the hall the other night."

So that's what this was about. "We—"

"She looks at you differently," he went on before Collin could offer up an explanation. "She talks to you. My daughter deserves happiness—someone who won't let her down."

He scratched at his jaw, trying not to squirm as he struggled with a fresh punch of guilt. If Jonathan only knew that he already had.

"Ly-Ly seems so strong. She can certainly take care of herself. But I keep hoping she'll find someone who can take care of her."

Collin gained his feet when he heard her voice mingling with Fedor's down the hall. "I don't exactly know what I'm supposed to say here."

"Just be careful with her."

He nodded, fully intending to fix the mess he'd made. "I will be."

———◆———

"Yes! Good, Lyla."

Lyla barely heard Fedor's compliment as she moved to the music she knew so well. Today her mind and body worked as one—each step automatic after the endless rehearsals. She soared through the air and closed her eyes, always exhilarated by the power of flight. This was what she needed, nothing but dance. She did her best, was always at her best, when there was nothing else in her life. To dance was easy. Her art demanded everything from her: time, energy, strength—all things she understood, all things she controlled. There was nothing confusing about *pliés* or *grand jetes*. Her craft often brought her pain, but it was an agony she was familiar with, one that could always be expected. Blisters, bruised toenails, and muscle strains were part of the sacrifice, but none of them injured her heart.

She'd made several mistakes over the last few days: spending too much time with Collin was definitely one of them. Letting him matter had proven to be her biggest blunder of them all, but luckily the entire situation could be rectified. For the remainder of her trip, they would attend her scheduled events, posing as a couple deliriously in love, and stick to their protocol of handholding in public. That was it. There would be nothing more.

She certainly had a mess to clean up here in Russia, and hiding at Spaso House wasn't going to fix anything. But while she and Collin were here at home, she would be focusing on *The Markovik Number* and her upcoming commitments to Geoffrey's show—as she should have been all along. Collin was her bodyguard, a man her father had hired to keep her safe during these uncertain times. She was used to security personnel. DSS Agents had surrounded her father for most of her life, but Dad didn't gallivant through the city with the men and women on his staff, and he didn't kiss the people who provided his protection. There was no need for things to be any different between her and Collin.

Twirling across the room, she executed her *arabesque penchee* into a *sauté* perfectly, again closing her eyes, lost in the dance. Reversing her position, she completed another series of turns as sexy smiles and edgy brown eyes floated through her mind, past her guard. Suddenly Collin invaded her thoughts—his firm lips capturing hers, his taste, the deep groan rumbling in his throat as he pushed her up against the wall. Her eyes snapped open, and she missed the timing of her final *pirouette*.

"What are you *doing*? Concentrate, *Lyla!*"

"I'm sorry." She shook her head, wiping at her sweaty forehead. "You're right. I'm sorry. I'll do it again."

"*Nyet. Nyet.*" Fedor waved a hopeless hand at her. "Enough for today."

"I can do it."

"You can, but will you do it when it counts?" He pointed at her, emphasizing every word.

"Yes—"

"Save your energy for the Bolshoi." He started for the door.

She followed, trying not to limp in front of him. "Please, Fedor."

"You must rest. Today was supposed to be a short practice." He twisted the knob and stepped out. "Sergei left hours ago."

She didn't want to rest or think. She didn't want to deal with Collin. "But—"

"Go soak your ankle and clear your head of that man who distracts you so easily."

She nodded as Fedor walked down the hall and let himself out, then glanced around, relieved to see that Collin wasn't waiting for her. She'd thought he might be, but luckily she was alone. Hobbling as quickly as she could, she made her way up the stairs and into her room, shutting the door and locking it. She stared longingly at her cozy comforter as she limped to her bed and collapsed against the mattress, caring little that she was sweaty, gross, and still in her pointe shoes. All she wanted was a nap.

She settled herself on her pillows and sighed as her muscles relaxed for the first time in hours. Last night she'd slept for thirty minutes—maybe forty-five—before her dreams reminded her that she'd made a complete fool of herself in front of Collin. Groaning, she closed her eyes, thinking of their messy situation, and dismissed it just as quickly. "Doesn't matter," she muttered and snuggled more truly against her pillow...until her stomach growled.

Sighing again, she sat up. She needed to eat. Reluctantly she gained her feet and showered, making certain to be quick. The last thing she needed was an even crankier ankle two days before the most important night of her career. She got out, toweling off, and immediately pulled on her compression sock. Comfy leggings and a baggy sweatshirt followed. Now it was time for *food*. Her stomach grumbled as she made her way down to the kitchen. "Oksana, my stomach is calling you."

Oksana smiled. "How's our ballerina today, other than ready for her lunch?"

"Good." She sniffed the air. "Something smells *amazing*."

"I've made you roasted sweet potato soup with quinoa and a salad."

She wrapped Oksana up in a hug and kissed her cheek. "Thank you. I don't think I tell you you're the best often enough."

Oksana laughed, returning her embrace. "You're a good girl."

"You spoil me, Oksana. How will I ever go back to cooking again?"

"Easily, I imagine." She patted her cheek. "You're talented in the kitchen. Sit now, my love, and I will dish you up your meal."

"I can do it."

"As can I. Sit now, dear. Sit." She ushered her toward the table.

Lyla nodded.

Within minutes, Oksana brought over soup, salad, and a thick slice of bread.

"Thank you."

"Ah, there's my girl."

She whirled in her chair as her father walked in with Collin following behind. Her shoulders tensed as their gazes met. "Daddy." She stood, smiling.

He hugged her. "Go ahead and eat. You worked hard today."

Her appetite was gone, but she needed the calories. With little choice, she sat down when all she wanted to do was go back upstairs. "The soup looks delicious."

"Collin, will you join us for lunch?" Dad invited as he took his spot across from Lyla.

She darted Collin a glance from beneath her lashes.

"Definitely." He sat next to her, moving closer as he pushed in his chair. "Hey."

She cleared her throat. "Hey."

Oksana brought over two more servings.

"Thanks, Oksana." Collin sniffed at the steam rising from his bowl. "This smells like heaven."

"Eat it all up, handsome one." Oksana patted his shoulder.

"Every bite." He winked.

Lyla shoved a spoonful past her lips and tried to focus on Dad instead of the scent of Collin's aftershave. "How's your day going so far?"

"Good."

She nodded, realizing that he seemed to mean it. "Are things settling down?" She gestured to the windows and the trouble she'd caused in the city.

"Yes. Everything's under control now."

She set down her spoon. "I'm so sorry, Daddy."

He frowned, taking her hand in a firm grip. "This isn't your fault."

She shook her head. "We both know it is. I should have kept my mouth shut and come home."

"You were upset."

"It was tough seeing Pasha like that. He's such a good

man."

"He's doing better today." Dad squeezed her fingers. "His condition is improving."

"You checked in?"

"Collin did. He went to the hospital after breakfast."

She looked at Collin, trying to shrug off the undeniable soft spot she had for his kindness. "Thank you."

"You're welcome."

As much as she wanted to ignore him for the next little while, she needed answers. "Is he awake?"

He shook his head. "They'll keep him sedated for a few more days."

"Oh."

He touched her hand, sliding his thumb along her knuckles. "He's going to be okay."

She wanted to pull away but knew her father was watching. Swallowing, she nodded and grabbed for her spoon, breaking their connection.

"How was rehearsal?" Dad wanted to know.

She sampled more of her soup. "Great. Sergei only threw one tantrum before Fedor told him he could go."

Dad chuckled. "It sounds like that might be one for the record books."

She smiled. "Fedor and I are celebrating. I've been given strict orders to rest until tomorrow."

"I hope you'll listen. Collin said you were up early."

She said nothing as she tore off a chunk of soft, warm bread.

"You two are in the papers again," Dad continued.

She stabbed a piece of leafy romaine with more force than she meant. "I'm sure."

"Russia's quite smitten with the two of you."

"Daddy," she said on a breathless laugh, hoping he would stop. "Your soup's getting cold."

"I don't think I ever told you that your mother didn't care for me much the first time we met."

Her gaze whipped back to his. "I thought it was love at first sight."

"Maybe more like at fourth or fifth sight."

"What?"

He shrugged as he smiled. "Your mom was pretty independent—pretty stubborn too. But the moment I laid eyes on her, I knew she had to be mine."

"You never told me that."

"I was actually dating another woman when your mom came to perform in Manhattan. I was so captivated by Mina Markovik, I forgot my date when I went backstage to introduce myself—left her right in her seat."

She grinned. "No, you didn't."

"I'm afraid I did."

She laughed. "Dad."

"I had a one-track mind: meeting the beautiful ballerina who enchanted me for her entire performance. Finally I stood face to face with your mother. I was fumbling my way through small talk—something about the weather or how nice the theater was—when my date found me and gave me hell. That was almost the end of everything right there. Your mother called me a toad."

She laughed again. "Why is this the first time I'm hearing this story?"

"I happen to like the other one better."

Shaking her head, she chuckled. "So what happened next—in the real version?"

"I kept coming back. I watched her dance three more times—went backstage three more times. I smartened up and brought her flowers. Luckily she gave me a second chance."

"I had no idea." She studied her father as she chewed the final bite of her salad. Why was he telling her this?

Dad finished his soup and pushed his bowl aside. "I'm glad I'll be able to see you dance on Tuesday. I've missed too many of your performances."

"You've watched me when you could."

"I've never forgiven myself for missing your opening night as a principal dancer."

"Your flight was canceled."

"My seventeen-year-old girl—the dance world's phenom, playing Cinderella, and I wasn't there."

"Stop."

"There was no one there to stand up and applaud for you. There was no one there at all."

"Daddy, please stop. There were hundreds of people clapping. And I told you all about it afterward."

"But it wasn't the same."

She took his hand this time, worrying. "Are you all right? Is everything okay?"

"I've been reflecting quite a bit over the past few days. Your mother would have been disappointed. Not in you," he added quickly. "In me."

She shook her head vehemently. "No."

"Grammy's illness was rough—too much for your shoulders."

"She needed me."

"You were a teenager. I should have been there more."

"I was grown enough to live on my own and have a career." She stood, disturbed to see her father aging before her eyes. She hugged him, resting her cheek on his hair as he continued to sit in his chair. "You're the best. The very best," she said to him in Russian.

He gripped her arms. "I want you to be happy," he responded in the same language.

"I am."

He shook his head. "Really happy."

"I am." She kissed his cheek.

"Go take care of your ankle and rest for the afternoon," he reverted back to English.

"Please be careful tonight. Come home safely." She kissed him again and left, heading upstairs. Moments later, footsteps followed her down the hall.

"Lyla," Collin called.

She closed her eyes, exhaling as she stopped. It was better to get this over with.

"I want to talk to you." He took her hand and pulled her into her room, shutting the door behind him.

She tugged free and stepped away, creating a wide berth. "I need to rest."

"I know. I want to explain about last night."

She shook her head. "There's no need."

"Yes, there is."

She held up a hand as he took a step toward her. "You're a nice man. You're also my bodyguard."

Heat snapped into his eyes. "Don't go there, Lyla."

"I'm not going anywhere. *We're* not going anywhere. I'm a dancer in the prime of my career. I simply forgot my priorities—"

"We've already established that you're not a very good liar."

"My intention isn't to be dishonest." Or maybe it was—whatever she needed to say to make him go away.

He pulled her against him. "Sydney means nothing to me anymore. I don't want Sydney, Lyla."

She breathed in the scent that was purely Collin, the one that clung to her clothes after they spent the day together, as his breath puffed against her lips. "I don't know why you're telling me this."

His nostrils flared as he clenched his jaw. "All I have to do is kiss you. I can see it in your eyes."

"But you won't." She tried to pull away. "There will be no more kisses between the two of us."

"I'm not like everyone else, Lyla. I see who you are."

She swallowed, afraid that he did.

"Rest up, because once you're finished with your dance, I won't make things so easy. I have no intentions of stepping out of your way."

"Even if that's what I want."

He shook his head. "It's not what you want."

"Don't tell me what I want," she whispered when she intended to shout.

"It's going to be my pleasure to show you." He captured her chin between his fingers, his mouth a whisper from hers.

Her breath shuddered out as their gazes held, and she closed her eyes, forgetting her promise to herself, eager for his lips to touch hers.

"Two days," he murmured and stepped back, walking out her door.

She blinked, staring after him, sliding her fingers against her lips, suddenly more worried about Collin than she was everything else that was going wrong in her life.

———◆———

Lyla stared out the window as she lay snuggled up in her blankets, waiting for her father to come home. She glanced at the clock glowing green on her bedside table and sighed, rolling over to face the wall. It was nearly midnight. Dad rarely stayed out late—usually not past ten thirty or eleven, so where was he?

She nibbled her lip, worrying the way she seemed to so much lately, and struggled to relax. No one had called. Oksana hadn't rushed up to her bedroom to tell her something was wrong, which meant everything was perfectly fine. Dad was more than likely enjoying himself at the party and lost track of time...or maybe his security detail had lost track of *him* in the crowds and he too was lying somewhere beaten and half-dead in the snow. She reversed her position, reaching for her phone to give him a call, but stopped, putting her arm back beneath her covers. She was being foolish. Her imagination was getting the better of her. But what if it wasn't?

She nestled her head more truly on her pillow as her gaze

wandered to the lights of Moscow in the distance. Dad was in the papers again, being smeared in the headlines. And it was her fault. If she had walked past the media after she left Pasha's bedside instead of verbally sparing with Roman Akolov outside the hospital, her trip with Collin to the NICU would have been the only thing filling the newspapers this morning.

Tomorrow she would fix it. Tomorrow after her interview with Roman, she and Collin would spend the afternoon out and about in the city. If she had to call the news stations and leak their planned locations herself, she would. Perhaps a visit to the jewelers needed to be on their agenda. And if she just happened to peruse the engagement rings while hungry reporters camped outside the glass... It was a risky plan. Her relationship with Collin was a mess. His promises to get in her way after she finished *The Markovik Number* still had her on edge, but she would do whatever it took to bring the attention back around to herself and the man Russia found as fascinating as she did.

Sighing, she looked at the clock again, realizing only five minutes had ticked by as she waited for the sound of Dad's footsteps to start up the stairs. "Stop," she whispered and forced herself to close her eyes. He would be... She frowned, straining her ears when she heard a noise in the hallway, then yanked back her covers when she recognized her father's murmurs mingling with Collin's.

Finally, he was home, but something wasn't right. Their voices were barely more than whispers, but still she could tell by their steady back and forth that something was wrong. Whatever they were discussing wasn't a casual conversation. She hurried out of bed and opened her door, not bothering with a robe despite the lime-green exercise bra and skimpy white boy-cut shorts she wore. "Daddy?"

He turned in Collin's doorway, still wearing his coat. "Lyla."

She saw the strain on his face, even as she blinked, waiting for her eyes to adjust to the brightness of the light. "Is everything okay?"

"No, honey, it's not."

She closed the distance between them, gripping his arm as her heart kicked up to a racing beat. "Is it—did Pasha's condition change?" Before Dad could answer, she spotted the horrible images playing on the small television in Collin's room and stepped inside.

"There's been another bombing. In Perm," Dad said. "It detonated a little over an hour ago."

She stared in horror at a woman, covered in ash and blood, sobbing as she ran toward an ambulance with a lifeless toddler in her arms, then at a man hollering for his family as he climbed through a mountain of rubble that had once been a housing complex. "Oh, my—Oh, my God," she shuddered out.

"They think two, maybe three hundred people might be dead."

She pressed her hand over her mouth as she shook her head. "They were at home sleeping. They should have been safe in their own beds."

Dad nodded. "It's a terrible, terrible thing."

Collin stood from the foot of his bed, dressed in his usual nighttime attire of athletic shorts. He grabbed his charcoal-gray zip-up hoodie slung over the chair and wrapped it around her shoulders. "You're shaking, Ly-Ly."

She glanced at him, breathing him in, and craved to walk into his arms as the news station continued streaming live footage of terrified, bloody citizens searching for survivors by flashlight in the dark. Collin would return her embrace, resting his chin on top of her head the way he often did, and somehow make the whole situation a little better, just by holding her close. Instead, she wrapped her arms around herself and took a step away. "Thanks."

"Do you think—" Collin frowned when the live coverage from Perm vanished from the TV screen. Seconds later, a man dressed in black clothing and a disguise took its place.

"What—did someone hijack the air?" Dad asked.

"Looks like it."

The man occupying the television started speaking in Russian.

"What's he saying?" Collin asked.

"Um, we—we've been forced to strike again. More citizens have had to die at the hands of Chechen Freedom," Lyla translated as she stared into the man's soulless eyes, the only part of his face showing with the large handkerchief wrapped around the majority of his head. "The government refuses to answer our demands to be our own nation. Since the death of hundreds brings no change, we will offer our next warning." She swallowed as the man paused. "No one is safe now. We can and will strike anywhere, as we have just proven: Big cities—small towns. Rich and the poor. Men and women this country holds dear—and their many supporters—are now our targets. Russia has endless options, and we will seize them all. Give us back the country you've stolen, and we will put an end to our carnage." She blinked as the masked image disappeared and static filled the screen.

Collin swore under his breath as he switched off the TV.

"I have phone calls to make," Dad said as he turned toward the door.

"Wait."

He turned back.

"I want you to come home with me. Please come home with me to New York when I go."

Dad shook his head and gave her shoulder one of his absent pats. He stood before her, but his mind was already focused on his job. "You know I can't do that."

"But—"

"The US will stand with The Federation against these cowards, and I'll be here to do my part."

"But what about *you*? What about your safety?"

"What sort of message would I be sending if I tucked tail

and took the next flight to The States?"

The terrorist's words echoed in her head, and she fought not to shout in her fear and frustration. "You heard what that man just said—"

He gave a decisive nod. "Loud and clear."

She scoffed out a quiet breath as she stared at the floor. There would be no convincing him to change his mind.

"Ambassador." Oksana walked in, her eyes bloodshot and her nose red and stuffy from crying. "There's a phone call downstairs—from Washington."

Dad nodded. "Thank you, Oksana. I need to see to this. I'll need to prepare a statement for the press and get in touch with my staff." He kissed Lyla's cheek. "We'll talk more in the morning." He hurried off with Oksana at his side, and Lyla stared after him, pulling Collin's jacket more snuggly around herself.

"Ly-Ly—"

She whirled. "I'm fine."

"No, you're not."

"Hundreds of people were murdered while they slept. I'm going to go see if there's something I can do to help. Oksana's very upset."

"So are you."

"This isn't about me."

"Let's go see what we can do—"

She shook her head. "I'll take care of it."

"If you're going, I'm going." He grabbed a fresh t-shirt from one of his drawers and put it on.

Now wasn't the time to argue. "Fine." She turned and started downstairs, eager to do what she could for her father.

cg CHAPTER SEVENTEEN &

L YLA STOOD BY COLLIN ON ONE SIDE AND HER FATHER
on the other as Russia's President asked his nation to
observe a moment of silence for the country's latest
victims of violence. The church was silent as a bell tolled, a
ring for each of the fifty bodies pulled from the rubble so far.
There were at least two hundred more sufferers to be found.
Hopefully a few would be brought out from beneath the
crumbled buildings alive, but since the detonation in Perm
fourteen hours ago, there had only been reports of death.

The Patriarch of Moscow and all Russia stepped up next
to the President, leading the cathedral full of worldwide
dignitaries in prayer. Lyla bowed her covered head, the re-
quirement for all women in an Orthodox church, and said
"amen" as His Holiness ended the hour-long service. Russia's national anthem began to play while everyone waited
their turn to file out of their pews.

Lyla clutched her bouquet in hand as she stepped from
the second-row seating with Collin following, both of them
dressed in black: her a stylish, no-frills dress and him a suit
and tie. He placed his hand on the small of her back as she
kept her head down, ignoring the rapid-fire click of the nation's preferred press corps hovering close by. Despite the
tragedy of dozens of families dead, the media was eager for
their pictures of the princess and anyone else among the

crowd worth mentioning. They didn't yell for her to "look this way" or ask her any questions today, yet the intrusion was no less maddening.

She stopped by the cross and set her bundle of red carnations among the dozens already piled on the floor, waited for Collin to do the same, then moved on, stopping by the president when their eyes met.

"Princess," he said with a curt nod as he extended his hand to her.

She accepted his greeting, and cameras clicked in a frenzy. This wasn't the first time they had spoken, and it likely wouldn't be the last. Being Mina Markovik's daughter somehow made her worthy of a Presidential handshake, yet standing with her father as a representative of the United States made her an enemy instead of a friend. "Mr. President, I'm sorry for the loss of so many."

"Thank you." He gave her another nod, then Collin.

She turned and walked away, down the exiting aisle, as she and Dad had agreed she would do once the service was over. At breakfast this morning, he'd tried to talk her out of attending the memorial event, but she wasn't about to sit home and watch the live coverage from Spaso House. If being at the church was safe enough for Dad and the others, it was safe for her as well.

She glanced over her shoulder, hoping Dad was close behind her and would be leaving soon, but he wasn't even in line any longer. Instead, he stood next to Russia's President, posing for pictures with him and the US Secretary of State, who had flown in from Washington to show his respect and offer support to a nation in mourning. Several more men and women, foreign officials from around the world, took their place next to the Federation's Leader—a stance of unity against terrorism. And an act of defiance with potentially deadly consequences.

"Are you ready, Ly-Ly?" Collin said close to her ear.

She wasn't, but it was time for her to go. There was nothing left for her to do here. She nodded as Collin settled his sunglasses in place, and they stepped outside into the frigid, sunny day. He kept close, his arm loosely wrapped at her waist as DSS Agents seemed to appear out of nowhere and whisked them off toward the car she and Collin had arrived in.

A new group of photographers snapped pictures as they walked quickly through the cold, but Collin's gesture had nothing to do with furthering their image as a couple in love and everything to do with the situation they were all dealing with. No one was safe, as Dad kept reminding her. Anyone could be a target, but as they settled in the back of the vehicle and the car took off, she looked back at the church, well aware that if anything was going to happen today, it was happening right there in the cathedral. And there was nothing she could do about any of it.

She stared out at the city of Moscow, usually bustling at the noon hour, but today its citizens were locked away in their homes, all glued to the television no doubt. How had she ever thought she could rectify such a retched situation? Her visions of settling tensions and violence with a foolish dance now seemed laughable. Dad worried about her safety, but there was no need. Didn't he realize that in the big scheme of things, she was nothing more than a ballerina with a ridiculous title? No one was planning to make an example out of Princess Lyla, but that couldn't be said for Ambassador Jonathan Avery, who had issued another harsh statement in this morning's papers, criticizing such cowardly acts of terror.

There was fear in the air; the extremists were getting exactly what they wanted. Everyone was holding their breath, waiting for their next move. And so was she.

She pressed her lips together, steaming out a long breath through her nose, wishing she'd never come for this year's visit. If she had stayed in New York, she would have been able to live under the cloak of ignorance instead of seeing what her father's situation had become. In a week and a half, she would leave, but he would stay behind. Her departure wouldn't be like all the others where they hugged and kissed at the airport then waved until the next time. When she boarded the plane in ten days, she would fly to safety and worry, always wondering if Oksana would call, or Washington, to express their sincerest regrets for the loss of her father. She'd tried again last night and this morning to make him see that it was time for him to come home, but the US Ambassador to Russia wasn't going anywhere.

"Hey," Collin said, sliding the back of his fingers down her arm.

Her gaze whipped to his as she pulled away and folded her hands in her lap.

"What are you thinking about over there?"

She shrugged. "Not much of anything."

He nodded. "Just looking out the window?"

"Yeah." She gestured to the glass, suddenly missing their bedroom chats where he rubbed her ankle and made her smile.

"I can't be positive, but I'm almost certain I don't frown when I'm staring out the window—unless there's something on my mind. I could be wrong though..."

Why did he have to notice *everything*? "I'm fine."

"No, you're not, but we'll go with that."

She sighed. "Collin—"

"I know I'm not your favorite person right now, but I wish you would talk to me—let me help you."

She wasn't about to cry on anyone's shoulder, especially Collin's, no matter how tempting the idea. "I don't need help. I just need to get ready for my interview with Roman." She had no doubt he would be out for blood. There were plenty of headlines to be made without needing a story from her. Roman was bound to make sure his time wasn't wasted, that the article he created was worth a passing glance.

He sat back, resting his head on the seat. "I'm sitting in

on your meeting."

She shrugged again. "If that's what he wants."

He laced his fingers, settling his hands on his stomach, as if he didn't have a care in the world. "I'm not interested in making your buddy happy."

"Roman's not my buddy, but this is his interview. His rules."

He turned his head, looking at her again. "I don't play by rules that don't suit me."

She couldn't see his eyes covered by the dark lenses of his sunglasses, but she imagined they were as edgy as the tone of his voice. "We're not calling the shots right now. The last thing I need is to make Roman angry. If it was possible, I would cancel this whole thing, but sometimes we don't get what we want."

He flashed her a lethal grin. "I always get what I want, Lyla—when it counts."

His double meaning was unmistakable as tense seconds passed. She turned her head and looked out the window again. Today of all days, she couldn't allow him to get under her skin. She didn't have time to think about Collin and his sensational kisses or his promises to get in her way after she finished *The Markovik Number*. She just needed to get through her scheduled hour with Roman Akolov.

Lyla sat next to Collin on the loveseat, across from Roman in the private quarters of Spaso House, much like she had just over a week ago. But this time she held a teacup in her hands and kept her posture ramrod straight, making certain that the inch-and-a-half gap separating her from Collin appeared casual.

"We'll get started right away," Roman said as he reached down and pressed "record" on his tape recorder, wasting little time with small talk and pleasantries.

She'd expected nothing less. "Sure."

He sat back in the plush chair and steepled his fingers as he typically did. "A lot has changed since the last time we spoke."

She nodded. "I'm afraid you're right."

"Tomorrow you dance."

"Yes. But it's hard to focus on ballet when Russia has suffered another tragedy."

"As an American, you must be able to sympathize after the horrible events that took place in your own country several years ago."

She set down her cup, realizing that Roman's games had officially begun: Paint Lyla Markovik-Avery as a foreign enemy. "As a citizen of both Russia and the United States, I'm equally heartbroken. It's terrible any time lives are lost to useless violence."

"How do you feel about the situation Russia faces presently?"

"I imagine I feel what everyone else does: shock, grief, anger," she replied, deliberately misunderstanding his question. She wasn't going to explore her political beliefs with Roman. She'd opened her mouth once already; she wouldn't be stupid enough to do so again.

"Fear?"

She nodded. "Worried certainly."

"For yourself?"

She shrugged as she sat back against the cushions. "I think we all have a right to be concerned."

"You especially."

Frowning, she shook her head. "I'm no more vulnerable than the next person, no different than anyone else."

Roman made a sound in his throat as he raised his brow. "You like to pretend this to be the case, Lyla, but I'm not sure I agree with you. No one else can say they're the Princess of Russia."

"A name given to me by the media on the night of my

birth," she reminded him.

"By your mother as well. By all accounts, she called you 'Russia's Princess' moments before her death."

She said nothing as Roman stared at her. How was she supposed to respond? She imagined she was supposed to feel a deep sense of grief, the way her father or other Russians who actually knew and loved Mina did, but she could only absorb the typical waves of guilty regret.

Collin reached for her hand and laced their fingers, silently offering her support.

She clenched her jaw, keeping her eyes on Roman, not daring to look at the man at her side. Didn't he know that his sweet gestures weakened her and made her vulnerable? Didn't he know that when he slid his thumb along her palm and wrist, as he did right now, it made her need him? She was used to dealing with Roman on her own—her entire life alone. She couldn't afford for that to change.

"You're an inciter of riots," Roman continued. "You speak a few words outside of Pasha's hospital room and have hundreds demonstrating in Red Square. You shook our president's hand just today. Your father, a powerful man in his own right, has been very vocal—not only against Regime policies he disagrees with, but also the recent acts of terror. Isn't it safe to say one might consider you and the ambassador high-value targets?"

"I can only consider myself a citizen." She scooted closer to Collin's side as her father's name came up, hoping to remind Roman that the story he sought needed to be about her and the man sitting next to her, not Ambassador Avery.

"A citizen who has millions of adoring fans."

"But a citizen all the same." She cleared her throat when Collin wrapped his arm around her shoulders and played with her hair. Her breath shuddered out when the pads of his fingers tickled her neck with every down stroke. She pulled away, sitting up and grabbing Collin's untouched mug. "Tea?"

"Nah, I'm good but thanks." He winked at her as he sat sprawled on his cushion with his ankle resting on his opposite knee, his tie loose and his collar unbuttoned, appearing completely at ease while she sat in the hot seat.

She held his calm gaze as she settled back in her spot, silently demanding he stop, then faced Roman again, smiling.

"There has been talk of canceling the Bolshoi event. How do you feel about that?"

"Um, I think—wouldn't it be a shame to stop living our lives for what-ifs?" she said as she tried to find her balance again. "But I understand the need for precautions. Safety is paramount. If government officials feel it's best to postpone, we certainly will, but until I hear one way or the other, I have every intention of dancing *The Markovik Number* tomorrow night."

"Are you afraid?"

"Didn't she answer that already?" Collin jumped in, twisting a lock of her hair around his finger this time.

"I refuse to be." She directed the attention back to her as she noted the spark of challenge heating Roman's eyes. "I refuse to be afraid to live my life."

"You'll go back to the US after you dance?"

She shook her head. "I'll stay for the entirety of my scheduled visit."

"Even if Collin, your personal security, suggests otherwise?" Roman gestured to Collin.

She barely suppressed a sigh. "I wonder why it is, Roman, that you're looking for a story that doesn't exist? Is there not enough going on in this country already? Why is it so hard to believe that Collin is my lover instead of my bodyguard?"

"Because it doesn't make sense. You bump into a man on a sidewalk in Manhattan, who just happens to be a security expert, and all of the sudden he's your significant other?"

"So if we'd bumped into each other and he was a chef or a doctor, that would make it more plausible? It's not always possible to help who you fall in love with, who you have a connection with. Collin and I clicked from the moment our eyes met. He makes me laugh. He's sweet and rubs my feet while we talk at night after I've danced all day. If that's not a relationship, I don't know what is. It's mere coincidence that he happens to be a former close protection agent."

Roman shut off his recorder. "We will end here." He stood.

That was it? She didn't know whether to be relieved or concerned. He hadn't hit her with his usual tough questions. Perhaps he'd realized this was a waste of his time. "Let me see you out."

"Thank you." They started down the hall, leaving Collin where he sat. "We'll speak after the parade Wednesday."

"Yes." She accepted Roman's kiss on the cheek and opened the door for him. "I look forward to it," she fibbed.

"Good luck tomorrow."

"Thanks." She waved as he walked down the steps, then closed the door, whirling when she sensed Collin behind her. "Why did—what were you *doing*?"

"Offering my girlfriend support while she was being grilled."

"I am not your—" She stopped, looking toward the hall-way where anyone could appear at any moment. "You know where we stand," she said in a hissing whisper.

"It's funny how you can be honest with that slime ball but not with me—or yourself, Lyla."

She scoffed as she shook her head. "I was trying to get through the interview."

He stuffed his hands in his pockets. "Did you hear what you said?"

"It was—it was for the paper. I just—"

He nodded and turned away, walking back down the hall toward the private quarters of the house.

She sat down on the chair in the entryway and closed her eyes. Having Collin here was no longer a comfort—just hor-ribly confusing. And they still had a week and a half to go be-fore they could get on their plane and go their separate ways.

LYLA ROTATED HER ACHING ANKLE, THEN LIFTED HER leg high, resting her heel against the wall as she pushed herself forward for a good stretch. She dropped her foot to the floor and did the same with her opposite leg, muttering the steps she would follow for the first four eight-counts of her dance.

The noise of the crowds out front filtered backstage, and the chaos of stagehands and other members of the crew running around were typical no matter where she was preparing to perform—and something she easily ignored. She glanced at the clock hanging in the corner and blew out a deep breath. Ten minutes and she could begin. In half an hour, she would be able to put this entire experience behind her.

She raised herself up on pointe in front of one of the many mirrors, keeping her muscles warm and studying the intricate sequins along the bottom of her costume—a replica of the elaborate tutu her mother would have worn if she'd lived long enough to dance the piece she and Fedor had created together. Her gaze wandered from the clean lines of the bold blue work of art to Collin's eyes meeting hers in the glass.

He was dressed in blue jeans and one of his snug long-sleeve tees, the supportive boyfriend waiting for his one true love to do her thing on stage, but he was unmistakably tense—his shoulders, his jaw—just like the dozens of other security agents she'd seen wandering around throughout the day. This morning she'd rehearsed with Sergei and Fedor behind the protected walls of the Spaso House compound, then she and Collin had arrived at the theater an hour after lunch.

At times it had been hard to keep her focus with all of the distractions: bomb-sniffing dogs hopping up on props and walking the aisles of seats where the audience would eventually sit, but she was determined to follow through with her renewed sense of purpose and be the example Roman Akolov had surprisingly made of her in this morning's paper.

To her amazement, he'd flattered and complimented, asking Moscow if Russia's Princess was the country's last hope for happiness. He'd talked of her upcoming dance at the Bolshoi as a beautiful distraction to ward off clouds of hopelessness and grief. And he'd made mention of her inevitable marriage to her Prince Charming as something lovely to watch and remind everyone to go forward with their futures during some of the worst times Russia had seen. Roman had even taken quotes from their interview—the part where she'd spoken of foot rubs and bedtime conversations and the way Collin made her laugh. But it was the picture filling the front page, one she'd never seen before, of Collin holding her close while they stared in each other's eyes after their unexpected kiss at the fundraising event, that had stunned her the most—and stayed on her mind for most of the day. The undeniable feelings and emotions captured in that photo couldn't possibly have been staged, as Roman had accused too often.

Roman's uplifting article quickly became infectious. By midday, the news stations had broken away from some of the depressing coverage in Perm to highlight many of the lighter moments Princess Lyla and Collin had shared during their visit in Moscow thus far. And Russia's citizens were heeding the message to go on with living—the packed theater beyond the curtains was testament to that.

She turned away from the mirror, moving in a series of *pirouettes*, testing her ankle, trying to concentrate on her dancing as Sergei walked down the hall in his black tights and silky white top. His makeup was as dramatic as hers.

"Are you ready to show the world that you are more than your mother's name?" he asked her in Russian. "Don't make me look like a fool tonight."

She ignored his "pep talk," focusing only on the first four eight-counts of *The Markovik Number*. If she made it through the intricate thirty-two steps that were Mina Markovik's trademark, she would be fine. She blew out another long breath, visualizing her nerves vanishing with each exhale.

Someone tapped her shoulder, and she turned, her eyes going wide as she stared at her mother's former instructor, the woman who'd made Lyla's days at Saint Petersburg Dance Academy a living hell. Eleven years ago Alina had seemed old; now she was ancient, but no less terrifying. "Alina. What are you doing—"

"Do not let your mother down." She jabbed her bony finger into Lyla's shoulder, punctuating each word. "Do not let Russia down, ungrateful child. She gave her life for you." Alina turned and walked off before Lyla could respond or Collin could intervene.

She swallowed, more shaken than she cared to admit. A full decade and a round of therapy couldn't quite bury the painful memories of Alina's constant ridicule and guilt trips for causing her mother's death. She glanced Collin's way and spotted her father, followed by two of his agents, coming to stand at his side.

Dad looked at her and smiled.

She smiled back and lifted her chin, shaking off the unpleasant reminder of the past. Tonight wasn't for Russia and had nothing to do with Alina. Tonight would be for her father. He'd lived the last twenty-four, almost twenty-five years of his life, without his wife because of her. She wanted to make him proud.

"Be ready," Sergei snapped, bringing her back to attention.

She nodded. "I am." The orchestra played the first dramatic notes of the piece as the curtain raised. Lyla made her graceful entrance to a round of applause, with Sergei not far behind. Her heart pounded as she held Sergei's arrogant gaze and began to dance.

———◆———

Collin stared in fascination, watching Lyla and Sergei move across the stage. Over the last few years, he'd spent plenty of time backstage. He'd watched Top 40 artists and various R&B superstars sing for thousands of fans, he'd witnessed more than a few actors and actresses accept their prestigious awards on Oscar Night, but he'd certainly never seen anything like this.

Sergei lifted Lyla high and set her down in a move they both made graceful. Sergei was an incredible dancer, but it was Lyla who captivated. The lighting was dim, the music dramatic and edgy—and she portrayed both perfectly with exacting movements that appeared effortless.

She smiled in the spotlight, her glossy blond hair captured in a tight bun, and Collin could see how the world compared her to her mother. They looked so much alike and moved similarly, but Lyla and Mina Markovik also had their differences. Lyla was more delicately built, yet her dancing packed a bigger punch.

Sergei left the stage, and the light changed, brightening, focusing on *The Markovik Number's* star as the music became gentler and Lyla's moves even more graceful.

She twirled several times, moving closer to where he stood. They made eye contact for mere seconds before she continued on, leaping then soaring high—flying, and landing on her right foot.

He winced, certain the impact brought her pain. Her ankle had to be screaming, but it was impossible to tell as she carried on with her flawless performance.

Their gazes met again and once more as the music faded. Lyla spun her final *pirouette* and held his gaze as the Bolshoi went nuts, clapping for her.

He nodded, winking before she looked away and grinned for her audience.

Sergei joined her center stage, clearly eager for his credit, and the crowd went wild again.

Collin studied Lyla next to the muscular man. She was petite yet strong. After the conversation he and Jonathan had in his office the other day, he realized she'd had no choice but to be. He overheard what that bitchy woman, her old dance instructor, said to her moments before she went on stage—or one of the stagehands had translated for him, anyway. Lyla may have been dubbed a princess, but her life had been tough—it came with a lot of baggage most people wouldn't want. She'd given him his out—kept pushing him away. And for the briefest of moments yesterday after Roman's interview, he'd been ready to give Lyla what she seemed to want. All they had to do was hold hands in public and get through the next few days, but as he studied the blond beauty accepting the flowers thrown to her, he knew he didn't want to let her go—couldn't.

She looks at you different. She talks to you.

Jonathan was right, whether Lyla chose to acknowledge it or not. He'd seen it for himself—in the Kremlin kitchen when they shared a cookie, in the hallway outside her bedroom when they kissed each other crazy, and on the front page of this morning's paper in the large picture of him and Lyla staring in each other's eyes as if there had been no one else in the gala ballroom. He meant what he said when he promised her it would be his pleasure to get in her way. He intended to start right now.

❧ CHAPTER NINETEEN ❧

LYLA STEPPED FROM THE SMALL SHOWER IN HER DRESS-
ing room and quickly pulled on panties and a bra, then
wrapped herself in her robe. She sat down in front of
her mirror and rubbed moisturizer on her face, happy to
be free of the thick pancake makeup she used on stage. She
slid a comb through her wet hair and began twisting her
long locks into a braid. Any minute now people would start
knocking on her door, eager to congratulate her on a job well
done—and she'd done one hell of a job.

Every performance had imperfections, spots that could
be improved upon for the next time, but technically, she and
Sergei had been flawless. If she were the type to gloat, she
might even say they *nailed* it, but she wasn't. Later, when
she had time to herself, she knew she would pick apart every
step she'd danced and think of all the ways she could have
made *The Markovik Number* even better.

She secured her hair tie in place as knuckles wrapped
against her door, and she smiled.

"Ly-Ly."

Her smile turned into a grin when she recognized her
father's voice and opened the door, stepping into his arms.
"Daddy."

"You were brilliant, Ly-Ly." He kissed her forehead. "Brilliant. Your mother would be so proud. *I'm* so proud."

"Thank you."

"I bumped into several people while I was trying to get back here to you. They're looking forward to seeing you at the party."

She wanted a bucket of ice water for her ankle and her bed, but after-parties were always part of the after-performance deal. "I can't wait."

"I know we're celebrating tonight, but that doesn't mean we can't celebrate again tomorrow—just you, me, and Collin. After you've slept in."

She laughed, loving the idea. "Maybe we can talk Oksana into making her scrambled eggs."

"Anything for you, my little darling." Oksana barged into the room, dressed to the nines in an emerald-green dress, skirting around Dad. "You have the gift." She gently patted Lyla's cheeks. "I haven't seen dancing like that in a very long time."

She understood the sentiment behind Oksana's words. Lyla had reminded Oksana of Mina. "That's very kind."

"I mean what I say. Perhaps you'll dance here in Moscow again?"

She nodded even when she was certain she wouldn't. "Yes."

"I need a picture of you and your papa, then I'll leave you to finish up. Your dress is pressed and ready for the party. I'll have snacks waiting for you in your room."

"Thank you."

"Smile for me." She held up a camera as Dad wrapped his arm around Lyla's shoulders, holding her close as they both grinned.

Oksana snapped her picture, glanced at the screen, and smiled. "Perfect." She hugged Lyla again and kissed her cheeks. "My love."

Collin stepped in as Oksana walked out.

"I'll let you finish up in here." Dad kissed her cheek. "We'll head home when you're ready."

"Thank you, Daddy." She hugged him for the second time, savoring such a wonderful moment. Dad rarely made it to her performances. It was always a special occasion when she could have him with her backstage.

"I'll see you in a minute."

"Okay."

He shut the door behind him, and the pandemonium beyond quieted.

She looked at Collin as he stared at her, leaning against the wall with his powerful arms crossed at his chest. "Hi."

"You were amazing."

She sent him a small smile, not sure how to act around him anymore. They hadn't spoken much since he walked away from her after Roman's interview yesterday—nothing more than small talk at the dinner table because it was expected of both of them in front of Oksana and the others. "Thanks." Unable to bear the awkward tension, she turned away, pressing her face into one of the dozens of flower arrangements that had been brought to her room. "I'm always amazed by the number of flowers I receive. It's like a garden."

"There's more in the hall."

"I'll have them sent over to the maternity hospital."

"Lyla." He stepped up behind her and rested his hands on her shoulders.

She whirled, finding herself trapped between Collin and the table.

"You and Sergei... I've never seen anything like that before."

She looked down, recognizing the hunger in his eyes as she breathed in the hints of his aftershave.

"I thought the billboard in Manhattan was magical..." He puffed out a small laugh. "Man, that sounds corny."

She shook her head. "No. It sounds lovely. Sweet."

"I've never seen anyone so beautiful." He clenched his jaw and hesitated before he skimmed his thumb along her cheek. "You're so beautiful, Lyla."

She grabbed his wrist, halting his movement as her heart started beating faster.

"I've never known anyone like you." He laced their fingers as he settled his opposite hand on her waist.

"Collin, I can't—we can't... This isn't the time," she whispered.

"I know I said tomorrow." He touched his lips to hers. "But I can't wait," he murmured against her mouth. "I don't want to wait, Lyla."

Instead of pushing him away as she knew she should, she closed her eyes and glided her hands up his arms, tired of fighting her need for Collin.

The kiss grew instantly deep, instantly hot. He dove in again, framing her face, easing back long enough to look into her eyes, and dove in again just as quickly.

She wrapped her arms around the back of his neck, meeting his edgy demands as he walked her backwards, bumping into her makeup chair.

Groaning, he turned and sat down, pulling her up into his lap.

She hooked her legs around his waist as he snuck his hands beneath her robe, sliding his palms up her thighs and around her hips to grip her ass.

Shuddering, she moaned.

"Lyla," he whispered as he pressed a kiss to her throat, then her chin. "Lyla, we have to figure this out."

Her breath steamed in and out as she kept her arms wrapped around him.

"We have to talk about the other night—the stupid crap I said that I didn't mean."

She nodded. "We will."

"Tomorrow." He pressed his lips to hers. "Tomorrow after you've had a chance to rest."

She nodded again. "I have to get dressed. Everyone's waiting for me. There will be hundreds of people waiting to see us off to Spaso House."

He caressed her back. "I'd rather stay here like this."

She smiled.

He stood and set her on her feet. "I want to dance with you tonight—all night."

She nodded. "Okay."

"I'll wait outside."

"All right." She sighed as he closed the door. So much for keeping her distance from Collin. Hadn't she predicted from the moment they met that he had the potential to be trouble? Maybe just for tonight she could enjoy his company and take things as they came.

———◆———

Collin stepped out of Lyla's dressing room and met Jonathan's gaze as he shut the door. He curved his lips, giving the woman setting more flowers on the table outside Lyla's room a polite nod. "Lyla mentioned that she wants these delivered to the maternity hospital," he said to Jonathan as he moved to stand by his side.

"Someone here will take care of that."

"Good." He cleared his throat as he looked at Jonathan again. It wasn't often he made out with a woman then chatted it up with her father directly afterwards. That had never happened, actually, and he wasn't sure he liked it.

"The crowd is huge outside—wrapped around the block. Everyone's waiting to see Lyla—and you."

He shook his head. "Tonight's about Lyla. She did a hell of a job." He smiled at another person passing by.

"I want her out of here."

Collin's gaze whipped to Jonathan's, surprised by the sudden change in his tone.

"DSS intercepted a package outside Spaso House fifteen minutes ago."

"What was in it?"

"A burnt American flag. No note or warning."

But a threat just the same. Collin blew out a long breath as he rubbed at the back of his neck, growing more uncomfortable as the stakes kept climbing higher. "Do they know who sent it?"

"No. And they probably won't figure it out." Jonathan shifted his weight to his other foot. "I'm taking my leave before Lyla. They have me exiting out the side entrance."

"Where's Oksana?"

"She already left to deal with the party." Jonathan waved to a couple leaving Sergei's dressing room down the hall. "We have agents assigned to stay behind with you. The Escalade's going to follow you and Lyla while she walks down the street and greets some of her fans. If a quick exit becomes necessary, you'll have one."

He nodded.

"I want you on Lyla every second."

He shoved his hands in his pockets, feigning a calm he didn't feel. "I know how to do my job."

"There will be new precautions for the parade tomorrow. And we need to talk about your departure. I want Ly-Ly back in New York by tomorrow night and for you to stay with her as we agreed."

"I don't know if she's going to go for that."

"I won't give her a choice. You're to stay on—whether she likes it or not—until we know she's no longer being followed. I think Roman had the best of intentions when he published this morning's article. Lyla is well-loved and an inspiration to many, but she's inadvertently taunting a group of madmen eager to make an example out of anyone they think they can. She needs to go home and get back to her life. Russia will forget about her soon enough—"

Lyla's dressing room door opened and she stepped out with her bag slung over her shoulder, smiling. She'd put on makeup—not the thick junk she'd worn on stage, but subtle Lyla makeup—and wore snug jeans, stylish boots, and a black wool sweater.

"Ly-Ly." Jonathan smiled, taking her hand.

Her smile faded as she looked from Jonathan to Collin. "Is everything okay?"

"Of course." Jonathan kissed her cheek. "I wanted to wait for you to come out before I started back to the house. I'm sure there are already people there waiting for you."

"No rest for the weary."

Jonathan chuckled, patting her hand. "That's all the more reason to sleep in tomorrow."

"Mmm." She closed her eyes. "I'm looking forward to it."

Jonathan kissed her cheek again. "I'll see you soon."

She grabbed Jonathan's hand before he could leave. "Walk with us. Drive home with us."

He shook his head. "Not tonight."

"Daddy—"

"This is for you. This is about you. Politics are for another day."

She nodded and hugged him. "I love you."

"I love you too." Jonathan walked off, swarmed by agents.

She glanced at the four men who hung back, stationed close by. "Isn't this overkill? I know there are men standing by outside too."

"There's a huge crowd. I can't handle that on my own if things get out of control."

She studied him with skeptical eyes.

"We have an Escalade that's going to follow in the distance and a couple of agents who are gonna walk with us as a precaution. That's all," he said as they both put on their coats and zipped up. They weren't about to discuss burnt flags and heading back to New York early right here in the hallway.

"Can't we leave in the car we came in? The Escalade seems so...superstar-ish."

He grinned. "Tonight you *are* superstar-ish." He took her hand as she rolled her eyes, kissing her knuckles. "Ready?"

"Yes."

They started down the long hall to the front entrance as

the security agent spoke into his wrist piece, alerting their driver. Once the man got confirmation that the vehicle was in place, he opened the door to the hundreds of people standing behind the barriers to the left of the huge theater. A round of cheers rang up as Collin and Lyla stepped outside.

He gripped Lyla's hand tighter as they walked down the steps, keeping her close in the pandemonium despite the gates and police presence. His explanation to Lyla about the added security hadn't been complete bullshit. A crowd like this could get out of hand quickly, and the extra backup didn't hurt. He raised his hand, waving as Lyla did.

More flowers were thrown their way as men, women, and children hollered to Lyla, all vying for her attention.

He kept her moving as they made their way down the one-way street, wanting her in the SUV and on the way back to Spaso House. He glanced over his shoulder as Jonathan's small motorcade moved toward the traffic a good hundred and fifty yards away and looked down as flowers landed at his feet.

"Those are definitely for you," Lyla said close to his ear as a group of girls screamed his name.

He smiled but he was on guard, constantly watching for threats as the DSS agent moved them forward.

"I think half of these people are here to see—"

A massive blast filled the air, shaking the ground and knocking Collin to his knees. Instinct kicked in and he pulled Lyla down, crouching over her body. Madness ensued as the masses ran away from the huge fireball and plumes of smoke. He looked behind him, realizing that Jonathan's car had just detonated, as he and the agent closest to him yanked Lyla up.

"Where's my dad?" Lyla screamed, turning toward the site of the explosion. "Where's my—Daddy! No! Daddy!"

"Lyla, let's go," he shouted, gripping her by the arm as she tried to run toward Jonathan's mangled vehicle.

The back doors on the Escalade opened, and he hooked his arm around Lyla's waist as she fought against him. He shoved her inside as the agent got in on the opposite side. "Go!" Collin shouted, shutting the door as he jumped in, pulling Lyla down into the vehicle's center cavity and covering her with his body.

"My dad!" She struggled to get up. "I can't leave my dad!"

He held her tight. "Stay right here with me, Lyla," he murmured next to her ear. "Right here with me."

A keening moan escaped her throat as the SUV screeched around the corner, heading right. Seconds later, another explosion sounded a hundred feet ahead, blowing out the windshield of the vehicle they were in.

Lyla screamed as glass flew into the backseat and their driver let out a high-pitched screech and slumped against the wheel.

"Fuck! Keep her down," Collin called to the agent at their side as he awkwardly dove to the front of the SUV and fought his way into the driver's seat, sitting half on the consul and the man's thigh, kicking the dead agent's foot off the gas as he steered them away from the building they were mere seconds away from slamming into. He stared at the second car that had blown up—the US Ambassador's decoy vehicle, the one he and Lyla had arrived in earlier this afternoon—and hit the brake, tossing the SUV into reverse, spinning the Escalade around in a J-turn, and heading in the opposite direction, as their driver should have done in the first place.

He shoved the corpse farther toward the door in an attempt to make more room for himself and entered the busy traffic to the blaring of dozens of horns, quickly cutting to the right and down another side road, taking them as far away from the Bolshoi and Spaso House as he could. The Averys were under attack. Jonathan was dead, and the second blast had been meant to take out Lyla.

Minutes ticked by as he struggled to keep control of the speeding vehicle while the frigid winds slapped at his face through the broken windshield. He took back roads whenever possible, zigzagging through the city and losing the tail he spotted, knowing that at any second they might catch up with him again.

He saw a sign for the Metro ahead and screeched to a stop, pulling up close to the shoulder. He grabbed the pistol from the deceased agent's holster, noting the lack of identification around his neck—that was standard for security working big events like the Bolshoi—and let himself out the passenger's side, then yanked open the back door, grabbing Lyla's hand. "Let's go."

Her eyes were dull staring into his as she got out.

"What are you doing?" The remaining DSS man asked—or was he? His identification was missing too.

"Protecting Lyla." He pistol-whipped the possible rogue agent, knocking him unconscious.

Lyla let out a startled whimper. "Why did you do that?"

"Because they were driving us the wrong way. Your father told me the plan if shit went south, and that wasn't it. Let's go." He pulled her down the sidewalk and yanked her into an office building when he recognized two of the vehicles that had been tailing them only minutes ago. The SUV and late-model car screeched to a halt next to the Escalade he and Lyla had just abandoned. "Come on."

They ran into the elevator before it could close and got out on the fourth floor. Collin walked with Lyla down a hall and pushed her through a door into a darkened room where he knew he would have a view of the street below. He looked out from the edge of the window, watching a swarm of men shining flashlights in surrounding cars and stepping in and out of the restaurants lining the block. He focused on the man who appeared to be calling the shots, trying to get a look at him in the dark, but it was no use. Who the hell were these people? This wasn't the work of The Regime and it—

Headlights flashed across the man he hadn't been able to take his eyes off of, and a rush of dread twisted his belly as he swore under his breath. "Ayub." They had to get out of here. Now. "Do you have a hat in your bag?" he asked Lyla as she leaned against the copy machine at his side.

"What?"

"A hat. Do you have a hat in your bag?"

She shook her head. "I don't—I don't know."

He pulled the bag off her shoulder and fished around, grabbing the pale blue beanie-style hat he knew she usually carried with her. "Put this on."

She blinked at him, her eyes foggy with shock.

He tugged the hat on her head himself and tucked her long braid beneath her coat. "I need to get you out of here."

She nodded.

"Come on." He took her hand and walked with her down the stairs instead of using the elevator this time. When they made it to building's entrance, he kept them away from the long wall of glass doors, waiting for the group of people heading down the sidewalk to get closer. "I want you to walk with them. Stay close to that group right there."

"What about you?"

"I'll be right behind you—just a few steps away. Go. Hurry. Don't run, but keep up, right with them."

She nodded and stepped outside.

He walked out only steps behind her, keeping his distance for one block, then two, until his gut told him someone was following them. They approached a dimly lit spot on the sidewalk, and he took her hand, hearing her gasp as he yanked her toward another group of people, leading them down another street and pulling her into an alleyway, then behind a row of trash cans. They crouched down, leaning against the brick wall at their backs, and he put his finger to his lips, signaling for Lyla to stay quiet.

Moments later, footsteps moved quietly in their direction, stopping, then continuing forward. Collin watched the shadow get closer, waiting, waiting, then stood, punching the man in the throat before his adversary had a chance to draw his gun. Their tail fell to the ground in a heap, and Collin grabbed Lyla's hand, running with her to the opposite end of the alley, heading toward the noise he heard ahead. The bar was loud, crowded, and dimly lit—perfect.

They went inside and Collin glanced around, honing in on the tables full of drunks. As they passed a group of rowdy women sitting on their barstools, he discretely snagged one their cell phones resting on top of a pack of cigarettes while its owner gave her attention to the man standing behind her.

Pulling Lyla farther into the back, he spotted the utility closet tucked in the corner by the bathrooms. He gave the doorknob a twist and ushered her inside with him. Wasting no time, he dialed Chase's number on the borrowed phone.

"Hello?"

"I'm in trouble," he said in Farsi.

"Jesus, it's all over the news. Are you okay?"

"They're after Lyla. I saw Ayub Umarov about ten minutes ago," he continued in the language Lyla didn't understand.

"*What?*"

He knew Chase would recognize the name immediately from his counterterrorism days with the FBI. "He's here in Moscow." Ayub Umarov had been on Collin's radar during his years as an Army Ranger. On more than one occasion, he and his team had aided in the search for the leader of one of the most brutal Chechen militant groups, the Chechen Liberation Movement. Twice they'd almost had their man, but Ayub had a large band of separatist supporters scattered throughout the Middle East.

"I thought Chechen Freedom was behind the bombings. Their flags have been in the videos they've been releasing. Their leader's voice has been verified as the man delivering the messages."

"I don't know what the hell's going on, but I'm one hundred percent positive I just saw Ayub Umarov."

"Do you think Chechen Freedom and Chechen Liberation Movement are working together?"

"No." He dismissed the idea immediately. "They have different agendas, different ideologies of what a free Chechnya should be." Which made this all the more confusing. If Chechen Freedom was responsible for the Saint Petersburg and Perm bombings, why was Ayub Umarov and his group suddenly on the hunt for Lyla? What was up with the foot chase—because that's what this was. It didn't make sense, but they appeared to want her all the same. "We need to get the hell out of here."

"Ethan's on it."

He glanced at his watch, knowing they couldn't stay here much longer. "I'll call back later."

"Stay safe, man. We're going to get you home."

"That would be great." He hung up as Lyla stared at him in the dark, her body racking with shudders. "Undo your braid and pull your hair back in a bun."

She blinked up at him as she had before.

"Lyla." He touched her cheek. "Ly-Ly, we need to get somewhere safe."

"Spaso House."

He shook his head, taking the elastic from her hair himself and undoing her braid. "Put your hair up so it looks different."

"They killed my father," she said, her voice as dull as her eyes.

"Yeah, they did."

"My dad is dead."

They didn't have time for this, but he pulled her against him anyway, holding her tight as she clung to him. "I need to get you out of here. Your dad asked me to keep you safe. Let me keep you safe, Lyla."

"Okay."

"Put your hair up for me."

She slid her fingers through her damp locks and pulled them back in a bun.

"Good."

He handed her his warm jacket. "Put this on."

"What about you?"

"I'm going to get a new one." He opened the door and looked out into the dim lighting. "Come on."

They walked back the way they came, and Collin put the phone back, leaving the woman who'd let him borrow it none the wiser. As they moved through the crowded space, he snatched another phone and snagged a jacket off the back of a chair on the way out the door, walking with Lyla into the night, knowing that their attempts to hide were useless in the city. There was surveillance everywhere, and Ayub would have the capabilities to access it. They needed to get out of Moscow.

ଔ Chapter Twenty ଓ

COLLIN CUPPED LYLA'S HAND IN HIS AND BLEW HOT AIR against her chilled fingers as they moved through the dark. They'd been walking for close to two hours, sliding in and out of busy nighttime establishments, trying to stay warm in between check-ins with Chase, who relayed information from Ethan. With every stop they made, he switched between Arabic and Farsi, making certain he and Chase were the only ones who understood what he was saying. He wanted Lyla—and anyone who might be eavesdropping—out of the loop for now.

When he last made contact, Ethan had been in touch with California's senator, who was feverishly working with the Department of State to secure him and Lyla asylum in one of Russia's European neighbors to the west. At some point while he and Lyla were dodging in and out of the shadows, the terrorists had hijacked the airwaves again, but this time it had been the Chechen Liberation Movement, claiming responsibility for the death of US Ambassador Jonathan Avery. Ayub Umarov had taken to the air to warn of more violence to come—Russian citizens and foreigners alike would suffer, anyone who supported The Federation and stood in the way of the liberation of Chechnya.

Collin guided them closer to another bar, knowing that every time they walked into any establishment they were taking the risk of being spotted. They couldn't keep doing this. Sooner or later someone would track them down. Moscow was huge, but even if they kept to the alleyways and shadows, they left a trail. He just needed to keep them two steps ahead of Ayub's men until he, Ethan, and Chase had a plan. "Hopefully this will be our last stop."

Lyla nodded. She'd hardly said two words since their quick hug in the utility closet. She needed a place to rest and grieve, but the shock of witnessing her father's death was working on their side for now. Eventually, she would fall apart, and he wanted her somewhere where she could do so in private.

He pulled opened the door for them. "Keep your head down," he reminded her as he ushered her through the crowds. He glanced around the busy place, searching for a phone to use, and lifted an iPhone peeking out of a man's back pocket as he and his date groped each other on the dance floor. Moving toward the back with Lyla walking in front of him, he looked for someplace to make his call in the crowded bar-and-grill-type atmosphere and found a coatroom with a janitorial closet beyond. "Over here." He dialed Chase immediately as they hid among the thick winter jackets.

"Hello?"

"How's it going?" Collin asked, choosing Arabic this time.

"I wish I had something good to tell you."

He clenched his jaw. "And that means what, exactly?"

"They're having a hell of a time securing asylum for Lyla."

"Why?"

"Jonathan's death and Ayub's warning have everyone jittery. No one's interested in Chechen revenge—and two different groups are willing to dish it out. It's clear Lyla was a target tonight—as well as her father. Bordering countries aren't touching that."

"This is bullshit—absolute bullshit. We just need an out. Lyla's the victim here, dammit." He exhaled a long breath, trying to keep his voice calm. The last thing Lyla needed was to realize they were fucked. "So what's The Federation doing to give their princess a hand?"

"What they can—or so they say, but I'm translating that to mean not much."

And why didn't that surprise him? Lyla was as big a thorn in The Regime's side as Jonathan had been, especially after the riots in Red Square. If a group of terrorists got to her and took her out, well... "The enemy of my enemy is my friend?"

"Sounds about right." Chase cleared his throat in Collin's ear. "Senator Farley wants you to go to the Embassy."

"That's not happening. DSS didn't do shit for Jonathan. The agent who was driving at the scene was moving us toward the next detonation, not away from it. Hell, we weren't even headed in the right direction from the start. Jonathan told me this morning that if things went wrong, DSS would take us to Sheremetyevo International and keep us there until they could get us home. The driver didn't have a badge either. I'm almost certain he and his buddy riding in the backseat with Lyla were locally engaged staff. The man I hit had an accent now that I think about it. I'm not about to make Lyla an open target again." But what were they going to do? They had no passports or visas and were stuck in a huge-ass country with no way out.

"If we could get you to Alaska, onto US soil..."

"No problem. We'll hop on the next available flight..." He trailed off as a thought occurred to him. "We need a flight."

"We're working on that."

"No. I'm going dark. Lyla and I are about to vanish. I'll find a way to get ahold of you when I can." He couldn't say anything more, knowing that every word he and Chase spoke was potentially being listened to.

"I take it you have a plan?"

"I think so."

"Stay safe, man."

"That's the goal." He'd spent six years behind enemy lines,

evading capture. He wasn't about to get caught now.

"Bye."

"See ya." He disconnected the call and looked at Lyla. "How about a ponytail this time?"

She pulled her hair from the twist she'd created the last time they stopped and secured it back in a simple ponytail.

He studied their options for coats, spotted a woman's non-descript black scarf and warm jacket for Lyla. "Here. Go ahead and trade."

"I don't like that we're stealing."

She certainly wasn't going to like their next move then. "We're doing what we have to for now."

He took a black jacket and hat for himself and opened the door to the janitor's closet, studying the small selection of tools, searching for the items he would need and shoving them in his pockets. "This is almost over."

"Where are we going now?"

"I'll tell you when we get settled." They stepped from the dingy little room and back out into the noise and commotion.

Lyla paused as her face filled the TV screens hanging above the bar. The news station showed her dancing with Sergei at the Bolshoi, then her holding Collin's hand while they grinned and waved to the crowds waiting to greet her. She flinched when cell phone footage captured the moment her father's vehicle exploded.

"Come on. We're getting out of here." He dropped the phone he'd just used, letting it fall on the dance floor close to the man who owned it, and they walked outside, moving along the row of cars lining the street. He stopped in front of a late-model Audi and tested the doors. Locked.

"What are you doing?"

He kept going, looking for something he could work with, spotting the old Toyota. He tried the doors. "Yes," he muttered when the back left door opened.

"Collin, what are you doing?"

He reached in and unlocked the front door. "Get in."

She shook her head. "No."

He sat down in the driver's side seat and leaned over, opening her door. "Get in, Lyla."

She took her seat. "We shouldn't be in here."

They should've been at Spaso House celebrating Lyla's big night, but that's not how things had worked out. Now he was going to do whatever it took to get them to Asha, Russia. He jammed the screwdriver into the ignition and twisted the flathead, turning over the engine.

Lyla stared at him, her eyes wide with surprise. "You're stealing this car?"

Lyla had watched her father die. She'd walked around in shock for much of the evening and had barely spoken more than a dozen words, but her conscience was still firmly intact. "We're running out of options. Buckle up."

She did as she was told, and he pulled away from the curb, needing to get them well out of the city before sunrise.

Lyla rested her head against the seat, staring out the windshield at snowflakes dancing in the headlights as Collin sped down the highway. For over an hour they'd sat in silence while Collin steered them toward Destination Unknown and she listened to talk radio rehashing the tragic events of Ambassador Avery's untimely death. The explosion of Dad's motorcade and the mysterious disappearance of Russia's Princess and her boyfriend were discussed in detail. Even the video surveillance of Collin pistol-whipping the DSS agent came up. According to the broadcaster, Russian authorities were worried because Princess Lyla and Collin hadn't been seen since. The listening audience was being encouraged to call local police with any information that might help them locate one of Russia's most important citizens.

She sighed as she turned off the radio, not wanting to hear anymore. Her father was dead, had been blown up after watching his daughter perform the only finished piece of his wife's last dance. She was sitting next to her bodyguard who'd knocked two men unconscious, spent much of the night speaking in languages she didn't understand, and had recently stolen a car like he was a seasoned professional. At any moment now, she was going to open her eyes and realize that this was all some sort of horrible nightmare. She blinked, waiting to wake up in her bed at Spaso House, and gripped her fingers tighter in her lap when nothing changed.

"Do you need something to eat?" Collin asked as he looked at her.

She shook her head. "You're probably hungry though."

He shrugged.

She dug in her bag. "I have an apple and some whole wheat crackers."

He grabbed them from her. "Thanks." He took a bite of the apple, then held it out to her.

"No, thanks."

"Take a bite, Lyla," he said over his mouthful. "You need something."

She did as he said, caring little to argue.

"I'm planning on driving through the night."

"Where are we going?"

"To find Sergei."

She frowned. "Sergei?"

"He's taking us to Alaska."

She shook her head. "I don't understand."

"We need to get onto US soil. Sergei has a plane."

"How do you know where to find him?"

"He said he was going to Asha—skiing. He told us at the banquet, remember?"

She shrugged. "Sort of. How do you know he'll help us?"

"He'll help."

She swallowed, studying the violent determination in his

eyes—something that scared her slightly.

He took her hand, kissing it, and the Collin she cared for deeply was recognizable again. "Try and get some sleep."

"I feel like I already am. I keep hoping I'll wake up."

He stroked his hand along her cheek. "I'm sorry, Ly-Ly."

Sorry didn't change much of anything, yet everything was different. She rested her head against the seat and watched the miles roll by.

☙ CHAPTER TWENTY-ONE ❧

COLLIN PULLED UP IN FRONT OF THE SMALL MOTEL IN the dark, ready for a hot meal and a bed. He and Lyla had been on the road for a solid eighteen hours, stopping only for gas, convenience store snacks, and quick bathroom breaks. Finally, they were close to their destination—just minutes away from the resort Sergei was most likely staying at.

Sergei's current dance partner had just suffered an unimaginable loss—the death of her father not even an hour after he and Lyla had exited the stage, yet something told Collin Sergei hadn't given Lyla a second thought. He'd probably considered it a lucky break that he didn't have to stick around for the parade after all, and headed up to Asha a day early to bask in the privacy he seemed to treasure so much.

"I'll be back." Lyla took off her seatbelt and reached for the door handle.

"Wait." He snagged her by the wrist before she could get out. "Remember, you're just going to ask for a room and pay with cash."

"I've stayed in a motel before."

"Not while you were on the run."

She sighed. "No, I haven't."

He wanted to go in with her and monitor for any snags in their plan, but being seen together from this point forward was suicide. "Be careful—casual."

She nodded, settling the black scarf more securely on her head, disguising the majority of her face without making it completely obvious that that was the whole idea.

He studied her jerky movements as she tucked a loose strand of her hair beneath the fabric. Lyla hadn't said much during the drive. She'd mostly stared out the window or dozed off for short snatches and occasionally translated the news for him while he constantly checked the mirrors for a tail. The police were searching for Russia's Princess, the media was speculating about their mysterious disappearance, and he was doing everything in his power to make sure they stayed hidden until he knew exactly how they were going to get the hell out of this country. "Hopefully we can get some food and a decent night's sleep." He couldn't offer her anything more than that at this point.

"I'll be right back." She got out, shoving the money from her purse into her pocket.

"Be careful," he said again as he readied his weapon—just in case—and kept his eye on the lobby door, waiting for Lyla's return while he glanced around, studying their surroundings more closely. Asha was tiny and nothing like the resort towns his clients were used to in The States. The derelict spot didn't offer much in the way of three-star amenities let alone five, but the gas station and small restaurant across the street would serve their needs for the night. Lyla had mentioned the signs for the regional airport a few miles back, which was a good first step. Now they had to confirm that Sergei was actually here.

His eyes darted to the rearview mirror when a car drove past the parking lot. He needed to get rid of this vehicle. Certainly the car had been reported stolen by now, and he had little doubt that with Russia's Princess MIA, foreign agents had hacked into Ethan Cooke Security's records. Contact wouldn't be safe from this point forward. Until he could guarantee that he and Lyla were boarding a plane for

Alaska, he wouldn't be reaching out to anybody.

Lyla walked out with a key in hand, holding it up, and opened the passenger-side door.

"Did you have any trouble?"

"No."

"No one seemed suspicious?"

She shook her head. "I don't think so. I asked for a room, paid, and got the key. It was pretty straightforward."

Nothing was straightforward anymore, but he would have to trust her instincts. For the next little while it was the two of them against the world. "Go ahead and get settled in. I'm going to move the car, and I'll get us something to eat across the street. Can I have your scarf?"

She unwrapped the black wool and handed it to him, then grabbed her bag.

"Hey."

She stopped and looked at him.

"I'm going to be keeping my eye on the room, but don't open the door for anyone. Unless you hear my voice, don't open that door."

She nodded.

He waited for her to go inside, then brought the car around the small five-room establishment, having to settle for a spot toward the side of the building. The last thing he wanted was to call attention to the vehicle. He pulled down the visor and adjusted the scarf around his neck, making certain that most of his mouth was covered, and tugged his hat low on his head—a decent disguise on a cold night. The language barrier was going to be an issue at the restaurant, but he was going to have to do the best he could. They just needed to hunker down till morning.

———◆———

Lyla stepped from the shower, dried off, and put on the leggings and sweatshirt she'd worn to the Bolshoi yesterday afternoon. She applied her moisturizer and ran a brush through her hair—normal, everyday actions she'd done thousands of times before, but nothing was normal anymore. Her father was gone. She'd witnessed his death, felt the heat from the fireball that had been his car, smelled the putrid scent of his vehicle burning, yet she still couldn't make herself believe it.

"He's dead," she whispered as she stared at herself in the mirror, hoping that voicing the truth out loud might make it real. "He's dead," she repeated, still brushing her hair. "He's dead," she said for the third time and dropped her hand to her side, studying herself. Her eyes appeared glassy and weary. The dark lines of exhaustion were present like bruises on her skin, but there were no tears on her cheeks. There was nothing in her heart either—no grief, no pain—only emptiness. She swallowed and glanced down at the floor. Dad had been her everything, her only family. Now she was alone. Knowing that she would never talk to him again via Skype or hug him as she said goodbye at the airport brought a quick wave of nausea but no sorrow.

A knock sounded at the door, and she tensed.

"Ly-Ly."

Recognizing Collin's voice, she hurried to the door and let him in.

"We've got eats." He handed her the bag and took off his winter gear, then turned on the ancient television. "Maybe we can catch the news while we have dinner," he said, twisting the dial through the meager rotation of channels. Wavy gray lines or static filled the screen, but there was nothing worth watching. "That's not going to help us much."

"No."

He shut it off. "But that will." He gestured to the meals she held.

The scents wafting from the containers were heavenly, but she didn't want them. Her appetite was as absent as her emotions. "It smells good."

"I'm not exactly sure what I ordered but I'm game for just about anything."

She made her lips curve.

He took her chin between his cold fingers, studying her, she knew. "I'm positive I got soup. That's a Russian word I've mastered."

She closed her eyes, touched by his thoughtfulness. "Thank you."

He took her hand and moved with her to the full-size bed—their table as well as sleeping arrangements in the no-frills room. "Let's see what we've got." He pulled out containers as they sat knee to knee in the center of the mattress. "Like I said. I'm not exactly sure what this is."

"How did you order?"

"I pointed to stuff."

She smiled this time, finding him adorable when she could feel nothing else.

"So, help me solve the mystery." He handed her the to-go bowl.

She sniffed the soup. "*Rassolnick.*"

He shook his head. "That's not helping me much."

"It's sour." She blew on a spoonful and held it up to his lips.

He sampled, moving his head from side to side as if considering. "Sour, but not half bad."

"It's made with pickled cucumber and barley."

"It's good."

She ate some herself, a soup Oksana had made several times for her and Dad.

"How do you say it again?"

"*Rassolnick,*" she enunciated.

"*Rassolnick,*" he repeated.

They opened the other containers.

"Dumplings." He rubbed his hands together and wiggled his brows.

"*Pelmini.* Dad's favorite."

The fun left his eyes, and he blew out a long breath. "I'm sorry, Lyla."

She shook her head, seeing the distress she'd caused by mentioning it. "You didn't know." She stabbed the doughy dinner with her plastic fork and brought it to his mouth. "They're good, I'm sure. You can make them a million ways, but Dad likes them best with meat."

He chewed. "Really good." He looked at the other meal with more caution.

"*Gollubtsy.*"

"Which is?"

"Cabbage rolls." She broke off a piece for him.

He redirected her fork, pointing the utensil in her direction. "You first."

She sampled, not loving the meat in the popular Russian dish, but she needed food, and Collin had done his best. "It's good. Oksana makes them with mushroom when I visit, which Dad tolerates." She smiled before it faded, realizing she kept speaking as if Dad was at home, safe and cozy in Spaso House. "Why didn't we go to the embassy or consulate? Dad always told me to go there if I was in trouble."

"Because the only people I trust right now are in Los Angeles."

"They can help us at the embassy."

He shook his head. "DSS drove us the wrong way—toward the danger and away from the airport where they were supposed to take us if something happened."

"He might've gotten confused—"

He cut her off with another shake of his head. "We know how to evacuate a principal. Whether you're DSS or close protection, you know how to get your man out of the line of fire. That's the whole objective—what we train for constantly."

"They were corrupt—part of the terrorist group?"

"I don't know, Lyla. I don't know what's going on. But we're not taking any chances. We're going to have to take some precautions—stay low, ditch the car. I'm going to let my beard grow out until we can get out of here."

Did he think that was a disguise? He was gorgeous whether he was clean-shaven or scruffy with two days of growth shadowing his jaw. "Is this what you did when you were a Ranger, hide and wear disguises?"

"Not quite. I did VSOs."

"I don't speak in acronyms."

"Village support operations."

"What is that exactly?"

"Most of the time I searched for bad guys."

"Did you find them?"

"Sometimes."

"What did you do when you found them?"

"My job."

She swallowed, holding his gaze, not needing him to explain any further.

"We should think about cutting your hair."

She paused with another spoonful of soup at her lips. "Cut my hair?"

"Maybe dye it."

"Oh." She set the spoon back in the bowl.

"It's kind of hard to disguise a trademark." He slid his fingers through the yards of damp, glossy blond. "Just to your shoulders."

"Okay."

"I wouldn't suggest it if I didn't think it was important."

She stood and walked to her bag, digging to the bottom until she felt the small sewing kit she always traveled with to fix her pointe shoes. She took the scissors from the case. "I have these."

He ate more of the dumplings. "Right now?"

"Yes." She walked into the bathroom, took off her bulky sweatshirt, and stood in her bra, wanting to get this over with.

He stepped into the cramped space behind her as she

grabbed her hair and made the first cut, tossing a good twenty-four-inch chunk in the trash. "Let me do it, Ly-Ly. I'll try to make it even." He draped her shoulders with a towel, then picked up her brush and slid the bristles through her hair. "Luna does hair when she's not reading her Tarot cards and auras."

"How do you read an aura?"

He shrugged. "Beats the hell out of me."

She smiled as he did.

He took the scissors and began to chop. Minutes passed in silence as the hair she'd let grow for years fell to the floor.

She watched Collin in the mirror as he frowned, concentrating and doing his best to even out her ends.

"Almost finished," he mumbled, making his final snip. "There."

She slid her fingers through her remaining locks, studying her hair now resting just above her shoulders. "It's different."

He turned her to face him. "You're still beautiful."

"My father's dead. I don't care about my vanity."

He sighed, cupping her cheeks. "I'm so sorry, Ly-Ly." He wrapped his arms around her, sliding his hands gently up and down her back beneath her towel.

She closed her eyes and returned his embrace, resting her head against his chest. "He's gone and I don't feel anything."

"You will when you're ready." He drew her away far enough to look her in the eyes and stroke his knuckles along her skin. "I wish I could snap my fingers and change everything."

But he couldn't. She stepped away and tidied up the mess they'd made. "You should eat your dinner."

"I'm going to. And shower too, but first we have to call the resort and see if Sergei's there."

"What if he's not?"

"Let's see if he is before we focus on what-ifs. We're a long way from Moscow, which is good. That was one of our biggest obstacles." He picked up her sweatshirt and helped her put it on. "We'll have you call and ask for his girlfriend."

She frowned. "Ava? Shouldn't I ask for Sergei?"

He shook his head. "He's looking for privacy on this trip. They won't be registered under his name."

"That makes sense."

They went out into the bedroom, and Lyla picked up the old phonebook, flipping through the pages until she found the number for the resort.

"Don't identify yourself. We just need to know if they're there."

"Okay." She snagged the ancient phone and dialed as Collin polished off the remaining dumplings.

"Asha Resort," the woman answered in Russian.

"Good evening. May I please speak with Ava Utkin?"

"Please hold and I'll ring her room."

"Thank you." She hung up. "They're there."

"Perfect. Tomorrow we're going home."

He seemed so certain Sergei was going to help. "I don't see how this will work."

"We just need to get on the plane. There are no customs to deal with or passport checks at a private airport. We won't have to worry about them when we land either, because someone from the Department of State is going to be waiting for us in Anchorage and make this whole problem go away." He took her hand, kissing her palm. "We're going home, Ly-Ly."

She nodded, trusting that he knew what he was doing.

ೞ CHAPTER TWENTY-TWO ೞ

COLLIN LOOKED BOTH WAYS BEFORE HE PULLED OUT of the motel parking lot and joined the light morning traffic. He glanced in the rearview mirror as he accelerated, making certain he didn't pick up a tail as they traveled father down the street. So far, things were quiet. Last night had been blessedly uneventful, which was exactly what they'd both needed. He and Lyla had even managed to catch a solid eight hours of sleep. But that didn't mean something couldn't go wrong today. Their only liability at this point was the stolen car, which he planned to ditch sooner rather than later. If all went well, they wouldn't need it anymore anyway.

With the coast clear for the time being, he snagged the last of the pastries Lyla bought at the restaurant and took a huge bite. They'd enjoyed eggs and toast, and he'd happily eaten both of their sides of bacon before they packed up and left their room behind. The goal this morning was to meet Sergei and Ava at the resort before they had a chance to head off to the slopes for the day. Since the sun was just now rising, he assumed the dancer and his girlfriend were still in bed. He bit into the pastry again, polishing off most of the glazed, raspberry-filled confection. "God, this is *good*. Want the last bite?"

"Sure." Lyla's lips brushed the pads of his fingers as she snagged the final piece.

He frowned. "I didn't actually think you were going to say yes."

She smiled as she chewed. "A token offer."

"Pretty much."

"I guess you learned your lesson."

He grinned. "I guess I did. How about some news?" He gestured to the dashboard.

"Sure." Lyla turned on the radio, lowering the volume as the unmistakable jingle of a commercial played through the speakers. "It's a commercial."

"Yeah."

"Do you think..." she cleared her throat, "do you think they've caught the men who hurt my father?"

He seriously doubted it. Now that he knew Ayub was behind this whole thing, it wouldn't surprise him if the authorities never caught their man. Ayub was a brilliant, evil son of a bitch who excelled at eluding capture and wreaking havoc wherever he went, but how could he tell Lyla Jonathan's murderer might never be found? Eventually he would spell out the truth for her, but for now she needed to believe Jonathan would get the justice he deserved. "It's hard to say. Hopefully we'll have an update in a minute."

"Hopefully," she agreed.

He came to attention when he spotted the sign Lyla had mentioned last night and took a left, heading toward the airport. Not being able to use the internet services on his phone was working against him. Instead of scoping out the area with a little technological assistance, he was stuck doing reconnaissance on the fly. He slowed, studying the short runway that catered to private jets and prop planes bringing skiers to the resort. A small, concrete building was the only structure on site along with two planes outside of a bay—one a twin-engine Cessna 310 and the other an older model Beechcraft. This was as basic as it got, which was perfect. Security measures would be non-existent. They would be able to park, get on the plane, and go.

Satisfied that this would work, he flipped a U-turn and started toward the resort. Figuring out which room Ava and Sergei were staying in was going to be a bigger obstacle than securing a flight to The States.

The musical sounds from the radio segued into a man talking. "Here it is." Lyla reached forward, turning up the volume again.

Collin glanced from the road to Lyla as the man spoke, not liking that she was frowning. "What?"

"They have nothing new to report about my father. The Federation and US are working diligently to capture the group who claimed responsibility for his death."

"It'll take some time." He took her hand, giving her fingers a gentle squeeze.

She nodded as she looked at her lap. "I know. I just thought—" She stopped, and her gaze flew to the dashboard when a familiar voice filtered through the speakers.

"Is that Oksana?"

"Yes." Her frown returned, growing deeper. "She says— she says she doesn't know where I am. She's heard nothing from me. If I was okay, I would have called to let her know. It's been too long. You seem like such a nice man—very loving, very good to me, but now she can't be sure."

"Wait. *What*?"

"Hold on." She settled a halting hand against his arm and swallowed, still listening as the newscaster's voice replaced Oksana's. "The media's starting to speculate that you might've had something to do with the bombing, that maybe I've been kidnapped. The US is firmly denying the accusations on your behalf, but the footage of you knocking out the DSS Agent and pulling me down the street..."

"Jesus."

"We need to fix this, Collin." She clutched at his shirt. "They think you killed my father—or helped at least—and abducted me."

"We'll get everything straightened out," he reassured instead of swearing as the stakes grew higher. Today had to be the day. They were running out of time to get out of this country. He wasn't about to let the police haul them in and separate them. There was no way in hell he was going to leave Lyla alone in DSS custody while he sat in a cell, waiting for the Department of State to get him released for boosting a car.

He glanced Lyla's way, watching her nervously nibble her lip as she stared out the windshield. She wore her shorter hair tucked in a tight bun beneath her hat, and her scarf disguised much of her face, but he feared she was still recognizable. Her heavy winter jacket added a little bulk to her slender frame, but her ice-blue eyes wouldn't allow her to go unnoticed. He slowed as they drove by a bakery and stopped along the side of the road. "Can you go in and order something, have them box it up for you?"

She gaped. "How can you be thinking about your stomach at a time like this?"

"It's not for me."

"For Sergei and Ava?"

"Yeah." He didn't want to make this stop at all. If he could, he would just hijack the damn plane and they would go, but he needed Sergei if they were going to pull this off. Hopefully a simple box of baked goods would be enough to get him and Lyla past the front desk at the resort.

She adjusted her scarf and put on her dark-tinted sunglasses.

"Keep those on," he said, touching the frames.

"I will."

She got out and moments later came back with a pretty pink box. The scent of heavenly breakfast treats filled the car as she settled into her seat. "Assorted options since I'm not sure what they like."

"Perfect." He pulled back onto the road and made his way toward their destination, his shoulders tensing with each mile they drove. Too many variables were out of his control. Too many things could go wrong. "When we get there, I want you to go up to the front desk and tell them that you're from the bakery."

"Okay." She played with the ribbon wrapped around the box. "What if they won't let me bring these to them?"

"They will. Adlib if you have to. They're a surprise for Ava—her favorites she and Sergei get every time they come in to ski. When we talked at the banquet, it sounded like he and Ava had been here before, so we'll work with that."

Sighing, she nodded.

"We're almost to the finish line," he said, reminding himself as much as her as he took her hand and kissed her knuckles. "We just have to get in the air."

"Okay."

He pulled into the parking lot, finding a spot sandwiched between two larger cars, and took the snacks from her lap. "Go ahead and grab your stuff. We won't be coming back to the vehicle."

She secured her bag on her shoulder and took the pastry box back.

"Hold up." He adjusted her scarf and pulled her hat farther down on her head, then did the same with his own. "You'll have to lose the glasses inside, but hopefully that will help a bit."

They got out and walked the path to the lobby, stepping into the warmth of Asha's only decent overnight establishment. Collin hung back a little as Lyla approached the front desk, smiling at the attendant as she spoke in Russian, gesturing to the box she held.

The woman behind the counter hesitated as she glanced from Lyla to Collin.

He sent her a friendly smile as Lyla spoke again, but something was up, and he didn't like it—the way the woman kept peeking up from under her lashes and looking at him.

The front desk attendant said something else, and Lyla turned, facing him. "Second floor."

They walked to the elevator and stepped in. Collin gave the button an impatient shove. "What did she say?"

"That her aunt and uncle own the bakery, and she didn't know they hired on a new employee."

Shit. They weren't even to Sergei's room yet and they were already in trouble. The woman had definitely been suspicious. If she called her aunt or uncle to confirm Lyla's story... He stabbed the button for the second floor again, as if that would make the elevator car go faster. This was going to have to be quick. "What room?" he asked as the door finally slid open.

"Two-fifteen."

They walked down the hall, stopping in front of the door, and he knocked.

There was no answer.

He knocked louder, pounding with the side of his fist despite the early hour.

Sergei's irritated voice carried through the thick wood.

"He said to go away, but not that nicely," Lyla translated.

"Tell him you're room service." The last thing they needed was for him to call down to the front desk.

Lyla spoke.

Sergei said something back.

Lyla spoke again, and the door whipped open, with Sergei standing in a pair of sweats and a pissed-off expression on his face.

Collin pressed his hand to the door, anticipating Sergei's attempt to close it, as Sergei's eyes registered surprise. He shoved Lyla inside in front of him and shut the door himself as he turned on the overhead light, needing to get the situation under his control.

"What the hell are you doing here?"

Ava hurried into the room, covering her bra and panty-clad body as best she could with her arms.

"Ava, call the police," Sergei demanded.

"Sergei, Ava, please don't," Lyla said.

"The police are looking for you." Sergei pointed his finger at Collin. "Ava, call."

"Ava, you don't want to do that," Collin assured, trying to bring a little calm to the tense room.

"Yes, she does," Sergei argued.

This wasn't going well, and he was done fucking around. He pulled the gun from the waist of his jeans. "Ava's going to come sit down on the bed, right next to you."

Ava made a sound in her throat as she instantly paled.

"Sit on the bed and stay quiet," Collin warned both his captors.

"Collin." Lyla stared at him as wide-eyed as Ava and Sergei. "What are you *doing*?"

"Whatever I have to."

"Put that away."

He ignored Lyla's request as he stared into Sergei's mutinous eyes. "The four of us are going on a little trip."

"I'll go nowhere with you." Sergei crossed his arms like a spoiled child.

"Collin, this isn't the way." Lyla stepped closer to Sergei and Ava. "We need help. My father was killed—"

"Do you think I don't know this? I can't find anything but your *face* to watch on TV."

"Collin didn't do anything wrong," Lyla tried to explain. "He's only protecting me."

"Then he won't have trouble talking to the police."

"We're not going to do that," Collin interrupted. They were getting nowhere with Sergei and wasting time. "Lyla, get Ava something to put on and pack them up. Toss bathroom stuff into a bag. Everything needs to come with us."

Sergei glared. "We won't go with you."

Collin walked closer to Sergei, aiming the gun at his head, bringing his point home to Sergei that he was the only one in charge. "You're going to do exactly what I tell you to do. Lyla, go pack them up."

Lyla stared at him in disbelief and hurried off.

"We're going to file a flight plan and get ready for an immediate takeoff. You're bringing us to Alaska."

Sergei's mouth dropped open. "*Alaska?*"

"You'll drop us off in Anchorage, then you can be on your way—right back to your vacation."

Sergei shook his head adamantly. "I want nothing to do with this. We'll be stuck in the US. Once the authorities figure out I took you across the border, they'll think we aided a fugitive."

"I'm not a fugitive."

Sergei raised his brow. "Is this not kidnapping?"

"I guess it all depends on how you look at it. If you weren't a dick, you would be taking us voluntarily because you know Lyla's in trouble and I've done nothing wrong."

"This is a matter for the police."

"You and I both know what will happen to Lyla if we go to the police. She's a target here just like her father was. If they bring me in, they'll separate us, and I can't let that happen."

"These things aren't my problem." Sergei locked his arms tighter across his chest.

"They are now. We're flying to and from untowered airports, and we're going to be sure to stay out of any controlled airspace until we're ready to cross the border. If we do this right, no one ever has to know you got us to the US. But I need you with me just in case we have to radio in. I don't speak Russian, and I don't want anyone knowing Lyla and I are in the air. You cooperate and I'll make sure the flight plan vanishes as soon as you're back over the Bering Sea."

"Why should I trust you?"

"Because you don't have a choice."

"They will find out!" Sergei stood and immediately sat again when Collin followed his movements with the gun. "The people who are doing these things are powerful. My government can't even stop them. If they know we helped—"

"They won't."

Lyla came back into the room with Sergei and Ava's suitcases and handed Ava an outfit to put on. "I think that's everything."

"Good." Collin gave his attention back to Sergei. "Which vehicle is yours?" Collin rested his finger on the trigger when Sergei refused to speak, even though the safety was on. "Which one?"

"The red Audi."

"Lyla, go out the back door and pull the red Audi around to the side entrance."

Lyla snagged the keys off the table and left.

Collin kept the pistol trained on Sergei. "When she gets back, we're going to file that flight plan."

Minutes later, Lyla walked through the door, slightly out of breath.

"Go ahead and open up Sergei's computer and set it in front of him so we can see what he's typing."

Lyla placed the laptop in front of Sergei, where Collin could see the screen as well.

"Sergei, go ahead and file the DVFR—destination Ted Stevens International in Anchorage. Put Fairbanks International as the backup." He watched Sergei enter the information, typing four passengers into the designated box. "Put two."

Sergei looked at him. "There will be four."

"Put two."

Swearing, he did as he was told and hit "enter" to submit the plan and make it official.

"Get dressed and let's go." Collin clenched his jaw, glancing at the phone on the side table when it started ringing— the front desk attendant calling to check in with Sergei, no doubt. This was going sour, fast.

Sergei put on his shirt, socks, and shoes. "Do you think I'll let this happen? Do you think I won't seek attention the second we open that door? I'm not afraid of you. The people who will hunt me, I'm terrified of them—"

Collin yanked him up by the collar and slammed him back

against the wall, shoving the gun under his chin as both Lyla and Ava gasped. It was time for Sergei to fear him as much as any terrorist group. "Listen real close," he said through his teeth as the hotel phone continued ringing. "You're going to get us to that airport and in the air without any bullshit. If you alert anyone—hotel guests, the police, air traffic control—that something's off, I swear to God I'll end you and you'll never be found."

Sergei's eyes were huge as he nodded.

"Not one wrong move."

Sergei nodded again.

"Grab your bags and let's go." He glanced at Lyla as she stared at him, clearly as terrified as Sergei and Ava. "Ly-Ly—"

"No." She shook her head, turning away from him.

He grabbed her arm, pulling her back. "Trust me."

"If I'd had any idea... I don't know you," she shuddered out. "Who are you right now?" She shouldered her bag, took one of Ava's duffles, then Ava's hand as they opened the door and started down the hall.

He clenched his jaw, reading the disgust in her eyes easily enough, but he would have to deal with that later. Right now, he needed them gone. He glanced at the phone that began ringing again and quickly shoved his weapon back in the waist of his jeans, then closed the door behind them.

A couple joined them as the four of them stepped into the elevator. Collin smiled politely and moved closer to Sergei, a reminder to his temporary hostage to keep quiet.

They got out on the first floor and headed out the side entrance, making quick work of transferring their items to the waiting car.

"We'll do a fast flight check," Collin said as he got in the front seat next to Sergei and they drove toward the airport. "How's our gas situation?"

"The tank's full. I had it seen to when we landed yesterday morning. Just take the plane. You're a pilot. Leave me and Ava here."

"That's not an option. Just drive."

Within minutes, they were pulling into the spot closest to the Cessna 310. Collin took the keys from Sergei and unlocked the plane. "Load up and let's get out of here."

Luggage was carelessly tossed inside, and Collin took his seat next to Sergei while Lyla and Ava settled in back. Sergei began his pre-flight check with Collin's assistance as the engines warmed up. "I should radio in for a weather update."

Collin shook his head, well aware of Sergei's game. There would be no contact with anyone from this point forward. "The weather's fine." He buckled in, then glanced over his shoulder at Lyla as he put on his headset, hating that she kept looking at him like he was slime.

"We're ready," Sergei said.

"Let's go."

The plane barreled down the runway, gaining speed, and Sergei pulled back on the yoke, lifting them into the air.

"Take her up to altitude. I want to maximize fuel economy," Collin said as he switched off the transponder.

"Why did you do that?"

"What?"

"Turn that off."

"Because we're going to disappear for a little while. Go ahead and head north."

"But that's not the path we declared."

"Do it anyway."

"If we crash, we won't be found."

"Then don't crash. As long as we identify ourselves before we hit the border, we'll be fine." They were going off grid for the next several hours to give everyone a chance to breathe—mostly himself.

Sergei leveled off at max altitude, and Collin sat back in his seat, staring down at Russia thousands of feet below. For the first time in over two weeks, he let himself relax. They had a long way to go, but they weren't on the ground. The police wouldn't be hauling him in and separating him from

Lyla. He looked away from the window and back at her.

She met his gaze and looked away.

He took off his seatbelt and headset, then turned, leaning over his seat, pulling off her headset as well in the noisy cramped quarters of the cabin. "Hey." He tilted her chin until their eyes met.

"What?"

"Don't look at me like that."

"Why did you do that? Why did you use the gun that way?"

"Because we need to get home. I need to get you home."

"You frightened Ava." She swallowed. "You frightened me."

He took a chance and cupped her face, stroking her skin. "I'm sorry. I went with what I knew would work. The front desk attendant was on to us. How long did you want to wait around and argue with him?" He gestured to their reluctant pilot.

She pressed her cheek into his palm. "Do you know how many laws you've broken? You're risking so much for me."

He eased her closer, kissing her forehead. "I'm going to get us home. Whatever it takes."

"I should've turned myself in so we could explain—"

"No." He drew her back, looking her in the eye. "Whatever it takes, Ly-Ly. We're in this together."

"You could have left me. After the bombing you could have left me, but you didn't."

"That was never going to happen."

"Thank you." She pressed a gentle kiss to his lips. "For everything."

He kissed her again, wrapping his arms around her as best he could with the seat between them. "Get some rest. We've got a long flight."

She nodded.

He glanced at Ava as she studied him, clearly still afraid. There wasn't much he could do to change that at the moment. He turned around and buckled his belt, glancing at the altimeter. At this point, all he cared about was getting Lyla over the border.

———◆———

Collin stood outside, freezing his ass off in eastern Russia's brutal tundra temperatures, watching Sergei ready the Cessna for the last leg of their journey. He waited for Sergei to seal the gas tank on the left wing, then followed him around to the right side of the plane, making certain he topped off that tank properly as well. Somehow the newbie pilot had never fueled himself up during the two years he'd been flying, which was absolutely insane.

Lyla's dance partner had lost another notch of Collin's respect when Collin realized Sergei had no idea what in the hell he was doing shortly after their rocky landing at the shitty-ass airport—and that was a generous name for this joke of a place: two fuel pumps, an ancient runway, and a nasty bathroom neither Lyla nor Ava had been excited to step into. "Make sure you put the grounding wire back when you're finished," he said as he glanced at his watch. He couldn't say what time it was for sure. They'd been flying for hours, moving through several time zones on their way across the country, but that didn't stop him from dialing Chase's number on Sergei's cell phone. They would be back in the air in less than ten minutes—the perfect opportunity to finally check in.

"Hello?"

He smiled, happy to hear a familiar voice. "Hey, man."

"Jesus, Collin. Son of a bitch, man. Where the hell are you?"

"At some shit-hole airport in eastern Russia, refueling Sergei's plane."

"We were all hoping your plan had something to do with you and Lyla heading closer to The States."

"We're probably four, maybe five hours from the border, depending on what type of weather we run into as we approach."

"That's not too bad."

"No, it's not. Things should go pretty fast once we cross into Alaska. How are things in LA?"

"I'm glad I can finally say I have some good news. The Department of State has been in touch with Moscow several times since we talked last. They've explained the situation—that Jonathan hired you as Lyla's personal bodyguard. Ethan's provided proof of contract, so you're clear with the government from a legal standpoint. You don't have to worry about any misunderstandings with the authorities from this point forward."

That was one monkey off his back. "That's good to know."

"On the other hand, you and Lyla sure know how to grab the headlines."

He closed his eyes, steaming out a breath. "What now?"

"The Russian media's going crazy. They've been interviewing the front desk attendant at the Asha Resort—the one Lyla spoke to."

"I remember her."

"There are all kinds of rumors and speculation about stolen cars and Lyla pretending to be a bakery employee, but the biggest question is whether the princess and her prince tagged along on Sergei and Ava's Alaska-bound flight since no one's seen either of you since you brought Lyla's dance partner donuts."

Why did it sound like Chase was getting a kick out of this whole thing? "So I'm her Prince Charming again, not her abductor?"

"At least for now. We'll have to see what they come up with tomorrow."

He was looking forward to putting the constant scrutiny of the press behind him. "We'll just have to keep them guessing for a while."

"I thought you should know Sophie's working on your crown. It should be ready by the time we get you back to LA."

He grinned, shaking his head. It was going to be a long time before anyone at the office let him live this one down. "Fuck you."

"And we've changed the nameplate on your desk. We weren't sure if you wanted to go with 'Royal Highness' or 'His Royal Highness' so we went with the simpler of the two."

"You're a tool."

"We can't all be royalty."

He chuckled. This right here was exactly what he'd needed—a little slice of normal: one of his buddies busting his balls. "Clearly." His smile faded as he looked at Lyla through the window while she and Ava talked in the back seat. Their female hostage had relaxed several degrees during the long flight, but it was clear both Ava and Lyla were tired. "Is there anything new on Jonathan?"

"No. Nothing. But I've heard through the grapevine that intelligence sources are concerned by the lack of chatter they're picking up on. For most of January, communications were nonstop—before and after the bombing in Saint Petersburg, the one in Perm, even Jonathan's murder. Now there's almost nothing."

Quiet terrorists were often more lethal than the noisy ones. "Ayub's up to something."

"More than likely."

He was willing to bet his life on it. "Sounds like it's a damn good thing we're getting the hell out of here."

"You're heading into Anchorage?"

"That's the plan. I've had the transponder off all day. I'm going to keep it that way." The Russian government might have cleared him of any wrongdoing, but he wasn't taking any chances until Lyla was safe on US soil. "We won't be making contact again until I have to clear the border."

"I'll catch a flight and head up. Someone from the Department of State and I will be waiting for you. We'll take care of everything for Sergei and Ava. We'll figure out what we need to do for Lyla as well."

He didn't doubt it. "Thanks."

"Just get back to us safely."

"Will do."

"Fly safe, man."

"You too." He hung up and opened the pilot-side door as Sergei walked back from returning the grounding wire to its designated place by the fuel pumps. "I'm flying."

"This isn't your plane."

"You're right. It's Ava's father's. I'm sure he wants it back in one piece."

"He's never worried about my abilities before."

"It'll be full-on dark soon. Are you instrument rated?"

"No."

And that settled that. Dad had taught him to fly by instrument before his tenth birthday. They were getting closer to Alaska, but before they landed in Anchorage, they would head through brutal terrain, over mountain ranges, and who knew what the weather would bring as they neared the Bering Strait. Coastal storms could pop up out of nowhere and offer fatal results just as fast. "You have to know there's no way in hell I'm leaving it up to you to be our pilot in charge. You can't fly safely—or legally—once the sun goes down."

Surprisingly, Sergei didn't argue. He moved around to the co-pilot's seat and got in.

Collin took his seat, firing up the engine and doing a quick instrument check as he buckled in and settled his headset over his ears. "Everybody ready?"

"I need a blanket or something," Ava said as she fidgeted. "This chair is quite uncomfortable. No matter how I sit, the spring pokes me in the shoulder."

"How about we trade?" Lyla offered.

Ava shook her head.

"I don't mind. It's the least I can do after you and Sergei have been so kind to us."

"We didn't have much choice," Sergei mumbled into his microphone.

"Let's switch," Lyla said again. "We'll both be able to say we rode halfway comfortably."

Ava nodded. "Thank you, Lyla."

"Of course." Lyla moved to the seat behind Collin.

When he was certain the ladies were buckled in, he accelerated down the runway, lifting off the ground and bringing them into the sky. The plane cleared the first thousand feet, and he grinned as they left Russia behind for the final time. "Hell yeah!" he shouted, following up his holler with a triumphant whoop as he looked back at Lyla.

"Alaska, here we come," she said, smiling at him.

"That's right, baby. I'm taking you home." He winked at her and returned Ava's cautious smile as he faced forward again. He glanced at the transponder, making certain it was still off, then guided them east, ready to finish this trip once and for all.

CHAPTER TWENTY-THREE

COLLIN GLANCED AT THE GPS AND MADE SMALL AD-justments, guiding the plane on the new path to Anchorage. They were making decent time despite the pockets of gnarly weather he'd been forced to fly around when they approached international waters. An hour ago, he'd had no choice but to turn on the transponder and identify their aircraft as they penetrated the Air Defense Identification Zone, but being a blip on air traffic control's radar screen was no longer a big deal.

He rubbed at the back of his stiff neck and stifled a yawn as he looked at his watch, which Lyla had reset to reflect the actual time. They'd had one hell of a long day, and there was still a ways to go, but at least they were flying over US soil on a clear, moonlit night. In a perfect scenario, he would have flown southeast and cut across the southern half of the state, but the unexpected snow and gusty winds being reported in Anchorage left him no choice but to redirect and move north across Alaska's interior, then head south toward Fairbanks. He would have to keep an eye on the gas gauge after their series of detours; otherwise, he couldn't complain.

By now, Chase and someone from the Department of State were waiting for them to land. He couldn't be sure what would happen next, how Lyla's situation would be handled from this point forward, but he was ready to stand by her side as they took the next step. There was a strong possibility they would deplane and be whisked off into protective custody for a little while, just until everyone was certain the threats against Lyla wouldn't follow her home, but hunkering down with his principal in an undisclosed location in Somewhere, United States would be an entirely different experience than running for their lives in Russia. There would be no language barriers to contend with, his co-workers would have his back the entire time, and ultimately Lyla would be safe and able to relax—maybe even let her guard down enough to start the grieving process.

The plane bumped about in a pocket of turbulence and glided through just as quickly. Within seconds, the plane shuddered again. "Looks like things are going to be a little bumpy as we move closer to this mountain range. Make sure your safety belts are secure." The jostling continued, and he glanced over his shoulder, checking on Lyla and Ava, smiling at Lyla as their eyes met in the dim blue glow of the instrument lights.

She smiled back.

They hit another rough patch, and he returned his attention to the front.

"Damn turbulence," Sergei grumbled as he rubbed his eyes.

"Welcome to Alaska."

"I should be in *Asha*."

How Lyla had put up with such a miserable man for the last couple of weeks was beyond him. Sergei Ploeski, dancer extraordinaire, was an absolute bastard. "Feel free to doze off again."

Sergei opened his mouth to respond as the twin-engine bounced in another pocket, giving them all a considerable jolt. Ava and Lyla's gasps echoed in Collin's headset.

"I'll take us up a couple hundred feet. That should smooth us out. We don't want Sergei losing his pastries."

"A pathetic dinner," Sergei complained.

"At least it was something." But after sixteen hours of endless travel, he was craving a steak, garlic mashed potatoes, and a beer. A huge salad wouldn't hurt either.

"The donut was stale."

"So get a fresh one when we land." He pulled on the yoke, nudging them up in altitude, and hit another rough patch, jolting them with such force, Collin pressed his hand to the ceiling, bracing himself against the impact as Ava squealed. "Sorry about that."

Sergei sat ramrod straight as his eyes went huge. "We lost forty feet."

"We might lose forty more before we get through this."

"You're supposed to know what you're doing. You should see this on the radar."

"Not if it's clear air turbulence, like we have right now." They took another beating, the deep pocket in the air current slamming them hard. Despite Collin's attempt to hold himself in place, his head connected with the roof, just as the GPS went fuzzy, then dark. *Shit.*

"What the hell happened?" Sergei smacked the dashboard. "Where's our GPS?"

Collin tapped on the screen. "We lost our panel."

"Lost our *panel*? What are we going to do?"

"Stay cool, stay our course, and maintain VFR." He took the plane down in altitude, using the trees and moon as his reference points to the horizon as their situation quickly became dangerous. The turbulence itself was no big deal. Planes were built to take one hell of a beating, but flying without navigational instruments was a huge damn problem. Depending on sight rules to guide them through Alaska's monster mountain ranges in the dark was bound to end badly.

"What if you become disoriented? Even seasoned pilots can lose their direction."

"It's a good thing I'm extra seasoned then, huh?" He ignored Sergei's panicked ramblings and focused on making radio contact with air traffic control. "This is nine-one-eight-four-bravo. We're experiencing multiple instrument failure and are flying blind."

"Nine-one-eight-four-bravo, descend in altitude and maintain VFR."

"Roger that. Maintaining VFR."

"Skwuak seven-seven-zero-zero if you have a transponder."

"Seven-seven-zero-zero," Collin said as he adjusted their code to reflect their emergency.

"We've just lost radar contact, nine-one-eight-four-bravo."

The air traffic controller's voice grew hard to hear. "Say again." Static filled his ears. "Acknowledge, air traffic control." Still nothing. "This is nine-one-eight-four-bravo. Repeat last transmission." There was nothing but static. He clenched his jaw as sweat dribbled down his back. And now things were officially worse.

Sergei clutched his seatbelt. "What the hell are we going to do?"

"Maintain VFR and hope we get our radio back."

"This is just great." Sergei pounded his fist against the GPS. "Come on you bastard."

"Keep that up and you'll break something."

"Break something?" He laughed humorlessly. "It's *already* broken."

Collin tossed him a cut-the-shit look. Clearly Sergei wasn't going to keep cool under fire. "I've lost my instruments before, and I'm still here."

"That was then."

"And this is now." He kept his focus on the moon and trees. "Lyla, Ava, we're doing fine, but I want you prepared for a rough landing if that's how things end up." Which it more than likely would.

"How?"

"I don't know what to do," Ava said as Lyla spoke at the

same time.

"Your feet would need to be flat and as far under your seat as you can get them. You'll rest your forehead on the seats in front of you, bracing your head with your arms. If I tell you to brace for impact, I want you to do it."

"Okay," Lyla responded, her voice tight with nerves.

"We're doing fine," he reminded everyone even as he went through a patch of low clouds. The last thing he needed right now was an obstruction in his visibility, especially when he was flying so low.

Minutes ticked by in tense silence as the Cessna passed in and out of the thickening cloud cover. The plane bumped and jostled slightly in the increasing winds.

"We still have no radio." Sergei pounded on the dashboard, then the GPS. "The clouds are getting worse, not better. Soon we'll be blind to our surroundings. There are mountains all around."

"How about you sit back, shut the hell up, and let me fly this plane?" The wind blew again as they passed through another patch of clouds then into a long stretch of clearing. "Be my co-pilot. Look out your damn window and find me a place to set down. Mayday, mayday, mayday. Nine-one-eight-four-bravo. Mayday, mayday, mayday," he tried again but still there was no response from air traffic control.

"I think I see—I see lights," Lyla said. "I think there's some sort of building or house down there."

"Where?" he asked as he stared at the odd-shaped mountain peak in the distance—his new point of reference for keeping his bearings. "Tell me as if the building you see was on a clock and the mountains ahead are twelve o'clock."

"Um, three—three o'clock."

The pockets of poor visibility came again, along with a huge gust of wind.

"Set us down! Set us down already!" Sergei hollered.

"Shut *up*!" If they landed now, they would be stranded without help on the way. If he didn't find somewhere to set them down, they were going to go down anyway. "Are you looking for a runway?" The wind pushed them toward the trees, and he lifted them up higher, afraid that one of the tall pines might take out the rudders.

"The cover is thick."

"So keep your eyes open."

"There's nothing. Just trees everywhere."

If he dared take his hand off the yoke, he would aim his fist in Sergei's direction. "Keep looking. There has to be something around here somewhere." Another gust took them hard to the right.

"Lift us up!"

Maybe Ava could pull off a chokehold from her seat in the back. "If I go higher, I can't see."

The wind toyed with them, knocking them left then right as he struggled to keep them level and straight. Another gust forced him into a sharp correction.

"We're going to crash," Sergei screamed and yanked up on the co-pilot's yoke, sending them soaring up in a quick adjustment.

"No!" The engine died with the stall, and sickening seconds ticked by as the wind gusted around them in the silence. There was no time nor was there enough elevation to correct the stall Sergei just caused. "Brace for impact!" Collin hollered, doing his best to steer them down easy as the plane collided with the forest of pine trees below. Lyla and Ava screamed in his ears seconds before the world went dark.

Lyla groaned, blinking her eyes open in the dark. She rubbed at the ache in her neck and realized she was dangling in her seat, caught in the tight tether of her safety belt. She squinted, trying to make out her surroundings, but it was impossible to see much of anything at all. Reaching out to the right, she grabbed hold of something—Ava's shoulder, maybe? "Ava?"

The moonlight broke through the cloud cover above, and she gasped, yanking her hand back and barely stifling a scream as she stared at Ava trapped among the wreckage and debris, punctured through her torso by a pine tree. "Oh, my—oh, my God," she shuddered out as her gaze wandered to Sergei, realizing he'd met the same fate. "Collin," she croaked on a broken whisper, squinting again to decipher his profile from the shadows, as he laid slumped forward in his seatbelt. "Collin?"

She waited for a response, for him to move, but he lay still while the bitter winds blew in through her shattered window. "Collin?" Her heart raced and her breath came faster as she frantically searched for the release on her buckle. "Wake up, Collin." She pushed the button and gasped as she fell the two or three feet onto the back of his seat, but he didn't move when the weight of her impact jostled his chair.

"Collin." She scrambled over the soft leather to the smashed metal on his side of the cockpit and screamed when her hair got caught up in Sergei's limp fingers as his arm dangled in her direction. "Let me go. Please let me go." She freed her tangles and sat on the damaged controls, hoping she wouldn't fall out the windshield with the plane angled down and to the left at an odd pitch, stuck in several trees.

"Be alive," she whispered as she brought her trembling hand to Collin's neck. "Be alive," she muttered again, expelling a breath of relief when she felt the strong, steady beat of his pulse. "Okay. Okay." She did her best to assess his condition, running her hands up his legs and the hip she had access to. Gently, she pressed on his stomach and ribs, not exactly sure what she was looking for, but when bones didn't protrude through his clothes, she figured that had to be an excellent sign. "Collin," she called louder, touching his cheeks and pressing her lips firm as the wet warmth of his blood trailed down her skin. "You're bleeding," she whispered, pulling away and trying to determine how bad the wound was as he groaned. Her gaze flew to his face and she moved in closer so she could see him better. "Collin."

His eyes fluttered open.

She feathered her fingers along his temple. "Collin."

He tried to move and winced.

She settled a halting hand on his shoulder. "Stay still. Stay still."

"Lyla."

"I'm right here."

"We went down hard."

"Yes."

"Sergei? Where are Sergei and Ava?"

"They're—they're dead."

"Did you check their pulses?"

She shook her head adamantly. "No."

"You need to check their pulses."

Perhaps she was a horrible human being, but she couldn't bear the thought of looking at Ava again. "There's a—there's a tree in them."

"What?"

"They're impaled."

He steamed out a breath. "Goddamn."

She didn't want to think about more lives lost, the horror of bodies alive only moments ago, gone. "You're bleeding. Your head."

"That's probably why I have one hell of a headache. Are you okay?"

She nodded. "I need—I need to keep you warm."

"We need to get out of here. I smell gas."

She shook her head. "We have no idea how badly you're hurt."

"I guess we should figure that out." He grit his teeth as he moved.

"Don't."

"Unbuckle me."

"Collin—"

"Unbuckle me, Lyla."

She did as he asked and helped him sit up on the dashboard next to her in the crowded space.

"Fucking-*A*."

She touched him gently, attempting to soothe him. "Your ribs?"

"No, my arm." He clutched his left bicep.

She unzipped his coat and felt beneath the bulky layers, making sure nothing protruded there either. "I don't think you're broken."

"It's probably just sore from the impact."

"You were out for at least three or four minutes. You have a concussion."

"Probably."

"How old are you?"

"Twenty-eight."

"Are you? I actually don't know your age. It never came up," she shook her head as she spoke more to herself than him. "Why did I ask you that? Um, where do you live?"

"Los Angeles." He stroked her cheek. "I'm okay." He looked past her shoulder to Sergei's seat. "Jesus."

She kept her eyes on Collin, not wanting to see the gore. "What are we going to do?"

"Get away from here."

"Where are we going to go?"

"Anywhere but here."

"We're in Alaska. I thought we just had to make it to The States."

"Mostly that's true, but we can't just sit and wait. We have no idea when they'll come looking for us. We lost radar contact about sixty, maybe even a hundred miles back. The wind was whipping us all over the damn place, throwing us off our original flight path, I imagine. We're a needle in a haystack." He looked to the sky. "And it's starting to snow."

"So we just run off into the dark, into the Alaskan wilderness in the freezing cold?"

"We get far enough away to assess the situation with cool heads. This thing could blow at any second. Sooner or later, animals are going to catch Sergei and Ava's scent."

She pressed her hand to her mouth as she shook her head. "Don't say that."

"I'm sorry."

"It's just—this is so...*awful*." Her teeth began to chatter as she struggled with a wave of fear.

"Yeah, it is."

"If we leave, they'll never find us."

"Air traffic control knows where to start looking. Chase and Ethan know we were coming home. The Department of State knows Sergei was flying us in. We sent out a distress call, but like I said, it'll take them a while to track us down. I'd rather take my chances looking for that cabin we saw before the crash. We don't want to get stuck out here in a storm."

"Do you remember the direction?"

"I have a general idea—west of the mountain range in front of us."

"Is that enough to work with?"

"I've worked with less before. Let's get what we can use and see what we can figure out. Can you crawl in back and grab the emergency kit? We should also go through the clothes: put on Ava's ski pants and boots—lots of layers."

"What about you? Sergei's not as broad as you."

"We'll use what we can. We need to hurry." He adjusted his weight on the dashboard as she fought her way into the back of the plane, and he tried to open the door, but it didn't budge. "You've got to be kidding me."

She grabbed the flashlight from the survival pack and sent the bag over the seat in Collin's direction. "What?"

"It won't open."

"We're stuck?"

He lay down in the small space, whistling out a breath

of pain, and kicked his feet against the door until the metal gave way.

She shined the beam of light among the mess and grabbed what she thought she could use of Ava's, feeling guilty as she picked through the deceased woman's items, and shoved them in her bag. She rifled through Sergei's stuff next, grabbing extra socks, ski gloves, a hat for Collin and long underwear she hoped might fit. "Here." She sent Sergei's boots over the seat.

"These should work." He handed her his shoes to bring with them.

"I think I've got what we can use."

He boosted himself up, cursing loudly, and dropped down the five or six feet into the deep snow. "Come on." He held out his hand to her.

She jumped, purposely avoiding his assistance, not wanting to accidentally hurt him any more than he already was. "What about Sergei and Ava?"

"There's nothing we can do for them right now. I can't bury them with my arm like this."

"It feels wrong just leaving."

"Hopefully search and rescue will be in the air soon. We're probably three hundred miles from Fairbanks. We'll make sure they get home to their families." He took her hand and the flashlight. "Let's go. We'll start toward the house you thought you saw."

CHAPTER TWENTY-FOUR

COLLIN'S EYES FLEW OPEN WHEN HIS CHIN HIT HIS chest. He blinked and scrubbed his hands over his face, listening to the crackle and pop of the fire as he sat leaning against a pine tree in the dark. He'd been struggling to stay awake for the last couple of hours while he and Lyla huddled beneath the emergency blankets in the makeshift shelter he'd dug into the snow. Constructing a full-blown snow cave hadn't been possible with the limited use of his arm and lack of tools, but the small recess they created and large fire he'd built were protecting them from the worst of the wind and on-and-off precipitation.

They'd walked for a good two or three hours, hoofing it through the deep snow, until Lyla's ankle started bothering her and she'd gotten cold. The clothes they scavenged from the wreckage were helping. The extra layers they added to their basic winter coats was definitely a bonus, but Lyla was tiny—a plus for a ballerina but a death sentence for surviving the brutal Alaskan temperatures.

He pulled off his glove and wiggled his fingers beneath her scarf, satisfied to find her skin warm as she breathed deeply, curled against his side while she used his thighs as a pillow.

He glanced around their desolate surroundings, peeking at his watch and yearning for a huge cup of coffee. They'd crashed nearly ten hours ago, and he had yet to hear a rescue chopper or plane searching the area. He and Lyla had walked five, maybe six miles at the most—eight if he wanted to be generous—but even at that distance from the wreckage site, he should have been able to hear help coming.

Unfortunately, only one of his passengers would be going home. He'd replayed the last few minutes of the flight a million times, trying to figure out what he could have done differently, but he couldn't find the answer. The altitude they'd been flying at had been too low to angle down, put the plane in a spin, and get the engine going again after the stall. He had blood on his hands—the loss of two lives and his biggest failure as a pilot. The only way he could make it right was to get Lyla to safety and make sure Sergei and Ava made it back to their families.

Something moved off to his left in the distance. He grabbed the gun close by his side as he whipped his head in that direction and watched snow fall from the tree branches. "Son of a bitch," he muttered through clenched teeth, cupping his throbbing head when his quick movements made the pain in his skull worse. His whole body ached from the jarring impact of the crash, but the discomfort in his head and left arm were damn near unbearable. The dose of ibuprofen he'd taken when they stopped to rest was barely touching the pain.

He moved his arm, bending at the elbow, trying to keep his tender bicep and tricep from stiffening up, and yawned, rubbing his tired eyes as his body craved for him to let them close. Lyla needed sleep—he needed to rest as well, but not while Lyla did. They were going to have to take shifts to keep the fire going, especially in this cold. Most of the brush was buried deep beneath the snow. Finding dead, dry wood hadn't been easy, even in the huge-ass wilderness. The fire was roaring hot, and he planned to keep it that way until they were ready to go.

They had a good couple hours before the sun started

creeping its way over the horizon—if it was even going to make an appearance at all through the thick cloud cover—but regardless, he and Lyla needed to be on their way once the sky brightened up in the stingy winter daylight. The scent of more snow hung heavy in the air, compounding their need for real shelter.

He glanced westward, toward the direction Lyla spotted the cabin from the plane. Hopefully they would come across the house sooner rather than later, but it didn't settle well with him that there were absolutely no signs of civilization. He had survival skills. He'd spent months in the military, training for scenarios like this—or not exactly like this—but he could get them through for a few days if he needed to. He just hoped it wouldn't come to that.

Lyla shifted against him.

He looked down, watching her eyes flutter open and her eyebrows furrow before she sat up in a rush. "This is really happening."

"Afraid so."

Sighing, she shook her head. "How is it possible that things keep getting worse?"

"I'd say our luck is in a bit of a downturn."

"I hope it rights itself soon."

Two of his passengers didn't survive the landing, he was hurt, and they were stranded in the middle of nowhere with unpredictable weather patterns. Things could only go up from this point. "Ditto."

She stifled a yawn. "I'm sorry I fell asleep."

He stroked her cheek, wanting to give comfort as much as he needed to take it. "I'm glad you did. I wanted you to."

"But you're concussed." She captured his hand, cradling it, and kissing his knuckles, once, twice. "I should be making sure *you* don't fall asleep."

"I've dozed off more than a few times and woken up just fine."

She sat up farther and leaned close, carefully pulling off

his hat and wincing as she examined his head. "That looks so sore, Collin."

He snatched his hat from her and put it back on, then replaced his glove he'd taken off. "Don't think you're cleaning it again."

She smiled. "I was thinking of an ice pack instead. It might help with the swelling."

He didn't want her touching his injury at all. Period. When she'd rubbed antiseptic on the gash, it had hurt like a motherfucker, even while she'd assured him she was being gentle. "Let me catch a half-hour first."

"You should sleep longer, but I'll wake you every hour." She lifted his arm, bringing his wrist close to her face, checking the time. "I'll wake you at seven forty-five, then again at eight forty-five, and so on."

He unzipped the backpack and pulled out one of the high-calorie energy bars in the survival bag they'd taken from the plane. He ripped open the packaging and broke the bar in half, giving Lyla her portion. "We'll have to be careful with our food until we see what's what."

"I thought they would've found us by now. It's been a long time."

"They'll come. The weather sucked in Anchorage, and there was a system moving toward Fairbanks before we lost our instruments." He polished off his bite and stood, ignoring the wave of dizziness as he set a couple more large pieces of dead tree and dry bark on the flames.

Lyla adjusted herself on their blankets, leaning her back against the tree he'd just abandoned. "You can rest on me." She patted her thighs.

Right about now he could fall asleep with a rock for his pillow, but he took her up on her offer as he settled himself on the emergency blanket they'd put beneath them and covered himself with the second she used as well. "Thanks."

"You're welcome."

"If you get cold, wake me up."

"I'll be fine."

"Getting cold out here is a death sentence, Lyla."

"I'll wake you." She gently pressed his head to her legs. "Sleep."

He rested his head again and closed his eyes. The fire popping and crackling was the last sound he heard before he surrendered to oblivion.

———◆———

Lyla's ankle ached as she walked as fast as the terrain and her makeshift snowshoes Collin had fashioned out of tree branches and shoelaces would allow. For the most part, his creations were doing the trick, but occasionally her foot sank into the powdery depths.

They'd been hiking for hours, taking advantage of the short window of daylight the Alaskan winter offered, but the cabin she'd spotted from the plane was nowhere to be seen. She'd tried ignoring the occasional trickles of panic while they waited for the sound of an airplane or helicopter to fly overhead or to see smoke rising from a chimney, but so far there was nothing.

She glanced toward the sky as the dismal gray clouds continued to thicken and threaten snow. Collin had assured her they were going to be okay. He knew what he was doing, but how long could they survive in these harsh temperatures? They had rations, and water surrounded them if they simply melted the snow, but eventually they would run out of food no matter how careful they were. And she was worried about him. His head looked awful—deep purple, raw and bloody: nasty. The goose egg had to be excruciatingly painful.

"How are your hands and feet? Are you staying warm?" he asked as he kept pace in front of her.

"I'm fine." She was exhausted. The stress and fear of the last few days was catching up with her, but she'd been tired before. "How's your head?"

"I'm trying not to think about it."

"Maybe we should get you another dose of medication."

"I'm fine."

"Okay." She stumbled a bit in an uneven spot and winced as her ankle protested the jarring movement. "I'm surprised we haven't found the cabin yet. I guess I didn't realize it would be so far away," she said, trying to make conversation in the quiet.

"It's around here somewhere."

When they stopped for a quick handful of nuts a while ago, Collin had estimated that they'd logged a good ten to twelve miles. Between what they walked last night and today, they had to be close to their destination...unless they weren't headed in the right direction at all. "Do you think—could we have gotten turned around somehow? The crash—"

"We were going a couple hundred miles an hour. It's around here somewhere," he snapped, stopping and turning to face her.

She blinked, surprised by his tone.

Tense moments passed in silence as he stared at her and huffed out a long breath. "I'm sorry."

She shook her head. "No. I'm sorry. I shouldn't be questioning you."

"You're fine. My head's throbbing like a son of a bitch. I'm feeling a little nasty."

Sympathy flooded her, and she stepped closer, placing her hand on his arm. If he was admitting his pain, it was probably close to unbearable. "Of course you are." She took off her glove, surprised by how quickly her hand grew chilly, and opened the bag, rifling through the packages until she found the ibuprofen among the other over-the-counter options. "Let's get you some of this."

"We should keep going. I don't want to spend another night outside if we can help it."

She handed him the capsules.

He popped them in his mouth and swallowed them dry.

"Thanks."

"When we get settled, we're going to try some ice. It's not lost on me that you weaseled your way out of an ice pack earlier."

"I'm sorry." He pulled her against him—as far as the bent branches of their snowshoes allowed—and tugged the protective barrier of the scarf, covering half of her face down past her lips, pressing his to hers.

She gave him a small smile. "I'll—"

"Hold up." He put his hand on her shoulder. "Do you hear that?"

She narrowed her eyes, listening as the distant drone of an engine moved closer. "A plane?"

He frowned. "No. A snowmobile." He took her hand. "Come on."

They moved toward the noise, quickening their pace.

"Hurry."

They walked as fast as their shoes would allow.

"Hey! Hey!" Collin left her behind, running in an odd gait, waving his arms as he ran through the trees. "Hey!"

The snowmobile slowed.

Collin continued waving, until the man dressed in thick furs stopped.

Lyla hurried over, standing next to Collin.

"What are you folks doing all the way out here?"

"Our plane crashed last night." He pulled off his hat, exposing the nasty bump. "Probably a good twenty miles east of here."

The guy grimaced as he stared at Collin's head.

"We saw a cabin from the sky. Does that belong to you?"

"You must be talking about Mikey's old place. You'll be glad I found you before you made it there. Old Mikey died a couple years back. His son stays on out there occasionally—mostly when he's hunting, but the place is pretty much empty and has been falling apart for a good while now."

Lyla's stomach sank. Now what?

"I'm bringing in the catch from my lines." He gestured to the dead animals in the cart attached to the back of his snowmobile. "My family and I live about thirty-five, forty miles south of here if you'd like to hop in the sled and come along."

"We appreciate it." Collin held out his hand to the stranger. "Collin Michaels. This is Lyla."

"Collin, Lyla, I'm Sam Ritter." He got off his snowmobile. "Let's clear a spot for you."

Lyla couldn't take her eyes off of the animal carcasses frozen stiff as Sam moved them around. "Go ahead and sit down."

Collin sat first and made a spot between his thighs for Lyla.

She settled in, covering them with their emergency blanket, trying to avoid contact with the staring, lifeless bunny.

"Warm up with this." Sam poured something hot into a cup. "Drink up quick or it'll freeze on you."

Lyla sniffed the steaming coffee. She didn't like coffee. The taste was too bitter, but today she took a deep sip. "Mmm. Thank you." She passed the cup carefully to Collin, and he drank, groaning. "Have the rest," she encouraged.

"You need more."

She shook her head, eager to get them to shelter. Collin was in rough shape. He needed to rest.

"Are you ready, folks?"

Lyla nodded. "Yes. Thank you."

Sam gunned the engine, and they were off through the wilderness, surrounded by at least a dozen dead animals as the sky opened up and the snow started falling.

The single-engine plane flew low in the snow and wind while Ayub peered through his binoculars, keeping his eyes open for signs of wreckage.

"The last transmission was here," Yunus said in Chechen from the backseat. "They disappeared from radar at these coordinates."

"Then maybe they're close. Keep looking," he responded in their native language, never taking his eyes off the tree-filled terrain.

"We should head back, or we're going to need a rescue mission for our rescue mission," said Gus, their scruffy, Alaskan pilot.

"Soon," Ayub assured, reverting back to English.

"Seriously, buddy, the weather's due to get worse—and this is bad enough."

"Keep going."

"Can't do that, I'm afraid." Gus tipped the wing left and circled wide, reversing the plane's direction toward Nome. "Last thing I want to do is crash and pull planes away from the rescue attempt going on for those two boys over on Denali. We'll head back out and search for your friends tomorrow if the weather clears."

"Take care of this, Yunus!"

Yunus pulled the gun from his coat and pressed it to Gus's temple. "Turn around and fly like you've been told."

"Shit. Shit. Shit." Gus's complexion paled as he immediately righted the plane in the direction Ayub demanded.

"My friends are very important to me, certainly worth your life."

"I, uh, I imagine your friends might have gone east from here. They would've wanted to stay away from the mountains if their instruments failed."

"Take us east then."

Gus nodded. "I'd feel a lot easier if you would put that gun away."

"Put it away, Yunus. We'll only use it if our pilot forgets how to listen."

"I can—I can hear you just fine."

Minutes turned into an hour as they circled, doubled

back, and ultimately kept moving in the only direction that made sense.

"There! The plane is there!" Ayub pointed to the mangled red and white mess that had once been Sergei Ploeski's plane. "Land us now."

"Nome Station, this is seven-four-three-seven-alpha," Gus said into his headset, calling the flight station.

Ayub whipped his head around. "What are you *doing*?"

"Calling in a mayday. We've found the—"

"No."

"If there are survivors—"

"We will help them. Just land."

"There's nowhere *to* land."

"Be creative."

"Go ahead, seven-four-three-seven-alpha," Nome Station called back.

Ayub gestured for Yunus to pull the gun again.

"Uh, I need...a weather update, Nome Station."

"Heavy snow accumulation—twelve to eighteen inches, low visibility, high winds."

"Roger that, Nome Station." Gus wiped his sweaty brow with his arm. "Let's see what there is up ahead of us." They continued on as the winds yanked at the wings, and eventually they passed a small spot mostly clear of the trees. "I can try there, but it's risky."

Ayub needed to see if she was alive. He'd waited a year for her—since her last visit to Russia. Twelve months of surveillance, of watching her every move, of planning the exact moment of when she was supposed to have been his. And now she might be dead. His lifelong dreams, his promise to his father potentially ruined. "Try."

Gus sighed. "Here goes." He took them down in a sharp decent.

Ayub swore as he smacked his head on the side panel as they bumped about from the rough landing. "Wait for us here." Ayub took the gun from Yunus. "If you return to Nome without us, my group will find you."

Gus nodded. "I'll wait, but we have to go soon or we'll be no better off than your friends."

"We know how to be quick." He jumped down to the ground with the pair of snowshoes they'd brought along and fastened them to his boots as Yunus did the same to his own. "Let's go."

They moved as fast as the blowing snow would allow, backtracking the two miles to the site of the wreckage. Ayub studied the mess hanging oddly in the trees—the broken left wing in pieces on the ground, along with several engine parts, half covered by the snow. It was hard to imagine anyone surviving the landing. "This doesn't look good." He took off the snowshoes. "Help me up." He stood on Yunus's shoulders, using the trees around him to lift himself into the cockpit, and stared at Sergei Ploeski and Ava Utkin, dead and frozen in their seats. But the princess was gone. "Fuck! Move so I can jump down." He gestured for Yunus to step to the side below him and paused when he spotted the smears of blood on the pilot-side seat and doorframe. The bodyguard, also a pilot, was hurt. He jumped down into the snow. "She's alive. And the man is injured. They can't be far."

"What should we do?"

"Find her." Ayub secured his snowshoes in place again. "Is that not why we came?" As soon as the newspapers began spreading rumors that Princess Lyla and her love took flight with Sergei to Alaska, he'd started paying attention. When news broke that Sergei's plane never landed in Anchorage and more than likely crashed, he made arrangements to cross into the United States.

"Russia is frantic for their princess. Even Roman Akolov is praying she and her prince are found safely. Imagine what The Kremlin will do to get her back once they know who has her."

"If they don't bend to your desires?"

"Then millions will be outraged when they watch Mina's beloved daughter die on TV. The president isn't stupid enough to let this happen. His position is too fragile with his people." And Ayub could only thank Chechen Freedom, his rebel rival, for their efforts to destabilize the region with the Saint Petersburg and Perm bombings. For once they'd done something right, and he'd jumped in at the most opportune moment to finish what his family started long, long ago. "Chechnya will be ours again—once and for all."

The wind gusted, blowing a plume of snow in their faces.

"Tomorrow we will come back," Yunus assured.

He shook his head. "No. Today. We must get to them before anyone else has a chance."

"Ayub, the snow falls harder with every minute." Yunus held out his hand as fat flakes fell on his glove.

"We *need* her, dammit. You know the stakes."

"And we'll have her when the weather clears."

Ayub looked back at the smashed remains of the plane and turned in a circle, trying to figure the path the princess and her bodyguard must have taken, but the wind had blown away any trail they left. "Fine. Tomorrow." They started back toward Gus's plane. Several minutes later, they settled into the warmth of their seats.

"Your friends?"

"Are dead."

"I'm sorry."

"Yes. It's a terrible loss."

"I'll call it in—call off the search and rescue."

"No, you will shut your mouth."

Gus frowned as he looked from Ayub to Yunus and back. "Who are you guys?"

"Your friend or enemy, which is up to you."

Gus nodded. "Let's see if we can get out of here." He started the plane and bumped ahead on the skis, lifting off seconds before they made contact with the trees. "Jesus Almighty that was too close."

"Circle around the area."

"Mister, I need to head back."

"Yunus, the gun."

"You can shoot me and we'll crash. We can fly around in this weather and we'll crash. Either way I'm dead just the same—and so are you."

"Circle once, then go."

They made a large circle over the wreckage site in the worsening conditions. Ayub swore his frustration when he saw nothing but trees and blankets of white. The flight back was bumpy, but he paid little attention, planning out tomorrow's mission. "How far could someone walk in this terrain in a day?"

"Ten, maybe fifteen miles."

"With injuries?"

"Half that, I suspect. The snow would make it difficult as well."

"You will say we searched the area and nothing was found."

"I don't understand—"

"You only need to do what I say. Tomorrow you will bring us back."

"If the weather cooperates."

Ayub let his finger brush the trigger in his lap as he watched Gus's eyes slide his way. "You'll say nothing about any of this, or you and your family will be missing your heads. That little boy who hugged you before we left, he must be your son?"

"I know how to do as I'm told."

"Good."

"Seven-four-three-seven-alpha, this is Nome Station. Any luck out there?"

Gus swallowed. "No. Negative, Nome Tower. I'm seeing nothing but trees and snow. My perimeter has been thoroughly searched and is clear."

"We're calling off the search for today due to the weather. Start back, seven-four-three-seven-alpha."

"Roger. We're—I'm on my way." Gus looked at Ayub.

"There's a drop about twenty miles outside of Nome. They have snowmobiles people can rent for hunting. They have cabins stocked with fuel to keep the engines full. It would take a couple days to get back out here, but it can be done easier than in a plane."

"Then drop us off today."

Gus adjusted his course slightly. "We'll head that way now."

"And you'll still say nothing, because I will be back to make sure your mouth stayed closed. If it didn't, my promise to you and your family won't change."

❧ CHAPTER TWENTY-FIVE ❧

THE SNOWMOBILE, OR SNOW MACHINE AS SAM CALLED it, slowed as they pulled up in front of a small, two-story log cabin lit up in the dark. Collin looked around, studying the four outbuildings scattered around the property, all within a short walking distance to the main house. He spotted a woodshed and a chicken coop, he was almost certain, but he couldn't be sure about the other two structures. His gaze whipped left and he blinked his surprise when several dogs stepped from their houses and began barking and howling their greetings.

"Oh my goodness. *Look* at all of them." Lyla smiled up at him as she still leaned against his chest. "Are they Huskies?"

"I'm not sure." He narrowed his eyes, trying to make out the breed, but it was impossible to see as the wind whipped large snowflakes around.

Their rescuer had come along at just the right time. The snow had picked up considerably, and the daylight faded fast after Sam pulled away with them in the back of his sled. The last ninety minutes had passed in an agony of jostles and bumps, but Lyla was going to have a roof over her head tonight, which made every nasty knock to his battered body worth it.

Sam killed the engine, got off the machine, and made a noise with his tongue, signaling the dogs quiet. "Let's get you folks inside. I'll introduce you to my family." Sam offered a hand to Lyla.

"Thank you." She stood and offered hers to Collin.

He gained his feet and grit his teeth as his blood pressure changed and his pulse throbbed in his head. "Thanks."

Lyla scooped up their bag.

"I'll get that." Collin snagged it and discreetly pulled the gun from the waistband of his ski pants. He shoved the weapon deep among their clothes before he shouldered the straps and took Lyla's hand, following Sam up the steps. They entered a mudroom where various coats and snow pants hung on hooks.

"The Arctic entryway." Sam gestured to the space they were standing in as he began taking off his snow-covered furs. Little by little, Sasquatch Sam disappeared, and a well-built, handsome black-haired man wearing Carhartts over white long johns appeared. "That's a touch better. Go ahead and follow my lead. You can get out of your things here— keeps the snow and worst of the cold from getting inside. Just make sure the outside door is closed before you open the interior. "

"Sure." He and Lyla pulled off their gloves, hats, coats, and the rest of their winter layers until they stood in their blue jeans, long-sleeve shirts, and socks.

"Come on in." Sam opened the door to a surprisingly large yet cozy, rustic open-concept room decorated with maroon furniture and navy blue accents.

They stepped into the blessed warmth and homey scents of a meal cooking on the woodstove as a pretty, raven-haired woman glanced over her shoulder, stirring something in a pot. Four kids—two boys and two girls—stopped playing their board game on the rug in the middle of the pinewood floor and stared up at them.

Collin smiled. "Hey."

"Leah, I found a couple of friends along the way."

"So I see." Leah smiled her welcome and grimaced as her

gaze wandered to Collin's wound. "Your head looks rough."

"It feels pretty rough." He stepped forward, holding out his hand. "Collin Michaels. This is Lyla."

Lyla smiled. "Hello."

"These are our children," Sam said as he gestured to the kids who all strongly resembled their father. "Nickolas here is our oldest. He's eleven. Then we have Gabriel, who's nine. Ellie's just about to turn eight. And my little Maisey's a great big four."

Lyla sent them a friendly wave.

"They're a bit on the shy side," Leah said. "It's not often we have visitors—maybe once or twice a year."

"We were headed to Anchorage," Collin explained, "Our plane lost its instrument panel, and we went down."

Leah gasped, pressing a hand to her chest. "I can't even imagine. We didn't hear about your crash on the radio—power's been off more than it's been on today. I've been try-ing to conserve the generator."

Collin slid his hands in his pockets. "We're just glad Sam drove by when he did."

"This has been a tough winter so far." Leah set a large cov-ered pot on the table as she spoke. "The news report I heard last night was talking about a search and rescue going bad over on Denali. A group of hikers got themselves stuck. A plane and chopper went down trying to get to them. Now rescuers are trying to get to the one pilot that's alive as well as the hikers. Getting to others in need right now is a struggle. They've been using private pilots to answer distress calls."

"Sounds like a mess."

"It is. We're just about to eat—split pea soup, some ham Sam traded for on his last jaunt over to the ocean a couple weeks ago, and hot fresh bread."

"That sounds amazing."

Leah smiled. "I'm not sure the children always agree—at least about the soup. Go ahead and settle in."

"We certainly don't want to be any trouble," Lyla said as

she smiled at the kids still gawking at them.

"Don't be silly. We'll add a couple of bowls and plates. Ellie, give me a hand please," Leah said to the oldest of the two girls.

"I'd like to help." Lyla stepped over, grabbing the two extra glasses Leah handed her to bring to the table.

"Collin, I'm putting you right here next to your lovely wife." Leah brought over silverware as her daughter put down the bowls and plates.

"Oh, we're not married," Lyla said as she took the extra napkins Ellie handed her.

"We're dating." He wanted to keep up that part of the story whether it was necessary or not. He caught Lyla's look before she gave her attention to her task.

"Why don't we all sit down to dinner?" Leah invited.

He took his seat, squeezing in next to Lyla on the bench, studying the pot of vegetable-laden soup, huge hunks of ham, and sliced golden bread in the center of the table. "This looks so good."

"We're so thankful," Lyla said as she winked at Maisey, who kept peeking at her from under her lashes.

"Eat a good meal and be comfortable." Leah offered Lyla first dibs at the ladle.

Portions were plated, and Collin was satisfied to see that Lyla had been generous with her own, even taking some of the meat she typically wrinkled her nose at. Salad and poached shrimp weren't going to be offerings out here. He dipped a chunk of bread into his soup and sampled it. "Wow."

Lyla made a sound in her throat and nodded her agreement as she chewed a mouthful of her own.

Collin took another bite of the amazing soup, trying to remember his manners when he easily could have tipped the bowl back and drained every drop. "This is really good stuff, Leah."

"I'm glad you like it."

"Love it." He cut into the tender ham. "So, we didn't see

much in the way of civilization on our ride here. How far are we to the nearest town?"

"About two hundred miles. Buckland's the closest spot," Sam said.

Lyla paused with the spoon at her mouth. "Two hundred miles?"

Sam grinned. "City folks. You won't see anyone around here for another couple weeks—until Fletcher brings in supplies on the plane—and that's if the weather behaves, which it doesn't sound like it's going to. Last report said we've got quite a line of storms blowing in."

"A couple weeks?" Lyla set down her spoon as she looked at Collin.

"At least," Sam confirmed, as if his news was no big deal. "We're a good couple hundred miles from the ocean, but we're high in elevation. The combination usually hits us pretty hard. It's difficult to get planes in here during the winter months when the clouds hang low for days."

"I didn't realize... I don't know..." Lyla looked at Collin again; the distress in her eyes was unmistakable.

"We're certainly not about to toss you out in the snow," Sam reassured with a chuckle.

Collin rubbed a comforting hand along her arm as his gaze trailed around the room and stopped on the radio unit hanging on the wall by the desk tucked in the corner. He wasn't exactly sure how he was going to get ahold of Chase with a radio, but he needed to try. "I'm hoping you might be able to help me get in touch with my friend in Anchorage so I can let him know we're okay."

"Internet's acting up—haven't had it for days," Sam said as he buttered his slice of bread

Collin raised his eyebrow as the surprises kept coming. "You have internet out here?"

"Depends on the day—satellite connection for our laptop." He gestured to the desk Collin was just looking at. "We have more luck in the summer, but you're welcome to try; although, I'm not sure you'll get through with all of the cloud cover. We might be stuck calling in a bushline."

"A bushline?"

Sam nodded. "We call a message into the radio station and they'll broadcast it out three times a day."

"Huh." He wanted to avoid that if at all possible. The internet was a better option—more secure than calling out over an open broadcast system. "I'll give the computer a shot first. Hopefully we can get someone in here to get us out of your way." Collin polished off his ham and snagged the piece off of Lyla's plate with a stab of his fork, recognizing that she was finishing up.

"You're more than welcome to try. As I said, I don't think you'll be going anywhere for a few days. It's not uncommon for Mother Nature to give us a good wallop this time of year."

Collin nodded, but he didn't like Sam's thoughts on their current situation. He wanted Lyla tucked away somewhere different than this. She needed some semblance of her life back. "We'll have to play it by ear."

"You try and get ahold of your friend. If that doesn't work, I'll contact mine and see if he thinks he'll be able to drop our supplies sooner. He could take you into Anchorage."

"That would be amazing."

"We can certainly get you squared away for the time being. We have a small loft above my workshop. Leah's family usually comes in for a week in the summer, so we have an extra bed you're welcome to."

"We'll take you up on it."

"But we wouldn't feel right about not compensating you for your trouble," Lyla added.

"I'll never turn down a working hand. There's a lot to do out here."

"Whatever you need," Collin assured as he set his fork down. "Have you always lived here?"

Sam and Leah smiled at each other. "For about ten years now. We were city folks too once upon a time, but we both had a pension for the outdoors. When Nikolas was one, we took a trip to Fairbanks and fell in love. I quit my practice, Leah gave up teaching, and we bought the land and had our home built."

"So you're a physician?" Lyla asked.

"No. I'm a retired attorney."

"You must live off the land then?" Collin continued his study of the simple home that had a fairly up-to-date feel despite the isolation from the rest of the world.

"We have chickens, and the boys and I hunt and fish. There's a lake we frequent about ten miles east of here. I'm also a trapper—sell extra meat when I can, and the furs. I also work with wood when time allows."

"Work with wood?" Lyla asked, then nibbled another piece of bread.

"I carve pieces that are sold in several gift shops."

She swallowed. "That sounds fascinating."

"Leah has a hand with knitting, and we make soaps that sell real well too."

Lyla's eyes brightened. "Knitting is one of my favorite hobbies."

Collin glanced at her, remembering her handing Charlie a hat for his friend in the alleyway, but he didn't realize the prima ballerina had made it herself. "Lyla's also one heck of a cook."

Lyla wiped her mouth. "I'd really like to be able to help out however I can."

"We'll see what's what when we're all up and fresh in the morning." Leah set her napkin in the center of her plate. "I imagine you must be exhausted."

Lyla stood as Leah did. "Let me help you pick up."

"Nonsense." Leah brushed her offer away. "The children clear the table."

"I can help wash the dishes."

"If you'd like."

"I would."

"Nikolas and Gabriel, why don't you gather some fire-wood and get Lyla and Collin's room set up for them?" Sam suggested.

"Sure." Nikolas and Gabriel stood, and the oldest of the two boys gained his tiptoes to grab a shotgun from the tall rack close to the door before the brothers headed out into the Arctic entryway.

Lyla's eyes widened slightly before she schooled her features and smiled politely at the adults in the room.

"Kids learn early how to protect themselves around here," Sam said with a smile. "Keeps them from becoming bear food."

"Oh." Lyla sent Collin an uneasy glance as she stacked their dishes when the girls started gathering dirty items from the table.

He touched her hand and stood. "I'm going to try the internet."

"Good luck to you," Sam said with a cautious smile.

He moved over to the laptop and opened the lid as he sat down, waiting and watching the internet trying to connect. "Looks like I might have a shot."

"How about that. You just never can tell."

He typed in the website, waited for what felt like an eternity, and was directed to log-in. He entered the username to his dummy account only he, Ethan, and Chase knew existed—in case shit went wrong overseas and he and Chase somehow got separated.

Hey man,
Crash-landed but I know you already know that. Instrument failure and a twitchy co-pilot made for a rough impact.

He sent his message off, knowing Chase would reply immediately. He wasn't disappointed when the computer alerted him to a new e-mail in his inbox.

Glad you're okay. You scared fifty years off of everyone's life. We're all in agreement you owe us a beer.

He smiled and started typing.

I'll happily toss one back as soon as you get us the hell out of here. We're staying at a cabin: coordinates are sketchy at this point, but I'll get you an estimated location as soon as I can. Unfortunately, we had two casualties. Sergei and Ava didn't survive the landing.

He hit "submit" and ignored the rush of guilt as he shared the news.

Sorry to hear about Ava and Sergei. You know we'll do whatever we can to get them back to Russia.

I wish it had ended differently, he typed then clicked over to another screen, searching for a map, trying to nail down a decent approximation of where in the hell they were. Seconds turned into minutes while he waited for the image to load. "Come on, dammit," he muttered, growing impatient with the slow, shitty connection. Finally, the image appeared and he located Buckland, but he wasn't sure where to go from there. "Sam, could you help me out with this? I'm not exactly sure where we're at."

"Sure can." Sam stuffed a log in the woodstove, secured the door, and walked over.

"I'm trying to pinpoint us on a map."

Sam pointed to a spot nestled among the mountain ranges that was truly in the absolute middle of nowhere.

"Thanks."

"No problem." Sam went back to his business as Collin sent off the information.

Got it but be prepared to stay put at least until tomorrow.

Weather's bad; visibility sucks here in Anchorage. Several private planes were looking for you today before they were called back in. Now that we know you're safe, we'll get you out when we can. At this point, the Department of State wants to keep this quiet while we wait for more information on the chatter going on overseas.

Whatever you guys think is best. We're good to sit tight here.

We'll charter someone in to get you as soon as the weather clears.

I don't see us going anywhere for a while. Let my dad know we're okay.

Will do.

I'll check back with you tomorrow. He sent his reply and waited for Chase's response, then realized his connection was gone. He closed the laptop and turned back to the noise of a family tidying up after a meal.

"I'm glad you were able to get through. I'll show you and Lyla to your room if you're ready."

Lyla was safe, his belly was full, and Chase knew they were fine. Now that he could relax, he was more than ready for bed. "That would be great."

"I imagine the fire will be roaring by now." Sam led them toward the Arctic entrance. "Let me show you, folks."

"Good night. Thank you again, Leah. Dinner was wonderful." He held out his hand to Lyla.

"You're welcome."

"I hope you'll put me to work in the morning." Lyla waved to the shy little girls with her free hand.

"There's always something to do."

He and Lyla put on their jackets and boots and grabbed

the rest of their stuff before following Sam through the cold to the building closest to the house.

The dogs roused themselves again, wagging their tails and barking.

"That's a lot of dogs."

"Alaskan Huskies. We mush more than we use the snow machine. Dogs don't break down, but engines certainly do."

They stepped into the garage-sized space that smelled of wood. Collin caught subtle hints of stain and polyurethane as they climbed the stairs to the charming, lantern-lit spot with a full-size bed and woodstove. The room was chilly still, yet cozy—a solid three hundred feet of living space.

"The woodstove should have you warm in no time."

"Thank you." He shook Sam's hand again.

"You're welcome. Get some rest. Can I get you something for your head?"

"We have some ibuprofen."

"See you in the morning then. Boys, we should get to feeding the dogs, and I need to put the snow machine away."

The kids nodded but still didn't speak.

"Good night," Lyla called as Sam and the kids left.

Collin watched Lyla eye the bed as she stood by the woodstove, warming her hands. "I can take the floor."

She frowned as she looked at him. "Absolutely not."

He set their bag in the corner. "The offer's on the table."

"We'll make this work just fine." She took off her jacket, then her hat, stuffing it in her sleeve. "The bed's plenty big enough for the both of us—just like it was in Asha."

He tossed his jacket to the floor then pulled off his shirt, ready to be comfortable and get a better look at his arm in the light.

Lyla gasped and hurried over. "Oh my God." She snagged him by the wrist and led him to the old-fashioned quilt on their freshly made bed. "Collin, this looks awful." She ran her fingers over the dark welt covering the majority of his left shoulder, bicep, and tricep.

"I'm in better shape than my other two passengers."

Sympathy filled her eyes as she met his gaze. "What happened last night wasn't your fault."

He stood, stepping away from her touch, and walked to the woodstove, not ready to forgive himself as easily as Lyla was. "It certainly feels that way." He shoved his hand through his hair. "A pilot is responsible for everyone on board." He sighed as he faced her again. "If he would have just let me fly the damn *plane*."

She stood, closing the distance between them. "It's not your fault," she said quietly and kissed his cheek. "You were doing everything right. You were trying to keep everyone calm and get us on the ground safely. Sergei caused our accident."

"That doesn't mean I don't wish it could be different."

"Of course you do. We both do."

"I don't know what I'm going to do about their families, how that's going to be handled. I kidnapped—"

"No." She shook her head vehemently as she took his hands, gripping his fingers. "No, you didn't. Sergei and Ava offered to take us to Anchorage. We sought them out in Asha and they gave us a hand. They died heroes—helping a friend in a terrible situation, paying the ultimate price to see that she made it home safely."

He clenched his jaw, blowing out a long breath, not sure he could live with the lie. "Lyla—"

"Heroes." She pressed her palms to his cheeks, holding his gaze, her eyes intense. "I'll make sure everyone knows they were heroes. I'll sit down with Roman the moment all of this is over and tell him of Ava and Sergei's selflessness."

He swallowed, touched by her desire to protect him.

"You've risked so much for me, put too much on the line. I wouldn't be able to live with myself if you faced consequences you didn't deserve because you were helping me. They would be alive if he would have let you fly." She kissed his cheek again. "Sergei and Ava are dead because of Sergei.

You saved me Collin. *You* saved me." She hugged him, resting her head on his chest.

Sighing, he returned her embrace.

"I'll be forever grateful for all that you've done."

"Thanks."

"No, thank you." She gave him a squeeze and stepped away. "You need to rest and heal. Why don't you settle into the long johns I found for you? I'll make you an ice pack, and we'll get you tucked in and comfortable."

He took her hand, playing with her fingers. "Are you taking care of me, Ly-Ly?"

"Haven't you been taking care of me?"

He moved his head from side to side. "*Touché.*"

"It's you and me against the world, right?"

"It is." He tugged her close again and kissed her.

She moved out of his embrace, sending him a small smile. "I'll go get something for your head and arm."

He nodded, watching her put on her jacket and hat and grab plastic bags from their supplies. They had yet to straighten things out after their misunderstanding that seemed like it happened eons ago, but they needed to regardless. "Stay close to the house."

"I don't plan to do much more than step outside the door," Lyla called behind her as she went downstairs.

He sighed again and rifled through the bag, looking for Sergei's clothes, eager to crawl into bed.

———◈———

Lyla opened the workshop door to a hearty gust of wind. She gasped as she lost her grip on the handle and reached out, catching the heavy wood by the doorknob before it slammed against the exterior logs. She looked up to the sky, at the fat snowflakes steadily falling—hardly a nasty winter storm, but Sam and Leah surely knew more about the Alaska weather than she did.

She glanced toward the sweet little cabin only a short distance away as the wind blew strongly again. Hurrying with her chore, she grabbed handfuls of snow and secured them within the plastic bags she'd saved from the emergency kit. An animal howled somewhere in the distance, and the dogs stirred in their houses. Her eyes slid left then right toward the desolate dark beyond the homestead, and she shuddered, finding their mountain surroundings suddenly creepy. She closed herself inside again and hurried up the stairs toward the warmth, comforted by the idea of Collin waiting for her.

She faltered on the last step and stopped, staring at him pulling back the covers on the bed, wearing the long-john bottoms she'd suggested he change into. She swallowed, trailing her gaze down his body, studying him in the lantern light. She'd seen him without his shirt on several times. His broad shoulders and powerful, muscular build were certainly worth a second and third glance, but she'd never seen him in snug pants that left *nothing* to the imagination. Clearly Collin was well-endowed... everywhere. Clearing her throat, she met his gaze as he turned his head. "I, uh, I have ice." She held up the bags, keeping her eyes above his neckline as she took the last step into their temporary bedroom. "Or snow, anyway."

"Great." He sat down. "I really appreciate it."

She took off her hat and jacket again in the now-toasty space and sat next to him. "Let's get you settled." She nudged him toward the pillows.

He refused to lay back. "Go ahead and get changed. You'll feel better for it, I promise."

She nodded and stood. "Okay."

"I won't peek." He looked toward the wall.

She glanced his way several times as she took off her jeans, pulled on her black yoga pants, and freed herself from her bra, then tugged on one of the white long-sleeve shirts that had once been Ava's. "I'm all set."

He turned and looked her up and down, far less concerned about concealing his appraisal than she'd been. "That looks much more comfortable."

"It is." She tucked her hair behind her ear and sat next to him, focusing on the ice packs and his injuries instead of his sexy body. This wasn't high school, after all. She wasn't a foolish teenager drooling over her crush. She grabbed one of the washcloths folded on top of the guest towels that had been left out for each of them. "You'll want this on your arm so we don't add frostbite to your list of booboos."

He grinned. "Booboos?"

She rolled her eyes at herself as she shook her head. "I don't know where that came from."

"We can call this a booboo if you want." He gestured to his arm.

She smiled, feeling herself blush. "One of the little girls at the YMCA calls her cuts and bruises 'booboos.'"

"It's catchy."

She nodded. "If you're four."

He chuckled. "You're pretty cute when you're embarrassed."

Her cheeks burned impossibly hotter. "Just hold this." She settled the ice on his arm, placing his hand over top to keep it where it belonged, and gently pressed one of the bags to his head.

He groaned, closing his eyes.

"Feel good?"

"Yeah."

"Good."

He opened his eyes, looking into hers. "I'm sorry for snapping at you this afternoon."

She shook her head. "You were in pain—are in pain, and you apologized right away. I'm sorry there's nothing more I can do for you than put snow in a bag."

He let the bagful of snow fall to the blankets and gripped her chin, pulling her face closer and capturing her lips. He kissed her tenderly, drawing out the sweet moment with a gentle glide of his tongue against hers.

She savored the moment, as she had in Spaso House then again at the Bolshoi Theater, before she remembered Collin's comments to his ex. They'd both agreed to talk the situation through, and he'd promised her that he had every intention of getting in her way, but that was before her life changed. She placed a hand on his shoulder and eased back, worried by how easy it was to get lost in Collin and forget that ultimately she was always better off alone. "I don't know how to do this," she confessed in a whisper. "I don't know that I want to."

He stroked her cheek. "I know things have been terrible for you." He kissed her again, chastely. "But when you're ready, I want us to figure this out." He gestured to the both of them.

"We're probably going home tomorrow." She thought of the big snowflakes and nasty whips of wind. "Or at least the day after."

He shook his head. "The Department of State isn't one hundred percent ready to say you're in the clear. We'll have to stay somewhere for a couple of days and make sure you're safe before you get to go back to your life. And I'm coming with you for a while even then. I told your dad I would."

"And when you go home to Los Angeles?"

"I can't think about California. All I want to think about is you."

She looked down. He was so good with words. Collin knew exactly what to say to weaken her resolve. "I have to focus on my career," she reminded herself and him.

He kissed her knuckles. "Let's go to bed."

She nodded.

He lay back against his pillow and made a spot for her next to him in the small bed.

She turned out the lantern on the antique chest close by and blinked, slightly unsettled. "I guess this is true country dark."

"We've seen that a few times lately."

"At least last night we had a fire so we could see *something*."

"We can leave the lantern on."

"No." Holding out her hand, she crawled closer to him, being careful not to hurt him, and lay down.

He hooked his arm around her and nuzzled his chin against the back of her neck. "Mmm. Now this right here is perfect. Night, Ly-Ly."

She hesitated then let her hand rest on his arm. They had held hands as they fell asleep next to each other in Asha, but she'd never spent the night wrapped up in a man before. "Night."

‹ Chapter Twenty-six ›

L YLA DIPPED ANOTHER DISH IN THE HOT, SOAPY WATER she'd heated on the woodstove after dinner and scrubbed another plate. She twisted on the faucet and rinsed the pretty country crockery in the icy cold water pumping into the house from a well somewhere on the property, then handed it off to Leah to dry.

"Thank you again for such a delicious meal." Leah set the dish on the clean stack. "It's certainly a treat to have someone else cook for a change, especially when it tastes so good."

Lyla smiled. "I'm glad you enjoyed my humble fish."

"*Humble*?" Leah chuckled as she shook her head. "I don't think the kids will ever be happy with my version of fish sticks again."

She'd made battered cod, garlic-herb potatoes, and roasted up a bunch of the broccoli she'd found on her trek to the huge root cellar beneath the house. Sam and Leah had a small grocery store only a few steps away—shelves full of vegetables and other perishables they'd harvested in the fall for the long winter months. "I can share the recipe." She handed off a bowl. "But I imagine they like your version just fine."

"Sam would never forgive me if I didn't write it down." Lyla grinned.

"And the hat you worked up today is *adorable*," Leah went

on as she put the silverware away in the drawer.

"You like it?"

"Sweetie, I *love* it."

"Good." Leah had reluctantly handed over a skein of yarn and two knitting needles when Lyla offered to help with the inventory the family sold in the gift shops scattered throughout Alaska. Lyla hadn't missed Leah's occasional glance her way as Lyla sat by the window, watching the snow blow about while the mother of four taught her children the day's math lesson. "It's one of my favorite patterns, and it's so easy."

"I hope you're willing to share that too." Leah gave her a gentle bump with her shoulder.

"Definitely."

"So you cook like a dream and knit like a woman with sixty years' experience."

Lyla chuckled and dunked a pot in the water. "I think I'm a ninety-year-old in disguise."

Leah laughed. "You're the best looking geriatric I've ever seen."

"I love to knit when I have the time—even when I don't. Sometimes I stay up later than I should so I can get my fix. I make tons of stuff that I could never use—hats, mittens, scarves—so I donate them to the homeless shelter a few blocks from my apartment."

"You said you're in Manhattan?"

"Yes."

"What do you do? I feel bad that I'm just getting a chance to really talk with you—ask you about yourself. With the laundry today and the children's schooling..."

"Leah, you have your hands full."

"More than I don't," Leah agreed. "So tell me about you."

"I'm a dancer."

"Oh, an instructor?"

"No." She rinsed the final dish. "I'm a ballerina. I dance for Manhattan Ballet."

Leah's eyes went huge. "Wow. That's impressive."

She shrugged. "It's a job." And one she didn't want to talk about. She'd loved her day today—knitting and helping Leah with the kids. There had been no rehearsals or unrelenting demands. She hadn't missed her physiotherapy sessions or the manic pressure to constantly improve her techniques. Instead, she'd cherished cozy chatter over board games at the kitchen table—a pastime she'd missed out on as a child.

"I thought I heard Collin tell Sam that he lives in Los Angeles."

"He does."

"So how did you meet?"

"I was walking back to my apartment after rehearsals one night, and we bumped into each other on the sidewalk. We kind of took things from there." She blinked, realizing she was smiling and her heart was beating faster from the memory.

Leah pressed her hand to her chest. "I love a good love story."

But she and Collin weren't in love. She had no idea what they were. "How did you meet Sam?"

"On a hiking trip. A few of my girlfriends and I went up to the mountains for a weekend and set up tents a few yards from Sam and his buddies. We got married a week later." She chuckled, rolling her eyes. "Everyone told us that it would never last, that we were complete idiots—and I imagine we were, but we've been together ever since."

"That's so sweet." And she envied her new friend. Love at first sight did exist. Magical things did happen when you found the right person.

"I guess you just never know, but somehow I think you do."

She made a sound in her throat as she wiped down the small counter space, afraid that she would never know what Leah spoke of. She couldn't deny that she had feelings for Collin or that something she'd never experienced before was going on between the two of them, but where would they end up when all of this was said and done? Her longest relationship had been a month—and that was years ago. She wasn't cut out for the complications that came along with dating. She didn't know how to let herself be vulnerable. It was so much easier to keep everyone at arm's length—to make friends instead of lovers.

"You must have been dancing in Russia?"

"Huh?" She shook her head, lost in her thoughts. "I'm sorry?"

"At lunch Collin said you were on your way back from Russia before your crash."

"Yes. We were visiting family. My father just passed away."

Sympathy filled Leah's eyes as she touched Lyla's shoulder. "I'm so sorry."

She tucked her hair behind her ear, hoping for the rush of grief she still didn't feel. "Thank you."

Sam, Nickolas, and Gabriel walked inside with their cheeks rosy from the temperatures outside.

"The weather's growing mighty nasty." Sam blew on his hands as he moved to stand by the woodstove. "Feeding the dogs was a real chore tonight. Lyla, Collin wanted me to tell you he's up in the loft."

"I should head over." She hung the dishcloth over the knob for drying.

"There's no rush," Leah assured.

She wanted to check on Collin's injuries. He'd spent much of the day outside with Sam, giving him a hand. They saw each other briefly at lunch, but otherwise they'd done what they could to help the family in their own ways. "I want to make sure Collin ices his head before we go to sleep."

"Men." Leah sighed. "Such a stubborn breed."

Lyla smiled as she picked up the matching skein of yarn she'd used today. "If you want, I can take this with me and make something else."

"You certainly don't have to."

"I would love to, actually. I think I could happily knit for days."

"Be my guest. Maybe a scarf to go along with the hat?"

She nodded, eager to get started. "I'll see if I can finish it up tonight." She moved toward the door.

"Lyla. Wait." Maisey hurried down the ladder from upstairs.

Lyla crouched down as the doe-eyed girl stared up at her. "What can I do for you, Ms. Maisey?"

"You're a ballerina."

She took the little girl's hands. "I am."

"Maybe you could teach me and Ellie to be ballerinas too."

She glanced up, noting Ellie peeking down from upstairs. She was older than the peanut of a girl standing before her and much more timid. "I would love to teach you both."

Maisey beamed.

"Tomorrow we could try if that's okay with your mommy and daddy."

Maisey looked at her parents.

"After you're finished with your lessons and chores, I don't see why not." Leah sat down with a steaming cup of tea.

Maisey bounced up and down. "I'm going to be a ballerina." She hugged Lyla. "I'll see you tomorrow."

She hugged her back. "Good night." She glanced up to the loft. "Good night, Ellie."

"Good night."

She grabbed her tools for the evening. "Goodnight, everyone."

"Should I walk you over, Lyla?" Sam asked.

"No. Thank you, though."

"Hold on to the rope as you head across. It'll guide you along."

"Okay." She hurried into her coat, hat, mittens, and boots and stepped out into the blizzard-like conditions. The cold took her breath away, and she gripped tight to the rope she'd watched Collin hammer into place earlier this morning before the snow started pouring down like rain. Her heart pounded as her gaze whipped around in the dark, realizing how easy it would be to get lost if she strayed too far. Looking up, she walked toward the blur of light shining through the loft window, and opened the workshop door, closing out the storm and breathing in the scent of wood and Collin as she ran up the stairs. "It's awful out there."

"It's rough," he agreed as he poured a huge bucket of steaming water into a tub piled high with snow.

"What are you doing?"

"Sam helped me bring this in. I thought cleaning up would be nice." He poured in the next bucket then picked up his dirty shirt from the floor and used it to toss the hot rocks into the large basin as well. "It's been a few days since we've had a chance to scrub."

A huge gust of wind battered the small structure. "A bath would feel great on such a cold night."

"Should we take one?"

She held his gaze. "Uh—"

"Your own bath, Lyla. I'm not asking you to share with me."

"Of course you're not." She cleared her throat as she tugged off her gloves and hat.

He grinned. "I was going to take our quilt off the bed and put it on the rope here." He pointed to the long twine of white strung high across the room. "You'll have some privacy."

She pulled off her jacket, cursing herself a fool. "You should go ahead."

"Nah, you go first. I'm pretty gross after today."

"Thank you."

She grabbed the guest towels and washcloths then her bathroom supplies she'd brought with her to the Bolshoi, as Collin settled the blanket in place. "I'll be quick."

"Take your time. I'll go down and get another bucket of snow and put it on to heat. We'll keep the water nice and warm."

"Okay." She undressed and settled herself in the tub that was almost big enough for her to lie back in, but she huddled in the center instead as goose bumps covered her body. The water was warm but only came up to her stomach, leaving her cold.

The door closed downstairs, and a gust of wind followed Collin up the stairs.

"Holy crap," she muttered, trying to sink herself into the heat of the water, finding her attempts at submersion unsuccessful. Instead, she cupped her hands into small bowls and began pouring water over her body, intending to make her bath quick. Cleaning up certainly wasn't going to be the relaxing, leisurely event she'd started to envision.

"Cover up for a second, Ly-Ly."

She pressed her arm to her breasts as Collin stepped behind the curtain to put the heaping bucket on the stove.

He stepped back out, keeping his eyes averted like a perfect gentlemen.

She leaned forward and dunked her head, taking the time to shampoo and condition, then washed quickly, wanting Collin to have his turn. She stood, drying herself off, and put on the clothes she wore to bed last night. As she pulled the shirt over her head, she caught the scent of Collin on her clothes. She'd slept in his arms all night. Would he pull her close again after his bath? She stepped from behind the makeshift partition, staring at Collin still dressed in his jeans and long-sleeve shirt as he lay on the bed with his arms folded behind his head and his eyes closed. "I'm finished."

He opened his eyes and looked at her as he sat up. "Feeling better?"

"Mmm. It's always nice to be clean."

"I'm looking forward to it myself." He stood, walking past her, and disappeared behind the curtain. Water splashed as Collin poured in the fresh pail of melted snow. "Damn, it's cold."

She grinned. "The water's nice, but not the temperature

outside the tub."

"A warning wouldn't have sucked."

She chuckled as she settled herself under the covers and got busy on the scarf Leah wanted her to knit. "Sometimes it's better to find out stuff like that for yourself."

"Damn. I can't believe they live without a shower—without a damn toilet inside the house."

"Creature comforts." The wind howled beyond the walls and she sighed, content to be cozy in her bed while Collin bathed close by.

"I'm a big fan of being comfortable." Collin stepped from behind the curtain with his hair wet and his beard still in place, wearing his long-john bottoms. She preferred him clean-shaven, but with the temperatures outside and the amount of time he spent in them, she couldn't blame him for letting it grow.

"Do you feel better?"

"I like being clean."

She studied his arm and head that still looked awful. "I should get you some ice," she said, pulling back the covers to stand.

"No. I'm fine. Stay in bed."

"You still have to be sore."

"I am, but I took some ibuprofen before you came in."

"Okay." She focused on her project again as he pulled the quilt down from the rope and tucked it back in place on their bed.

The mattress jostled as he crawled to his side and settled beneath the blankets, letting loose a groan. "Man, this is the place to *be*."

She smiled. "I agree."

He rolled, facing her. "So, how was today? I didn't see you much."

"Good. The kids are sweet—not so shy anymore—and Leah's really nice."

"Dinner was incredible."

"I'm glad you liked it." She met his gaze and quickly looked back at her knitting. There was something in his eyes as he stared at her that unsettled and excited her all at the same time. "How did your arm do with all of the chores?"

"It's a little achy, but it'll be fine." He rubbed at it as he spoke.

"No word from Chase today?"

"No. Hopefully the internet will be up and running tomorrow."

She settled more comfortably against her pillow as their easy flow of conversation relaxed her. "I told Leah I'm a dancer with Manhattan Ballet."

"Okay."

"It didn't seem like it made too much of a difference all the way out here... Since you guys aren't sure if I'm safe yet."

"I think you're fine. You were a target in Russia, but I think you're good here. Taking you away for a few days is more precautionary than anything else."

She nodded. "I told her that we were visiting family and that my father passed away."

He bent his arm on the mattress and rested his head in his palm. "All right."

Seconds passed in silence.

He settled a hand over hers as she created the next stitch. "What's up, Lyla?"

She shrugged. "Leah said she was sorry about my father."

"I'm sure she is."

She nodded.

He reached up and tugged gently on her chin until her eyes met his. "What's bugging you?"

"Why don't *I* feel sorry? Why don't I feel *anything*—grief, emptiness, loss? I feel nothing, absolutely nothing but this huge void." She set the needles down with a frustrated huff. "What kind of person feels nothing after their parent's death?"

"You've been through a lot. You just need time to process

everything."

She pulled away from his grip, growing impatient with herself as Collin tried to rationalize. "He died in a fiery explosion. Horrible men blew up his car, and I saw the whole thing."

"I'm not a psychologist, but it seems logical that you're in shock—you know, distancing yourself from your emotions. You saw something most people never see—should never see. That was your father, Lyla."

She shook her head. "What if I'm cold—devoid of normal human emotion?" More than one person had told her so.

"You're not cold, Lyla. You're sweet and caring. You take care of homeless men and old ladies with too many cats."

She made her lips curve, unappeased by Collin's theories on her as a person.

"Maybe you're unhappy."

She frowned. "I'm not unhappy. I'm not anything. That's the problem."

"If you could have anything or be anything, what would you choose?"

She shook her head, baffled by his question. No one had ever asked her that—not even herself. She'd always been expected to be exactly what she was. "I have no idea."

"Would you dance?"

"Yes," she said, hesitating. "Of course," she added with more conviction. "Of course I would."

He narrowed his eyes as he pursed his lips. "Were you convincing me or yourself?"

She yanked the blankets back and stood, wondering the same thing. Why did he have to see her so clearly? "I should get this dirty water out of here."

"It's too cold right now. I'll take care of it in the morning."

Too restless to be still, she wandered to the window, staring at her own reflection as the deep, dark night threw her unhappy expression back at her.

The mattress squeaked when Collin got up and stood behind her. "You don't like it when I make observations."

She shrugged. "It doesn't bother me."

"Yes, it does." He turned her, giving her little choice but to look him in the eye. "You don't always have to say what you think is the right thing. You don't have to try to make me happy. If you don't like what I'm saying, you can tell me to kiss your ass."

"Okay, kiss my ass." She tried to skirt around him.

"Hey." He snagged her arm. "I'm not going anywhere. I have no intentions of walking away because we disagree."

"Your reassurances are unnecessary."

"Are you sure?"

She glared as her temper started heating up. "Is this some sort of free therapy, Collin? I thought we established that you don't hold a psychology degree."

"I'm backing you into a corner."

"No. You're annoying me."

"Then I won't stop now."

She scoffed and walked away from him in the small space, not looking forward to listening to whatever it was he felt he needed to say.

"I think you're repressed, that you're afraid to disappoint or go after what you really want, because you want to give everyone else what you think they need."

She whirled, more than finished with this conversation—especially when he hit the mark so perfectly. "I don't see a plaque on the wall. And where's your shrink's chair?"

He smiled, playing with the tips of her hair. "Anger's a perfectly healthy emotion."

She swatted his hands away. "I'm feeling pretty healthy then."

"There's nothing wrong with taking what you want, what you need. It doesn't make you a bad person."

"Your opinions are duly noted. Now I'm going to sleep." She turned to the bed and yanked the covers farther back.

"Ly-Ly—"

"You don't know me that well." She turned, pointing her finger at him. "You barely know me at all."

"I certainly know you better than you like." He stepped closer to her.

She stepped back. "You like to think you do."

"You don't like people in your space—in your bubble." He moved until she had no room of her own.

"So? There's nothing wrong with that."

"Not usually—unless someone wants in. I want in, Lyla."

"What if I don't want you? Maybe I don't want *you*."

"Yes, you do. I can see it." He slid his fingers down her cheek.

"No." She shook her head adamantly, bothered by the lack of conviction in her voice.

"Take what you want, Ly-Ly."

She swallowed as her breath came unsteady and fast, as his meaning became perfectly clear.

"Take what you want," he encouraged again.

She lifted her hand, eager to touch him, and dropped it.

Holding her gaze, he grabbed her by the wrist and pressed her palm to his quickening heartbeat. "Take it," he whispered.

Tired of fighting, she stood on her tiptoes and pressed a quick kiss to his lips.

"Is that all you want?"

"No."

He traced his fingers up her neck, pausing on her hammering pulse. "So take more."

She rose up on her tiptoes again, touching his waist and pulling her hands away.

He settled them back against his warm skin, staring, waiting.

She pressed her lips to his, surrendering as he cupped her cheeks. She sagged against him, no longer interested in denying herself, only in taking what she wanted for the first time in her life. Unsure of what to do, she trailed her hands up his back.

He groaned, letting his own hands slip beneath her shirt. "I want to touch you, Ly-Ly. I want to take what I want."

She nodded, trying not to stiffen up, and sighed her pleasure when he palmed her breasts, brushing his thumbs over her nipples.

He tugged on her ear with his teeth, then kissed her neck as his hands continued to bring her pleasure. "Is this okay?"

She'd never been touched like this. "Yes."

He pulled her shirt over her head and looked his fill as he continued tracing her skin. "I want to take you to bed."

Her breathing became increasingly unsteady as she gripped his hips.

"Let me take you to bed, Lyla."

"Yes."

He walked her back, laying her on the mattress, instantly bringing his mouth to her breasts.

She whimpered, curling her fingers in his hair and arching as flutters of sensation grew to life in her belly.

"Are you on the pill?" he asked as he worked his way down her body, kissing her stomach and tracing her belly button with his tongue.

"No." She moaned as goose bumps puckered her skin, relishing the delicious sensations Collin made her feel so easily.

"I don't have any condoms. Are you comfortable with me pulling out?"

"Mmhm."

He nipped at her hips as he peeled off her pants, taking her panties with them.

She swallowed, stiffening, feeling completely exposed as he stared at her.

He frowned. "What's wrong?"

She shook her head. "Nothing."

"Ly-Ly—"

"Nothing." She held out her hands out to him.

"If you don't want to—"

"I do."

"We don't have to."

"Yes, we do." She took his hand and placed it back on her stomach.

He stroked her skin and her muscles quivered. Their gazes stayed locked as he pulled off his long johns.

She swallowed as she stared at him, huge and fully aroused.

"Lyla, why are you looking at me like you've never done this before?"

She sat up and covered her face as her first experience was quickly turning into a disaster. "Because I haven't."

"You're a virgin?"

She made a V with her fingers, peeking at him, noting his eyes huge with surprise. Her cheeks burned hot as she covered her breasts with her arm and reached over the bed for her shirt.

He caught her by the elbow. "I thought you said you've been in a relationship before."

"I was for a few weeks. When I wouldn't give it up, he stopped calling." She grabbed her shirt and pulled it over her head, drowning in the wretched waves of humiliation. "Let's just go to bed."

"No. Wait a minute. I had no idea."

"Now you do." She tugged up the covers and lay on her side, still pantiless. As soon as the light went out, she would put those on too, but right now she just wanted for him to stop looking at her. "Good night."

"Uh-uh. You're not about to turn over and let this one go."

"I just did."

"There's nothing to be embarrassed about. I just didn't know."

She still refused to look at him. "I'm almost twenty-five, and I've never had sex."

"So?"

She scoffed out a laugh, as close to tears as she'd been in

years. "Good night, Collin."

He got under the blankets and pulled on her arm until she faced him. "Something like that's worth mentioning. I could've hurt you." He kissed the top of her head.

She closed her eyes. "I just wanted you to see me like you would any other woman."

"You're not any other woman." He slid the hair back from her temple. "If we're going to do this, I want to be gentle."

Her eyes flew open. "You still want to?"

"Only if you do. Only if you trust me. Your virginity's a one-shot deal."

She swallowed. "I'm nervous, but I do want you. I guess I've wondered how it could be—how you would be."

"So we'll take our time."

She nodded.

"Are you sure?"

She nodded again.

He grabbed a towel off the floor, then kissed her, keeping the pace gentle as he brought his palm back beneath her shirt. "Can we take this off?"

"Yes."

He lifted her shirt off as he had before and traced his tongue around her nipples.

She snagged her lip as she moaned.

He slid his hand down, touching her.

She tensed.

"Relax," he whispered, stroking her gently. "If I do anything that hurts or makes you uncomfortable, just tell me."

So far everything he'd done felt amazing. "Okay."

He touched her again, tracing and sliding the pads of his fingers over her, until her breathing grew faster, until the butterflies battled in her stomach again.

"Does that feel good?"

"Yes."

"I want to put my fingers inside you."

She nodded. "Okay."

He dipped his fingers in and groaned as she gasped. "You're so wet, Ly-Ly."

Her breath came in harsh trembles as he swept his fingers, as if he motioned for her to come here. She realized her hips moved with his movements. "Collin—"

"Let yourself relax."

She strained, reaching for what had to be an orgasm, and clutched at the sheets as she called out to him.

He kissed her neck and chin, then her mouth, swallowing her moans.

Her eyes fluttered open, looking into the intensity in his. "I don't know what I'm supposed to do."

"Enjoy the way it feels. You can touch me too." He took her hand and gripped it around him. He closed his eyes and clenched his jaw as she moved her palm.

"Am I doing it right?"

"Yeah." His breath came fast as he touched her again, sliding his fingers in small circles that had her orgasming for the second time. "I want you to be wet." He settled himself between her legs as he kissed her. "Are you sure, Ly-Ly?"

She nodded, ready for the rest, eager for what he would show her next. "Yes."

He inched his way inside, stopping to kiss her as he slowly pushed himself farther.

She whimpered as his girth filled her.

He tucked her hair behind her ear, staring into her eyes as he lay perfectly still. "Are you okay?"

"Yes. I think you're big, though."

He smiled. "I think you're perfect." He kissed her again, deeply, sweetly. "Let me show you the rest."

She nodded again.

He began to move, and she waited for the pain, but there was only the glory of him sliding back and forth inside of her.

She fisted her hands against his hips as his slow, deep thrusts brought the butterflies back, and her breathing came faster.

"Are you going to come?" he panted out.

"I—I think so."

He grit his teeth and curled his fingers in her hair while he kept his pace steady.

The rush of heat came, flooding her, and she gasped, stiffening as she called out.

He kissed her knuckles and clasped her hand. "Lyla, I'm going to come." He yanked the towel up, dragging it onto her stomach.

"Okay."

He pulled out and took her hand, curling it around him, groaning long and loud as she finished him off. His breath came in ragged pants as he bundled up his mess, tossed it to the floor, and let himself rest on top of her again.

She smiled.

"I was going to ask you if you're okay."

Her smile turned into a grin. "I feel pretty okay."

"I didn't hurt you?"

"It hurt a little at first, but only for a couple of seconds."

He kissed her. "I'm sorry it hurt at all."

"Thank you for being so kind and gentle with me."

He didn't answer, just kissed her before he reached over, twisted off the lantern, and snuggled himself close, much the way he had last night. "Good night, Ly-Ly."

"Good night."

A strong gust of wind slammed against the work shed, rattling the windows and waking Collin. He opened his eyes in the darkness, breathing in Lyla's shampoo as he held her close. He lifted his arm and glanced at his watch—seven a.m.—but it easily could have been midnight in the pitch-black Alaskan winter.

He pulled Lyla closer as she slept deeply, enjoying the feel of her warm, naked body fitting snuggly against his, and nuzzled his face into the crook of her neck the way he liked best. She was so soft, so beautiful, and she'd given him her virginity.

He and Janine Henderson had been each other's firsts, groping and fumbling their way through the entire experience one hot July night when he'd been sixteen, but being with Lyla had been entirely different. She'd taken him by surprise when he realized she'd never been touched before, and he debated for about thirty seconds whether he wanted the responsibility of taking something she'd waited so long to give. But when he'd stared into her humiliated eyes, he knew that he wanted nothing more than to be her first partner, to show her how it could be. Lyla deserved gentleness; she deserved someone taking care of her for a change, and he'd tried his best to do just that.

He slid his hand down her side, knowing they had to get up. Their new subsistence lifestyle started early. Leah and Sam would be expecting their help sooner rather than later. "Ly-Ly," he whispered against her skin.

She moaned her protest as she nestled her head farther into her pillow.

"We need to get up."

"I'm on vacation," she mumbled.

His eyebrows shot up. They had very different ideas of what constituted a vacation. Snow up to his thighs and working his ass off for twelve hours a day was a long way from umbrella drinks and white sandy beaches. "Well, it's time to get out of bed." He gave her butt a playful swat.

She gasped and quickly turned, facing him, not that they could see much of each other. "You just spanked me."

"I'd say tapped." He kissed her, eager for her taste and the feel of her lips. "Good morning."

She held him in place a moment longer, touching her mouth to his again. "Good morning."

"How are you feeling today?"

"Good."

"Are you sore?"

She shook her head. "Everything feels pretty normal—maybe even a little better."

He grinned. "I'm glad to hear it." He crawled over her and turned on the lantern when he wanted nothing more than to stay put, but Lyla needed a chance to get used to the way things were. She was skittish at best, and he was in no hurry to push her...yet. He grabbed two pieces of wood from the dwindling pile and tossed them in the woodstove, then turned to look at her.

She sat up and quickly covered her breasts with the sheet.

He frowned. "What are you doing?"

She shrugged. "Thinking about getting dressed."

"You don't have to be shy around me, Ly-Ly. You're beautiful."

She looked down, playing with the edge of the blanket.

He sat next to her, worrying some that she was already building her walls back up. "Are you sure you're okay?"

"Yes."

"You're not having regrets?"

"No." She met his gaze again. "I like being with you. I've just never done anything like this before."

"What?"

"Slept with a man I've only known for three weeks."

"They've been pretty intense weeks."

She nodded. "They have."

"Are you going to let me be with you again?"

"Yes." She sat farther up, clutching the blanket tight against her.

He tugged the cover down, exposing her to him, bothered that she seemed so guarded.

"Collin." She pulled it back up.

He yanked it down for the second time. "I like looking at you." He reached out, caressing her breast, finding satisfaction when her nipple instantly hardened. "I like touching you." He leaned forward and kissed her. "You don't have to be shy."

"You're clearly very comfortable walking around in the nude, but I *am* shy."

"You don't have to be with me. I wish I could explain to you what it is that you do to me." He kissed her knuckles. "I want to touch and taste every inch of you." He nudged her back and found the angle at which they laid brought the blood rushing to his tender forehead. "Let's try something different." He rolled, bringing her with him. "I want to be with you right now."

"Oh."

"Is that okay?"

"Yes."

"Will you ride me?"

"I'm not exactly sure..."

"It's pretty easy. Go ahead and sit up." He adjusted her so she straddled his stomach. "When we're ready, you're going to sit down on me and rock."

She nodded.

"But I want to touch you first." He cupped her breasts, groaning when she arched forward and her cheeks went pink. He tickled her stomach with soft slides of his fingers, watching her muscles jump, then trailed farther down, rubbing her, loving that she was so responsive, so open to his advances whether she realized it or not. He moved his fingers faster and her hips jerked. "Are you going to come?"

"I think so," she gasped.

"Your chest gets blotchy when you're turned on."

"Oh," she said, gasping again while he continued playing her.

"Take me in, Ly-Ly."

She rose up and sat down, moaning.

He clenched his jaw, steaming out his breath as she sunk him into her wet warmth. "God, you feel so good."

She moaned as she rocked, slowly, sinuously, snagging

her lip with her teeth as she closed her eyes. "Like this?"

"Yeah. Open your eyes."

She stared down at him as she moved faster and her breath steamed out.

She was close. He wanted to watch her, fascinated by Lyla lost in pleasure. He grabbed her hips and pumped up.

Her eyes grew wide and she went stiff, gripping his biceps and crying out.

Christ, she was sexy. He pumped faster, harder.

She clutched at his shoulders, crying out louder, frenzied.

He waited as long as he could, shoved himself deeper one last time, and yanked her off of him, groaning as he let himself go in the towel instead of inside of her where he wanted to be.

"Collin," she gasped. "Oh my God, Collin."

He sat up and cupped her face in his hands, kissing her passionately, tenderly. It was easy to be both with Lyla.

She wrapped her arms around him as she took what he offered and gave back just as much.

"Ly-Ly," he murmured against her lips as he slid his fingers through her hair. "You don't have to be shy."

"Okay." She pulled his mouth back to hers. "I know—" she cleared her throat, "I know there are other positions."

He grinned. "All kinds of them."

"Maybe we could try them?"

He nipped at her ear, tempted to lay her back and eat her alive. "I'm looking forward to showing you all kinds of things."

She snagged her lip. "Now?"

He grinned again. "I think Sam and Leah are probably wondering where we are."

She sighed. "You're probably right." She kissed him once more. "Let's go help with breakfast."

CHAPTER TWENTY-SEVEN

LYLA SAT IN THE CHAIR BY THE WINDOW, CLEARING HER throat and pressing her lips firm when she caught herself humming again. She fought a smile as she looped the yarn around the knitting needle and started the next row of stitches on the intricate blanket Leah had asked her to make.

The clouds hung low, almost touching the Ritter's roofline, while the wind howled as if Mother Nature screamed. The power had flickered on and off throughout the day, and helping Leah fight against the elements to bring in a fresh supply of wood had been an aerobic activity, yet she couldn't remember the last time she'd felt so...relaxed.

Just hours ago, she'd officially cashed in her virginity card, easily trusting in Collin to take care and be gentle with her. He was the only lover she'd ever had, the only person to touch her body so intimately, but she had no doubt she'd experienced the very best sex had to offer. She nibbled her lip, remembering the way he'd stroked her skin, and felt the same rush of butterflies he seemed to incite so easily. He was such a big guy—tough and a little rough around the edges, but he had a way with words, and he was always so sweet.

Collin assured her he had a lot more to show her, and she couldn't wait to experience everything he was willing to share, but she wanted to be good for him too. This wasn't his first go-around in the sack, and unfortunately, she was years behind the other women he'd probably taken to bed. There was no doubt she had a lot of catching up to do if she planned to satisfy her lover in the bedroom. Luckily, it seemed they would have plenty of time to practice.

She focused on her current project, pleased with the initial results of the complicated pattern and her contribution to the Ritter's gift-shop inventory. Tonight dinner was her responsibility as well. After a search through the kitchen cupboards this morning with sweet little Maisey by her side, she'd decided on a hearty black-bean soup and homemade focaccia bread.

She sighed her contentment as Leah and the girls' voices melded quietly in the background. Could life really be this ideal? Snow still came down—sporadic flakes instead of the all-out shower of hours before, but the visibility was terrible. As much as she needed to get back to Manhattan and make her father's arrangements, it didn't bother her any that the weather was making their departure impossible. Collin had yet to get ahold of Chase after their initial e-mail the first night they arrived at the cabin, but soon enough someone would come for them, and she would have to deal with her life again.

She glanced out the window when the dogs barked, as Collin and Sam guided the Huskies to their houses from the sled and fed the animals a hot meal after a day of mushing and ice fishing. Nickolas and Gabriel brought a cooler into one of the sheds, and she smiled as she watched Collin speak to one of the dogs and give him a rub behind the ears. He'd been gone for hours...

"Ly-Ly." Maisey poked Lyla's leg.

She blinked and looked at the little girl.

"Will you show us now? Will you show us how to be ballerinas?"

She set down her project and smiled. "You're finished with your lessons for the day?"

She nodded solemnly. "Mmhm."

Lyla looked to Leah for confirmation.

"We're all set. I'm going to head out to the chicken coop and make sure its staying warm enough in there."

"We'll be fine in here." She looked to Ellie, who stood by her mother's side as Leah got to her feet. "Ellie, do you want to join us?"

She stared down at the floor, curling her hair around her finger. "Yes."

"Come on over."

Ellie hesitated, then started their way.

Lyla waited for her reluctant dancer and smiled when Ellie stood by her side. "Okay." She steepled her fingers in her lap. "We have a very important thing we have to do before we can even think about dancing."

"What?" Maisey bounced about. "What is it, Lyla?"

"We have to put your hair in a bun."

Maisey's eyes brightened.

"If you get me a couple of hair ties, I can help you. I brought over some of the bobby pins I used at my last show to share." She patted her jeans pocket. "I'll have you looking like official dancers in no time."

"Okay." Maisey rushed off, climbing the ladder to the second story so quickly that Lyla winced.

"Be careful."

"She's like a monkey," Ellie assured. "I saw a video about them when we were learning about primates, and Maisey definitely climbs just like them."

Lyla smiled. "I guess there's nothing wrong with having a sister who's part wild animal."

Ellie grinned.

Lyla winked, thrilled to see Ellie coming out of her shell. Every day she was slow to warm up, but once she did, she was as chatty as her younger sibling.

Maisey hurried back, handing over two hair ties and a brush. "Here you go."

"Thank you." She smoothed out Maisey's hair and twisted the long ponytail up on the crown of the little girl's head as she'd done a million times to her own. "There." She held Maisey at arm's length and narrowed her eyes. "Yup. Definitely a ballerina." She tapped Maisey's chin as the four-year-old grinned, then turned her attention to Ellie. "Ready?"

"Yes."

She tied Ellie's hair back and secured it with the remaining pins. "I feel like I'm back at work in Manhattan, surrounded by professional dancers."

"Is it a very big place?" Ellie wanted to know.

Lyla nodded. "A *very* big place. There are millions and millions of people who live there."

Both of the girls' eyes widened.

"It can be noisy, but it can be pretty exciting too."

Maisey nodded.

"Should we start?"

"Your hair isn't up," Ellie pointed out.

"You're right." She tied hers back quickly. "Okay. Now that we all look like ballerinas, we need to learn to dance like them. There's a lot to know about ballet, especially when you're beginning. It's not just about posing your hands and twirling around. It's also about the music's mood. You have to be able move your body the way the notes tell you to."

"How do we do that?" Maisey asked.

"When we listen to a song, we have to think about how it makes us feel. Kind of like when you look at someone's face." She pouted. "How do you think I feel when I look like this?"

"Sad," Ellie said.

She scowled. "What about this?"

"Mad," Maisey answered with relish.

She grinned. "And this?"

"Happy," Ellie and Maisey said at the same time.

"See? You knew my moods by looking at my face. I didn't have to tell you how I was feeling, you just knew. When you listen to music, your ears will help you do the same thing. It's called being musical." She chose a classical song on her MP3 player. "Let's move around the way your ears and body think the music is telling you to."

Maisey walked in slow motion, tiptoeing about.

"I like it," Lyla encouraged, noting that Ellie stood still. "Ellie, what do you think the music is telling you to do?"

She shrugged. "I don't know."

"Is it fast?"

She shook her head.

"I think Maisey's on the right track. The notes are telling us to go slow." She did some simple steps and made her way to Ellie, taking her hands and turning with her. "Yes, a lot like this."

She smiled as Ellie started to dance on her own. This is what she loved: helping children fall in love with dancing—the way Carla and Jenette had helped her at the studio close to Grammy's house so long ago, when dancing had been for pleasure, not obligation. She dismissed her negative thoughts, finding her happiness dimming.

"Lovely, girls. You're both so graceful." She selected a different song with a hip-hop beat. "Now what should we do?"

The girls bounced around, laughing.

Lyla took turns taking their hands and doing some of her favorite steps she and Moses had practiced dozens of times. "Let the music talk to you."

"You can dance fast too!" Maisey hollered in her excitement.

"There are all kinds of dances, not only ballet. My friend, Moses, teaches hip-hop. And there's tap." She bopped her head. "Five-six-seven-eight." She moved her feet in a series of shuffles and kick ball-changes she remembered from her early days of dancing. "But my most favorite is ballet." She took pose and lifted her leg high to her side, enjoying the stretch and the movements as familiar to her as breathing. She glanced behind her, doing a double take, realizing Sam and Collin stood in the doorway watching them. She smiled, then gave her attention back to the girls as she selected pia-no music next.

"Okay, now that our muscles are nice and warm, we're going to get ready for some basic positions. Can you point your toes?" She pointed hers in her sock, noting that Ellie had an excellent arch as the girls copied her. "Very nice. Now let's try first position." She showed the girls how they should stand and made small corrections as she took them through the stances up to fifth, glancing Collin's way from time to time as Sam went upstairs and he sat down at the computer. "Excellent. You've worked so hard. Now we need to rest our bodies."

Both of the girls groaned their protest. "We have to stop?" Ellie asked.

"For today, but we can try again tomorrow. We'll get right into positions and add *pliés* and *releves*."

"What's that?"

She showed the girls a basic *plié*, a *grand plié*, and a *releve*. "Now I'm going to wash my hands and start getting dinner ready. The soup and bread will take some time."

"I want to help!" Maisey offered.

"Okay. Give me a minute."

"We'll go change." Ellie started up the ladder before her sister could.

Lyla walked over to Collin as he opened the laptop. She stopped at his side, seeing that he was busy.

He paused, glancing up. "Hey."

"Hi."

He surprised her when he pulled her onto his lap. "How was the dancing?"

"Good." She framed his cheeks in the quiet room and kissed him, trying hard to give him what she'd never given anyone else. "I thought about you today."

"Oh, yeah?"

"Mmhm."

"I thought about you too."

She smiled at the idea. "How was mushing?"

"Incredibly fun. I also caught a huge-ass fish." He held his hands out a good foot. "The kids are out cleaning it in the shed."

"Congratulations." She kissed him again.

He pulled her closer, taking her attempts to be affectionate to another level as he wrapped his arms around her.

She eased back, listening to the girls clamoring around upstairs, knowing they would be down any second. "What are you up to over here?"

"I thought I would try to check in with Chase."

"The clouds are hanging pretty low."

"They are but I'll give it a shot anyway. Sam heard back from his pilot friend over the bushline. He's going to try to fly in sooner with the supplies and get us out of here."

"Oh."

"We're ready, Ly-Ly. We're ready to cook." Maisey hurried back down the ladder.

"Tell me about it later?"

"Sure." He pressed his lips to hers again.

She stood and walked over to where the girls eagerly waited. "Who's ready to make soup and focaccia bread?"

"Me!" they said at the same time.

"Let's get started." She glanced over her shoulder and grinned when she realized Collin was staring at her.

He winked, then gave his attention to the laptop.

She looked toward the window in front of the sink, noting the clouds thickening and the visibility diminishing in the darkening skies, hoping she would have another day or two of this. If she was lucky, Collin would tell her later that Chase or Sam's friend wouldn't be here to get them in the morning.

———◆———

Collin watched Lyla as she and the kids gathered up the

ingredients they would need for tonight's meal. She helped the girls slide two chairs over to the counter to stand on and caught Maisey by the elbow just before she fell backward off the seat.

"Are you all right?"

Maisey nodded.

"You have to be careful, honey. I can't have my assistant bakers getting hurt."

Maisey nodded again. "Okay."

She was as sweet with Ellie and Maisey as she was with homeless men and old neighbor ladies, and it was tempting to join in on the fun and come back to the computer later, but he stayed put, hoping he might be able to get something through to Chase even if the low clouds were making outside communication pretty much impossible.

The children giggled when Lyla touched each of their noses with her floury finger, then helped Maisey stir with the wooden spoon while Ellie added the cupful of water they'd measured out to the bowl. He gripped the edge of the desk, suddenly yearning to stand up and wrap his arms around Lyla. Her hair would be soft against his chin and she would smell good if he leaned close to breathe her in.

Swallowing, he felt himself frowning as he realized he'd never craved Sydney the way he did Lyla. Even during those first few weeks of their relationship, when they hadn't been able to get enough of each other, he'd never ached for her. His once-upon-a-time desire for Sydney paled in comparison to his need for Lyla now. He'd been Lyla's first in the bedroom, but she was constantly showing him new things—who and what he wanted to be.

He tore his gaze from the cute scene in the kitchen when the screen lit up with Google's famous insignia. It was about damn time. He typed the e-mail server into the address bar and waited again, glancing Lyla's way as the group of three began shaping the big blob of dough. He looked down at the laptop and read *Unable to connect to the Internet.* "Son of a bitch."

Lyla's head whipped around. "Little ears," she scolded.

"Sorry." He tried connecting again, waited another eternity, but it was no use. Giving into his need for Lyla, he stood and walked to her as he'd wanted to before and hooked his arms around her waist as he rested his chin against the top of her head and inhaled the scent of her shampoo. "What's going on over here?"

She leaned back against him. "We're making everyone a delicious dinner."

He sniffed the air. "It smells pretty good already."

"It's bread. A different bread we've never had before," Maisey told him.

"I like different bread." He spotted the candies in a jar by the window. "I spy a jar of gumdrops."

"Sometimes we get to have one."

"Huh. Maybe we should have one now."

Maisey smiled.

He leaned farther forward and opened the lid, grabbing a small handful. "One for you." He held it out to Maisey and dropped it in her mouth. "One for you," he offered to Ellie who blushed as she opened up and took one as well. "And one for you." He popped one past Lyla's lips and followed it up with a noisy kiss on her cheek.

"And one for you." Maisey snatched one. "Open up."

He did, growling as she brought it close to his mouth.

She squealed and threw it more than let him take it from her fingers.

"Yuck." He grimaced as he chewed. "This one's black-licorice flavored."

The girls giggled as he shuddered.

"That's some nasty stuff."

They giggled again.

Lyla tipped her head back, looking at him as she smiled.

He smiled back and kissed the top of her head, happy to stay right here for a while and listen to her patiently direct the kids as they moved on to soup preparations.

Ayub tossed the rickety chair back and let it smash to the scarred wood floor as he realized the dilapidated cabin was empty. But it hadn't been. Someone had been here recently. The *Alaska Herald* on top of the paper pile by the rusted woodstove was dated early last week.

"This place belongs to Michael," Yunus said as he walked out of the bedroom, shining a flashlight on some sort of bill.

"Tell me something I don't know. Did we not read the sign that said Mikey's Place on the door?"

"Mikey's not here."

He clenched his jaw as he grew impatient with Yunus and their fruitless search for the princess. "If she is not here, she must be close."

"Maybe Mikey took them for help."

He shook his head. "We would have gotten word that she was found."

"Perhaps she is dead."

He shook his head more adamantly. "She's is *alive*. She must be alive. The man she is with knows how to survive. His military experience makes him a worthy opponent."

Yunus turned and went back into the room.

"Fuck!" He slammed the side of his fist on the ancient table. For two days, they'd searched a tight perimeter around the crash site. Twenty miles had been circled with no luck, but he refused to believe that his plan was falling apart. Capturing Lyla Markovik-Avery was the key to freeing Chechnya.

"Look what I've found." Yunus came back with another yellow-tinged paper.

"This had better be of use this time."

"You will approve."

He yanked it away and shined his light on the area map,

studying the small circles of red pen on various spots in the mountain ranges. "Wagleys, Ritters, Farmingtons, Jacobys, Truesdells." He looked at Yunus. "Should we assume these are Mikey's neighbors?"

"But they are far away."

He shrugged. "Some very far. Others, not so much." He pointed to three of the closer dots as the wind gusted, howling through the cracks in the wood on the battered cabin. "Tonight we will stay here and tomorrow we will start making our visits. Perhaps the Farmingtons or Truesdells or Wagleys know where our princess is. Eventually, Yunus, she will be ours."

CHAPTER TWENTY-EIGHT

LYLA WASHED THE FINAL DISH AS THE BLUEBERRY COB-
bler she'd prepared cooled on the countertop rack.
They wouldn't have ice cream or even whipped cream
to go along with tonight's dessert, but they would make do
without it. Once a week, the children were afforded a special
treat. During lunch this afternoon, Lyla suggested creating
something with some of the wild, frozen blueberries she'd
spotted in the freezer. The entire table had unanimously
voted for blueberry cobbler.

She caught herself humming again and shrugged, carry-
ing on. The cabin smelled of delectable sweets, the blanket
she started making yesterday was coming along beautifully,
and Maisey and Ellie were eagerly awaiting their next afternoon dance class. Snow fell for the fourth day in a row, and
she was perfectly happy... She paused, frowning, as she realized that she was absolutely, perfectly happy.

The typical weight usually settled so heavily on her shoulders was gone. Her chronic, dragging sense of obligation to
others ceased to exist. Her father was dead—had been murdered in a most horrific way—but she was the "truly happy"
he'd wanted her to be when they spoke in the kitchen at Spaso House two days before he died.

She dried off her hands and walked to the living room
window, smiling as she watched Collin handle the dogs. She

pressed a quick hand to her chest, feeling her heart soar. They'd made love several times last night, waking after a couple hours' rest then driving each other crazy again. He'd kissed her this morning, telling her to have a good day before they parted ways after breakfast and he headed off to work—like a typical couple sharing their lives together. She glanced over her shoulder, watching Leah sitting with all four of her children as the day's lesson started winding down, and she knew exactly what she wanted. Today she knew exactly what she planned to have.

Collin headed toward Sam's workshop, and she hurried into the Arctic entrance, shoving her feet into her boots, and rushed out the door. The cold cut through her sweatshirt, and the snow fell in sheets, sneaking down the back of her neck with every step, yet she moved forward, opening the door.

Collin looked behind him, frowning and stopping on the top stair. "Jesus, Lyla, what are you doing outside without your coat?"

She grinned and ran up the stairs. "I know what I want. The other night you asked me, and now I know."

His frown was still there. "Is this some sort of cabin fever thing?"

She flashed him another smile. "No." She took his hand, tugging him into the loft with her. "Come here. Come with me."

He studied her through slightly narrowed eyes. "What?"

"Come on." She gestured with her head, pulling off his hat and unzipping his jacket, then yanked it to the floor as she walked him backward to the bed. "I want to tell you all about it."

"Lyla—"

She shoved him back, and he lost his balance.

He chuckled as he fell to the mattress. "What's gotten into you?"

"I'm not exactly sure, but I feel so *alive*—maybe for the

first time. All of the sudden these feelings...this rush..." How could she describe this newfound liberation? She crawled on top of him, straddling him at the waist.

He gripped her hips. "Lyla, someone could walk in at any minute."

"So they'll leave." She leaned over and kissed him. "I know what I want, Collin."

"Clearly."

She shook her head. "Not just that." She pushed his shirt up.

He placed a halting hand on hers. "I'm gross. Sweaty."

She kissed his stomach anyway. "Salty."

"Gross."

"Perfect." She worked her way up to his neck and went after his lips.

Groaning, he deepened the kiss, then drew her slightly away. "So tell me. What do you want, Ly-Ly?" he asked quietly as he held her gaze.

"What I don't want is to dance—not professionally, anyway." She let loose a small laugh of amazement. "God, do you know how good it feels to *say* that? I've never actually let myself think it, let alone say it out loud."

He smiled at her and laced their fingers.

"I want to teach kids in a studio—my own studio. I want to have a whole classroom full of Maiseys and Ellies."

"You can definitely make that happen."

"I *know*." She laughed again. "And I want to knit and cook and garden and have a house—a home of my own. I want friends that talk about something other than physiotherapy or pointe shoes or how much rehearsal sucked."

"Who doesn't?"

She grinned and slid his shirt over his head, then kissed his neck again. "I don't want to live in my mother's shadow anymore and constantly be measured by her success. It makes me tired. I'm so *tired* of it." She brushed her lips against his chest and stomach, then shimmied her way down, going to work on his belt. "But do you know what I want the most—more than anything?"

His fingers found their way into her hair. "What?"

"You."

"Sounds good." He reared up, wrapping his arms around her. "Sounds perfect."

She kissed his cheek. "I also want a family."

His grip loosened.

"I want the whole white-picket fantasy." She nibbled on his ear. "That's what I want." She nipped his jaw. "Make love with me again, Collin. Right now." She fought with his jeans and unzipped his pants.

"Wait a minute."

She sunk her teeth into his healthy shoulder. "I don't want to wait. I want you so much I think I might explode."

"We can't do this."

"Sure we can." She pushed him back again, unbuttoning her pants as she smiled down at him. "You lay right there and I'll take care of the rest."

He sat up. "Hold up."

She read the intensity in his eyes, not the typical desire she usually saw there, but something entirely different—the exact opposite of desire. Wariness. "What's wrong?"

"Nothing. I just—you caught me a little off guard. That's all."

She swallowed and crawled off of him as her mood plummeted from sheer joy to...uncertainty. "I'm sorry."

He stood as well, zipping his pants and pulling his shirt back on. "You don't have to be sorry."

"I've said something that's upset you."

"I just think you've got a lot going on, maybe you're not thinking things through."

"You're right. I'm not. For the first time in my life I'm not. I'm not overanalyzing and weighing in on what everyone else wants or thinks—how my choices will affect them before I think about how they'll affect me."

"You want a family."

She nodded. "I do."

"Babies are a huge commitment."

"I know."

"They cost a lot of money."

"I have a lot of money."

"Children deserve a stable life."

"I'm a very stable person. When I settle down, I'll have a stable life—no more constant travel."

"There would be two people involved in your equation: you and me."

"There would."

He puffed out a long breath as he shoved his hand through his hair. "This is pretty new, Lyla."

And something he clearly didn't want.

"I want a family, but I want it to be right—not some spur-of-the-moment thing that can't be taken back. I don't want to wake up like my mom and dad did and decide I can't stand my spouse's sight."

She swallowed as she absorbed the quick rush of hurt. "I understand. My wants aren't yours."

"No, they are. It's just... I think we need to slow things down."

"I didn't ask you for a ring, Collin, or for a commitment." She'd only wanted to share her happiness with him, to tell him what was in her heart. She turned and looked out the window as tension filled the room, and she frowned as she spotted Maisey standing outside in her boots and no jacket, hat, or mittens.

"Ly-Ly—"

"I have to go."

"No." He grabbed her wrist. "Wait."

She pulled away from him. "I can't. Maisey's outside without her coat on. She'll freeze." She ran downstairs and hurried into the snow and frigid winter winds. "Maisey, honey, what are you doing out here dressed like this?"

"I was looking for you."

She picked her up, holding her close. "You have to stay inside where it's warm. It's not safe to be outside by yourself. Promise me you won't come outside by yourself again."

Maisey nodded as she played with Lyla's hair.

Lyla kissed her cheek and snuggled her closer, shutting her eyes for a second as the void of emptiness she was so used to replaced the sheer joy she'd felt for such a short time. "Let's go inside."

"Okay."

———◆———

Collin sat at the dining room table, playing a round of Go Fish with the kids while Lyla helped Leah wash the dessert dishes. Once again, dinner had been delicious. The fresh fish from yesterday's catch had been cooked up tender and flaky, the wild rice simmered to perfection, and the cabbage Lyla doctored up with herbs and spices made the nasty vegetable edible. All in all, he couldn't complain: a safe place to hunker down every night, a warm house, and good company. Now if only he could get Lyla to talk to him or even look at him the way she had not even four hours ago.

She wasn't happy with him; they'd certainly hit a snag, but she wasn't bitchy about it. She didn't glare at him or mutter potshots under her breath. Lyla spoke to him politely enough and even smiled, but they were her fake smiles that didn't reach her eyes—the one's that masked her emotions and drove him fucking crazy.

Sydney had been a fan of knock-down-drag-outs, shouting matches that could make a man's ears bleed—and he'd hated it. But Lyla's cautious friendliness was twenty times worse. He clenched his jaw, remembering the way she'd apologized and curved her lips when their elbows bumped during dinner, or the way she'd handed him the tartar sauce he'd asked for and immediately went back to her conversation with Sam instead of letting her fingers linger as they brushed his, the way she typically did.

She grinned at something Leah said, and he wanted her to smile like that at him—like she had in their loft when she kissed him brainless and told him about all of the things she wanted...and spooked the hell out of him in the process. Three and a half weeks ago, he'd sworn himself off women and vowed only to concentrate on himself for a while; now he was sleeping with a sexy ballerina who wanted kids and a lifetime commitment.

Sydney had kept him at arm's length, always putting off the marriage conversation—until they hit the year mark, when she confessed in one of her screaming fits that she had no interest in marrying him or giving him children until he ditched his lame job—the beginning of their ending. Was there no happy medium? Sydney had been willing to wait him out, and Lyla wanted it all right now. But did she really? Not even a week ago, she'd been keeping her distance, reminding him that her career came first and last. Today she wanted a dance studio and a white-picket fence.

Lyla had a lot going on, many unresolved issues to deal with. She had yet to grieve for her father. What if her sudden desires were simply confusion? Her life was a mess, and they were sharing something pretty intense in the bedroom. He was Lyla's first—maybe in many ways. She found him safe to be vulnerable with. But they had to have more than good sex and a few deep conversations to build a life together. He wasn't kidding when he told Lyla he had no intention of ending up like his mother and father.

"Go, Collin," Nikolas said, giving his arm a nudge.

"What?"

"It's your turn," Ellie said, sitting in the chair to his left.

"Right. Sorry. Uh, do you have a goldfish?" he asked Gabriel.

Gabriel shook his head. "Nope. Go fish."

He picked up a card as the kids carried on with the round,

then set down his hand when he noticed the last of the dishes put away and Lyla drying her hands, still deep in conversation with Leah. "I'll be right back."

"Maisey just won, anyway." Nickolas gestured to his little sister.

"Oh." He glanced at her matches sitting on the table and her triumphant grin. "Yeah. Congratulations." He stood and stepped up behind Lyla, wrapping his arms around her waist.

She stiffened.

"Sorry to interrupt," he said, refusing to give her space when her body language clued him in that she wanted nothing more.

"That's okay," Leah said. "I'm going to go get things set up."

"Okay." Lyla turned to face him, breaking their connections and taking a step back.

"Hey," he said, shoving his hands in his pockets.

She crossed her arms, clearly uncomfortably. "Hey."

"I was going to head over to the workshop. Are you coming?"

She shook her head. "Not yet. I promised the kids I would help them make popcorn. Sam's going to set up a movie for them."

"How are they going to watch a movie? The internet's down. Still."

"They have an old TV and VCR. The kids like *Chitty Chitty Bang Bang*."

He raised his eyebrow. "*Chitty Chitty Bang Bang*?"

She shrugged. "That's what they like."

"Isn't that from the sixties?"

"As far as I know."

"We need to talk, Ly-Ly."

She nodded. "After the movie." She skirted around him. "Who's ready for popcorn?"

"Me!" the kids shouted.

Lyla grinned when Sam raised his hand as well. "I'll make

a big batch." She walked away from him, effectively dismissing him in her own subtle "fuck you" sort of way.

He sighed. It looked as though he was in for a wait.

———◆———

Collin leaned against the window frame, crossing his arms at his chest as he stared out the glass from his room above Sam's workshop. Thick clouds covered the moon and snow threatened to fall yet again while the woodstove burned hot, keeping the small space warm. But he was cold nonetheless as he watched Lyla sitting curled beneath a blanket on Sam's favorite chair, knitting away in the dim lantern light despite the fact that it was almost three o'clock in the morning. Clearly Lyla wasn't coming to the loft tonight. She'd assured him she would be right over after she read the girls a quick bedtime story...six hours ago.

He exhaled a long breath, slightly afraid that she was going to keep avoiding him. Lyla was definitely making it clear that she wanted nothing to do with him. During the kids' lame-ass movie, he'd eavesdropped on Lyla and Leah's conversation from the couch while they sat at the kitchen table, munching on popcorn and talking about Lyla tendering her resignation with Manhattan Ballet and renting studio space with Miles. She was moving forward with her plans whether Collin was along for the ride or not.

He clenched his jaw, watching her fingers manipulate the yarn and needles as the impressive blanket she was working on continued to grow in length. She should have looked lonely sitting there on her own, but she didn't—wasn't. He knew for a fact she was happy—not just because she told him so when she tackled him to the bed, but because he could see it for himself. Her father was gone; she'd lost so much, but every time she danced with Ellie and Maisey or worked her magic in the kitchen, her eyes lit up.

She didn't need him. He rubbed at the tension in his

neck, worrying about his revelation. Lyla was a self-made woman. She was completely capable of following through with her dreams on her own. She'd done just that for all but the last few weeks. Maybe her declarations today were due to the fact that she was repressed and confused, or maybe she was truly taking what she wanted for the first time in her life. One thing he knew for sure was Lyla was going to be just fine—with or without him. But would he be just fine without her?

"Goddamn," he muttered, shaking his head, already knowing the answer.

✂ CHAPTER TWENTY-NINE ✂

COLLIN STARED AT THE COMPUTER SCREEN, AS HE DID every morning after breakfast, hoping and waiting for a damn connection to the world beyond the Ritter's homestead. Google loaded with ease, and he blinked. "Huh." He typed the URL for his email server into the address bar and pressed "enter," finding himself cautiously optimistic for the first time since he'd made initial contact with Chase five days ago. Surprisingly, the link opened almost immediately, and he looked to the sky, wondering how. The snow finally stopped, but the wind still gusted with enough power to rattle the windows, and the clouds hung low and thick, much like they had ever since he and Lyla arrived in Alaska. Shrugging, he shook his head, thankful for whatever anomaly made this moment possible. "It's about fucking time," he muttered, and winced, glancing around the busy living room, making sure none of the children heard his cursing.

He clicked open the e-mail from Chase before his connection decided to stop playing nice and swore again as he scanned the message dated early this morning.

...raid went down late last night in Moscow—pretty fierce gunfight... four men killed... several computers and other evidence confiscated... fairly certain deceased are connected to Ayub and the Chechen Freedom Movement... more details to

follow as I get them.

Finally. Some initial progress was being made, which was far more than he thought would ever happen.

Awesome news! Glad to hear it's all starting to come to-gether. We should be heading your way soon—when we get a break in the weather, which could happen the day after to-morrow if the next line of storms stays north of here. Our host has a man flying in supplies. The pilot has agreed to bring us into Anchorage ASAP. Keep me up to date. I'm checking in whenever I can.

Collin sent off his reply and glanced out the window, catching sight of Lyla heading toward the rear of the house. Logging out, he shut the laptop and hurried into the entry-way, shoving his feet into his boots and snagging his jacket on the way out the door. He zipped his coat as he moved along the short path to the chicken coop, eager to catch Lyla alone. He'd bided his time, stalling over his morning meal and cup of coffee. Then he'd waited while checking the sta-tus of Sam's finicky internet, only to hear Lyla tell Leah she would happily go out and grab a few logs for the woodstove and collect the day's supply of eggs—an attempt to avoid him, he knew.

She'd bundled up and walked outside a good fifteen min-utes ago. By now, she had to be finishing up. And he was going to be right there waiting when she did.

He opened the door, slowly, silently, and stepped into the small space, smiling as she talked to the chickens.

"That's the wrong attitude, Gertrude." She yanked her hand away when one of the hens tried to give her a peck. "I'm just trying to do my job." She attempted to reach under the chicken again.

Gertrude gave her jacket a couple of nasty digs with her ugly black beak.

"Gertrude," she said in a warning tone. "Stop that. No one else is giving me these problems." Lyla reached under the irritated hen, clearly in a battle of wills. "Ha!" She triumphantly pulled the brown egg free. "I told you this is how it was going to be. Hopefully we can put this behind us—" She looked over her shoulder and gasped as she did a double take and whirled, stumbling back a step. "Collin." She pressed a hand to her heart. "You scared me half to *death*."

"Sorry."

Lyla let loose a surprised squeal when Gertrude gave her ass a spirited peck.

He bit the inside of his cheek, fighting back a grin. "Chicken problems?"

"Just a hen who woke up on the wrong side of the nest." She eyed the ill-tempered bird.

Damn she looked good enough to eat all bundled up in her winter gear. Her cheeks and the tip of her nose were pink from the cold, accentuating the startling blue of her eyes. And she'd braided her hair in two pigtails. "I thought I should tell you that I got through to Chase."

"Is he coming?"

"No. We'll wait for Sam's buddy. He's flying in from Fairbanks sometime in the next couple of days."

She nodded. "That makes sense."

He shoved his hands in his pockets, expelling a long breath. "So, there was a raid in Moscow last night. Four men were killed—possible terrorists—and a bunch of evidence was confiscated."

"Oh." She dropped the basket she was holding to her side.

"The authorities think they may be connected to your father's murder."

"Oh," she said again as she blinked and stared down at the floor. "I guess I don't—I don't exactly know what to say."

"They're not one-hundred percent certain yet..."

She looked at him. "But they're pretty sure?"

He nodded. "This is definitely a positive sign—a move in

the right direction. The computers should have a lot of good information on them if the men didn't get a chance to destroy anything. Hopefully something will point them toward other members of the cell. If they're lucky, maybe even to their number one."

She frowned. "Their number one?"

"The insurgent's senior leader."

Her brow furrowed deeper. "I thought you said the men were dead."

"There are more. This faction is known for working in small, independent groups of about ten to twelve. It makes sense that a few would have hung back in Moscow—keep an eye on developments, keep their group informed, lay the groundwork for the next attack if that was their plan."

"Do you think the authorities will find them?"

"It's hard to say. We can hope so, but it's really hard to give you a definite yes. The higher ups probably hopped over the border shortly after..." He cleared his throat, not needing to say the rest. "Most likely they're in hiding for now." That was Ayub's MO—destroy people's lives in the name of his causes, then hide out like the pussy he was.

"Thanks for letting me know." She gave him one of her false smiles, far dimmer than the usual wattage she often sent his way, and turned back to the animals. "I need to get this finished up."

Tense silence filled the small space as she carried on with her chore.

"Lyla, I just told you the men who more than likely murdered your dad are dead."

"I know. It's a lot to process. I appreciate you sharing the news."

"If you need to talk about it—"

"I'm fine."

His nostrils flared as she tossed him her typical line. They were back at square one. He stepped up next to her, getting in her way. "Ly-Ly, why are you avoiding me?"

"I'm not."

He raised his eyebrow.

She slid him a guilty glance out of the corner of her eye and cleared her throat. "I'm helping Leah with the children. She rarely gets a break."

"She doesn't need help when the kids are asleep."

"No, she doesn't."

"So why did you crash on the couch?" He stopped her movements with a hand on her arm before she could reach under another hen. "I missed sleeping with you last night."

She pressed her lips together. "I think—I think maybe we made a mistake."

He shook his head. "No, we didn't."

She took a step away from him as their eyes met once again. "I tried to warn you that I'm not good at this stuff. I don't know how to be part of a couple. I'm a much better friend. Let's go back to being friends."

Screw that. "I don't want to be your friend—or not just your friend."

"I've realized a lot of things over the last few days. This is the first time I've ever let myself be happy—or at least since I was a very little girl. I plan on staying this way."

"Good. You deserve to be happy."

"Thank you." She turned, getting back to her work.

"But I want you to be happy with me."

She paused, sighing. "We're looking for different things. I'm changing careers—taking on my own studio."

"You mentioned that, but what does that have to do with whether or not you can be with me?"

"We live in different places, and I'm planning on starting my family in the next six months. I want to be a younger mother."

"You typically need a partner for that."

"No." She grabbed the final egg. "I'm going to look into donor insemination."

His eyes went huge as her words sank in. "*What?*"

"Donor insemination."

"Yeah, I heard you the first time." He jammed a hand through his hair as their conversation took on a whole new life. He couldn't keep up with her. "You want a sperm donor, Lyla? What the hell happened to white-picket fences?"

"Maybe I'm not cut out for white-picket fences. I'm certainly not cut out for relationships. I'm better off on my own—alone. I always have been."

"You and I were doing fine."

"Three and a half weeks isn't exactly a barometer for success, especially when you consider where we're at right now and the issues we had in Russia."

"Lyla—"

She passed the basket back and forth between her hands. "You just got out of a relationship."

"Six months ago."

"But you and Sydney are still involved."

He clenched his jaw in frustration as she brought up his ex's name. "No, we're not."

"It was your kneejerk reaction to tell her that I meant nothing more to you than a job."

He stuffed his hands in his pockets. "I've apologized for that. It was a mistake."

"I'm not trying to pick a fight." She moved the basket faster. "I'm being honest whether you want to hear it or not."

He turned away then back. "This is *bullshit*."

"It isn't. I'm not going to be your mistake—your rebound."

"Whoa." He stepped closer to her. "You are *not* my rebound."

She eased back. "I think I am, and I don't want to play the game."

"I'm not interested in games either. That's Sydney's forte, not mine."

She blinked at him patiently.

His temper went from bubbling to flashpoint. "Damn it, don't look at me like that—all smug, like you just proved a point."

"I'm not going to be *the* person in your life until the next one comes along...or until you and Sydney decide you're going to give things another try."

"We're not."

"Haven't you said that before?"

Son of a bitch, she didn't fight fair with her simple logic and unending calm. "Yeah, but we were trying to hold onto something that wasn't there. I don't—"

"No, Collin. I'm new to a lot of things, a lot of experiences, but I'm not an idiot." She stepped out through the pen door, waiting for him to follow, then closed the animals in and secured the latch. "I need to get back inside."

"Lyla."

She kept walking.

"Lyla, stop." He snagged her wrist, forcing her to turn around. "Stop." He pulled her close and backed her against the wall. "You are *not* a rebound. When I left California a few weeks ago, I was in a pretty rough place. I was a damn mess. All in all, I was downright pathetic. I told myself I was going to concentrate on me for a while, until I got my head screwed on straight—"

"Which makes perfect sense."

"But then you bumped into me on the sidewalk and took my breath away—literally took my breath away." He stroked his knuckles along her cheek. "I found you, and nothing's been the same."

She closed her eyes.

"Will you look at me?"

She opened her eyes.

"You spooked me a little yesterday. I can admit that, but it's not because we're not looking for the same things. We were moving along at a nice pace—building something strong and solid. I wasn't expecting such a big change so quickly."

She swallowed. "It wasn't my intention to—"

"Please don't tell me this is over before we've even had a chance to start. Please."

"I don't know—"

"It's your birthday," he said quietly as he held her gaze and continued sliding his fingers along her skin, needing to touch her.

"It's just another day."

He shook his head, relaxing a little when he recognized the desire in her eyes—the vulnerability she never wanted him to see. "I can't take you out for dinner right now or buy you flowers or do the hundred other things I want to do, but I can bring you with me today."

"Where are you going?"

"Fishing. I told Sam I would take some of the dogs out to the lake and see if we can get some more fresh fish while he rides his trap lines."

She sighed. "I don't think—"

"Please, Ly-Ly. We'll have fun—a date. Your first and hopefully only Alaskan ice-fishing birthday date."

She smiled—a real smile.

He smiled back, wanting to kiss her, but kept his lips to himself. "Please, Ly-Ly."

She sighed again. "Okay."

He grinned his relief. "Let me get the team hooked up and we can go. We'll build a fire—"

"On the *ice*?"

"It's really thick. Trust me. We're going to have a hell of a time. Trust me," he said again. That's what today was about after all, showing her that she could trust him again.

———◊———

Lyla sat in her chair next to Collin as the fire spewed and sparked, raging a few feet behind them despite the latest round of snowfall. She moved her fishing line up and down in the small hole Collin had made with the nasty-looking auger and looked across the frozen, empty miles toward the snow-draped pines, knowing huge mountains towered somewhere beyond, even if they were impossible to see in this weather.

"You feeling anything yet?"

"No." She and Collin had been on the ice for over an hour—and had nothing to show for it. Hopefully something would nibble at her bait so they could enjoy another fresh-fish dinner. "Maybe they're not hungry today."

"They're hungry." Collin leaned forward, using the large spoon he brought with them to clean out the slush forming over the hole.

"You're quite the outdoorsman—musher, master ice fisherman, fire-starter extraordinaire."

He smiled. "Sam's a good teacher."

"You made a fire before you met Sam."

"The Army taught me plenty of survival skills too." He picked up the coffee he'd recently poured from the thermos, sipping at the brew already losing its steam in the bitter temperatures.

"Maybe Alaska's the place for you."

"Uh, no." He held out the cup to her.

Smiling, she shook her head. "You're not a big fan of the snow?"

"Snow's okay. I prefer warm weather—surfing, palm trees."

"What if I said I wanted to live in Alaska?"

He puffed up his cheeks before he blew out a long breath.

She grinned. "I'm just kidding, Collin." Or mostly she was. At this point, she was trying to feel him out. After their conversation in the chicken coop, she didn't know what was going on between them. She'd given their relationship a try, felt about Collin the way she'd never felt about anyone else before, but after her confessions in the loft yesterday and his stunned reaction, she'd forced herself to accept that he didn't want her the way she wanted him.

"Right." He bobbed his line. "What about LA?"

"LA?"

"Yeah. What about setting up shop in Los Angeles?"

"I—I don't know. I've never given it any thought." Maybe it had crossed her mind for the briefest of seconds when things seemed different between them, but then they'd changed so quickly, she'd dismissed the idea before it had a chance to truly bloom.

"You should think about it."

She swallowed as she stared at the hole, focusing on keeping her line moving.

"What?"

She looked at him. "What, what?"

"You're frowning."

She sat up taller in her chair and relaxed her brow. "I didn't realize I was."

"What are you thinking?"

She shook her head. "I don't know."

"Sure you do."

She met his gaze as he stared at her. "I just—I can't keep up with you. I can't figure out what you want."

"I want you."

She sighed quietly. They had different ideas of what "want" meant. He wanted a partner in bed; she wanted more.

"I want *you*, Ly-Ly."

She shook her head. "Let's not talk about this—our relationship or non-relationship... I don't want to be confused today. Let's just fish."

Silence filled the air and she bobbed her line faster.

"Then let's talk about your birthday. How does it feel to be twenty-five?"

She smiled, aware that Collin was trying to clear the awkwardness swirling between them. They'd been doing pretty well with small talk, chatting about things that didn't matter. "Pretty similar to twenty-four."

"If we weren't stuck in Alaska, what would you be doing

to celebrate your big day?"

"Laying flowers on my mother's grave."

He stared at her with sincere shock written all over his face. "Jesus, Lyla. That sucks."

Why did she say that? She also went out for dinner with her dad and had chocolate cake Oksana always made for her. Why was that the first thing that popped out of her mouth? "I've done it for so long..."

"On your *birthday*?" He shook his head. "Jesus," he muttered again.

"Ever since I started visiting Russia regularly."

"I'm sorry."

"I hated it," she confessed quietly, letting her pole sag toward the water. "I hated knowing that each year when we celebrated my life, my father mourned her death. For some reason, I never equated her passing with my life until I was ten. Before I went to school in Russia, I would wake up to chocolate-chip pancakes and my grammy singing to me. My day would be about me—cake and friends and presents. Then I went to Saint Petersburg and Alina told me what Dad and Grammy never had."

"What did she say?"

"The truth—my birth caused my mother's death."

"Lyla—"

"Isn't that what happened?"

"It's probably not that cut and dry."

"The results are still the same."

"Yeah, but—"

"When I turned eleven, my father surprised me and brought me home from school for a long weekend to celebrate at Spaso House. I woke up early the next morning, imagining Oksana preparing pancakes in the kitchen since Grammy couldn't. I hurried down to Dad's room and stopped in the hall. He was staring at my mother's picture in a frame he kept by his bed. That was the first time I ever saw his shoulders slumped and his eyes sad. He didn't look like US Ambassador Jonathan Avery. My mother's death had never hit me hard until that moment. It took eleven years to realize the significance. What kind of person does that make me, Collin?"

"Fourteen years ago it made you a child, a child who never should've been burdened with something that wasn't your fault."

"I'm alive. She's not."

"It sucks that it worked out the way it did, but it's still not your fault."

She stared at their fishing hole as her memories took her back in time. "I still remember thinking that I didn't miss her the way he did. I've always been curious about Mina Markovik. There's always been a sense of loss for not knowing her when so many people adored her, but the emotions I feel for her have never been deep."

"She was gone before you had a chance to develop a bond."

"I've always—I've always wondered why they didn't fight harder to save her instead of me."

"Lyla—"

"She had a life and a husband. They could have made more children..."

"Lyla, look at me."

She couldn't, not while she said all the things she'd never voiced before but needed to. "I knew he was sad and missed her terribly. He talked about her all the time, but never on that day. I went and sat next to him on the bed and I told him I wanted to put flowers on her grave. His eyes watered, and I thought I said the wrong thing, but then he hugged me and I knew it was right."

"For him, but not for you."

"We went every year that I lived in Russia. After, we would go out for dinner and come home to Oksana's delicious chocolate cake. When I was eighteen and started flying over from New York, I made sure I came during my birthday so he wouldn't have to be alone."

Collin sighed. "I'm sorry, Lyla, but that sounds like a pretty shitty birthday."

She shrugged. Somewhere along the way, she'd just accepted it.

"The instructor at the school in Saint Petersburg, she was tough on you."

She shrugged again. "I guess she thought I deserved it. I was the reason why the woman she cherished as a daughter was gone. Russia lost its queen the night I came into the world."

"Ly-Ly."

"Hmm?"

He touched her arm. "Will you look at me?"

She met his gaze.

He pushed his chair closer to hers and took off his glove, skimming his finger down the inch of her exposed cheek. "I don't want you to have any more birthdays like that."

She expelled a long breath and rested her forehead against his chin. "I don't think I want to either."

He set his pole down and wrapped his arms around her. "When we get out of here, we're going to do it up right."

"This is fun."

He shook his head. "Not even close. You deserve so much better than this, than what you've had."

"He loved me."

"He did. A hell of a lot, but he never put you first."

"He did the best he could." Her voice trembled, and she closed her eyes, suddenly terrified by the rush of emotions wanting their freedom—the weight of her pain so huge she locked it deep, into the numbing abyss she always kept at the ready when life became too overwhelming.

"I want to do better." He eased back, tugging on her scarf, finding her lips and pressed them to his tenderly. "I want to show you what it's like to be first."

"I'm afraid," she admitted.

He twisted her braid around his finger. "I know."

"I don't want to talk about birthdays anymore either."

He kissed her again. "I don't either."

"Can we just fish?"

"Yeah."

"Thanks." She smiled and bobbed her line.

Collin stayed close as he scooped another pile of slush away then settled his arm around her.

She leaned against him, resting her head on his shoulder until something nibbled at her hook. Gasping, she sat up straight, gripping the pole tight. "Something—"

"You've got one."

"I don't know what to do."

"Give your line a good tug." He made a yanking motion with his own in demonstration.

She did as he'd just done, feeling the fish resisting.

"Good. Now start reeling in."

She began cranking the reel as the fish on the other end gave her a workout. "He's fighting."

"He's probably realizing he's shit out of luck."

"But—"

"Keep reeling, Lyla."

She twisted the reel again and pulled the floundering fish from the hole. "Look at that. I got one!"

"Yeah, you did. This sucker's huge."

She grinned. "I really got one."

"A real beaut. Probably twelve, maybe fourteen pounds." He grabbed hold of the animal and stuck his fingers in the fish's gills, ripping a small flap of flesh, causing a rush of blood to pool on the snow and instant death.

She winced. "Oh."

"It's fast and humane. We don't want to just let him flop around out here and suffer."

"Of course not." She stared at the mess. "It's not—this isn't exactly like a grocery store."

"Not quite. It's actually better if you ask me. You can't get any fresher than this."

"No, you can't."

"Do you want to keep going?"

"I think it would be hypocritical to say no. I eat fish all the time. I just don't partake in the dirty work."

"Catching your own food helps you appreciate the animal's sacrifice."

She touched the dead animal. "Thank you, fish."

"Do you want to call it a day?"

"Is this enough to feed everyone?"

"It wouldn't hurt if we got a couple more. The Ritter boys can eat."

"Then we should stay."

Collin's line started dancing. "Shit." He grabbed the pole, giving a yank, and reeled in their next one. He pulled the fish free from the hole and let it land next to hers. "Looks like we're getting closer to a hearty dinner."

"It also looks like my fish is bigger than yours."

His gaze whipped over to hers. "Are you looking for a little competition?"

"Maybe."

He grinned. "Bait up your hook, Markovik-Avery, because it's on."

She chuckled, planning on kicking Collin's butt.

❧ CHAPTER THIRTY ❧

LYLA STOOD IN FRONT OF COLLIN, RESTING HER BACK against his chest as he steered them home on the sled. She grinned beneath her scarf while the wind rushed cold over the bridge of her nose, and her heart pounded from the thrill of the ride. The dogs weren't particularly huge, and Collin only brought six of the usual twelve, but they were *fast* working as a team, pulling them along the path through the trees.

"Gee!" Collin yelled, and the Huskies took them right.

"This is *amazing*." She laughed, tilting her head up to look at him.

He smiled, then made a kissing noise, signaling to the dogs to move even faster.

"Collin," she gasped and faced forward, holding on tighter as they hit a long stretch of open snow. "We're going to crash."

"They know what they're doing."

And so did he. She was as amazed by the man standing at her back as she was the animals. This was hands-down the best birthday she'd ever had. Never before or again would she be able to say she'd ice fished, caught two huge lake trout, and ridden on a dogsled back to a sweet little cabin in the middle of the Alaskan wilderness.

The team pressed on for several more miles, taking them

over hills and deep dips of land, until the landmarks of the homestead became familiar and Collin hollered, "Easy!"

Like magic, the dogs slowed their pace. Soon she and Collin would pull up to the Ritters' with a cooler holding this evening's meal, and she would tell the tales of an adventure new to her but one the family had undoubtedly partaken in before.

"Whoa!" Collin commanded, and the Huskies stopped several feet from their doghouses, barking and howling back at the group of dogs who hadn't been able to go on today's journey.

"That was *indescribable.*"

"It's pretty fun, huh?"

"I've never experienced anything like it." Something she could say about most of the moments she and Collin had shared together over the last few weeks.

"Good. He tugged down her scarf and kissed the tip of her nose, then her mouth. "These boys and girls are going to want their dinner." He gestured to the dogs as he stepped off the back of the sled and dropped the anchor. "I'll get—"

She gasped when the team accelerated forward despite the heavy spiked metal sunk in the snow. "Collin!"

"Hold on!"

She couldn't be convinced to do otherwise.

"Whoa! Whoa!" he yelled, diving for the edge of the sleigh and grabbing hold. "Whoa!" he shouted again as the team dragged him along and stopped a good twenty yards from their original spot.

Her breath heaved as she stared down at Collin still lying facedown in the snow.

"Son of a bitch," he muttered, gaining his feet and dropped the anchor harder into the snowpack this time. "Are you okay, Ly-Ly?"

She nodded, realizing her heart was beating hard enough to pound right out of her chest. "Are you?"

"Yeah."

She studied Collin's beard and eyebrows clumped with snow and fought back a smile as the rush of stark terror dissipated. "Let me..." She tugged his face closer to her level and gently brushed away the worst of the mess.

"That wasn't supposed to be part of your birthday experience."

She gave into her grin. "A bonus."

"Something like that."

She snorted out a laugh she could no longer hold in. "You sort of looked like Santa Claus there for a minute."

"Ho, ho, ho."

She let loose a peel of laughter at his less-than-enthusiastic rendition of Old Saint Nick's infamous line.

He grinned. "You think that's funny?"

She nodded, laughing harder. "I'm sorry, but I'm afraid I do. It's just the way you dove to my rescue and your beard—I'm sorry," she said again.

"Don't be." He pulled off his hat, shaking loose the tiny snowballs attached to the wool. "I haven't heard that sound in a while."

She took a steadying breath. It felt good to let that go, to let herself enjoy a humorous moment.

The front door opened. "You're home," Maisey called, standing in the doorway dressed in jeans and a pink-knit sweater.

She grinned and waved. "Hi, sweetie."

"It's your birthday."

She looked at Collin. "You told them?"

He shrugged. "Why wouldn't I?"

She shook her head. "I don't know. I guess—it's just another day."

"We made you a cake," Maisey hollered next with her hands cupped around her mouth, even when her voice projected just fine. "A chocolate one."

She blinked, surprised yet again. "They made me a cake."

Collin wiggled his eyebrows as he grinned mischievously.

"I can't wait to eat it."

"I made you a card too. I spelled your name all by myself. L-Y-L-A." Maisey's voice carried through the air.

"I can't wait to see it. Go inside, sweetie. It's cold. I'll be right there." She looked at Collin as Maisey closed the door. "Maisey made me a card."

"She's a sweet little girl."

"And you took me ice fishing."

"It's your special day, baby." He winked. "Just for you."

Just for her? When was the last time her birthday had been just about her? And why did not knowing make her suddenly unbearably sad? She gave her head a small shake, struggling to deny her feelings, fighting to push them away when they were too huge and overwhelming. She touched her cheeks, realizing tears were rushing down her skin. Wiping quickly, she blinked, alarmed when they wouldn't stop. "What am I doing?"

The humor in Collin's eyes vanished. "Are you okay?"

Her lips trembled, and her chest heaved with every breath. "Yes." But she wasn't. Turning away, she closed her eyes, battling for composure.

"Ly-Ly." Collin tugged on her arm, pulling her around to face him. "What's wrong?"

"I don't—I don't know." She yanked off her gloves, sniffling as she wiped at her face for the second time.

The front door opened again, and Gabriel and Nickolas started their way, bundled in their winter clothes. "Mom said to come help with the dogs."

"I can't—I just need a minute," she mumbled to Collin and hurried toward Sam's workshop, pulling off her scarf, hat, and coat once she stepped inside. "You're okay," she assured herself, pressing her hands to her chest, hoping to remedy the pressure building there. "You're okay," she reminded herself again and clutched the banister, squeezing her eyes shut as a rush of images flashed through her mind—Dad sitting at the kitchen table at Spaso House, telling her he wanted her to be happy; their last hug at the Bolshoi; then the horror of his black car engulfed in a fireball. Dread filled her stomach and pain shocked her heart with the agony of emotions she'd craved and now wanted to go away. "Oh God. Oh God."

Collin walked inside. "Lyla?"

"I just need a minute." She held up a halting hand to hold him off as her breath continued to steam out in unsteady torrents. "I just need a minute," she repeated as she hurried up the stairs.

"Lyla." He followed her, taking off his hat and jacket. "Lyla—"

She whirled as she stepped into the loft. "Please go away."

"I'm not going to do that."

She pressed her hands to her face. "I can't make it stop."

"Come here."

"No!" She shook her head as he advanced toward her, not ready to be touched. "No," she said more gently, moving to the window, gripping the ledge as she stared out at the endless acreage of trees, trying to banish her devastating thoughts.

Collin took another step toward her, his boots echoing on the floor.

She spun back around. "Why wasn't I enough?"

"What do you mean?"

"Just once I wanted to come first, but I never did. Not one time."

"Lyla."

She shook her head and stepped back, smacking into the wall. "I understand why he didn't—couldn't pick me. I can't resent him for dying, for refusing to come home to New York even when it was the only thing I ever asked of him." She impatiently wiped at more tears. "He couldn't stand leaving Moscow, not even for short visits, because that's where he felt connected to her—where they'd lived and loved. I took that away from him—I took her away, the stranger I never knew and have somehow grown to resent."

"You have a right to the way you feel."

She shook her head again, finding her words and his completely unacceptable. "I'm the reason he had to live without her, the reason he fought so hard to preserve her memories and make her dreams come true."

"That's not fair," he said gently.

"You're absolutely right. It was never fair. He had to wake up and face each day alone because of me, Collin—because I lived and she died." She covered her face with her hands when her voice broke. "*God.* If he just would have listened. If I could've made him need me more just one time..."

"Come here." He closed the distance between them and pulled her against him.

She clutched at his shirt, desperate to get away, desperate to stay. "My dad..." Another trembling sob escaped.

"It's okay, Ly-Ly."

She shook her head. "He's really gone," she choked out.

He held her tighter. "He's really gone, Ly-Ly."

The confirmation of what she already knew, of what she'd seen with her own eyes days ago broke her. And she wept wildly.

"I'm right here," he murmured against the top of her head. "I'm right here, Lyla."

She burrowed against him, clinging as the anguish she'd buried deep finally escaped.

"Come here." He sat her on his lap on the rickety chair next to the woodstove, never letting her go.

"I can't—I can't make it stop," she struggled to say as she sobbed.

"It's going to be okay." He rocked her and stroked his hand up and down her back as another dam of grief burst.

She wasn't sure how long she sat there, resting her cheek on his chest, shaking and shuddering, while he cocooned her. She blinked at the walls in the quickly fading light, weak and worn, hardly able to move after such an intense emotional purge. "I don't know how you do it," she said dully.

"What?" he muttered against her hair, kissing her head.

"What power do you hold over me that makes me admit things to you—say them out loud, when I can barely think them to myself?"

He tilted her chin up, looking into her eyes, and kissed her lips.

"I don't know why that happened, but I'm okay now. I can get up."

He shook his head. "You should stay right here."

"I'm sorry for bawling all over you."

He wrapped his arms tighter around her. "I'm only sorry it took so long."

She frowned.

"It's okay to cry, Lyla, to let go of the pain."

Her lips trembled again as she thought of her father. "I don't want him to be gone. Why did they have to take him away from me?"

"I don't know." He captured the tears trailing down her cheeks with his thumb.

"It just hit me—something about the chocolate cake and you and the Ritters making my day special—knowing I'll never share another birthday with Dad, even if he couldn't get past his grief to make my day about me instead of my mother."

"It's a tough situation—the way everything worked out."

She nodded. "He was a good man."

"He was."

"I watched him blow up, and it's just sinking in that I'm never going to hear his voice again. He's never going to ask me about my ankle." She sniffled. "I'm never going to tell him it's okay even though we both know it's not."

He kissed her forehead.

"I'm so sad." Another tear fell, followed quickly by another. "I feel so sad, Collin, and I hate all of this pain I can't seem to get rid of."

"It's going to take a while before everything feels all right again."

She nodded.

"But I'm going to be right here—right next to you."

She nibbled her lip, as afraid as she was soothed by his declaration.

"I'm sorry you're going through this, Ly-Ly." He reached forward, pulling off her boots, and stood, bringing her with him.

"What are you doing?"

"Putting you to bed."

"I can't sleep. I don't want to. It's the middle of the afternoon."

"You don't have to." He pulled the covers back and set her down, then tugged off the snow pants she still wore.

She took his hand. "Do you want to—do you want to have sex?"

He gripped her fingers. "No. I want to take care of you."

"Make love to me." She nudged him down next to her and kissed him. "I want you to make me feel something different than what I do right now. I don't want to feel like this anymore. Every time we're together, there's this freedom wrapped up in all of the intensity..." She shook her head. "I can't explain it."

He cupped her cheeks and kissed her sweetly. "I'm not going to take advantage of you."

"You wouldn't be. I'm asking." She reached for one of the buttons on the plaid shirt he was borrowing from Sam.

He pulled her hand away and intertwined their fingers. "Rest for a few minutes first."

She didn't want to rest, couldn't possibly relax but she nodded anyway. "Okay."

"Lie back," he said quietly, covering her up as she did. "Close your eyes, Ly-Ly."

She nodded, rolling onto her side, capturing his hand again. "Do you think they're together? My mom and dad?"

He stroked her temple. "I'm sure they are."

"That's what he wanted—what he needed. Always. They only had a few years together before I ruined everything."

"You didn't ruin anything. You were a baby, Lyla—as innocent as any child coming into the world."

"He loved her desperately."

He kissed her knuckles, once, twice, three times then four. "Rest."

She nodded.

He pressed her palm to his cheek and let her go. "I'll be right back. I want to get some more firewood." He grabbed his jacket and walked down the stairs.

"Tell Leah I'll be over to help with dinner."

He didn't answer.

She closed her eyes and was asleep before the door shut.

———◆———

Collin put the last of the four snow-heaped buckets on the woodstove, listening to the cold drops of water hiss and sizzle as they trailed down to the hot cast-iron. He glanced Lyla's way as he carefully slid the bathtub closer to their only heat source, making certain she would have a view out the window if she chose to take advantage of a rinse in the tub. When he was satisfied that he'd done all he could for now, he sat in the chair next to their bed and took her hand while she slept, sliding his thumb over her knuckles as she breathed deep in the dim lantern light.

She'd been out cold for close to two hours. After their busy afternoon and her breakdown, he'd had no doubt she would crash hard. Poor Ly-Ly had cried in a way he'd never witnessed before. Her sobs racked her body while he held her in his arms, her endless tears drenching his shirt. Even now the tip of her nose was pink and her eyes swollen.

Sighing he bent down, kissing her forehead, wishing he could offer her more than a tinfoil dinner and a bath in a lame metal basin, but their isolated location left him stuck.

She stirred, stretching, and blinked open her eyes.

He rested his elbows on the mattress, studying her face as he lifted her hand and cradled it between the two of his. "Hi."

She smiled. "Hi."

"How are you feeling?"

"A little worn out."

He considered it progress that she didn't paste on another smile and tell him she was fine. "I bet." He kissed her fingers, eager to comfort her. "Are you hungry?"

Her eyes went huge as she sat up. "I need to help Leah."

"No, you don't." He settled his hand on her shoulder as she tried to pull the covers back. "Dinner's all set. I have ours right over there." He gestured to the tinfoil-wrapped meals staying warm on the woodstove.

"I should've helped."

"I told her you weren't feeling well."

"I'm fine."

"Leah's capable of taking care of her family. She's been doing so for at least ten years."

"But we're supposed to be helping. I don't feel right—"

"They're fine, Lyla." He gave her arm a gentle squeeze of reassurance. "They're fine."

She nodded, tucking loose strands of hair escaping her braid behind her ear.

"Are you hungry?"

"I could eat."

He stood, grabbing their meals and the flattest log he could find, placing their dinner on the wood as he set it on her lap. "Here you go. Dinner in bed—Alaskan style."

She smiled. "Another first."

He sat back down in the chair, handing her one of the forks and a knife. "It's chicken. I know meat's not your thing..."

"It's fine." She peeled back the foil, yanking her hands

away as a rush of steam plumed from the packet along with the heavenly scent of peas, carrots, and potatoes in the natural chicken juices. "Was our fish bad?"

"No. Leah and I thought we could eat it tomorrow. The boys cleaned them up after they finished with the dogs, and the girls think we should wait to have it with your cake."

Her eyes softened. "That's so sweet."

"They're good kids."

She smiled again. "They really are. I'm going to miss them when we leave." She cut into the tender breast and took a bite.

He opened his own packet, watching her. "How is it?"

"*Really* good," she said over her mouthful.

"Like you might consider partaking in a chicken dish every now and again? That kind of really good?"

"Definitely."

His eyes widened with his surprise. "Yeah?"

"No."

He laughed.

She grinned. "How about you can eat all the chicken you want when someone else prepares it at a restaurant or a barbeque, and I'll eat my vegetables and seafood."

He sucked in a breath through his teeth as he considered her words. "I guess we have a deal." He frowned as a thought occurred to him. "What do you eat on Thanksgiving?"

"All kinds of stuff."

"But no turkey?"

"No turkey."

"Man, Thanksgiving without turkey..." He shook his head. "I don't know about that one."

"It works out fine for me."

"Ethan's family throws a huge bash—more food than you can even imagine. You would definitely find your fair share of veggies. And the pies... There's literally a whole table dedicated to dessert."

"Are you inviting me to Thanksgiving?"

If he could convince her to come home to LA with him, he had no intention of letting her go. "If I'm not being too forward, or if you don't have something else in mind."

"I don't know. Nine months doesn't leave me much time to cancel on Moses and Charlotte."

He smiled as she did and dug into his meal. Minutes passed in silence while they both ate, and he studied her eyes while she chewed. She looked tired.

She stabbed a tender carrot and half of a potato wedge, pausing with the bite halfway to her mouth. "Please don't look at me like that—like I'm delicate or broken or...damaged."

"You're not broken or damaged, but you are a little delicate right now—vulnerable. And there's nothing wrong with that."

Her brow furrowed as she opened her mouth to speak.

"There's nothing wrong with that," he repeated before she had a chance to say whatever it was she had on her mind.

"I'm just used to—"

"Taking care of yourself and shouldering everything on your own."

"Yes."

"Well, that's not how it's going to be anymore."

Her frown returned as she toyed with a pea.

"You're mourning your father, Lyla. You're allowed to be sad and devastated, and I'm allowed to make sure you're okay."

"I'm going to be fine."

"I know you are. *We're* going to be fine too."

Her gaze whipped up to his.

"We got off track for a couple of days, but I want us back on the right one." He barely suppressed a sigh, hating that fear filled her eyes at the mention of them as an "us." "Eat up, Ly-Ly."

"I'm finished. I'm—"

He stabbed another slice of potato and held his fork up to

her mouth. She'd eaten fairly well, but a couple more bites wouldn't hurt.

"Collin."

"Lyla."

She rolled her eyes and snagged the food off of his silverware.

"Thank you." He ate more himself.

She held his gaze as she chewed, then slid a glance toward the window and made a sound in her throat.

"What?"

She swallowed. "Look outside." She set down their makeshift tray on the floor and scrambled from the bed as a flash of green lit up the occasional patch of clearing sky. "Did you see that?"

He stood behind her, staring out as she did. "The Northern Lights."

"The Northern Lights," she repeated reverently, clearly in awe. "I've heard of them, but I've never seen them." Brilliant swirls of pink and yellow joined the flashes of green. "It's magic."

She deserved a little magic. "They've been flickering off and on for a little while." He wrapped his arms around her. "Maybe we'll head home tomorrow if the clouds keep clearing."

"Maybe." Sighing, she leaned back against him, lacing their fingers. "This land is so harsh yet so beautiful all at the same time."

"You're right about that." He kissed the top of her head. "I thought it might be nice to set you up with a little rustic luxury. You could enjoy the show." He twisted at the waist as she looked back, offering her a view of the bathtub.

She smiled up at him as her eyes went soft again. "You did this for me?"

"I was thinking I could put the quilt up on the rope like we did the other night—"

She turned and stood on her tiptoes, kissing him. "You're

such a good guy."

"I think you make me want to be a good guy."

"Aww." She hugged him. "A bath sounds really great."

"Good. I'll get the blanket and the—"

She shook her head. "You don't have to put that up."

He slid his hands down her arms as he held her gaze.

"Or maybe we do." She sighed. "I don't know what you want anymore, Collin," she said quietly. "We keep dancing around the situation. You're confusing me."

He moved his palms to her shoulders and pulled the bands from her braids, combing his fingers through her hair as he freed her twisted locks. "There's no confusion here. I want you."

"So you've said, but I don't exactly know what that means. I'm looking for more than a partner in the bedroom."

"So am I."

She closed her eyes, resting her head on his chest. "I feel like I'm pressuring you—that I'm ready for things you aren't."

Maybe she was, but she wasn't all at the same time. "I want to get married. I want a white-picket fence just like you do. I've been ready to start my family for a few years now. I just need it to be right. I hate the idea of divorces and custody battles."

"That's the last thing—"

"I don't want you making babies with strangers when I want you having mine," he blurted out, needing to get that off his chest.

She kissed him.

"I want you having mine," he said again, stroking her cheeks.

"I think that sounds perfect."

"How about we just go with the flow for a little while? Take things as they come, take a step when it feels right for us."

"I can live with that." She nudged him closer. "It wasn't fair for me to put a timeframe on everything. I guess I'm just eager to have all of the things I told myself I couldn't."

He nodded. "I can understand that."

"I'm sorry if it felt like I was pressuring you. That wasn't my intention." She kissed him as she stood on her tiptoes, trailing kisses along his jaw to his ear. "I'll wait for you, Collin," she whispered, "for as long as you want." Easing back, she stared into his eyes. "For as long as you need."

He swallowed as their gazes held. This was what he'd been searching for. There was no anger here, no pressure, just a sweet woman he absolutely adored. "Right now I feel ready for everything."

She started unbuttoning his shirt. "Will you take a bath with me and watch the lights?"

He blew out a breath of relief as she peeled off his first layer of clothing. "I can't imagine wanting to be anywhere else."

She pulled off his long-john top and let it fall to the floor. "We could skip the bath and go to bed."

He shook his head as he slipped her shirt up and off, exposing her sexy pink bra. "There's no rush. I want to be able to say that we took a bath under the Northern Lights."

She pressed his palm to her cheek. "How did I get so lucky?"

"I think your dad called mine."

She smiled sadly. "He did."

His intention wasn't to bring the unhappiness back to her eyes. "He told me he thought we were good together—your dad."

"He did?"

Collin nodded. "He said that you talked to me and looked at me differently. He was hoping I might be the man for you, that maybe I might be the man who would actually take care of you for a change."

She sniffled as a tear fell down her cheek.

He wiped it away with a gentle slide of his hand. "I want to be that guy, Lyla."

She sniffled again. "What is *wrong* with me? I don't cry in front of people. I can't remember the last time I let myself cry at all—"

"Why?"

"I don't know exactly. Maybe I'm afraid I'll never stop."

He clenched his jaw and wrapped his arms around her. "You're doing just fine."

She held on tight, then eased back. "I don't want to be sad anymore tonight."

"I want you to be whatever it is you need to be."

Her eyes softened as they stared into his. "You always say the right thing. You're so good to me—so good for me."

"I love you, Lyla."

She swallowed. "I—you do?"

He nodded.

"I love you too."

He grinned.

She smiled back. "Are we crazy? We've known each other for such a short time."

"It feels right. I've been around the block a few times, and it's never felt like this."

"Leah and Sam married after a week of dating. She said sometimes you just know."

"I knew the minute you smacked into me on the sidewalk that you were special. Deep down I knew you were going to change my life."

She took his hand. "Come and watch the show with me before it fades away."

"Okay." He left her bra in place. He wouldn't be undressing her tonight, not with the intensity swirling between them. That wasn't what this was supposed to be about. Instead of taking off her clothes, he got to work with setting up the tub, pouring the buckets of water into the snow he'd put into the bottom of the basin. He picked up one of his dirty shirts and tossed in the hot rocks, then tested the water, finding it to be slightly too warm. "It's a little hot."

"That won't last long."

He smiled. "It certainly won't. Go ahead and grab what you'll need."

She nodded and went to her bag, digging for the towel she'd washed the other day.

"Is that your MP3 player?"

"Yeah, it's getting low on batteries though."

"Let's use it anyway." He grabbed it up and searched her playlist, selecting a Norah Jones album. "Perfect." He hit "play."

Lyla smiled. "Perfect." She dipped her hand in the water. "I think this should be good."

"Hop in."

She peeled off the rest of her clothes and sunk her feet into the water that came up to the middle of her calves. "Nice."

"Yeah?"

"Oh, yeah."

He twisted the lantern light down to its dimmest setting and took off his remaining clothes as she sat down.

"Come on in," she invited, scooting forward and making room for him.

"Thanks." He settled in behind her and wrapped his arms around her, easing her back against his chest. "Is this okay?"

"I don't know how it could be better."

"Mmm... I'm thinking a hot tub, ocean waves a couple hundred yards away, a toilet that's actually located *inside* the house—"

Chuckling, she swatted his hand. "This is what we have for now."

"It's not too bad." He nuzzled her skin, breathing in the scent of her hair.

"Thank you."

"For?"

"For making today so great."

He scooped her hair out of the way and kissed her neck.

"I wanted it to be better."

"I'm happy with this."

"You don't ask for much."

"I don't need much."

"Well, you've come to the right place."

She grinned and laced their fingers as the music played and the lights flashed outside in a rainbow of colors. "It's so pretty."

He wrapped his arms tighter around her. "It is."

She sighed. "I love this. I want to remember this moment forever."

"Do you want me to wash your back? Maybe I could rub your shoulders too before the water gets too chilly."

She looked up at him. "I usually start with my hair."

"I've never washed anyone's hair."

"That's okay. I can do it."

"I can too." He picked up the cup bobbing about in the water and filled it, letting the water cascade down the back section of her head and onto his chest.

"Mmm," she purred. "That feels good."

"Yeah?"

"Very relaxing."

He did the same thing several more times, working his way closer to her forehead, careful not to get her face wet. "Shampoo?"

"You don't have to."

"I want to."

"Okay, then yes, shampoo. Just a little though."

He squirted a small dollop into his palm and worked it through her hair.

She purred again. "We should add 'amazing hair washer' to your list of talents."

He smiled. "You think?"

"Definitely."

"I'll have to ask Ethan if that's worthy of a bump in pay."

She laughed.

He loved hearing that sound. "I figure it's a marketable skill."

"With your magic hands, you could be rich and famous."

"It's always good to have a backup plan."

She chuckled.

"Ready for a rinse?"

"Yeah. But we can skip the conditioner. I'll use the spray-in stuff I have in the bag."

He tipped her head slightly and suds ran down his chest and stomach. "Tonight is for you. We can condition as well."

"We need some warm water for you too."

He poured water until her hair ran clean. "There. I think you're all set."

She squeezed out the excess drops and reached for her bag, spritzing stuff through her hair.

He sniffed. "Smells good."

"It reminds me of spring." She set the bottle down and turned, straddling him, using his thighs as her seat. "Do you want a turn?"

He rested his hands on her hips. It would be so easy to pull her closer and let her take him in. "You'll miss the show." He gestured to the sky.

"I want to return the favor, Collin."

He sat up farther and scooted them into the center of the tub. "It's your birthday."

"Yes, it is." She wrapped her legs around his waist. "The best birthday I've ever had."

He couldn't wait to show her that they were only going to get better. "Good."

"Tip your head back a little."

He did as she asked, and she poured water on his head. Moments later, she lathered shampoo through his hair, and he closed his eyes, groaning as her gentle fingers relaxed him as much as her breasts rubbing against his chest excited him. "This feels amazing."

"I knew it would." She began the rinsing process, cup after

cup of water raining over his head as they stared in each other's eyes. "This should be the last one." She gave him a final rinse. "There we go."

"Thank you."

"You're welcome." She nipped his bottom lip. "I can't wait to get that beard off of you."

"We can take care of that too."

She shook her head. "Not tonight. Besides, you need it until we leave—to keep that beautiful face of yours warm."

He winced. "Beautiful?"

"Mmm. Beautiful."

He held her gaze, reading perfectly what she wanted. Grabbing the bar of soap, he rubbed it over her body, stopping and circling her breasts, teasing her perky, sensitive skin.

She whimpered, nibbling her lip as she slid her hands up and down his back.

"Feel good?"

"You know it does. Keep going." She closed her eyes as he continued his caresses.

"You've gotten a little bossy."

Grinning, she opened her eyes. "And you love it."

"It *is* pretty damn sexy."

She chuckled as she took the soap from him, rolling it in her hands and sliding them down his chest. "You like assertive women."

"I like your different moods—sweet, quiet, sexy, bold. They all work for me."

"That's good to know." She let her hands sink beneath the water and wrap around him.

He sucked in a breath through his teeth.

"Do you want me, Collin?"

"Yes." He gripped her butt. "But not in here like this." He splashed water on their chests, washing away the suds, and locked her arms around the back of his neck. "Take this and hold on." He handed her the towel and stood.

She gasped. "Holy crap, it's cold."

"I have every intention of warming you up." He sat on the mattress.

"We're going to get our covers all wet."

"They'll dry." He kissed her, instantly taking it deep.

She moaned, wrapping her arms tighter around him.

He adjusted her legs so they no longer hooked around him and laid back, bringing her with him, sliding his arms down her sides, causing a riot of goose bumps.

She shuddered.

"Still cold? I'm going to have to do better."

She shook her head. "I'm definitely not cold."

Damn, she turned him on. He rolled over, lying on top of her. "I've missed this—feeling connected to you like this."

She brushed his hair back. "You're so good with words. You always know just what to say to make my heart melt."

"It's not hard to tell you how I feel."

She smiled.

"Happy birthday, Lyla."

"Thank you for my day."

"You're welcome." He kissed her nose. "When we get home, we're celebrating again."

"Will we end the evening like this?" She walked her fingers over his ass.

He traced her earlobe with his tongue. "If you want it to."

She turned her head, giving him more room to explore. "I think it should be part of the deal."

"You've got it." He played his fingers over her mouth. "How do you say 'lips' in Russian?"

"*Guby.*"

"*Guby,*" he repeated, kissing her.

"And what about 'neck'?"

"*Sheya.*"

"*Sheya.*" He trailed his lips down her neck, stopping on her racing pulse. "You're always so soft, Ly-Ly. I can't get enough of the way you feel." He caressed her chest. "How do you say 'breast'?"

"*Grud.*"

He pulled her sensitive skin into his mouth, taking turns with each breast, teasing until her nipples were pebbled points.

She tipped her head back, moaning as her palms moved up and down his back.

"Does this feel good?"

"Yes."

He inched his way down, nibbling. "How do you say 'stomach'?"

"*Zheludok.*"

Her muscles shuddered and her breath hitched as he teased her with delicate brushes of his lips before he moved farther down, holding her gaze as he settled himself between her legs. "How do you say 'taste'?"

"*Vkus.*"

"*Vkus,*" he whispered as he traced her with his tongue.

Her eyelids fluttered closed as she gasped.

"God, Lyla, I love the way you taste." He continued his work, lapping, suckling, sinking his fingers deep inside.

"Oh. Collin." She brushed her fingers wildly through his hair. "Collin."

He brought her to the edge. "Ly-Ly, how do you say 'pleasure'?" Before she could respond, he gave her plenty, sending her over with a final flick of his tongue.

She arched her back and her legs tensed around him as she called out. "Oh my God. Oh my God."

He kept her going, revving her higher and sent her over again.

"Collin," she whispered desperately as she clutched the bedding and turned her head from side to side. "Collin."

God, he had to have her. He worked his way back up her body, kissing her damp, dewy stomach, then her breasts and neck.

"Collin," she said again, pulling his mouth to hers, kissing him wildly.

He pushed himself inside her, groaning and sinking deep into her heat.

She bowed up on a moan and rocked her hips in a frantic pace.

"Slow," he whispered. "Slow."

"Okay." She pulled his mouth back to hers and trailed her hands down his arms, eventually intertwining their fingers.

They stared in each other's eyes as they moved together.

"I'm getting close again," she shuddered out.

He arrowed deeper, and her fingers were a vice on his as he kissed her, swallowing her loud cry of pleasure.

"I'm going to come," he panted out.

She nodded.

"What do you want, Lyla?"

"You." She kissed him sweetly.

"Are you sure?"

"I want all of you."

He rested his forehead against hers, tensing and shuddering as he filled her.

———◆———

Lyla rubbed her hands up and down his back as they both struggled to catch their breath. "You didn't have to do that," she whispered, kissing his damp temple. "You didn't have to, Collin."

He eased himself up, resting on his elbows. "It's what you wanted."

She nodded. "Yes." She stroked his face. "I thought we weren't going to rush. We have time."

"We're going with the flow, right?"

She nodded again. "But where I'm at in my cycle. We might have just—"

"I'm going with what feels right. Everything about you feels right, Ly-Ly. Looking into your eyes, being with you...

What we did just now feels exactly right."

"Even if—"

"Even if."

She smiled as her heart soared.

"I love you, Lyla. From this point forward, you're stuck with me."

"I love you too." She kissed him. "How did I get to be the luckiest girl in the world?"

"You are pretty lucky, huh?" He winked as he smiled at her.

"Definitely." She nibbled at his chin. "So what should we do? It's still pretty early."

"We could eat the rest of the chicken."

She wrinkled her nose. "I hate that idea."

He laughed. "You pick then. It is your birthday."

She chuckled as she kissed his neck. "We could make love again."

He raised his eyebrows. "That might work."

"It's one of my very favorite things." She pushed on his shoulder. "Lie on your back."

"So bossy."

She smiled. "I promise you're going to love it."

"Ly-Ly, I already do."

They both laughed as he rolled with her, reversing their positions and letting her have her way.

CHAPTER THIRTY-ONE

LYLA SLID THE SCALLOPED POTATOES INTO THE OVEN, half-listening to the weather report broadcasting over one of the AM stations. She looked toward the ceiling where the boys played Chess in the loft above, while the nasty wind battered the house, much like it had all day. Poor Gabriel and Nikolas had come in minutes ago, cold to the bone and eager for one of the warm peanut-butter cookies she and the girls had made, then bee-lined it up the ladder for a game by the second, smaller woodstove.

"Are you ready?" Maisey asked from her seat at the table while Ellie twisted her sister's hair into a bun.

"Almost. Let me bring Collin and your daddy a cup of coffee before we get started."

Maisey let loose a long-suffering sigh. "Okay."

"I'll just be a minute, sweetie. It's really cold out there. We need to warm them up."

She nodded. "All right."

The girls had been patient, helping her in the kitchen for most of the afternoon, but they were buzzing with excitement, eager to share the little dance routine she put together for them in celebration of their last night together at the cabin—weather permitting. Sam's pilot friend sent out a bushline this morning, letting the Ritters know that he was going to attempt to fly in today, but she wasn't optimistic as she stared out at the gloomy skies. "Five minutes. I promise."

"Five minutes." Maisey held up five fingers.

"That's right." Lyla poured coffee into the thermal mugs the family kept at the ready and added to Collin's cup a few drops of the reconstituted powdered milk that substituted as a creamer out here in the boonies. "Four minutes," she said, flipping the "off" switch on the small countertop radio on her way toward the door.

"Four minutes." Maisey held up four fingers this time.

She walked out into the entryway, making certain she closed the interior door behind her, and pulled on a hat as she slid her feet into her boots, being sure to tuck her jeans deep inside. She tugged her jacket over her thick Manhattan Ballet sweatshirt and stepped outside into the frigid temperatures. Gasping in shock, she coughed when her throat instantly dried. Last night's small reprieve from the winter misery was short lived. "It's *awful* out here," she called as she hurried up the path to Collin and Sam chopping away at the dead tree they'd felled earlier that morning.

Collin stopped his work and pulled his scarf down to his chin as she moved closer. "You shouldn't be out here in this, Lyla. Go back inside."

"I plan to, but I want to give you these first." She handed off the mugs. "Coffee and cream—sort of. And straight up for you, Sam."

"Thank you, Lyla. This is a treat."

The wind whipped the snow around, and she hunched her shoulders in defense. "Do you think the pilot's going to make it in?"

Sam looked toward the darkening sky. "He said he was. It's hard to say though."

She nodded. "I planned on an extra plate at the table just in case." The wind blew again, howling with its ferocity. "Don't stay out too long. Dinner's a little more than an hour away."

"Everything okay in the house?" Sam asked, lifting his

cup for another sip.

"Perfect. The girls are eager for their makeup, the boys said something about a game of Chess, and Leah's upstairs finishing her project—the mukluks she needs to have ready to fly out when we do."

"Warmest boots a man could ask for." He held out his foot, showing off his own pair. "Leah has a real talent."

"You're a lucky guy."

"That I am." He winked as he smiled. "We shouldn't be too much longer."

Collin pulled her close to his side. "Thanks for the warm-up drink."

"You deserve it."

"Go back in, Ly-Ly." He rested his cheek on top of her head. "It's too cold."

"Okay." She smiled at him and hurried toward the house, stepping into the warmth, happy to be out of the misera-ble temperatures. She opened the main door and smiled as Maisey waited for her.

"Ellie says you were gone for seven minutes."

"Well, then we should get started right away." She took Maisey's hand, walking with her to the table. "Hop up and get comfortable." She waited for Maisey to settle onto her seat and unzipped the small makeup kit she'd brought with her from the guest loft, selecting the lightest shade of blush-er and fattest brush among her items. "This should do the trick." She slid a hint of pink along Maisey's porcelain cheeks.

"Does it look nice?"

"Beautiful." She picked up the tube of mascara. "You have to hold still while I do this. I don't want to poke you in the eye."

"Okay."

She swept the brush along Maisey's upper lashes once. "Now for some gloss and you'll be all ready."

The little girl grinned. "Like a real ballerina."

"You *are* a real ballerina." She dabbed clear gloss on little lips, knowing she would have to apply more shortly. The girls weren't even set for their recital until after dinner, but they were both excited. "Rub your lips together."

Maisey did as she was told. "I'm not a ballerina like you."

"It takes years and years of practice to dance with a company." She handed her eager dancer the small mirror that had somehow survived the impact of the plane crash.

Maisey studied herself. "I'm wearing real lipstick. I'm so pretty."

Lyla laughed as Ellie rolled her eyes at her sister. "You're both very pretty."

"Ballerinas wear makeup when they dance," Ellie said, patiently waiting her turn, but her eyes were just as eager as her sister's.

"That's right. The dancer's makeup helps tell the story. It's part of the costume."

"We're performing." Maisey bopped up and down in her seat. "We're performing tonight."

She smiled. "You're going to do a wonderful job."

"I know."

Lyla grinned, loving Maisey's confidence. "And you're going to have fun, which is even more important."

"I know," the little girl said again.

"You're all set. Ellie, come have a seat in the makeup chair."

Maisey stood and Ellie took her place.

Lyla repeated the same process and smiled as the subtle makeup enhanced Ellie's natural beauty. "Now we just need to do your hair. You did a great job with Maisey's bun."

"Thank you."

She pulled Ellie's hair back, securing a few stubborn stray pieces with bobby pins, then stepped back, appraising her students. "You both look beautiful—wonderful dancers ready for your show."

"You're leaving tomorrow." Ellie touched Lyla's hand.

"I am. If the weather improves."

"Maybe it will be too cloudy again. It's not safe to take off in a plane if there are too many clouds. And the wind..."

"We'll have to wait and see, but if I *do* have to go, we'll keep in touch on the internet." She leaned in closer. "And I can always send you packages with books and new board games and gumdrops."

Ellie's shoulders slumped. "We only get the mail a few times a year."

"Then you'll have stuff waiting for you when they're able to bring it in."

"Will you send me pictures of New York?"

"I'm going to be living in Los Angeles."

"With Collin?"

She smiled, still trying to get used to the idea. "With Collin. But when I go pack up my stuff in Manhattan, I can take some pictures for you."

"Will you send me a palm tree?" Maisey wanted to know.

Lyla grinned. "I don't think it would live very long out here in the bush, but I could plant one in my yard and name it after you."

Maisey's eyes grew huge. "Really?"

"Really."

"Maybe—maybe we can come visit you," Ellie said.

"I would love that. We would love to have you come stay with us any time you want."

"Will we meet movie stars?"

"I don't know any movie stars, but I think Collin does."

Ellie's eyes went huge this time. "Collin knows *movie stars?*"

She nodded. "He helps keep them safe. That's his job."

"He *does* have big muscles—bigger than my daddy's."

Her stomach fluttered from a quick wash of pleasure as she thought of Collin's excellent, beautiful body trapping hers on the mattress. "He's very strong. Should we warm up *your* muscles for your dance?"

"Yes." Maisey took her hand. "But when do we get to eat your cake?"

She smiled. "After dinner."

"I'm glad you're feeling better today," Ellie said.

"Me too." It was hard not to feel on top of the world. She and the man she loved—who loved her back—were starting their life together. "Thank you. Let's get ready for our dance." She walked with the girls to the rug, smiling as she looked out the window, spotting Collin and Sam back at it after their quick break. Their axes moved in unison, splitting through huge logs that would keep the fires burning for the long weeks ahead. "All right." She gave her attention back to the kids. "Let's get ready—" She stopped, looking over her shoulder when the rumbling motor of a snowmobile penetrated the sturdy glass. A black machine stopped along the path Nickolas and Gabriel made after the last snowfall.

"Who's that?" Maisey asked, gaining her feet and walking to the window.

"I'm not sure," Lyla said as she watched Collin and Sam stop what they were doing and walk toward the man wearing a black helmet.

"It's probably one of the Wagley boys," Ellie said as she sidled up next to Lyla and Maisey.

"Wagley boys?"

"They're our neighbors."

"I didn't realize you have neighbors."

"Yeah. They live about ten miles north of here. Sometimes they trade us bear meat for eggs or if Mom has extra vegetables, we'll trade for honey from their bees."

"Oh."

"But the Wagleys' snow machine is blue, not black." Ellie shrugged, and the girls walked away, clearly uninterested.

Lyla turned away. "Let me get us some music. We should stretch our muscles." She plugged in the MP3 player that had run out of battery long before she and Collin had finally fallen asleep. "Go ahead and take your seats on the floor and we'll get ready to touch our toes."

Collin split one of the final logs in his pile, hoping the massive tree he and Sam dragged back to the house with the snow mobile would be enough wood to get the family through the rest of February and maybe even into March. He and Lyla had used a decent portion of the family's supply by fueling the woodstove in the guest loft. The least he could do was help restock the woodshed and hopefully add quite a bit more—even if the weather today absolutely sucked.

"I sure am going to miss your strong back, Collin."

"Nickolas and Gabriel do a good job," he said as he slammed down the ax and lifted the wood stuck on the blade, then smashed it down again, splitting the thick piece in two. "You're teaching them well."

"Thank you. I'm proud to say they're mine, but they're a few years away from helping me the way you've been able to."

He hefted another log onto his chopping stump. "Anytime you guys feel like getting away, I hope you'll think about a visit to Los Angeles. We would love to have you."

"That's a nice thought."

"The kids could spend a day down in Anaheim at Disneyland. And the ocean's close."

"Unfortunately our lifestyle doesn't afford us the opportunity to vacation, but the kids might enjoy a break."

"Send them down—" He braced himself against a huge gust of wind blowing strong enough to push him forward a step and looked to the darkening sky. "Your buddy's got balls flying around in this." Or maybe Sam's pal was simply an idiot, scud running passengers out in conditions not fit for a small plane.

"Fletcher's been at it a long time, but if he doesn't get in soon, I'm afraid we might have another search and rescue on our hands."

He'd hoped for an early landing and maybe even an opportunity to get Lyla into Anchorage tonight, but with the strong gale-force winds and storms popping up again farther Southeast of the homestead, they would have to wait. He wasn't taking chances with her. Departing tomorrow would have to be good enough—if the weather allowed even that. "I'm sure he'll make it."

"He may have turned back after he dropped off that group of hunters he had on his books."

"Maybe, but the forecast for Fairbanks sounded more treacherous than this. And this is bad enough."

Sam shook his head. "Damn fool. And it will be full-on dark before long."

He set himself up a log from Sam's share, wanting to get this finished up before the daylight faded. If it was cold now... He raised his ax as Sam did, and brought it back down when he heard a snowmobile heading their way.

"Must be the Wagley boys wanting some sort of trade." Sam secured his tool in the tree trunk. "Although now that I think about it, the boys and Missy are supposed to be in Buckland with Ron." He frowned as the snowmobile stopped. "That's not one of the Wagleys."

Collin walked with Sam to the driver sitting on the back of a slick-looking Polaris.

"Good afternoon," Sam said with a friendly smile. "Can I help you?"

"You live here?" the man asked in a thick accent that set Collin on guard.

"Yes," he answered.

"A plane crashed. We are looking for survivors—a man and woman."

Sam slid a glance toward Collin.

Collin pushed his scarf down, exposing his mouth so he wouldn't have to raise his voice to speak. "You're part of the search party?"

"Yes. Search party."

"When did the plane go down?"

"Few days ago—five or six."

"If you're talking about the mess over on Denali..."

The man shook his head. "No, a different one."

"We haven't seen anyone out here."

Sam nodded his agreement.

Who the hell was this guy? Chase and the Department of State knew he and Lyla were alive and would be flying in when the weather cleared. Fletcher was on his way to pick them up, so who was this? His accent gave Collin a good idea. "Best of luck with your search; although, I hate to say you'll more than likely be on a recovery mission after the snow melts. People don't live long out here without shelter, especially with the storms we've been having." The wind blew another mighty gust. "And the wind."

"We must search anyway. She—they are very important to us."

He clenched his jaw. "They're your friends?"

"Yes, my friends."

"We'll keep our eyes open and radio in if we see anything," Sam assured.

"You're name?" Collin asked.

"Uh, my name is Bob."

Like hell it was. "Bob. Good luck."

Bob nodded as he put his helmet back on and drove off.

The sound of the engine faded in the distance, and Sam looked at him again. "You in some kind of trouble?"

"You know what, Sam? I sure as hell think we are."

"Who was that?"

"I don't know, but his name isn't Bob, and he's not part of any search and rescue team Lyla and I are leaving with. Since I've never seen him before, I can assure you he's not my friend." His gaze flew to the sky as the droning of a plane moved closer, flying low overhead. He sucked in a breath and winced when the single-engine Beechcraft tipped dangerously to the right as the wind sent up another pounding.

"Jesus Christ, I hope he lands that thing before the wind

lands it for him." Sam shook of his head. "Crazy son of a bitch. I'll go down to the clearing and get him—be back as soon as I can."

"Sure. We'll be fine here," Collin called over his shoulder as he jogged toward the house, no longer concerned about the Ritter's woodpile. He walked inside and straight through the entryway, not bothering to take off his boots and snow gear before he made his way over to the desk.

Music played in the warm, cozy space, something bright and friendly while Lyla sat on the floor with the girls, stretching.

"We're getting ready to dance for you," Maisey said.

"Awesome," he answered absently, pulling off his gloves as he sat down and flipped open the laptop. He'd tried to connect this morning without luck; he wasn't holding out much hope that right now would be any different, but he prayed to God he would be able to get through to Chase and figure out what in the hell was going on. "Come on," he muttered, waiting for Google to appear on screen the way it had yesterday morning.

Lyla walked over, tugging off his hat as she crouched down next to him. "Is everything okay?"

"Yeah. Fine." He wasn't going to say otherwise until he got in touch with Chase. Something was definitely wrong, but what good did it do to scare her? He tore his gaze away from the computer and looked at her. "How's the dancing?"

She held his stare, studying him. "Who was that on the snowmobile?"

"Bob." He kissed her forehead. "Everything's fine, Ly-Ly."

"Are you coming, Lyla?" Maisey asked. "My legs are stretched." She kicked them up in example.

"Yup." She stood, smoothing his hair. "We're still leaving tomorrow?"

"As far as I know. Sam's friend just landed."

"Okay." She opened her mouth, clearly intending to say something, and shut it again before walking over to join the girls.

He glanced over his shoulder, sending her a small smile when he realized she was still looking at him, then gave his attention back to the computer, gritting his teeth when the words *Unable to connect to the Internet* popped up. He steamed out a breath and slammed his hand on the table. "Damn it."

"Collin." Lyla stood and hurried over. "What is going on?"

"Nothing." He rubbed at his jaw. "I'm frustrated. Why can't this thing just *work*?"

"I couldn't say, but I do know you're scaring the girls."

He looked their way as the pretty Ritter sisters watched him from their spots on the rug. "Sorry," he said to Lyla. "Sorry about that. I was hoping to get through to Chase, that's all. Come here." He tugged her closer with a hand at the back of her neck and kissed her lips. "Go have fun."

"Yeah?"

"Yeah. I'm going to give this one more shot."

She nodded and went back to attend to the girls as he attempted to connect again. Seconds rolled into a solid minute-and-a-half before the same message popped up again. "Son of a bitch," he muttered and got to his feet. "I'm going to go take this stuff off."

"Okay."

He eyed the shotguns on the rack by the door and stepped out into the entryway, pulling off his outside gear, trying to figure out what to do now. Communication with Chase wasn't happening. Leaving tonight wasn't an option either. He hung up his jacket and tucked his boots out of the way, then went back in, moving quickly to the window when he heard a snowmobile approaching in the dark. Sam and his friend. Not Bob.

Moments later, Sam and a large, scruffy man with a gray beard—Fletcher, he presumed—came in.

"Fletcher!" The girls hurried up from the rug.

"Hello, my ladies." He gave them a hug and handed them

both some sort of packaged candy—gummy worms, maybe.

Maisey jumped up and down. "Thank you, Fletcher."

"You're welcome." He gave her a kiss on the cheek, then Ellie.

"Girls, go back with Lyla now," Sam said. "Collin, if I could speak with you for a moment."

"Sure."

He, Sam, and Fletcher stepped into the now-crowded entryway, and Sam closed the door behind them.

"Collin, Fletcher was telling me about some news he heard before he took off."

Why did he already know he didn't like this? "What news?"

"Dropped a group of hunters up in Noatak this afternoon. Had to fuel up so I landed in Kotzebue—got out, took a leak while Skinny Jimmy helped me out with my tanks. Grabbed a quick snack too—some of those nachos with cheese. Saw some news on the TV."

He imagined there was a point to Fletcher's ramblings.

"Anyway, happened to catch a story about that double-engine that went down somewhere in Alaska last week—how no one's really been searching for it: real mysterious circumstances, I guess. Some Russian princess was on board, and dancers. Some guy named Sergee or Sigmund or—"

"Sergei Ploeski."

"I think that's it."

"Anyway, some source leaked information to the Russian media a couple hours ago, saying the guys who blew up the princess's father are still looking to get at her too—if she's even alive, which she might not be."

He narrowed his eyes. "What do you mean they're still looking to get at her too?"

Fletcher shrugged. "That's all I heard, but it's quite a tale. Like to keep Sammy Boy here in the loop since he doesn't get out much." Fletcher gave Sam a jab to the arm with his elbow.

Sam looked at Collin. "I feel like we need to know what the hell's going on around here, Collin."

"Yeah, I think you do too." He rubbed at the back of his neck and sighed. "Lyla and I are involved, but I'm also her bodyguard."

Sam raised his brow. "Bodyguard? Lyla's the princess?"

"No. Not really." He shook his head, not wanting to take the time to explain. "It's her nickname. Her mother was a famous dancer. They called her the queen. When Lyla was born, the media dubbed her 'Russia's Princess.' Her dad was the US Ambassador to Russia and died last week in a terrorist attack."

"Your friend in there's father was the US Ambassador?"

"Yeah. She saw the whole thing."

"Dear God," Sam said with an apologetic shake of his head.

"The security team giving me a hand with Lyla wasn't following protocol, so I thought something might be up. I got Lyla on a plane with her former dance partner and brought her across the border here to Alaska. We were flying to Anchorage to meet up with my buddy and a man from the Department of State. Apparently, someone from the terrorist group followed us here."

"Bob?" Sam said.

He nodded. "Bob."

"He didn't seem to know who you were, and he doesn't know Lyla's here."

"I sure as hell hope it stays that way."

"Why do they want her?"

"I can't be sure. It's hard to guess their motivation. All I know is they can't have her."

Sam shook his head. "No, they can't."

He shoved his hands in his pockets. "Fletcher, are you going to be able to get us out of here in the morning?"

"As long as the weather gives me a little wiggle room. I guess we can try even if it don't."

"We'll sit tight for now and decide how we'll play it when the time comes." He glanced at his watch—only eighteen more hours until daylight.

They went back inside.

"Excuse us." Lyla snagged his hand before he could take two steps and pulled him right back out, shutting the door with a snap. "What is going on, Collin?"

"We need to get out of here."

She crossed her arms. "Why? Who was that on the snow-mobile? And don't you dare say Bob."

He sighed. "I'm not exactly sure who he is, but I think he might be here from Russia."

Her eyes went wide as she gripped her arms tighter across her chest. "That doesn't make any sense. Why would he be here? *How* can he be here?"

"It's not hard to get on a boat and smuggle over the border. We're not far from the ocean, all things considered. After our plane crash hit the news..."

"Okay, but why?"

He steamed out another long breath, taking her hands. "They're looking for us." And had clearly hoped to get to them at the wreckage site, kill him, and do whatever it was they planned to do with her before rescuers could extract them from Alaska.

Her hands went limp in his. "They're looking for us?"

"I think so." He gripped her fingers. "But he left. Sam and I told him we hadn't seen anyone in the area. He has no idea who I am or that you were inside." He touched his beard. "This thing's pretty thick now, pretty grown in. I don't look like I did when we were in the news all the time in Russia."

She sighed. "You look the same, just a little more scruffy." She exhaled another long breath. "Will he come back?"

"Probably not." He kissed her. All he wanted was to gather her up and flee, but there was nowhere to go. "Tomorrow we're leaving. Fletcher's going to get us out of here."

"If the weather cooperates."

"Tomorrow we're leaving." They had to go. The plane could be risky, but so was staying here. "I'm going to keep trying to get a message off to Chase and fill him in on what I think's going on. Fletcher's going to get us to the airport, and the Department of State is going to take care of things from there."

"We won't be able to go home."

He shook his head. "Probably not."

She stared down at the floor.

"We're going to be together." He hooked his arms around her waist. "However this ends up, we're still going to be together."

She nodded.

Maisey opened the door, looking from Collin to Lyla. "Are you sick again, Lyla?"

"No, honey." She shook her head and tried to smile. "I feel just fine."

"Everyone's fine. Everything's going to be just fine," he told Maisey and the woman he loved. He caught Sam's eye across the living room as they stepped back inside, following his gaze to the rack full of weapons. Before the evening was over, he, Fletcher, and Sam would be talking again. Just in case.

—◆—

Emin pulled up to the cabin Ayub had decided to make his own and turned off the snowmobile, blinking in the deep, dark wilderness. His hands and feet were frozen; it had been hours since his last hot meal, yet he dreaded the thought of going inside to give his leader the news. Taking a deep breath, he climbed the steps and opened the door.

Ayub and Yunus looked up from their card game and relaxed their hands on their guns resting by their sides on the table. "Any luck?" Ayub wanted to know.

"None."

He set down a full house. "We will search again."

"That was the last house, Ayub. She's dead."

Ayub stood in a rush, knocking his chair back to the floor, sending Emin's heart racing. "She is only dead when I *say* she is dead."

"The wind is harsh," Yunus added. "The temperatures are enough to freeze a person solid. They didn't live long in the snow, no matter how worthy you believe your opponent to be."

"Shut up!" Ayub pointed his finger at Yunus, then Emin. "She is *alive*! She must be alive!" He paced away and back.

"And if she's not?" Yunus questioned, playing with fire. Their boss had become more crazed as the days passed with no progress.

"She is."

"And if she's not, Ayub? Then what? What is next?"

Ayub smacked his glass of whiskey to the floor as he hollered, "Fuck! This is falling apart! This is not the way it was to be! They have our computers, our plans to conquer what belongs to us. I need her." He rushed around the room in his fit of rage, shattering glasses, winging delicate figurines against the opposite wall. "They would have made a deal for her! Moscow would have given us the world for their princess!" He tipped over the bookshelf, then swatted at the file close to Emin, knocking several pictures to the floor.

Emin looked down at the sheet facing up, one of the hundreds of pictures they had of the princess, and crouched down, yanking it up, staring into the eyes of the man he'd just seen—Markovik-Avery's lover. "She's here."

Ayub whirled. "Are you mad?"

"No. Him." He pointed to the picture of Prince Charming in a tuxedo, waving with his ballerina by his side at some stupid event. "He was at the house not far from here, chopping wood. I did not recognize him. He wears a beard. But I talked to him. He is here."

"Then she is too." Ayub yanked the paper away and

laughed. "Chechnya is mine! Tonight Chechnya will be one step closer to gaining its freedom. Go tell the others to come now." He gestured to the homestead's outbuilding. "We will make our plan."

CHAPTER THIRTY-TWO

COLLIN SAT BACK ON THE COUCH, CROSSING HIS AN-
kles on the coffee table, paying the navy blue curtains
closed over the living room windows more attention
than Sam's hunting magazine on his lap. He sipped his luke-
warm coffee, listening to the cabin creaking and groaning
as the winds gusted wildly outside the Ritter family home.
Luckily he and Lyla were warm inside.

"I don't think I've ever heard the wind *blow* like this before." Lyla tucked herself closer against his side, cozy in her
typical yoga pants and Manhattan Ballet sweatshirt, as she
knit a pale purple hat and scarf set for the girls.

"It's pretty intense." And the constant whistle and whirling made it impossible to hear what was going on beyond the
sturdy cabin walls. Fletcher was taking up residence above
Sam's workshop for the night and keeping his eyes open for
anything suspicious, but Collin always preferred his own
eyes and intuitions when it came down to it. "That's a pretty
little thing you're making there." He tugged her closer with
his arm around her shoulders, sensing her nerves despite
her smooth, steady looping of yarn around her needles.

She smiled. "Thanks. I feel bad that Maisey and Ellie's
special night was overshadowed by everything that's going
on."

"They had a good time. I don't think they even noticed

that anything was up."

She shook her head. "Kids are smart. They know something's going on."

"They had fun, Lyla. You taught them a lot in just a couple of days. All three of you did a nice job." He kissed her temple and glanced at his watch. "You know, it's past one. You should try to get some sleep."

"I don't think I'll be sleeping any better than you will tonight."

He wouldn't be sleeping at all, even if he, Fletcher, and Sam were as ready as they could be if anyone decided to head back toward the homestead. Sam's stash of weapons had been gathered and assigned. During the evening chores, Collin had briefed his temporary backup on Ayub Umarov and the insanity that was his liberation movement. He also taught the non-military men how to secure their perimeter all while bedding down dogs, grabbing extra firewood for three different woodstoves, and topping off the generator. Despite their lack of formal weapons training, Collin was assured that both men, and even Leah, were excellent shots. "I'm going to turn in soon."

She slid him an uncertain glance.

"They don't even know we're here. Staying in the cabin is just a precaution," he reminded her.

She sighed.

"Hey." He gripped her chin, nudging her his way until her eyes met his again. "We're playing it safe."

She nodded. "When we leave, how long—how long do you think we'll have to hide?"

"For as long as it takes."

She closed her eyes and puffed out a breath. "That's not an answer."

"It's the only one I can give you right now."

"What about the Ritters?" She gestured to the loft where Sam, Leah, and the kids had headed shortly after the birthday cake celebration and conclusion of the girls' recital. "I've put them in danger."

"You haven't done anything. And they're only in danger if there's an association between them and us, which there's not. We'll be out of here at first light."

The wind gusted its mighty power, making the logs creak once again, and she let loose a quiet, humorless laugh. "It certainly doesn't sound like we're going anywhere any time soon." She set down her knitting and stood in a rush. "Why can't—why can't..." She paced away and back, shaking her head. "For a few days, everything was okay, Collin. Everything was fine."

He took her hand and pulled her down next to him. "It still is."

She rested her forehead against his chin. "I thought once we left Russia..."

"I know." He slid his fingers through her hair and kissed her. "I know."

She gripped his wrists and sighed. "I'm not making this any easier, whining and asking questions you can't possibly answer."

"I'm not worried about it."

She sent him a small smile and nodded. "How about some tea—or more coffee? And I could cut you another slice of cake."

"Maybe in a minute." He wrapped his arms around her. "We're okay, Ly-Ly," he assured her again.

She returned his embrace, holding on tight. "You're right. Everything you've said makes perfect sense." Her shoulders relaxed as she released a deep breath. "There was only one man anyway."

He debated whether to let her go on believing that, especially when she was finally starting to relax, but if Ayub's men came back, he needed everyone on the same page. Ignorance was not bliss in this situation—just deadly. "That we could see."

"Hmm?" She slid her hands up and down his back.

"There was only one man we could see."

She drew away. "What does that mean?"

Son of a bitch, he hated this, scaring her like this. "The authorities killed four men in Moscow, which is a great start, but do you remember how I told you the leader probably went over the border after your father's murder?"

She nodded. "Yes."

"Ayub Umarov. That's his name—the leader." He shook his head, wanting to explain better. "There are several rebel groups that would like to see a free Chechnya. You know that."

Swallowing, she nodded again.

"Most of them work independently—are rivals—wanting to be the first to make it happen. The group who succeeds gets the power and control—at least initially. Ayub wants it to be his. He leads a small group of about ten to twelve men. They're pretty small, but they're dangerous: smart, determined." And he didn't like the odds.

"So there are potentially six to eight men here in Alaska? Somewhere close to the children?" She looked toward the loft as her eyes filled. "Collin—"

"Potentially." He took her hands.

She shook her head. "That's so many—too many."

"Potentially," he said again, giving her fingers a gentle squeeze.

"Look what they did to my dad. I don't know what I would do if something happened to the kids—or you."

"We aren't going to have to worry about that. I promise. I'm promising you that, Lyla. Nothing's going to happen to anyone."

"You sound so confident—"

"Because I am."

"This is what you did in the military? Searched for men like this?"

"This is exactly what I did."

"But now they're searching for you."

"But I'm on to them—that's half the battle right there."

She pressed her lips together. "I don't like any of this. It's like a horrible game."

And he had every intention of winning. "I've got this. I know this group well, the Chechen Liberation Movement."

"I've heard of them before."

He nodded. "I don't doubt it. Ayub's been trying to free his country for a long time; his father before him."

"Chase told you all of this?"

"He didn't have to. We tried to bag him a couple of times when I was serving overseas. He likes to stir things up all over the Middle East—cause unrest wherever he goes. It pays for him to keep the entire region unstable. He's not just an enemy of Russia's."

She swallowed. "Oh."

"But none of that matters, because you and I are going home tomorrow—or at least somewhere where we have access to help—and this family is going to stay safe. That man on the snowmobile is long gone, Ly-Ly." He kissed her. "Long gone."

She nodded.

"How about some of that cake?" He didn't want any. He wanted to keep her close by his side, but she needed an outlet for her nervous energy.

She stood and walked to the kitchen, busying herself with their late-night snack.

He stared at her rigid shoulders, watching her exacting movements as she prepared two mugs of tea. "Damn," he mumbled in frustration. Just this morning, they'd been laughing before they got up to start their day. Lyla was in the early stages of mourning, but she was getting through it and slowly moving on with her life. That's what he wanted her focusing on, not the extremist bastards who were hunting her.

He glanced at the laptop he'd brought over from the desk and grabbed it off the side table, settling it on his thighs

and opening it yet again. Rescue at this hour, in these conditions, was impossible, but letting Chase know what was
going on was vital. So far, his efforts to make contact had
been a venture paved in frustration, getting him nowhere.
He couldn't count the number of times he'd tried to connect
over the last few hours, but he had to keep trying. He waited,
tapping his fingers against the cushion, watching the familiar gray screen and message pop up: *Unable to connect to
the Internet.* "Son of a bitch." He slammed the lid closed and
rubbed at his jaw.

Lyla walked out with a large slice of cake on a plate, set it
down on the coffee table, and went back for the mugs of tea.
"Here you go."

He reached up, taking the steaming cup. "Thanks."

She pulled the laptop off his legs and set it back on the
table. "Talk to me about something other than this awful
situation."

"You got it."

She forked up a bite of the moist cake and thick chocolate
frosting and held it up to his lips. "Open up."

He took the bite she offered. "Thank you," he said over his
mouthful.

"You're welcome."

He stroked her cheek. "I love you, Ly-Ly."

She smiled. "I love you too."

He tugged the fork from her fingers and brought a bite to
her mouth. "Your turn."

She accepted his offering. "So good."

He helped himself to some more. "Very good." He put the
plate down and tugged her against him. "Come here."

"Mmm." She settled herself between the V of his legs,
snuggling on her side against his chest. "Perfect."

He pulled the blanket off the back of the couch and covered them, then wrapped his arms around her. "Pretty close.
Give me a bed in our own place and palm trees for a view."

"That sounds *amazing*. We're going to need a house—unless you have one?"

He shook his head. "I've got an apartment—a mostly empty one."

"I guess we won't have to do a lot of packing."

He smiled. "Definitely not." He played with her hair, twisting her soft locks around his fingers. "Most of my co-workers live in the Palisades."

"Is that where you'd like to be?"

He shrugged. "It's quiet. The schools are good. We would be close to our friends."

"Your friends."

"They'll be our friends soon enough. Everyone's going to love you. Trust me."

She nodded. "Homeowners in the Palisades, it is."

"As soon as everything settles down, we'll set something up with a realtor."

"I'll need to look into studio space too. I'd like something close to our home—maybe a couple miles or so. I want to be able to zip back and forth."

"There's lots of retail space in the area—classy, upscale."

"I'd still love to work with Moses."

"Are you thinking New York?" He'd always just assumed they would go to LA.

She shook her head. "You have a life in Los Angeles. I can start over anywhere." She sighed. "I need to figure something out for Mrs. Franelli. I can't just leave her without any sort of care. And I'm not sure how I'm going to be able to help Charlie."

"We'll get everyone and everything squared away." He kissed the top of her head. "You should shut your eyes."

She nuzzled her face into the crook of his neck. "I think I might."

"I'll see you in the morning."

"You need to sleep too."

"I will," he said as he eyed his pistol on the coffee table and the rifle Sam had unearthed for him, which was now resting on the highest rung of the gun rack. When they were safe he would rest, but not until then.

"I love you," she mumbled.

"I love you too." He trailed his hand up and down her arm as the wind blew against the house and the clock ticked away the endless minutes. He settled his head more truly on the arm of the couch, listening to Lyla's breathing steady out.

He and the woman sleeping in his arms were buying a house. They were renting studio space, carving out a life, starting a family. His hand paused against her sweatshirt. What if she was pregnant now? Last night they'd thrown caution to the wind time and again, before he realized she was still an active target of an extremely dangerous terrorist organization. They clearly wanted her. Somehow they believed Lyla could further their agenda, which was absurd, but desperation didn't have to make sense. It just made the situation all the more hazardous.

Clenching his jaw, he snuggled her closer as this whole damn thing made his blood boil. She just wanted to live a normal life, and he had every intention of giving her a pretty white-picket fence in one of LA's higher-end neighborhoods. As soon as they were in the clear, they would have their house. She would have her business.

He glanced down, making certain she was asleep, and adjusted their positions a bit, reaching for the laptop as the lamp flickered on and off on the side table before the power completely died. He blinked in the pitch dark and extended his hand, feeling around on the table for his gun, grabbing it up and holding it as he schooled his breathing to hear, even as his heart raced.

Sam had gassed up the generator. He'd watched him do it himself, so why did they suddenly lose their electricity? Seconds ticked by, then minutes as he strained his ears, but he heard nothing but the wind...and the dogs beginning to bark—first one, then the entire pack. He rushed up to sit on the cushion.

"What?" Lyla said. "What?"

"Shh."

"Something or someone's out there," Sam whispered from the loft. "Something has them worked up." Feet pounded overhead as the children were moved to the corner in Sam and Leah's bedroom—part of the plan. "The shed's on fire."

"*What?*"

"The shed. My snow machine." As Sam spoke, there was a loud pop.

Lyla gasped, jumping. "What was that?"

"Probably the gas tank exploding." Collin stood and led her to the ladder by the dim glow of firelight shining through the window on the woodstove. "Go upstairs. Help Leah with the kids."

"No." She gripped his shirt. "I want—I want to stay with you."

He kissed her. "Go, Ly-Ly. I need you to go."

"Okay. Be careful." She hurried up the ladder and disappeared into the dark with the rest of the family.

Moments later, Sam came down. "Hopefully Fletcher's got himself set up."

"If he does what we talked about, he'll be fine." Collin moved across the room, grabbing his second weapon, positioning himself opposite of Sam as the dogs' barks turned into vicious growls. "Just like we talked about. If they enter, it's more than likely going to be a three- or four-man formation—depending on how many men are actually here. Get a shot off immediately or they *will* get you."

"I'm not planning on dying tonight."

"That makes two of us." He crouched low and ready with his finger on the trigger, aiming at the door. Ayub was here, and he was going to end this once and for all.

———◆———

Lyla sat in the corner of Leah and Sam's bedroom, cradling Maisey and Ellie in her arms while the boys huddled close by her side. She held her breath as her heart throbbed in her chest, waiting in the torturous silence for something horrible to happen.

"It's okay," she whispered to the girls as they shook and shuddered. "We're going to be just fine," she assured with more conviction, even though she didn't believe it herself. Wasn't it only minutes ago that Collin had stared in her eyes, consoling her with the very same words? If she lost him, if the children were harmed in any way because of the men outside, nothing would ever be okay again.

"The bad guy's here," Ellie choked out. "He set our shed on fire."

"Dad'll get him. Dad and Collin are going to shoot him dead," Nickolas said, his eyes fierce in the orange-tinged glow of firelight flickering in through the half-drawn shades Leah had opened to see by. "I want to help."

"You're going to stay put," Leah warned, holding the shotgun trained on the long curtain draping the doorframe in lieu of a door.

"I can help, Mom. I can—"

The downstairs doors burst open with a thundering crash, and gunshots exploded in deafening, rapid pops, lighting up the dark. Maisey and Ellie screamed, pressing their faces to Lyla's chest as she fought back helpless whimpers of her own, more terrified for Collin than she was for herself.

"They're fine. They're fine," she chanted in a mumbled whisper, squeezing her eyes shut, needing it to be true.

Her eyes flew open again, meeting Leah's in the shadows when glass broke in the tiny sewing room across the hall.

Nickolas's terrified gaze slid from his mother's to Lyla's. "They're here."

"Cover your ears." Leah settled her finger on the trigger. "Keep them covered," she shuddered out, her voice tight and breathy as cautious footsteps moved through the girls' room, then the boys' before starting in their direction.

"Sam?" she called quietly despite the ungodly noise coming from downstairs. "Is that you, Sammy?"

No one answered as boots stopped in front of the curtain and the fabric rustled.

Leah fired, and a man screamed, falling backwards with a thud.

"Leah!" Sam hollered.

"We're fine up here! We're fine!" She sagged against the wall, gasping in each breath as she reached for another shell with her shaking hand. "Somebody's dead, but everything's fine!"

"Stay put," Collin shouted. "You stay put up there."

"Thank God. Oh, thank God," Lyla said, blinking back tears with the quick rush of relief. He was okay. Collin was alive. And it was tempting to do the opposite of what he asked, to run to him, but she held the children close while they sobbed, knowing that if she didn't listen, the situation would only get worse.

She swallowed, holding Leah's gaze, waiting for Collin to speak again or for Sam to say something else, as the homestead suddenly grew quiet, except for the vicious barking from the pack of Huskies. The wind died down; no one fired their weapons. The tension became unbearable as the eerie stillness stretched on. When were Sam and Collin going to let them know that the worst was over? When would Collin hold her close and say they never had to worry again?

"What's going on? Why don't we hear anything?" Gabriel wanted to know as he wiped his eyes, scooting closer to Lyla.

"They got all of them," Nikolas whispered. "Dad and Collin got them—"

Everyone jumped and the children screamed when gunfire echoed outdoors again in the same rapid-fire momentum as before.

"Put down your gun," someone said with a thick accent from the hallway.

Leah gasped and raised the shotgun, pressing the trigger

blindly, sending another bullet through the cloth barrier, but this time no one screamed; no one fell to their death with the same sickening thud as before.

"That's not what I said to do."

"Leah?" Sam shouted for the second time.

"Tell him you are fine or I promise to make it a lie."

"We're okay," Leah answered with far less conviction. "False alarm."

"Now put down your weapon or I will start shooting. I want to hear you set it on the floor. I have a general idea of where your children are in the room."

Leah looked at Lyla.

Not willing to take any chances, knowing there was no way to signal to the men downstairs that there was trouble among the constant blasts of gunfire, Lyla nodded, and Leah set the gun on the floor.

"No games." A tall, broad-shouldered man pulled back the curtain, keeping to the shadows, but the outline of his gun was unmistakable as a second set of footsteps approached and a stranger soon stood by his side. "Do not think of reaching for your weapon."

Leah raised her hands in the air, shaking her head. "I won't."

Lyla fought to free herself from the clinging children and sat in front of them, shielding the Ritter boys and girls as best she could, well aware of what these men could do— would do if they felt it necessary. There was no regard for human life here.

"Stand, Princess."

Her heart thundered against her ribs and her legs felt like jelly, but she got to her feet immediately. "You will not hurt this family," she said as firmly as her quaking voice would allow. These men were here for her, needed her. She planned to use that to her advantage. "You will leave these children alone."

"How well you listen will determine that."

"I'm standing."

"You will come with me, and your friend will stay quiet or Yunus will spare no one."

She took a step toward the man, and Maisey grabbed hold of her leg, crying harder.

"No, Lyla. No. Don't go."

"It's going to be okay. Everything's going to be just fine." Or it would be as soon as she was gone. Ayub Umarov was getting what he came for.

"Let's go."

With little choice, she walked from the room on her watery legs, stopping short and gasping when she almost tripped over the dead body sprawled in the hallway.

"Go." He gave her a shove to the back.

She stared straight ahead, skirting around the lifeless man as she moved to the broken window in Leah's tiny hobby room, studying the nasty shards of glass still intact along the frame's edges with dismay.

"Go out."

She knocked the deadly spikes away with her sweatshirt, already shivering as the bitter winds blew strong against her cheeks. If she went outside like this, she would freeze to death in her stocking feet.

"Go!" he demanded quietly. "You will hurry, Princess, or people will start dying."

She spotted the fur boots Leah had been finishing up on the table, probably two sizes too big, and snatched them from the carefully folded tissue paper, accidentally knocking the box to the floor. "I need these." Quickly, she slid them on then did her best to dodge the worst of the jagged pieces as she stepped through the empty frame, covering her hands with the cuffs of her sleeves to protect her fingers from the frigid rungs as she descended the metal ladder.

Her captor chuckled as he followed: Ayub himself, perhaps? "Your lover guards the door while we flee. This is much too easy."

She dropped down into the deep snowdrifts, absorbing the breath-stealing shock of snow coating her yoga pants well past her knees.

"Come this way." He grabbed her by the arm and pulled her into the darkness of the forest, moving with her through the trees. She flinched, gasping her surprise when Yunus, the other man from inside, stepped up behind her moments later.

"Leah? The kids?" she said to Yunus who ignored her. They had to be okay. They had to be fine. She hadn't heard any more horrid explosions coming from upstairs.

"We must hurry."

She stumbled and fell in the depths, unable to keep up with the men's steps in the large mukluks, afraid she might lose her borrowed footwear if she lifted her feet too fast.

"Let's go," Yunus demanded in Russian.

"I can't go any faster," she automatically answered him back in his language.

"Move! We have a long journey after we make it to our snowmobiles. The boat waits for us at the border."

She fell again, catching herself on the side of a pine tree. The impact of the bark against her skin should have hurt, but she hardly felt anything at all as the burning agony in her freezing hands quickly turned into a terrifying numbness. Righting herself, she fought to put one foot in front of the other as her teeth began to chatter and her body shook with wracking trembles in the debilitating temperatures.

"A blanket waits for you if you hurry."

She wanted to stall. She yearned to drag out the endless journey in hopes that Collin was going to find her, but she would be dead before the night was over if she didn't get to the blanket her captor promised her. "How—how—much—?"

"We will be there soon enough."

She tried to keep pace, moving farther away from the cabin, listening as the sporadic pops of gunfire grew distant.

Looking behind her, she hoped to see Collin coming to her rescue, but he was at the house, protecting the family. At this point, he probably had no idea she was gone.

———◆———

Collin was sweating his ass off as he maintained his designated position by the open window and the protective barrier of the woodstove. He kept his finger on the rifle trigger, biding his time with his next shot while he, Fletcher, and Sam took turns firing toward the tree line to the right of the cabin when necessary, hoping to hit their last stronghold while conserving their supply of quickly dwindling ammunition.

By his estimation, most everyone had to be dead. Leah had taken out someone upstairs, and four more bodies lay staggered in the entryway where he and Sam had shown no mercy. So where was Ayub? It was doubtful he was holding cover in the woods while three guns were firing his way, and he sure as hell wasn't among the deceased blocking the doorways down here. Could he be the corpse upstairs? Collin immediately dismissed the idea. Ayub wasn't stupid. This wasn't the rebel leader's first ambush. He never would have put himself in the position of being the first man to gain entry in an unknown situation, so what was his plan?

"They have her!" Leah yelled, shattering the tense silence. "They have her, Collin!"

His gaze whipped up to the ceiling as a wave of dread twisted his stomach. "Keep cover," he said as he and Sam both gained their feet. "Lyla!" He scrambled to the ladder, the journey up the twelve rungs seemingly taking forever. "Lyla! Leah!" He ran toward the bedroom, shouldering his weapon, ready to take down anyone waiting in the dark. "Leah!" He spotted the dead man in the hallway, paying him little attention as he yanked back the curtain, holding up his free hand when Leah lined up her shot. "Whoa, whoa."

"Oh, God." She sobbed, dropping the gun to her side. "They took her." She slid down the wall to the floor. "I'm so sorry, Collin. They took her."

His gaze traveled over the children, huddled and crying in the corner under a thick blanket, hardly able to believe that Lyla was really gone. "Where?"

"Out the window. In the hobby room. Two men."

"When?"

"Five, maybe ten minutes ago at the most. I didn't dare call for you until I was sure they were gone. They said they would hurt the kids." She wiped at the tears streaming down her face. "She's not wearing any gear—just her pajamas and maybe the mukluks. I think I heard her take them."

"Mukluks?"

"The fur boots I made for an order. On the table in a box."

He rushed into the room, spotting an empty box on the floor by the tiny table as he cautiously approached the window from the side and peeked out, catching sight of the ladder that had been used and taken down. It was tempting to jump to the deep snowdrifts several feet below and follow behind, but being stupid wasn't going to save Lyla.

He took the dozen steps back to the bedroom. "Stay up here. Stay armed and ready. This isn't over yet." He hurried down the ladder to the living room, spotting Sam in the corner by his open window, holding his post. "They have her. They fucking took her out the back." The one spot where he'd needed a fourth man. The lack of back-facing windows downstairs—only the one above the kitchen sink—had left him and Sam at a disadvantage and the women and kids vulnerable despite Leah's skills with a weapon. He should have *known* the first man to enter upstairs was a guinea pig. The moment he heard Leah's shot, he should have gone running, but he'd had his hands full at the front of the cabin—Ayub's plan all along.

"Fuck!" He rushed into the entryway despite the door half-open to the outside and put on his boots, coat, hat and gloves as Sam fired three quick shots out the window—their mayday signal between the two structures that didn't have any other way to communicate.

"We'll get her back, Collin. God as my witness we'll get her," Sam said as Fletcher opened the workshop door a crack and ran for his life down the short path when Sam shot a steady stream of bullets toward the trees to keep their enemy at bay.

Fletcher took the stairs in twos, stumbling over the dead as he attempted to step farther into the cover of the house. "Goddamn. It's like the wild west around here."

"They took Lyla," Sam explained to Fletcher. "Stay with Leah and the kids. Stay right here with them. Don't let anything happen to them."

Fletcher nodded, still struggling to catch his breath. "You can count on me, Sammy. You know that."

"I do." He set down his rifle and piled on his own gear in record time as Fletcher kept watch. "We'll need these." Sam grabbed two pairs of snowshoes hanging on the pegs and headlamps.

"We have to go out the kitchen window," Collin said, settling the lamp in place on his still-tender forehead as he considered their next move. "We aren't going to do Lyla any good if we get ourselves shot." He gestured toward the bastard in the trees assuredly still keeping watch.

"Let's go."

Collin hurried over to the countertop and twisted the locks, yanking up on the pane of glass before he awkwardly climbed into the sink and dropped down to the snow. He waited impatiently for Sam to throw down their stuff and join him. They both took the time to secure their snowshoes in place, knowing the few moments lost now would easily be made up with the aid of their winter equipment.

"Come on." They adjusted their headlamps from white light to red, which would allow them to enhance their vision in the dark yet stay less visible to their enemy, and took off into the trees with Sam leading the way, running and picking up on the trail that was quickly vanishing as the wind blew the drifts about.

"She doesn't have a coat," Collin said as the first waves of pure panic started kicking in now that he had more time to think. Time was ticking by—and it was not on their side. "She's fucking tiny and wearing pajama pants and a sweatshirt."

"But she's wearing Leah's boots. It was smart for her to take them. It's cold. The wind's a bitch tonight, and she's surely miserable, but she's not at risk of freezing to death in this short amount of time, especially if her feet are warm and dry and she's walking."

He nodded, needing to believe Sam was right as they stumbled their way through the forest, keeping their ears open and weapons ready to fire.

"They have to be heading down by the clearing," Sam said. "That's the only way to get a snow machine up around here from this angle of the range. And since that's the only way I can figure them getting out of the area... I'm going to cut around, see if I can head them off. You stay this path just in case I'm wrong—straight ahead."

"Sure." This was Sam's turf. He knew this area better than anyone—their advantage. "If you get a clear shot, take it. Kill those fuckers."

"I'll be close."

"Hurry. Please." He watched Sam disappear to his left and kept a fast pace despite the dark, finding it hard to make out the path Lyla and her abductors had made as the wind continued to distort the snow, but he'd traveled this way with his host more than once, making the land slightly familiar, and trudged on.

Time passed, probably only a few short minutes, but it felt like hours before he faltered, shutting off his headlamp and stopping when the hairs stood up on the back of his neck. He automatically moved closer to the cover of a tree and raised his gun, peering through his night-vision scope and relying on his instincts when he couldn't hear what was going on around him in the wind. Someone was here—was close, but where? He searched for tracks with the aide of the green tinge and settled his finger more truly on the trigger when a branch snapped fifteen yards to his right.

Whirling, he spotted the single figure moving closer, away from the cabin—the last of the stronghold by Sam's house, no doubt, and hesitated with his shot, knowing that once he fired, Ayub would be on to him and know he was coming. "Fuck," he muttered, conflicted by his lack of choices, and dropped the body with a shot to the head anyway. Second guesses and contemplations wouldn't get him to Lyla before she disappeared for good.

He turned and kept a steady pace, straining his ears for any odd movements or sounds among the forest, walking quickly, but he no longer dared to run. One wrong move and he could very well be on the receiving end of the next bullet. He slowed when he caught the faint hum of an engine and voices in the distance, then approached swiftly yet cautiously. Eventually, he fell to his knees and inched forward on his stomach, ignoring the cold bite of snow creeping down his jacket as he spotted two men and Ayub shoving Lyla toward the grouping of snowmobiles. "There you are. There you are."

But his relief was short-lived as the logistics of their current scenario became apparent. Lyla was within his sight, but she was still a good fifty yards away and in the middle of a clearing, which meant he wasn't getting any closer without someone knowing about it. Just because he had eyes on her didn't mean he was getting her back at this point. Ayub still had the advantage with the snowmobiles warmed up and ready to whisk Russia's Princess off into the night—and his men with the fucking machine guns...

Tucking his fear away, ignoring his doubts, Collin concentrated on his next objective, lining up his shot as one of the bastards moved toward the closest snow machine. He landed his first kill, listening to Lyla's scream, and repeated his mission before the second man had time to raise his gun and return fire. He pulled the trigger several more times, obliterating the back sprockets on the snowmobile, making the tracks useless on two of the three getaway vehicles—the only ones he could reach from his angle. Then he focused on Ayub Umarov holding his pistol to Lyla's temple.

"Drop your weapon," Ayub yelled. "Drop it now!"

"Don't—come—out!" Lyla struggled to yell as her teeth chattered and she shivered uncontrollably.

"Come on. Come *on*," Collin muttered, struggling to line up Ayub in the crosshairs of his scope, but no matter how he moved the gun, Lyla's trembling made a clean kill impossible.

"Now!" Ayub demanded.

"Fuck." With no choice, Collin stood and put his hands up, stepping out from behind the trees. "Let her go."

"No!" Lyla cried. "No, Collin. Go back."

Staring into her eyes, he shook his head.

"Where's your friend?" Ayub asked.

"I don't know."

Ayub pressed the barrel harder to Lyla's temple, making her cry out in pain.

"I don't know, Ayub," he said as calmly as he could, not wanting to add to Ayub's gain by letting his fear show.

"Months of my work is ruined. *Months*! Perhaps the princess isn't worth my time anymore."

"She is." He took another step closer as his heart stopped, certain Ayub would kill her before he could do anything to prevent it. "She's worth it. We have a plane. A man flew in—"

"You beg for her life?"

"If that's what you want. If that's what it takes." He stepped out a little farther, still too far from Lyla to do her any good, but he needed to keep Ayub talking. Sam said he would be close. Now he could only hope that was true. "I'll get down on my knees right here."

Ayub shook his head. "Pathetic."

"You know you'll get what you want—"

"Perhaps I'll still get what I want if pictures of the princess's brain spattered about on the snow make it to the television."

"No," he said more quickly than he should have, growing more frightened as Ayub's thoughts became increasingly irrational. "You'll just piss people off. No one's sympathetic to an asshole. Think about it, Ayub. You have the Kremlin by the balls if you keep her alive."

Ayub laughed as his finger moved toward the trigger. "Right now, Sergeant Michaels—American *pig*—I have *you* by the balls."

An explosion echoed to Collin's left, and the side of Ayub's head erupted in a mess.

Lyla screamed and fell forward, struggling to get up in the depths of the snow and run away.

"Lyla." Collin rushed ahead, scooping her up as she fought to breathe.

"Collin—I can't—I'm so—cold."

"We'll get you warmed up." He set her back down when he wanted to keep her close and yanked off his jacket, putting it on her and zipping it, then he gave her his hat and picked her up, kissing her forehead, once, twice, certain he would never let her go again. "We're going to warm you up."

Sam stepped from the woods, running toward them and grabbing a blanket from one of the machines.

"Wrap her up good. Wrap her up, Sam. She's gotta be getting close to full-on hypothermia".

Sam pulled off his bulky fur hat and stuck that on her head as well while they cocooned her in three wool blankets and secured a fourth around Collin's shoulders.

"You found me," she choked out. "You found me, Collin."

He stared into her terrified eyes as he fought to keep his own trembling in check, thinking of what almost happened, what would have been if Sam hadn't pulled the trigger when he did. "I was never going to stop looking."

"The children," she shuddered.

"Are fine. They're fine. It's okay now. Everything's okay. It's over."

She nodded and settled her head against his shoulder.

"Let's get back to the cabin," Sam said. "We'll get her warm by the woodstove."

"Come on." Collin took his spot on the back of the last working snowmobile, keeping Lyla tucked in his arms as Sam sat behind the handlebars.

"I'm ready—I want to go home."

"That's where we're going. Just a few more hours and I'm taking you home." He kissed her cold cheek and nuzzled her face into the crook of his neck, offering her any extra warmth he could give her. "I love you, Lyla. I love you so much, Ly-Ly," he whispered next to her ear again and again as Sam plowed them through the narrow spaces, taking them back to safety and the carnage they left behind.

∝ Chapter Thirty-three ∾

LYLA PARALLEL PARKED HER NEW LEXUS RX AND reached in back for the handful of bags she'd accumulated throughout her busy afternoon. She was running behind, but what else was new these days? For five weeks straight, she and Collin had been living in blissful chaos. From the moment Fletcher dropped them off in Anchorage, they'd been on the move. Their first stop had been to Portland, Oregon, for a forty-eight hour stay at some secret location while the Department of State and several other agencies made certain she and Collin were free and clear of any further terrorist threats. Luckily the desire to kidnap and hold Princess Lyla ransom for the freedom of a would-be independent nation had lived and died with Ayub Umarov.

From Portland, they'd jetted off to Manhattan to pack up her apartment, help Mrs. Franelli settle into her new room at her son's house in New Jersey, and sit down with Roman Akolov for a lengthy interview—the last she planned to give for a very long time.

And finally, three and a half weeks ago, they landed in Los Angeles for endless realtor appointments in search of the perfect home, all while working around each other's crazy schedules.

She shut the door, wearing tailored black slacks and a simple white blouse, and armed the vehicle, smiling as she stepped up on the sidewalk and passed the pretty pots of thriving purple verbena she'd planted last Tuesday. Reaching out, she struggled to twist the doorknob, fighting with her shopping bags when all she wanted to do was get into her new studio. "Come on now," she muttered, giving a little extra effort and eventually succeeding. "I'm back," she called, hurrying through the cozy entryway decorated in pale shades of green that accented the glossy pine benches and cubbies that would hold dancers' street shoes during their classes. "I'm back," she said again, stopping and staring at the beautiful space reflecting back at her in the mirrors as Collin tapped the last nail into the cream-colored wall.

"There she is." He turned and smiled, dressed in his favorite pair of blue jeans and a navy blue tee.

"I'm sorry that took so long. The traffic was *awful*."

"It always is." He put down the hammer and walked to where she stood, setting her pile of bags on the floor and pulling her into his arms. "Hey, you."

She sighed, letting herself relax against him. "Hi."

"Did you find the napkins and tablecloths you were looking for?"

"I did, which means we're officially ready for the grand opening." She wrapped her arms tighter around him and kissed him, admiring the work he'd finished today: the hanging of the pictures of her mother, her friends, and herself, dancing in various ballets. "This looks so good. You've done such a nice job."

"*We've* done a hell of a job."

"Yes, we have." She nuzzled his neck, breathing in his aftershave. "I can't wait to get Moses in here and get started."

He slid his hands up and down her back. "A couple more weeks and you guys will be rockin' and rollin'."

"We will."

"I have something to show you," he said as he eased back far enough to pull his phone from his front pocket and fiddle with the screen.

"What's this?" She grinned as she stared at the Ritters smiling by their rebuilt shed and brand new snowmobile. "Aw, they finished it up. Leah said they were close when I e-mailed her the other day."

"Looks like they did it—and added a little square footage. Apparently Maisey still has her countdown going on. Only sixty-nine more days until they come down for their visit."

She grinned again, looking at the sweet family she could never properly repay for all that they had done for her and Collin. Purchasing Sam a new snow machine and helping Leah arrange long-distance therapeutic sessions for the children via Skype was the least she could do. "I can't wait to have them with us for a couple of weeks. Disneyland, here we come."

He chuckled. "Should be fun." He took his phone back and shoved it in his pocket.

"I'm counting on it." She traced her fingers along his ears, always eager to touch him. "I heard from Jennifer on the drive over."

He frowned. "Jennifer?"

"My ballerina friend in New York."

"The redhead?"

She nodded. "The redhead."

"What did she have to say?"

"Well, besides being bummed that I'm not still dancing with the company, she wanted to tell me that Charlie ended up taking the janitorial job we tried to get him. She's seen him around in the halls a few times over the last couple of days."

He raised his brow. "No kidding."

"I'm so glad he changed his mind."

"I know that was bothering you."

She nodded. "It was."

"And now it's all set."

"It is."

"Good." He kissed her. "So, we have one more picture to

hang."

She looked at the glossy poster-sized shot of Ellie and
Maisey posing in first position, wearing jeans and sweaters
with buns twisted in their hair—Alaskan ballerinas: A dance
for all walks of life.

"Do you want to do the honors?"

"Sure." She picked up the large, light frame and slid it in
place. "How does it look?"

"You tell me." He took her hand and they stepped to the
middle of the room.

She grinned, nibbling her lip as she studied the dance
bars and mirrors, the new flooring, and pretty curtains Wren
had helped her pick out. "I've seen this in my head so many
times, always sure I could never have it. And now it's real."

"And you already have full classes."

She laughed. "I keep pinching myself."

"You should let me do that." He growled and nuzzled her
neck.

She laughed again as her heart kicked up a beat and she
gave a playful push to his chest.

He grinned.

She hooked her arms around the back of his neck, staring into his beautiful eyes. "I made another stop on the way
back."

He slid his hands in her back pockets. "Yeah?"

"Yeah."

"For food?"

She rolled her eyes as she smiled. "*No.*"

He chuckled. "Where'd you go?"

"To see Reagan."

He frowned. "Reagan? Why did you go see Reagan?"

"Because she's working at the clinic today. We were talking
at Ethan and Sarah's party the other night. She was telling
me a little bit about her experience in Eastern Kentucky—
the lack of opportunity she saw there, which got me thinking. I made some flyers and we hung a couple in her waiting

room. I would love to welcome a few scholarship students who might not be able to attend otherwise."

"Oh, yeah?"

She nodded. "A lack of money should never be a reason not to dance."

He rested his forehead against hers. "Have I ever told you you're amazing?"

She smiled. "I think a time or two."

"You are, Ly-Ly. I think that's what I love most about you: your generous spirit."

"I thought you said you loved me best because I made good pancakes."

"That was this morning. This is now."

She laughed.

"You and Reagan are really hitting it off."

"Mmhm. I like her. I like everyone, especially since they don't talk about pointe shoes."

"Bonus." He wiggled his eyebrows.

She chuckled. "She invited me to next week's girls' night—babies and toddlers included, of course."

"Of course. They're everywhere these days."

"It's exciting."

He nipped at her chin. "It is."

"I'm looking forward to us having our turn."

"Now *that* will be exciting." He went after her neck, trailing kisses along her skin.

"How does—how does October sound?"

He stopped what he was doing and met her gaze. "October?"

She nodded. "Maybe on or around the twenty-third?"

His eyes grew huge. "You're—you're pregnant?"

"Mmhm," she said as she nodded again. "Just a little over seven weeks."

"Ly-Ly, you're pregnant?"

Her heart melted as the shocked wonder played all over his handsome face. "Reagan kind of confirmed that for me today too."

He yanked her against him and hugged her, spinning once. "We're having a baby?"

She grinned. "We are."

He set her down carefully. "We're going to have to paint the bedroom and buy a crib. When can we find out if it's a boy or girl?"

"Not for a few more months. I'm going to make an appointment with Sarah's dad. All of the ladies say he's a great obstetrician."

"Are you going to be able to do this?" He gestured around the studio with his head. "Have the baby and work?"

"We'll make it work. If I keep things part-time as I get bigger. And I was thinking about asking Oksana if she might like to come stay with us. She seems so lost without my dad."

"Like a nanny?"

"Like someone who could help us out while we're at work. Someone we know and love and trust. She doesn't have any family. Every time I talk to her, she cries. And maybe we can plan a little memorial for my father together. She could fly over with Pasha next month when he comes for his new job with the LA Times." Eventually she would have to take her father's remains to Russia to be buried by her mother's side, but she would wait until the time felt right, until she was ready.

"I guess we could convert the space above the garage into an apartment. Stone might be able to give us a hand."

She grinned. "I was thinking the same thing."

He took her hands in his, holding them up to his lips. "We need to get married. Marry me, Ly-Ly. I don't have a ring on me or some fancy spiel I've rehearsed a million times, but marry me anyway, because I love you more than I've ever loved anyone."

She smiled. "That sounded like a fancy spiel to me."

"Not even close." He closed the distance between them and slid his thumbs along her jaw. "My life hasn't been the same since you bumped into me on the sidewalk, when I found the love of my life. Marry me, Lyla."

She blinked as tears filled her eyes. "Yes."

He swung her around again, letting loose a triumphant whoop. "This is turning out to be one hell of a *day!*"

She beamed. "I can't think of one better."

He kissed her. "Let's go drive by the new house and see which room we should make the baby's."

"It's not ours for two more weeks."

"So we'll look from the curb. I think the room that looks out over the old tree in the backyard should be his or hers—the one with the little window seat."

She nodded, already able to imagine their child growing up there, staring out at the cozy view. "That's a good one."

"Let's go look, Ly-Ly."

She glanced over her shoulder at the picture of herself and her father, snuggled up and grinning—the last special moment they shared at the Bolshoi before he died—and smiled even as her heart ached a little, knowing that this was exactly what he'd wanted for her. Finally, she had everything she'd ever wanted. Finally she was truly happy. "Come on."

They laced their fingers and locked up the studio on the beautiful sunshine-filled California day and hopped in the new SUV, starting toward their soon-to-be home...with the white-picket fence.

THANK YOU!

Hi there!

Thank you for reading *Finding Lyla*. What did you think of Collin and Lyla's story? Did you love it, like it, or maybe even hate it? I hope you'll share your thoughts by leaving an honest review.

I'll see you again soon when we catch up with another installment of the Bodyguards of L.A. County series.

Until next time,

~Cate

About The Author

Cate Beauman is the author of the international best selling series, *The Bodyguards of L.A. County*. She currently lives in North Carolina with her husband, two boys, and their St. Bernards, Bear and Jack.

www.catebeauman.com
www.facebook.com/CateBeauman
www.goodreads.com/catebeauman
Follow Cate on Twitter: @CateBeauman

Morgan's Hunter
Book One: The story of Morgan and Hunter
ISBN: 978-0989569606

Morgan Taylor, D.C. socialite and wildlife biologist, leads a charmed life until everything changes with a phone call. Her research team has been found dead—slaughtered—in backcountry Montana.

As the case grows cold, Morgan is determined to unravel the mystery behind her friends' gruesome deaths. Despite the dangers of a murderer still free, nothing will stand in her way, not even the bodyguard her father hires, L.A.'s top Close Protection Agent, Hunter Phillips.

Sparks fly from the start when no-nonsense Hunter clashes with Morgan's strong-willed independence. Their endless search for answers proves hopeless—until Hunter discovers the truth.

On the run and at the mercy of a madman, Morgan and Hunter must outsmart a killer to save their own lives.

Falling For Sarah
Book Two: The story of Sarah and Ethan
ISBN: 978-0989569613

Widow Sarah Johnson struggled to pick up the pieces after her life was ripped apart. After two years of grieving, she's found contentment in her thriving business as photographer to Hollywood's A-list and in raising her angel-faced daughter, Kylee... until bodyguard and long-time friend Ethan Cooke changes everything with a searing moonlight kiss.

Sarah's world turns upside down as she struggles with her unexpected attraction to Ethan and the guilt of betraying her husband's memory. But when blue roses and disturbing notes start appearing on her doorstep, she has no choice but to lean on Ethan as he fights to save her from a stalker that won't stop until he has what he prizes most.

Hailey's Truth
Book Three: The story of Hailey and Austin
ISBN: 978-0989569620

Hailey Roberts has never had it easy. Despite the scars of a tragic childhood, she's made a life for herself. As a part-time student and loving nanny, she yearns for a family of her own and reluctant Austin Casey, Ethan Cooke Security's best Close Protection Agent.

Hailey's past comes back to haunt her when her long lost brother tracks her down, bringing his dangerous secrets with him. At an emotional crossroads, Hailey accepts a humanitarian opportunity that throws her together with Austin, taking her hundreds of miles from her troubles, or so she thinks.

What starts out as a dream come true quickly becomes a nightmare as violence erupts on the island of Cozumel. Young women are disappearing, community members are dying—and the carnage links back to her brother.

As Austin struggles to keep Hailey's past from destroying her future, he's forced to make a decision that could turn her against him, or worse cost them both their lives.

Forever Alexa
Book Four: The story of Alexa and Jackson
ISBN: 978-0989569637

First grade teacher and single mother Alexa Harris is no stranger to struggle, but for once, things are looking up. The school year is over and the lazy days of summer are here. Mini-vacations and relaxing twilight barbeques are on the horizon until Alexa's free-spirited younger sister vanishes.

Ransom calls and death threats force Alexa and her young daughter to flee their quiet home in Maryland. With nowhere else to turn, Alexa seeks the help of Jackson Matthews, Ethan Cooke Security's Risk Assessment Specialist and the man who broke her heart.

With few leads to follow and Abby's case going cold, Alexa must confess a shocking secret if she and Jackson have any hope of saving her sister from a hell neither could have imagined.

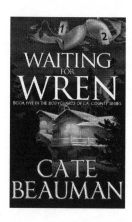

Waiting For Wren
Book Five: The story of Wren and Tucker
ISBN: 978-0989569644

Wren Cooke has everything she's ever wanted—a thriving career as one of LA's top interior designers and a home she loves. Business trips, mockups, and her demanding clientele keep her busy, almost too busy to notice Ethan Cooke Security's gorgeous Close Protection Agent, Tucker Campbell.

Jaded by love and relationships in general, Wren wants nothing to do with the hazel-eyed stunner and his heart-stopping grins, but Tucker is always in her way. When Wren suddenly finds herself bombarded by a mysterious man's unwanted affections, she's forced to turn to Tucker for help.

As Wren's case turns from disturbing to deadly, Tucker whisks her away to his mountain home in Utah. Haunted by memories and long-ago tragedies, Tucker soon realizes his past and Wren's present are colliding. With a killer on the loose and time running out, Tucker must discover a madman's motives before Wren becomes his next victim.

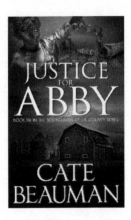

Justice For Abby
Book Six: The story of Abby and Jared
ISBN: 978-0989569651

Fashion designer Abigail Harris has been rescued, but her nightmare is far from over. Determined to put her harrowing ordeal behind her and move on, she struggles to pick up the pieces of her life while eluding the men who want her dead.

The Mid-Atlantic Sex Ring is in ruins after Abby's interviews with the police. The organization is eager to exact their revenge before her testimony dismantles the multi-million dollar operation for good.

Abby's safety rests in the hands of former US Marshal, Jerrod Quinn. Serious-minded and obsessed with protocol, Ethan Cooke Security's newest agent finds himself dealing with more than he bargains for when he agrees to take on his beautiful, free-spirited client.

As the trial date nears, Abby's case takes a dangerous turn. Abby and Jerrod soon discover themselves in a situation neither of them expect while Jerrod fights to stop the ring from silencing Abby once and for all.

Saving Sophie
Book Seven: The story of Sophie and Stone
ISBN: 978-0989569668

Jewelry designer Sophie Burke has fled Maine for the anonymity of the big city. She's starting over with a job she tolerates and a grungy motel room she calls home on the wrong side of town, but anything is better than the nightmare she left behind.

Stone McCabe is Ethan Cooke Security's brooding bad boy, more interested in keeping to himself than anything else—until the gorgeous blond with haunted violet eyes catches his attention late one rainy night.

Stone reluctantly gives Sophie a hand only to quickly realize that the shy beauty with the soft voice and pretty smile has something to hide. Tangled up in her secrets, Stone offers Sophie a solution that has the potential to free her from her problems once and for all—or jeopardize both of their lives.

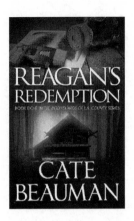

Reagan's Redemption
Book Eight: The story of Reagan and Shane
ISBN: 978-0989569675

Doctor Reagan Rosner loves her fast-paced life of practicing medicine in New York City's busiest trauma center. Kind and confident, she's taking her profession by storm—until a young girl's accidental death leaves her shaken to her core. With her life a mess and her future uncertain, Reagan accepts a position as Head Physician for The Appalachia Project, an outreach program working with some of America's poorest citizens.

Shane Harper, Ethan Cooke Security's newest team member, has been assigned a three-month stint deep in the mountains of Eastern Kentucky, and he's not too happy about it. Guarding a pill safe in the middle of nowhere is boring as hell, but when he gets a look at his new roommate, the gorgeous Doctor Rosner, things start looking up.

Shane and Reagan encounter more than a few mishaps as they struggle to gain the trust of a reluctant community. They're just starting to make headway when a man's routine checkup exposes troubling secrets the town will do anything to keep hidden—even if that means murder.

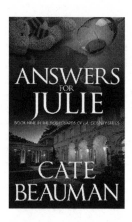

Answers For Julie
Book Nine: The story of Julie and Chase
ISBN: 978-0989569682

Julie Keller relishes the simple things: hot chocolate on winter nights, good friends she calls her family, and her laid-back career as a massage therapist and yoga instructor. Julie is content with her life until Chase Rider returns to Bakersfield.

Bodyguard Chase Rider isn't thrilled to be back in the town where he spent his childhood summers. His beloved grandmother passed away, leaving him a house in need of major repairs. With a three-week timetable and a lot to do, he doesn't have time for distractions. Then he bumps into Julie, the one woman he hoped never to see again. Chase tries to pretend Julie doesn't exist, but ten years hasn't diminished his attraction to the hazel-eyed stunner.

When a stranger grabs Julie's arm at the grocery store—a woman who insists Julie's life isn't what it seems, Chase can't help but get involved. Julie and Chase dig into a twenty-five-year-old mystery, unearthing more questions than answers. But the past is closer than they realize, and the consequences of the truth have the potential to be deadly.

34414001R00278

Made in the USA
San Bernardino, CA
28 May 2016